2

Taming the Wilderness Historical Fiction Series

JOANN KLUSMEYER

Published by Innovo Publishing, LLC
www.innovopublishing.com
1-888-546-2111

Providing Full-Service Publishing Services for Christian Authors, Artists & Ministries: Books, eBooks, Audiobooks, Music, Screenplays, Film & Curricula

Taming the Wilderness
Historical Fiction Series

Volume 2

GUIDING WINDOW
&
SUNLIGHT

ISBN: 978-1-61314-719-1

Cover Design & Interior Layout: Innovo Publishing, LLC

Printed in the United States of America
U.S. Printing History
First Edition: 2022

Contents

Guiding Window

One

God told you to WHAT?"

Kathleen Palmer stood with her soapy hands spread apart in amazement as she stared at her new husband of six months. Her rosy red-gold curls had been pushed back with her sudsy hand, leaving a glob of white foam on her forehead. The clump of foam was sliding, unnoticed, down toward her lovely pink ear.

Hapgood Palmer, new husband, sighed and began again. He had known it would be this way. He had tried every way to get out of it, but he had no better luck than many before him, when they had tried to get out of a direct command from above. No amount of ducking away or attempts to move sideways removed him from the direct command that came down on his head and resounded around within himself, like the water wheel that drew water for the cattle.

He had repeatedly explained to God that He was talking to the wrong person.... as had Moses and Gideon before him. He explained to His maker that it was surely a case of mistaken identity, but God had not been successfully convinced and remained stubbornly adamant, succinct, and well centered with His wishes. Just as He was with Gideon and Moses. His attention was absolutely not to be drawn aside by a mere mortal.

The young man knew, however, that his wife deserved the best explanation he could give her. He began, "There don't seem to be no way to git around it. I got'a be a preacher."

Kathleen expertly stripped the foamy suds from her hands, flinging it into the tub containing her embroidered unmentionables, still bright and pretty from her bridal trousseau. She wheeled around on her shapely barefoot heel and led the way from the washtubs of wet clothes to the door of the mountain cabin. This news was clearly something that should be taken sitting down and with full attention.

Hapgood, usually called "Hap," brushed back his coal black hair with a nervous hand and followed her.

Plopping herself onto the handmade wicker settee, she demanded, "Now, tell me again. Just exactly what was it that went on 'tween you and God?"

Hapgood, not feeling that he deserved to sit on the settee beside her, at least until this new directive from above had been absorbed, settled for a low stool at her feet and planted himself tentatively upon it.

"Lena, honey, don't think I ain't been a'tryin' to get away from it. I know what it's like bein' a preacher… livin' with one in the family I did. I know what it's like on the preacher's wife, and her bein' the innocent party to it all. Learned it all watchin' my ma. I talked to God, and I talked to God, and Him not seemin' to care how I feel about it all. Didn't notice that he took much notice's you, either."

Kathleen bent her lovely head forward and studied her toes, slightly muddy from the slopped over wash water and the rich, black dirt of the mountain farm. "You sayin' to me that this ain't a new thing to you? That you been hidin' all this from me? Now, Hap, you know we promised to not do that." The rebuke was gentle, but firm.

Hap had remembered. It had been easy to promise anything to the beautiful Kathleen O'Keen. The best day of his life was when he had stood in the parlor of his parent's house and promised to love, honor and protect her… and that was all he wanted to do, but there was no way to protect her from this. They were clearly in it together.

"Lena, honey, I wasn't in no hurry to talk to you, thinkin' it could be that I misunderstood what God was a'sayin' to me. I kept hopin' and hopin' I misunderstood."

She studied him for a moment. "How could a body misunderstand God?" Kathleen studied his pleading, open face, with a puzzled frown on her own.

Hap sighed, long and knowingly. "Ain't hard to misunderstand what God says if He's a'tellin' you to do somethin' you don't feel capable'a doin'. Wasn't hard at all."

Kathleen still struggled to understand. "Why'd you not be feelin' capable'a doin' what you was told to do?"

With a sigh, he began. "Well, I ain't studied, and I…"

Kathleen interrupted, "I 'spect they was a time your pa hadn't studied, neither. Wouldn't that be right?"

"Yeah. That was one'a them things I thought of."

Kathleen pressed unmercifully forward. "What was the other thing?"

"Huh?"

"The other thing you thought of? What was it?"

He sighed. "Gideon, in the Bible. About him bein' a farmer and God told him he was gonna have to be a general in the army. He didn't believe God, neither, and wanted a sign. 'Member, how he put the wool fleece in the bowl and asked God to make the fleece wet with dew and the grass dry? God did, and Gideon still wasn't sure, so he asked God to make the grass wet and the fleece dry and God did that."

"You sayin' you put out a fleece to God?"

"Yeah, you might say."

"What was it?" she demanded.

Hap hesitated. "Aw, Lena…"

"Tell me!" his wife demanded more sternly.

"I said to God if'n you didn't start in a'cryin' when I told you, I'd take it for a sign, for sure, that I hadn't been hearin' wrong. You bein' in the middle'a makin' baby things, like you are, I figgered cryin' was a cinch. Figured that'd give me the perfect out."

"You was expectin' me to cry? About words you was hearin' from God?"

"I thought it might be an even chance."

The girl nodded with understanding. "You wanted me to cry, to let you out'a doin' God's will."

"Well…" he hesitated, painfully. "I wouldn't put it like that, exactly. But they was another thing I thought of."

"Let's have it."

He summoned his courage and began, "You know, Gideon, he put out two fleeces to God. I only gave God one chance to back out'a callin' me. God ought'a be given another chance, wouldn't you think? Could be He's changed his mind."

Kathleen nodded, slightly, and turned her gaze out of the cabin door. Her white teeth caught her lower lip, as they often did when she was thoughtful. The color of her eyes turned from the pale blue of the summer sky to the deep swirling slate blue of a Kentucky mountain lake.

Hap waited. Ever since they were children in school, this color change had often brought on an idea. Some good, some not so good, but a thoughtful idea, just the same. It seemed to be worth the time, waiting to see what came forth.

"Now, Hap, I know the Bible didn't say nothin' about no Mrs. Gideon, but since this here thing affects me, too, I'd think it was fair if I was to get to put out the second fleece."

After a slight hesitation, Hap nodded. Why not? Seemed only fair, all right, and that'd put some of the responsibility on her.

Kathleen nodded and continued, "I want God to give us a sign so powerful that we know we didn't make no mistake. That'd seem fair to ask, don't you think? And I want it to happen tomorrow, before noon."

"Before noon?"

"Yeah. Gideon asked for his fleece to be wet over night. Seems like it'd be fair for me to put a time on it?"

"And what'd that sign be?"

"What it can be is for God to decide. He'd know how to make it big enough that we didn't make no mistake about it. We'd just have to trust 'im on that."

Hapgood Palmer watched the tiny smile creep into the edges of his wife's lovely mouth, and he saw the sparkles dance in her eyes. Once more he was thankful for the gift of this lovely creature. As soon as she understood the problem, she shifted the responsibility of it neatly back onto the shoulders of God… where it belonged.

What was it that could possibly happen that would be so big, as to be unmistakable, and occur before noon tomorrow? Especially in the tiny log cabin perched on the Kentucky mountainside so far from any main road to anywhere?

Hap breathed a sigh of relief. He would never have thought of anything so wonderfully hard for God to do. Nothing of such great importance and no surprises ever happened on this mountaintop.

He reached out from the stool where he sat and clutched the two bare feet before him, still slightly muddy and pulled them toward him.

"Now, Hap, you be careful!"

"I am! You notice I didn't grab a handful'a that hair. I'm bein' careful on account'a there being two a'you." He did, however, tug gently on the feet until she was removed from the settee and onto his lap.

Two

Kathleen's wash water had cooled considerably before she returned to it and rinsed her unmentionables, hanging them on the line to dry. But she spent some very thoughtful time beside the washtub, before her dresses, and Hap's overalls had spent their time on the rub board and were on the line beside the underwear.

Hapgood went back to his fence mending. If a fellow aimed to keep his hogs from wandering the mountains and getting long legged and skinny, he must be diligent with the fences and plug up the holes they rooted along the edges. Fence mending was good for thinking and he had some of it to do.

He had his plans. Good plans. He and Kathleen'd likely need to spend two, maybe three years here on the mountain, and then he'd sell out and be able to get something larger closer in to town.

This cabin was a nice place for two people. Nice, until they decided to go somewhere in rainy weather. The mountain roads, and especially the one leading up to his house turned slick as glass and ran red rivulets as the rainwater washed potholes into the clay. That was good, in a way, because it had made the cabin affordable. But, he reasoned, pigs weren't going anywhere, anyway, except to market. Humans would just have to deal with it.

Wintertime meant there wouldn't be much going, anywhere. There'd come a time when coming and going would be more important, like when their children would need to be educated.

He whistled a lighthearted tune as he drove stakes into the ground at the site of the latest hog wallow. He occasionally glanced over the fence at the noisy rooters. They were looking good, this batch of hogs. If he could just keep them penned up, and not out running off all their meat, he'd make a nice profit when they were sold.

With that, and the money from the sale of the wicker chairs and settees he made, he should be able to afford a nice place in town in a couple of years, three at the most. His plans were firmly set.

He circled the hog pen, checking for other rooted-out escape holes and moved on to another enclosure, also filled with grunting Hampshire sows. Their white hair was now dyed red with the mud from the wallow, but their characteristically patterned white "jackets" over the black body were still evident. He liked Hampshires. They put on weight very well, the boars were fairly even tempered… for a male hog, that is… and the little white jacket pattern made them look like they were dressed up. When they weren't covered with mountain mud, that is.

He had done all the right things, hadn't he? God had said in His book that the man who did not provide for his family was worse than an infidel. Well, he was not one of them. He was as prepared for marriage as any 21 year old, maybe better than most, and Kathleen's pa had been first to say as much.

As he headed back to the cabin, he walked through the patch of corn that he grew to feed the hogs. The shiny, flowing leaves on the cornstalks reached his armpits, just as they should this time of the year. Ears were beginning to head up all along the stalk. There would be corn kernels for weight gain in the hogs and plant stalks for roughage.

This spring's litters of baby squealers were beginning to put on weight, and his highly-bred sows were still young. Clearly, everything was working out, and it had seemed that God approved and was on his side.

Next spring…? Well, anyway, things were looking very good.

Now this...

Three

The pitch of the Kentucky mountain, leaning toward the south, as it did, created a lovely, cool night breeze blowing up the mountainside. The white starched curtains at the wide cabin window moved with the force of it.

It would be so pleasant to lie in the bed in the mornings, now that Kathleen was over the worst of her sickness, but they had already heard the flap of the rooster's wings, preparatory to the morning serenade. What with the crowing of the Barred Rock roosters, the mooing of the jersey cow, and the scratching of the dog at the door, it seemed time to get out of bed. They were clearly outvoted.

Besides, it was almost light in the east. Sunrise came early on the hilltop.

Another thing. God had until noon to do or not do what He wanted to get done. After that, they could settle into their planned routine without any upsetting problems to concern them. Their baby would be born, the farm would be in better shape than when they bought it, and they would get a good price for it. Then they would move down closer to the valley and their parents and friends.

But now it was time to get up. The corn could use another plowing before it got so tall the horse couldn't get through it. That should probably be the duty for today.

Hap pulled on his clothes and followed Kathleen to the kitchen. It was a pleasure to watch her cook. In addition to the knowledge that good food would be served, watching it being prepared was akin to watching a pair of orioles in flight, dipping and spinning in their courtship dance. Or a doe running through the trees, her fawn at her side. Or maybe a squirrel bounding about on the tree limbs, so nimble its feet hardly seeming to touch the limb. The whole thing made him feel poetic.

She stood there at the stove, his Lena, stirring the oatmeal with one hand, while dumping biscuit ingredients in the pan with the other. Sliding the oatmeal aside, she moved the skillet over the flame and plopped in a dollop of bacon grease, followed by four thin-cut pork chops. Then, both hands joined over the biscuit mixing bowl, and in seconds, the doughy globs were formed, popped in their pan and shoved into the oven.

The pork chops, crisp and brown, were fished from the skillet with the long-handled fork and put into the overhead warming oven to stay the right temperature while the eggs were cooked. One hand skillfully broke the eggs into the skillet, while the other hand set the jelly and honey down from the cupboard above the stove.

Milk, honey, jelly, and butter came to the table. The eggs got turned. Silverware arrived, followed by bowls of oatmeal and plates of meat and eggs. Lastly, on came the pan of biscuits, the tops as evenly tanned as a jar of bee tree honey. Hap could have gone on to the barn and already had the milking done, but then he would have missed watching the breakfast preparation. That surely would have been a pure waste of lovely viewing… maybe even a sin of wastefulness.

With a flourish and a swirl of her apron, Kathleen seated herself in the sturdy cane-bottom chair, made by her husband, and bowed her head.

Hap's voice intoned, "Dear Lord, we thank you…"

He had just picked up a biscuit and opened it for the butter when a light rapping sounded at the door. He and Kathleen looked at each other with surprise. How did anyone get past the dog without it setting up a racket?

Kathleen whirled from her chair and went to the door. The old man on the porch tipped his hat and smiled a snaggle-toothed smile.

"Mornin' Miss…"

"Mornin' to you, Mister. You come to see my hu…"

"You're fine, Miss. I come a'askin'."

"Askin'?" She was apprehensive.

By this time, Hap had managed to put down his biscuit and join his wife at the door. If someone needed directions, then they were certainly and hopelessly lost because the mountain cabin was not on the way to anywhere.

"Help you, Mister?" Hap asked, politely.

"Yes, Son, you can. Me and my missus, here, we come about as far as we can go. She's ailin' and we're two days short'a our destination. She was sayin' if there'd be a body close by that'd let her rest on their porch, maybe stretch out a bit without the swayin' of the wagon, it'd be a comfort to 'er. Maybe an hour… or two. Then, if there was a bite to eat that could be spared, that'd get us on our way."

Hap looked quickly at Kathleen's worried expression. She had only cooked the usual amount for the two of them, but they had two pork chops each in their plates, untouched. There were always biscuits…

"You folks come on in. We was just fixin' to sit. Your missus in the…?"

"There in the buggy," he supplied.

"You needin' help…"

"Yes, Son. A little help with 'er, if you will. My old arms, they ain't so strong nomore."

Hap followed the old man to the buggy in the yard, and Kathleen surveyed the table. Sliding two of the pork chops onto fresh plates, she opened four more eggs in the skillet. Two more oatmeal bowls… there was plenty of it. She always made extra for the dog. Biscuits? …enough. Jelly? ….honey? …enough. Yes!

She peeped through the curtain and saw the old woman being guided toward the porch steps. So thin, she was, that she was practically skin and bones, and her claw-like hands shook with palsy. Oops! Better fry them eggs a mite longer. Them old hands would never manage runny yolks.

Then they helped her through the front door, and the old woman was even worse off than she had appeared to be through the curtain. Her skin was darkened with age, her teeth, nonexistent. Her sparse gray hair was wadded into an inept knot on her head.

She smiled her toothless smile and settled into the chair designated for her. Kathleen slid the hard-fried eggs onto the plates and set them in front of the old couple.

Hap, the comfortable host, instructed them. "Dig right in, folks. It's done been prayed over."

Even eating as slowly as they could, Hap and Kathleen finished before the old woman, and finally Hap had to excuse himself to take care of the bawling cow. After the milking, he carried grain and water to the buggy horse.

Kathleen tried to keep from staring, and wanted, more than anything, to offer to feed the old woman with her own steady hand, but she kept silent until the food was gone. Finally, the toothless mouth was gumming its last bite of biscuit.

"Honey," the old woman said, smiling at Kathleen. "You been so good, I hate to ask one more thing, but I ain't got use'a my hands like when I was young, and getting' my hair combed, it's right much of a chore. If you could comb…?"

"Sure. I can comb your hair for you." Whereupon Kathleen picked up her comb and stood behind the old woman's chair, relieved to have something to do to keep her eyes off the pain in the old face.

Drawing the comb through the strands of oily hair disturbed her sensibilities. "Ma'am, you want I should wash out your hair? Bein' on the road like you was…"

"Honey, if you'd do that, it'd be a blessin'."

Draping the thin old shoulders with a thick wedding-present towel, she dipped water from the reservoir and moistened the gray strands. Massaging gently with her fingers, she brought out the dirt and oil, rinsing it off by holding the old head with one hand, and pouring water through her hair with the other, catching it in the dishpan. She blotted off the moisture and swished the comb through the soapy water.

Gently pulling through the snarls, she combed the hair until it was silky dry, and then skillfully twisted it into a stylish figure-eight knot, securing it using a few of her own pins. It helped the old lady's appearance quite a lot.

The old woman again gave her a toothless smile. "Now, Honey, if I could rest a mite. Your nice front porch'd be good. Just a little rest to get away from the swayin'a the buggy."

"Oh, no, Ma'am, you got'a lay on the bed. It's a good bed. My ma and me, we stuffed that mattress ourselves. My ma, she keeps geese just for the feathers. Says, otherwise, she'd not bother with the worrisome, noisy things. Here, you come on in here." Kathleen grinned, conspiratorially, "Them geese do make right smart of a tasty Sunday dinner, though."

Insistently, she guided the old woman into her bedroom. "Your Mister, he could come, too. He could likely use rest the same time as you."

She helped the old legs to straighten out, then covered them with a wool afghan knitted for her by her grandmother when she was a little girl. It had rested for years in her bridal chest. She stretched it to cover the feet of the old man, too.

"Now, you just rest and I'll be quiet as I can. Maybe them old roosters'll shut up."

Slipping back to the kitchen, she dipped water from the reservoir but it wasn't very hot. She had used most of it for the hair wash. Stirring up the firebox, she poked in several sticks of wood. She brought a pail of water from the well and dumped it into the stove reservoir. While it heated, maybe she'd stir up a little cake. Yes, an apple cake. If the old couple could rest until dinner, it would be a good desert to send them on with.

When the cake was ready for the oven, the water in the reservoir was hot again, so she could wash the dishes. Thoughts bubbled in her head. How did these people get to the porch without the dog barking, and how did they get so far off the main trail? If they were two days from their destination, would the old woman even make it? They must not have any food with them, so when they left her house, she'd need to put in enough to get them where they were going. Disturbing thoughts niggled themselves in the back of her mind, but she shoved them aside.

So what would two days worth of food be? Boiled eggs, cornbread, biscuits, cake, butter, canned peaches (did they have a jar opener?), a baked sweet potato… they were good even served cold, and… Well, what else?

She found the right size basket and packed the food inside so it would be ready. She even took it out to the buggy and set it on the floorboard, so there would be no argument about taking it. She felt a tinge of regret that she would loose that particular basket, but Hap could make her another one.

Glancing around in the buggy, she was amazed that they had so little in the way of comfort. Actually, they had nothing. But they'd get where they were going in two days, and for certain, they'd have plenty to eat.

By then, it was ten thirty. What for dinner? Fried potatoes, ham, green beans, spiced apples, and the cake? Good enough.

By eleven, the old couple was stirring, and Hap came in wearing dirty overalls.

His wife held her nose. "Been wrestlin' them pigs agin?"

Hap grinned as he changed. "I like them Hampshires, but they're the stubbornist critters for rootin' under the fence, that was ever made by God. Or whoever it was that made 'em."

By eleven twenty, the four of them were at the table, once more.

"Where ya headed?"

"Uh, down Louieville way," was the noncommittal answer.

A slight hesitation. "Well, ya ought'a make it. Good weather."

Four

At ten to twelve, the old woman was settled onto the buggy seat, exclaiming over the wealth of food in the beautiful basket. At five to twelve, they waved goodbye and the buggy moved toward the gate.

Hap and Kathleen stood on the porch as a good host and hostess would, waiting until they were out of sight before going back into the cabin, but instead of pulling through the gate, the horse was reined in and turned around to come back to the house.

"Young man," came a call from the saggled-toothed mouth.

Hap walked out to the buggy.

"All I got to give you for the help is my thanks, bein' I got no money. But I got this other thing, been savin' it for the right person. Figger that person must be you. Reach around here back'a me, and get that box."

"Mister, you don't…"

"I know that, but you're the right person to have it. I'm sure of it. Lift it on up there. I'd help, but my old arms… There, Son, slide it on over. I figger you and your bride might like lookin' at that, and time might come it'd mean somethin' to you. Be careful and keep it from bumps till it's opened. Wouldn't want it to break."

"Well, thanks… Mister."

"Don't mention it. God bless you."

Kathleen left the porch and joined her stunned husband who stood holding a box made of rough wood, about 3 1/2 feet by 4 1/2 feet, and only 8 inches thick. It was a bit heavy, as well.

"What ya got?"

"I don't know. Right now I'm tryin to figure where this was. There weren't enough room in the back'a that buggy for it. You can look at and see, it's too big for the space that was in that little old buggy."

Kathleen nodded, soberly. She, herself, had looked around, nosily, when she had loaded the lunch basket, and if the box had been there, she would surely have seen it. It was now twelve o'clock.

Taking the box to his workshed, Hap carefully lifted the shiny new nails and pulled the boards apart. Inside was a window… heavy glass… made of several glowing colors. He carefully lifted it from the box and held it up to the light. The Kentucky sun shone its light through the prisms of colored glass and created a picture of a baby lying in a manger. Each new color of glass was piped in a thin casing of lead. A lot of work went into making this picture.

Splinters of golden glass created the hay in the manger, and a silver halo crowned the baby. Far away into the blue sky, tiny angels of white glass filled the heaven. A slight movement of the window, and the angels seemed to move. The rough stones of the stable were each a different shade of brown or gray, and the white covering over the baby seemed to have sparkles captured within the glass.

It was just too beautiful for words, and they stared at it, until seven minutes after twelve.

Hap tilted his head to view the picture from a different angle. "This here's purty enough to go in the parlor… when we get one."

Kathleen was silent.

"Don't you think so, Lena?"

"Hap, don't you think this here picture's big enough?"

"About three feet by four feet, I'd say. How big ought it to be?"

"You ain't thinkin', Hap. It come to us before twelve o'clock, and it didn't come from nowhere in that buggy."

"But…"

"I know. You ain't a'wantin' to think on it, but that don't keep it from bein' right there in front'a you. It'd seem to me, we're fixin' to change our plans."

Hapgood Palmer gently placed the beautiful picture back into the box that was obviously made for it and pressed the boards back in place. Twitchy itches played along his arms and neck. Turning, he scooped his arm around his wife's somewhat expanded waist and led her to the kitchen of their two-roomed cabin.

Without a word, she pulled the kettle over the fire to brew a batch of tea. It would be ginger and hibiscus flowers in a background of raspberry leaves and a pinch of oregano. Zinger Tea. They would certainly need its slight bracing effect.

Kathleen was first to speak. "What now?"

"I haven't settled on a thought, but the first thing'd be to go down and get pa's study books. Seems I'll be puttin' in the winter a'studyin'."

"And practicin'."

"Now, honey, you know we can't get down that mountain in bad weather."

"Don't have to. Me'n the baby'll be your congregation. I've listened to sermons all my life, chances are I could even be a help to you, here and there. Leastwise I'd be interested. You'll not do much better'n that."

The colored tea flakes steeped in the hot water, releasing their flavor. The steaming liquid swirled around in the cups, pink from the flowers and spicy from the ginger. Kathleen added a spoonful of sugar to each cup, stirred briskly, and slid one across the table to her husband. It was time for serious thought.

She began. "I just thought on somethin' bout that picture."

"What was that?"

"It ain't no picture. It's a window. It ain't made for havin' the wallpaper showin' through it. It's got'a have outside light to show up the colors. As many pictures of church buildings as I've looked at, I should'a knowd it from the start."

"It's a window…?"

"Yeah, it's a stained glass window. Next thing is, what do we do with it?"

Dimpled chin in hand and elbows on the table, Kathleen stared into the dregs and leaves of her tea.

Beside his wife, the young Kentucky farmer slouched in dejection in the solid and attractive chair he had made with his own hand and tools. His arms hung from his sides, and his eyes drooped, staring at nothing. It seemed there would be a turn in the road where he had mapped… and the Zinger tea was sipped in thoughtful silence.

Five

The serious thinking at the table extended well into the afternoon.

The horse did not plow the corn, and the goose feathers for the cradle mattress did not get aired in the sunshine.

"Reckon tellin' the folks'll be the next thing."

"Won't be necessary to tell my pa. He'll know when I borrow the books. Could be, he knows already. It'd be just like God to tell pa first so's he'd help get me at it."

Kathleen ignored the mild sarcasm. "Yeah. And you'll need a place to study without no distractions."

"I can study right here."

"No. I'd distract you."

"Honey plum, you don't never distract me."

Kathleen ducked her head, peering at Hap with her sky-blue eyes half peeking out from under her curled rosy-gold lashes. Her pink lips formed themselves into her very best pout. Then she began to smile, turning up the tiniest outside corner of her mouth.

"All right! All right! You distract me. I'll study in the shop."

"It'll get too cold."

"Not for two more months."

"Then we'll figger somethin' else."

"How many books is in that set you got'a get?"

"I don't remember, for sure. It's called, 'THROUGH THE BIBLE, BOOK BY BOOK," and they's 52 books in the Bible. I'd guess there'll be a fair sight'a the study books to do a good job of it."

"You'll have to cut back on the willow weavin.'"

"We want the money."

"We wanted the money for what we wanted yesterday. Things is changed now. Reckon we'll still get to do what we planned?"

"Pa didn't."

Kathleen bit her lower lip, thoughtfully. "See there?"

Hap nodded agreeably. "I could cut back on them big settees and chairs and make more baskets and rug beaters. They're fast."

"How well'd they sell?"

"Don't know. We'll have to see."

Having time for study still concerned Kathleen. "You figger to get through the books by spring?"

Hap shrugged. "Could depend on how smart I am."

Kathleen nodded, thoughtfully. "First'a February'd be about right."

"How'd you figger that?"

"You was smart in school when you set your head to be. You still got the same head. You just got'a get it set right."

Hap let that pass. "Pa might not want to let some'a his books go. He uses 'em all the time."

"Then we got'a buy 'em, 'cause you'll need to use 'em all the time. At least for the first few years. We'll make a list when we go see 'em."

The senior Palmers took the news thoughtfully. The Reverend stroked his chin, meditatively, and his wife bowed her head moving her lips as though in silent prayer. The young couple waited.

Finally, Hapgood, senior, formed his words. "All this set well with you, son?"

After a slight pause, "Reckon it has to, Pa."

"And you, Kathleen?"

No hesitation, here. "I made a promise before God, didn't I? I promised I'd do what was needed for our marriage. I ain't one to go back on a deal."

"The baby?"

"I reckon he's just stuck with us. He'll have to take his chances."

"You take the books, son, and welcome. Later down the line I'll let you take a service or two in the church, here, just for the practice."

"Couldn't ask for more'n that, Pa."

At the O'Keen's, the conversation took a different turn.

"God told you to WHAT?"

Hap involuntarily flinched at the stern voice. "Weren't my idea, Sir. I told God he was makin' a mistake."

"Tell 'im agin," came Mr. O'Keen's best advice.

"Scairt to." And that was the honest truth.

"What's your pa say to all this?"

"Still in shock, Sir. Reckon he'll say more later."

"So will I. How about them plans with the hogs and your willow weavin' business?"

"Have to see how it goes, I reckon."

"And here I thought you were smart and on your way to getting' ahead."

"Yes, Sir. It'd been fine with me if God'd seen it like you do."

Mr. O'Keen paused. Trying to knock sense into this kid was like throwing a rubber ball against a wall. What he threw kept coming back at him.

"Kathleen, where you think you're gonna have that baby?"

"I was hopin' for a house, Papa."

"You sayin' you're goin' along with this, willingly?"

"I made a promise, Pa. You was there and heard me. You'd know I'd not go back on a promise."

"Have you thought what kind of a life the baby'll have?"

"Yeah, Pa. Likely it'll be the same kind'a life Hap had, and I ain't got no problem with the way he turned out. You didn't neither, up to now."

The older man sighed. His daughter had obviously been coached. Her answers were as impertinent as his own. While he considered his interrogation, Hap had questions of his own.

"Sir, you ain't likin' the way my pa turned out? You bein' lifetime friends…and all?"

"That's got nothin' to do with it."

"Because'a him bein' a friend'a yours?"

The older man bowed his head, knowing he was defeated. He had, indeed, been a boyhood friend and had seen the Rev. Palmer, senior, struggle through the exact same problem.

Sensing her husband had finished with his questions, Mrs. O'Keen added, "Is there any way you'll be movin' down from the mountain a'fore… well?…"

"Could be, Ma. We're workin' on it."

Taking the encouragement she was given, Mrs. O'Keen resorted to what she did best.

"I got food ready. Come on in and eat, and we'll feel better. I got cinnamon berry cobbler, honey, just like you like it."

At the sound of the words, Kathleen clamped her hand over her mouth and fled the room. Her startled mother looked toward Hap for an explanation.

Hap shrugged. "That particular food ain't been her favorite, of late. 'Speck she'll get over it soon. I'll eat her piece."

In the late afternoon, after being duly fed, advised and loaded with books, the pair turned the buggy horse toward the mountain and settled back for the climb.

"Lena, I keep thinkin'. Your pa…."

"Forget it. He's had his say. I counted these here books and they's only twenty four of 'em. They're not as thick as I'd'a thought. You could do one'a these every week and be done in twenty-four weeks. Maybe twenty-five weeks, takin' a week off for Christmas."

"While you're figgerin', could you go on ahead and do the studyin'?"

"Don't be tacky. I had to know so's to figger around it."

"Reckon you're right."

Kathleen, the practical, always knew she could handle anything, as long as she knew in advance it was coming. It was all in the planning. Before the day was out a workbench had been cleared in the tiny workshop, and a cane bottom chair from the kitchen was set before it. It was study time.

For a month, Hap dug into his work, bettering his wife-set goal by a narrow margin. While he studied, his fingers worked. The simple rug beaters made of light-weight willow limbs were easy to construct, and he could practically make them without looking. Which he did, as he read the text. Kathleen administered the tests and prepared them to be sent in to the denominational headquarters.

When he was weary of rug beaters, he made children's stools. They were cross sections of a ten-inch tree trunk, sawed into two inch slices, sanded satin smooth and fitted with four spraddling legs. Some children's stools had only three legs, and they were quicker to make, but they also tipped over with the wriggling and squirming that small tots did.

Hap's stools had four legs. More value for the same price. It was just the little extra he liked to give.

When he finally went to bed at night, after the barn chores and tending to the hogs, the words, phrases, and passages of his day's studying swam about his head in crazy formations. So much to learn.

Kathleen's girth expanded. Her dresses were replaced by the amply cut style, belted in as necessary, expanded as needed. Her increased girth did not greatly restrict her activities.

Hap had cut and stacked a heap of willow limbs beside the workshop, and when he was weary of making stools, he went back to rug beaters. His wife watched with concern as the supply of willow limbs dwindled.

The mountain stream that rushed downhill near the cabin, puddled behind a rock outcropping making a pool of a good size for soaking the willow whips. Days, sometimes weeks, of soaking were required to twist the limbs into the pretzel shape necessary to make the rug beaters. Hap always kept a good supply cut ahead of time, and it was evident the stache was getting low.

It was not her business to comment on the low supply, but she could do something else, even better. She could cut some more. Slipping silently into the workshop and removing the cutting loppers was simple. The bowed head with the mop of dark hair was bent studiously over a book.

Loppers were easy to operate. They were just like odd-shaped scissors, and she had often used them to rid the paths of a greenbrier vine, stickery blackberry sprouts or a patch of the Virginia creepers that threatened to knit the Kentucky mountains into a web of greenery.

The willow whips, she knew, must be longer than six feet. Kathleen crawled through the underbrush to examine the young willows. She could see where Hap had harvested them… the tall ones had been cut, and the new ones had not yet grown to six feet. She'd just have to climb higher up the mountain and find the right size. Even in her condition, managing a six-foot long willow whip, hardly bigger around than her thumb, should be no trick at all.

Willows like water. They grow as close to water as they can, and, because of this, piles of debris become heaped around their roots during high-water rains. Leaves, twigs and trash washed down a fast moving stream and lodged against the willow roots, making more soil for the tree. It was a good deal, really.

It was a good deal for the frogs, too, because they could hide under the sticks and leaves and still be close to the water. It was also a good deal for the snakes, because they could be close to the frogs, who were a tasty lunch.

In order to see the willows better, and to avoid the underbrush, Kathleen pulled off her shoes and leaving them safely on the bank, she stepped into the stream. It was a lot easier to walk in the shallow water flowing over the rock-bottomed stream, than to fight her way through the underbrush beside the flow.

Climbing the layers of rock like a staircase, she studied the willows that leaned out over the water, cutting one here, and another there. It was an easy job, and she hummed a tune as she worked. Occasionally, she paused to rest her arms, unaccustomed as she was to using the loppers to this extent.

There is a reflex that becomes ingrained in the mind of every mountain child from toddler size upward, and that is to stay clear away from the slither movement of a snake. As she leaned through the brush to clip a certain whip, the corner of her eye saw the dreaded movement. Reflex action set in.

LOPPERS… throw them clear! SNAKE… get as far away as possible as quick as possible! FEET… watch out for the slick, mossy rocks! REMEMBER THE BABY… don't fall down!

The clipped willow whip fell toward the stream, descending over her head and shoulders… the lopper handle caught on a vine… and the sudden movement of her feet activated the slippery surface of the mossy rock. Smacking against the rockledge on her backside, the fabric of her skirt soaked instantly, dragging her downward.

Across the sloping rock she scooted, finally squirming to her right side, but was still unable to grab a passing root or stump.

Ordinarily, she would have been able to grab a handhold, and was dismayed that her unaccustomed lack of balance kept her just out of reach. Down two of the rock stair steps she slid at considerable sacrifice of the skin on her legs and forearms, and now the short waterfall creating the pool was just below her.

Reason told her a 14-foot fall would do no good to either her or the baby, so she made a frantic lunge toward a short stump of a harvested willow and caught it, only to have it become tangled in her sleeve. The stump caught the fabric of the sleeve's underarm, pulling it tight and immobilizing her entire arm by the tightness of its hold.

Her legs dangled over the edge of the fall, touching nothing but mossy rocks, and the cold water entered her dress at the neck and flowed over her entire body, finally reaching her bare legs, and washing away the blood from her scraps and snags.

She strained to look behind herself and could see nothing of the snake… probably scared it away with her flounderings and screams.

"Hap! HAP! Come help me!" Reason also told her that her voice would not carry for the quarter of a mile distance it was to the cabin, and especially not above the babbling of the steam and the splash of the waterfall. Desperation, however, is never reasonable, so she continued to yell.

"HAP! HAP!…"

Hap heard only the sound of the birds in the trees and the continuously barking of the redbone hound, Roscoe. What in the world was wrong with that dog! Here he had let those people (ghosts? angels?) get into the yard without a sound, and now he barked at his own shadow.

"Shut up, Roscoe!"

He realized it would take more than a shout to silence the insistent racket, so he shut the book and stepped outside, only to bump into the dog leaping toward the workshop door. When the animal saw him on his feet, he wheeled around and headed back into the woods.

Hap watched with concern. Wildly running dogs often meant an outbreak of hydrophobia, the highly contagious disease they called rabies. Where was Kathleen? He ducked in the back door and knew instantly she was not there, so she was obviously outside.

"KATHLEEN! Where are you?"

No answer. Next action, follow the dog. Grabbing the axe from the wall of the shed, he tore out in the direction of the animal, racing down the familiar path to the call of the dog's yapping voice. If he didn't know Roscoe better, he'd swear the dog was barking "treed" as though he had an animal up in the limbs.

Straight for the water the dog ran. Didn't dogs with hydrophobia hate water? Or did they run to water? Which? He couldn't remember, except that it had something to do with water.

The dog still sped ahead of him, and he could hear the small roar of the falls just ahead. Finally, he heard her voice.

"HAP! HAP! Come help me!"

Kathleen's voice!

"I'm coming! Where are you?"

"HAP? Hurry! The waterfall!"

Hap paused at the edge of the pond to look up the mountain and to see his dangling wife. The dog had now stopped barking and looked from Hap, up to the pair of bare legs swinging clear in the flowing water.

"Don't move! I'll get you down!"

"Don't worry! I can't move!"

Clutching at roots and low limbs, Hap clawed his way to the top of the falls and carefully crossed the slippery moss, plans shifting in his mind. If he reached for her and loosened her, they'd both go over the falls. He had to brace himself, first.

Removing his overalls, he fastened the gallous straps securely in their buckles and hooked them over a limb. Then spreading the overall legs, he looped them around his waist, tying them tightly. Thus secured, he could almost reach her.

"You got'a turn a little and reach my hands."

"I can't."

"You got'a! There ain't no other way! Six inches'll do it!"

Gurgling as her face went under the water, she lunged toward the left and extended both arms. The fabric of her dress separated, loosing her from the stump just as Hap clasped her wet, slick hands.

"HOLD ON!"

Pulling against the toughness of the overall fabric, he held her as she turned over to her rounded abdomen and secured a toehold on the stone ledge of the fall. Spitting water, she pushed her toes against a submerged willow root, straining herself upward toward him.

Hap grabbed one wrist, then the other, and drew her onto the flat ledge of solid stone. After that it was only a short scoot on the ground to reach the path. Neither of them saw the dog's quiet tail suddenly whip into satisfied, sweeping arcs as if a job was well done, and his panting tongue drooled excited moisture.

"What in the world were you… ?"

"I tore my dress."

"I didn't like that dress anyway! You almost killed yourself! The baby…? Lena, baby, sweetheart…have you gone daft! You could'a got your head cracked open fallin' in that pool! What got into you to do a crazy thing like you done?"

"I was loppin' willow whips to help you. This wouldn't'a happened if I wasn't expectin'. Threw my balance off… a mite."

"I got a secret to share with you, Lena. Killin' yourself and our baby, that ain't no good way'a helpin' me. Likely, it'd'a totally done me in if I was to lose you. How're you feelin'?"

"Wet and cold."

"I mean…?"

"I don't know."

"We're goin' to the cabin, and I ain't lettin' you walk!"

"You can't carry me. I'm too big!"

"Yeah, and that's why you're sittin' right there on the bank till I get back with the wheelbarrow."

"HAP!" she wailed, dismally.

"YOU HEARD ME!"

"Please?"

"No. You scairt me enough for one day. I'm gonna scoot you to the bank, and you're gonna sit there till I get back!"

Whereupon he did just that.

Kathleen sat on the bank watching her husband stalk angrily through the underbrush toward the cabin. A little smile played about the corners of her mouth. He was so handsome when he got mad, but it took a lot to make him mad enough to glare and get red-faced, the way he was now. Not that she had done it on purpose, she had only meant to help, but it was nice, really nice, to see him so quick to take charge when it was necessary. She nodded with satisfaction. Really nice, it was! And besides, just sitting quietly helped the way she felt. Her cuts and bruises hurt everywhere, and some were seeping blood again.

As he disappeared into the leafy undergrowth, sudden panic hit her. Seven months! Seven month babies did not live! Oh, what a terrible thing she had done! To atone for her wickedness, she sat still as a snowman, hardly daring to breathe. When the wheelbarrow appeared, she was pale with terror!

Pillows lined the conveyance. Hap worked the single wheel between the trees to her side, and now lifted her, gingerly, into it.

"Don't you move!" he commanded, harshly.

He needn't have worried. She was practically afraid to breathe.

Finally reaching the cabin, he lifted her again, struggling up the steps and into the bedroom. Placing her on the bed, he reached for the scissors and cut away her the remains of her dress, staring at the bruises, scrapes, and jagged cuts hidden beneath it.

Watching his frightened expression, Kathleen's heart melted for him.

"Hap…?"

"Don't you talk to me!" he glared angrily at her. "I'm still mad. I'm gonna do something to you that'll teach you never to pull a fool stunt like this, ever again!"

"Hap…?"

"You're gonna stay in that bed for two whole days and put up with my cookin'. You're gonna eat my biscuits and oatmeal and not say a word. What I ought'a do is go get your ma and bring her up here to talk some sense into you. What did you think? That carryin' a 20 pound weight on your belly didn't mean nothin'….?"

"But, Hap…?"

"It'll be ham and eggs for supper. I can do both them things tolerable well, so it may be ham and eggs for two days. Only thing

I hate about your punishment is that it affects me, and I didn't do nothin' wrong. Now, you behave yourself and think about what you almost done."

With that, Hapgood Palmer, the second, turned and stalked out of the bedroom, returning with the jar of medicated petroleum jelly, a pan of water, and a soft cloth. Kathleen O'Keen Palmer said nothing as her wounds were cleansed and anointed with the salve.

Baby Palmer, cuddling against his mother's right ribs, heaved himself up and turned, cuddling against her left ribs, the sore ones. He stretched his legs twice, dragged his elbow painfully down the inside of his mother's abdomen once, then he shivered slightly and went back to sleep. His mother bore the discomfort without flinching, figuring it to be her due for what she had almost done to him.

Hap's ham and eggs were not bad, his biscuits were oversized bullets, his beans like buckshot, and his oatmeal a gummy mess. His cornbread made the dog turn away and hunt himself a rabbit in the timber.

Hap, himself, considered making Roscoe share the rabbit with him.

Six

Six weeks later, Mrs. O'Keen packed her bag and waited for a call. After a week of waiting, she demanded to be taken up the mountain immediately.

Three days later, Hapgood Palmer, the third, made his howling way into the world. Four days after that, Mrs. O'Keen deemed her daughter to be fit to take over her household, and she descended to her convenient life on the valley floor.

Hap was now in his tenth study book and was forced by the weather to move into the cabin. He studied books number eleven and twelve with one foot rocking the cradle at his feet.

His wife assured him, "It'll be part of your trainin'. No sermon in a church ever gets finished 'afore at least one baby starts to howl. That rockin', it'll teach you to keep your mind on two things. God and the people."

Then it was Christmas. After a week of pleasant sunshine, the snow began to fall.

Hap carried baskets of dry leaves to fill the hog houses. Damp chill can take off weight faster than grain can put it on.

He worked in the shop until his hands were stiff from the cold, then moved his work in the kitchen. Baby Happy learned to sleep with the background of tap, tap, tap, from the hammer, and the squeak of wood pulled against wood to form the twists and curls that decorate good willow furniture.

The snow continued off and on for a week and before it could melt, a layer of frigid northern air froze a sheet of ice over the top. The weak winter sun broke through the clouds for an hour or so each day, not nearly enough to melt the crust.

Sundays came, and the lighter furniture was pushed aside. Chairs were placed appropriately and Kathleen took her place as the audience. Hap set a stool on the table to create a pulpit and after three songs, he took up his stance behind it.

"Friends and neighbors, we will open with prayer. Dear Lord, we come before You…"

Occasionally, half the congregation was forced to tend the baby, but the service went on. The beginning… the middle… and the closing. His carefully researched thoughts were introduced, outlined, and summated, and were lengthened or pared away to fit within the prescribed forty minutes customarily allotted to the delivery of a sermon.

All of January they were marooned on the mountaintop, and by mid-February the road could be traveled on a surefooted horse. By the second week of March, they began to pack their belongings for the move into town. He was now freed of his study regimen and allowed to do the interesting things, like create sermon outlines.

Kathleen stood before the giant cast iron cook stove with an ache in her heart and moisture in her eyes. The stove was clearly too big to take. Too heavy and bulky to start moving from here to there, as they would certainly have to do at first. The only thing to do was to leave it.

The hogs were taken to market. It was with an ache in his heart that Hap had to let his young, carefully reared sows go, just when they were ready to start being profitable. Swine could not be moved into the city, and the only thing to do was sell them.

The willow wicker business was something else, though. Through his period of winter isolation, he had built a small trailer, four feet wide and six feet long, just large enough to hold all of his hammers, clamps, pulleys, glues and varnishes. His forms for stretching and bending the willow whips were packed together and fitted into the trailer, and a hinged lid closed them in. By careful packing, a supply of the willow withes, themselves, could be wedged in.

He hitched the team to the buggy, put his family aboard and made his way through the slick, red mud to the valley town of Lafette. Riding a horse back up to the cabin, he came down with a wagon full of belongings, the shop trailer and the redbone hound.

The rented three room house was much more comfortable than the mountain cabin. It even had a water pump in the kitchen, a proper parlor, though small, and neighbors on both sides.

Hap began to fill in for his father at various times, occasionally taking one of the Sunday service, and it gave him some much needed experience at looking at more than one face while he talked.

Members of the church, who had known him since he was born, were free with encouragement and advice. Both of which, his father instructed, he was obliged to graciously listen to, and then do as he thought best about it. As his pa pointed out, it was difficult to make a sermon both longer and shorter at the same time, and to speak more softly at the same time he must speak up for those hard of hearing. It was all very good practice.

They went uneventfully through the late spring and summer, and a need arose in a small mission church over the mountain. The new congregation would need help for a while, and who better to furnish the help than Brother Hap, the second?

The town consisted of ten houses, total, with a large surrounding population dwelling in cabins that were clinging to the mountainsides, and Hap would be with them, on his own, for the next six months. The furniture and the stained glass window were moved to the two-room cabin beside the tiny church, and Kathleen and little Happy were installed there. Kathleen was well on her way to producing her second child.

Young Happy Palmer was a solemn faced lad with pale skin, rosy cheeks and his father's coal black hair. He stood up at six months, walked at nine, and made almost no noise. He spent his days creeping along the floor, amusing himself with this and that.

When he was fourteen months old, his sister joined the family. Charity Palmer was a pink bundle of noise with a rosebud mouth and the curly golden fuzz of the O'Keen's covering her round little head.

Seven

The stained glass window was an ever-present apprehension. There had to have been a reason for it to have come to them under such unusual circumstances, and they were most impatient to learn what it was. They were also reluctant to be parted from it.

"Hap, you don't reckon this here is our church, and when it has to be made bigger, that window'll be part of it?"

"Thought about that, myself. Don't seem to be workin' that'a'way. Countin' noses that live on this mountain, I can't see that this church'll ever need to be bigger than it is, and the other fellow's comin' in less than a month when he gets through school. When he gets here, we'll be gone."

"It'd be good to know what we was to do…" Her voice trailed off, as usual, following a discussion of the window.

Hap tried to put his best words on it. "Yeah, but we're told to have faith. If we knowd what we was to do, where'd be the faith?"

"I know. It'll be good to be back in Lafette and have more room." There had to be something good about leaving the mountain.

The year turned over to 1885, and the seminary student graduated and came to claim his starter church, releasing Hap to go back to his father's parish.

It was comfortable life, there in town, and they could have happily settled in, except there was the thing with the window. By late spring, Kathleen was again becoming very round.

"Hap, you think we'll be here a while? Cause I need to do some cannin', and if I do, I'll need to get that window out from under our bed. Got'a have a place to put the jars. What could we do with the window?"

"Slide it out, and I'll figure a place. Thought I'd go hammer a few tacks in the willow. We could use the money."

So Kathleen pulled the glass window from under the bed and leaned it against the wall by the door so Hap could take it the next time he went out. Bending her thickening body to the task, she wielded the broom under the bed to clear out any lingering dust bunnies.

Young Charity Palmer had just learned to crawl and was constantly on the move. She gathered a handful of bust bunnies and sampled them for taste. Passing them by, she moved on toward the brightly reflected colors of the window.

Big brother Happy could now toddle quite expertly, and he saw her destination. When she sat up and reached out to pat the glass, he pulled on her dress tail, moving her back away from the window a few inches. She yelled, and crawled forward again. When she reached out her hand once more, he pulled her back again, and once more she yelled.

Happy glanced toward his mother, who must certainly have heard the yell, and he saw her make no move to stop the activity. He made an executive decision. If mother was not concerned, then he needn't be, either. It must be all right for her to pat the glass, so he moved away to his own play.

Now that her brother and his restraining hand were gone, Charity squealed with glee and proceeded to crawl behind the glass. Happy looked from his sister to his mother, and clapped his hands over his ears as the window began to pitch forward toward the floor.

The heavy glass hit the edge of a small stool, flipping it over. The frame of the window fell flat against the floor, landing with a crash, and Charity responded with a scream of terror and a flood of tears, crawling away on all fours.

Happy crept behind a chair and sat down, looking at the wall lest someone think he had something to do with the confusion.

"Oh, merciful heaven! What did you do?" Darting her glance between the Charity and the window, Kathleen rushed as quickly as possible to the child and comforted her while scanning the window with her anxious eyes. It looked as though all the pieces were still in place… but they couldn't be! Patting her hand along the leaded seams between the colors, she could feel they were still solid.

Setting the child aside, she raised the frame and looked at the other side. There appeared to be no damage at all. Whoever made this window did a mighty good job! But she'd better not risk another accident.

Struggling her arms around the frame, she hugged it to her rounded abdomen and headed for the barn where Hap worked. Seeing her coming, he dropped his tools and ran to meet her.

"You shouldn't be a'carryin' that! It's too heavy! I said I'd get it!"

"Yeah, but I didn't know if it'd still be there when you came. Charity pulled it over, and it fell flat on the floor. Scairt her, but didn't seem to hurt the glass. Didn't want to risk nothin' else happenin'."

Hap tested the glass and came to the same conclusion as his wife. Well, he'd take care of it right now.

Slipping it back into the box it came in, he tapped the boards shut and carried it to the barn hayloft, setting it carefully on a deep bed of hay. Nothing could happen to it there, because he was the only one who ever climbed into the loft.

Kathleen rushed back to the house and found Happy feeding a bread crust to his sister, obviously relieved to see his mother return.

Kathleen glanced at the clock and realized food preparation should start. Once again, as happened at least once a day, she bemoaned the loss of the giant, firewood-gulping stove she had been forced to leave on the mountain. There was clearly something wrong with this dinky little misshapen, misbegotten piece of metal.

It looked good, sure, but it released smoke though the seams of its firebox, the reservoir was useless because it was much too far from the heat source for the water to warm. The oven was big enough actually, but the heat was uneven. Anything being baked must be turned every few minutes to make it brown properly, and each time the oven door was opened, valuable heat escaped out of it and into the kitchen, which was already too hot.

Something had to be done about a stove. That was the trouble with living with other people's furniture, but it seemed popular, now, to leave the stove with the house, when it was either rented or for sale. If she could just look at the stoves in the store, surely there was something else available.

The more she looked at the stove in her kitchen, the more dissatisfied she got with it.

The more Hap thought about the stained glass window, the more dissatisfied he got with his life. The odd part of it was, he should be very happy. He was doing what he knew that God had specifically told him to do. Working with his easy-going father was pleasant, and he was learning a lot about conducting services. And about people.

Also, Lafette was a nice town, full of friends. The O'Keen's were almost happy with him… again. You'd think that would be enough to make Hap relaxed and content.

But there was that window. He would wake up in the night, conscious that it was on the floor under his bed, and then in the hayloft. And now, as he tapped the willow whips into place over the armrests of a fancy yard chair, his mind was on the crated window lying on a bed of hay in the loft directly overhead.

Perhaps he should do his own mountain missionary work. He had enjoyed his time at the small mission church, and the mountains were full of opportunities. If the window could only talk, he would ask it what it thought! If the window had been a sign or a message from God, it had obviously been God's last word on the subject. God must be pleased with him, now, but if so, why was he so restless? He could, maybe, apply for a mission position…and…what? Move Kathleen in her current condition?

But he did apply, and permission came, but not before Baby Mercy made her appearance. A new copy of Charity now occupied the cradle. Round and rosy, with her mother's mouth and the halo of red-gold curls, Mercy fitted herself comfortably into the three roomed house.

"We're movin'? Agin?" Kathleen's voice reeked with dismay.

"Well, we got permission to start a mission. Will you…?"

"No," she shouted, adamantly. "They's somethin' gonna change. I been patient, and I really tried, but I ain't plannin' to do it no more. I done had enough. More than enough. You can't be expectin' me to go on like this. Movin' somewhere new, and all."

Hap stared with speechless horror at the emotional outburst.

"I mean it," she yelled. "I thought it all out, and I'm not going to do it again."

Hap, with careful and lowered tones, knew he must talk some sense into her. "But, Lena, honey, you remember the fleece… and all… that we talked on?"

She stared at him. "Yeah. I remember. What's that got to do with me needin' a decent stove so's to make food that's fittin' to eat?"

"Stove?" Where did that come from?

"Yeah, what did you think I wanted? You been tastin' what's been comin' out'a the kitchen? Most times it ain't decent to put on the table."

"Well, I didn't notice…"

"'Course you didn't notice, worryin' about that window 'stead'a what went in your stomach. Now, about the stove. What I'd like is one like I had on the mountain, but movin' around like we are, I know I can't have that. Take me to the store, and I'll pick one out, and when I do, it goes where I go. Promise?"

He promised. Gladly.

Then he began to scout around to find a place where he was needed, and the weeks seemed to roll by. Little Mercy could twist herself over and push herself up, laughing gleefully at the accomplishment. Charity playfully pounded her sister on the head with her small fists, while Happy watched, quietly disapproving.

The stove shopping was successful. The new appliance was installed in the rented house, and the rented stove was moved to the porch. Hot water again became available, pastry was evenly browned, and the smoke was sucked up the chimney where it belonged and disposed of.

Then came the summer storm.

The air had been heavy and still all afternoon, with flies buzzing against the screen doors and birds too stupefied to make a sound. Roscoe, the redbone hound, walked from tree to tree looking for cooler shade that was not to be had. The girls fussed and would not go to sleep, and Happy finally left the house and tagged after his father in the barn.

The sun finally set, but the air was no cooler. Kathleen sponged the children with wet cloths and set a pan of water on the porch for them to splash their hands in.Youngens in wet clothing were bound to be more cool and comfortable. Then, finally, the day was over.

By early evening, the clouds had begun to pile up on the mountaintop, and the growls of distant thunder began. By dark, the lightening strikes were continuous, making the mountains seem to be on fire. Kathleen pulled the curtains together to darken the room and finally got the children to sleep. Taking advantage of the quiet, she also went to bed.

Hap in his restlessness, sat at the kitchen table with his Bible opened before him, staring out into the backyard, trying to get his thoughts together.

He felt the force of the lightning strike before he saw it and jumped up and ran to the door in time to see the spear of flame lick down from the lowering cloud and jab itself into the roof of the barn, not fifty feet from his face. A second fire bolt landed on the roof, scattering blazing shingles in all directions. A blaze arose instantly from the dry, weathered wood of the barn and shocked him into action. The horses!

Dashing out to the barn, he threw open the stalls and drove the animals into the yard, and, in the darkness, bumped squarely against his workshop trailer. He couldn't afford to let that burn, so he pitched tools, forms, braces and clamps into it and slammed down the lid. There was not time to hitch up the horses, so he lifted the tongues and dug in his heels. Slowly, then faster, the wheels began to move, rolling the trailer out of the barn doors.

He pulled it across the yard and turned serious attention to the house. If the rain would just hurry, it would be safe. If not, the burning barn would send up sparks…!

Just then another jab of lightening stabbed the now-flaming barn, exploding another large section of the roof. A flaming blaze of hay shot from the hayloft window and landed in the yard, just as the rain hit.

The first drops sizzled against the flames like eggs dropped in a hot skillet, and the next drops cut like silver knives through the smoke. He stood in the driving rain, staring at the scorched glob that had been blown from the barn loft.

Wiping streams of water from his face, he walked over to the dark pile, and in the light from a distant lightening flash, reached out to touch it. It was rough and hard and had a very familiar feel, for hadn't he carried it with him for the last four years?

Working the crate from the soggy mass of burnt hay and drenching rain, he carried it to the back porch just as Kathleen appeared at the kitchen door with a lighted lantern.

"Hap? What're you doin' out there, Hap?"

Silently he put the crate on the floor and sat down beside it. "Lena, honey, bring that light on out here, will you?"

Working his fingers under the often-pried-up panels of the crate, he pulled back the strips and felt inside. His panic subsided somewhat as the interior of the crate felt cool and smooth. The light from the lantern spread over the colored panes of glass, and the angels in the blue sky sparkled with silver lights from the lantern.

The golden straw of the manger seemed to be made of shafts of brightness.

Kathleen edged closer. "I'm glad you got that down. It could'a burned up."

"I didn't get it down."

"Huh?"

"It got itself down."

Hap pushed the protective paneling back in place and brought the crate into the kitchen, plopping himself wearily into a chair. Kathleen had dipped hot water from the reservoir and set it over a burner to boil. With an expert jab, she resurrected life into the coals, and flames reached up to the bottom of the kettle of water.

From the cupboard, she took down two cups and the tea. Zinger tea, it would be. Ginger root and hibiscus flowers for zip, raspberry leaves for body, and a pinch of rosemary for aroma. Hap watched her, silently.

She poured the bubbling water into the cups and swirled it with a spoon to gather the leaves to the bottom of the cup. A spoonful of sugar, each, and she set a cup in front of her husband. He circled the hot cup with both hands as if to pull strength from it. He gazed down into the steaming pinkish liquid as though it was his lifeline… a thing to pull him forward.

After two minutes of silence while his wife waited, knowingly and respectfully, he found he could form words.

"Tomorrow I go to the mountains to get things started and find us a place to live. When I come home, I'll remake the workshop wagon so we can move your stove. We're going to the missions, Lena, my darling, the five of us."

Kathleen swallowed, thoughtfully, and set her cup on the table. "You do what you have to do, Hap," she said thoughtfully. She sensed this was not the time to tell him there would eventually be six of them.

He had enough to think of. There was a limit to what a man could bear, and God had known it, so he made woman. She, herself certainly had no idea of what she was promising, there in the Palmer living room, but she could not imagine having done other than what she did.

Eight

The mountain community of Acorn was nestled in the saddle of the Appalachian Range, near the headwaters of a rushing creek bound noisily for the river in the valley below. It roared past the mountain church in a froth of foam and a gurgle of bubbles.

A two-room log cabin was the best accommodation to be had. The first services were held in the feed room of the spacious barn behind the cabin. Hymns were sung to the whine of the violin and the pulled-out tones of the accordion. Several harmonicas were in accompaniment. It seemed half the congregation were musicians.

Song after song competed with the chirp of the barn swallows under the eaves. Even the small children listened without undo squirming. After the first month, Hap and Kathleen had begun to think in terms of permanence. Logs were being gathered for a real church, a large, 24 foot square building. Here would be the place for the beautiful stained glass window to help these wonderful, musical people worship God.

Sundays were a thing of hope and harmony. Happy sat with the other young boys on the log benches in the feed room. Charity and Mercy were confined in the large feeding mangers, along with others of their age. Hap's voice arose to the rafters, and most of the congregation begged for longer sermons. Could a pastor possibly ask for more!

After three months, the foundation for the new building was laid, and the walls were rising. A building of that size required skill in notching logs for the longer spans and for the windows. The skill was there. Supporting columns were required for the span of the roof, but it seemed that every skill that was needed, this congregation was able to provide.

At the end of five months, the men of the new church were having "shingle" parties. The women brought pot luck dinners, the children played, and the men wielded their hatchets and shaped shingles, laughing and telling tales of hunting and family get-togethers. After the work party, the music started and lasted long after the most wakeful child had gone to sleep in the loft.

Two weeks later, they received word that a graduate student would be assigned to them, to work with Hap, and eventually take over the church. Hap was crushed and dispirited, and walked away into the woods so Kathleen would not see his most unmanly tears.

Kathleen had no private place to hide, so her tears flowed freely down her rosy cheeks. Happy climbed onto his mother's lap and hugged her to make them go away. Finally, they did.

Two months later, another rosy-cheeked little girl with spun gold hair came to fill the cradle. She came at the lowest period her parents had ever faced, and, after a short conference, she was named Faith. Perhaps she would help restore faith into her parents.

When Faith was four months old, the Palmers came down the mountain and moved into a four-room house near the church in Lafette. Hap found plenty to do, but nothing brought him the satisfaction he had felt in the mountains. Before he had gone to Acorn, he had felt he was performing the service God expected of him, but in that little mountain town, he had also found happiness along with it.

The happiness he felt must have stayed on the mountain, however, because it was surely not with him anymore.

Young Happy was now five years old. He rode with his father, holding the reins correctly and calling to the animals in his best grownup voice. He trudged up the hills under the leafy canopy as his father hunted squirrels. This was the year he was given a toy BB "rifle" and encouraged to practice accuracy.

His father printed the alphabet on a sheet of paper, and together they worked on it as they twisted the willow whips, tacking them into trimming for chairs, settees, decorative screens, rug beaters and a variety of other things. His father even bought Happy his own small hammer.

Life was pleasant around Hap's parents, and his younger sister, Lydia, now fourteen. Even the O'Keen's were almost happy with him again. Hadn't God made it clear where he should be by not letting him stay in Acorn? Perhaps he could now stay here with their families where he belonged.

Hap, however, did not take the window crate from his workshop wagon, because he knew it had no place in his father's church. As he thought about his future life, he seemed to be drawn toward the west, now, in the direction of the Mississippi River.

Perhaps a river town was the place to go, and without any approval or direction, he packed his family belongings into an oversized wagon pulled by two strong mares. His workshop wagon was hitched to an old reliable stallion and trusted to the skillful hands of his son, now age six. Happy's strong fingers held the reins properly, and he practiced the deep, commanding voice he needed to direct the animals.

With his wife and three daughters behind him and his son bringing up the rear, Hapgood Palmer, the second, started out on his own self-appointed missionary journey to some town on the river. His restlessness must be satisfied somehow.

For safer keeping, he had bolted the window crate to the underside of the first wagon. In this way, it would not fall over or be rammed by any shifting item inside the wagon. It was packed carefully within the crate to avoid juggling and scooting around.

Very often, Hap glanced behind him and noted with pride the serious and solemn face of his son as he concentrated on giving signals and direction to the animals entrusted to him.

They had been riding along a valley road, and had fjorded a shallow, rock-bottom creek when the road began to climb. The team leaned into the traces and drew the wagon steadily up the hill, but as Hap began to realize, the grade was steeper than he had thought it would be. Wondering about the little boy, he looked behind him at an open road.

No stallion, no Happy, and no wagon.

When he found a place to turn around, he retraced his steps to the first little pull-up out of the valley road. There in the middle of the road was the horse and the boy, staring at the ground.

Hap jumped from the wagon and went to investigate. There in the road lay the stained glass window. Minus the crate.

Smoothing his hand over the pane, he was not surprised to find it undamaged but was scratching his head over how it got there. Crawling under the big wagon, he saw the end of the crate was completely open, though still securely bolted to the wagon bottom. When the wagon had tilted uphill, the pane of glass had simply slid out. Simple?

The only thing was, he knew as a positive fact, that he had securely fastened all sides of the crate. The bolts could not have jiggled loose. As he stood staring thoughtfully at the bright picture, Kathleen joined him.

Her clear and firm voice summed up the matter without ado. “The window didn’t want to go that way, huh?”

He looked at his lovely wife. Her red-gold curls sparkling in the afternoon sun, and her sky-blue eyes were looking up at him. The rosy mouth was sober as she waited for a response.

“I reckon you’re right on that. We’ll spend the day here, and then we’ll go south. Maybe the window will want to go that way.” He pitched the small tent beside the road, and with the chain pulley, lowered the small cast iron cook stove to the ground where it set solidly on its platform.

“Happy, Charity, Mercy? You youngens go pick up dry sticks for the stove.”

After supper, the children played among the trees, and Hap and Kathleen sat by the stove, holding their teacups in their hands, breathing the spicy steam and trying to make sense of their lives.

“Seems clear to me. We ain’t to go no farther.”

“Stoppin’ here for a while? Ya think?” Her voice was tentative and unsure.

“Well, we got the tent here, and you packed food for a week. At the end’a that, we’ll see what goes on.”

“Times I get to thinkin’. It be so nice to have a burning bush like Moses had, or somethin’ that says what it wants, not leavin’ us to guess. Even a pillar of cloud and flame of fire would be nice. It’s an unsettling thing to be guided by a window that don’t seem to say nothin’ till we make a wrong move.”

“Yeah, you’re right. But ‘member how the Israelites wandered the wilderness forty years, followin’ the cloud and the fire. All we done, so far, is try to understand the window for a few years.”

“I know. It takes faith. We got’a have more of it. I wonder why it let us come this far? There ain’t a soul, livin’ or dead, within the sound of a voice.”

And then came the sound from the valley below them. “Git up, there! Haw on around! Pull! Git on up!”

Kathleen looked at Hap. “Looks like that’s fixin’ to change.”

They watched down the road they had just traveled, and finally the source of the sound appeared. The mules were bowed low under the weight of a wagon full of hay. Perched high atop the load was an overalled, straw-hatted figure, bouncing along on the load as the animals climbed the hill.

Hap walked over to stand in the road.

"Evenin', friend!" came the cheery call from the top of the load. "Found yerself havin' trouble?"

"No trouble. Just mostly wondered where we were. Is there a community or town near here?"

"Here? Well, no…'course there's Peaceful Island. Couldn't hardly be called a town….though…" His voice drew out, thoughtfully.

"Peaceful Island? How far away."

The hay hauler stared upward toward the sky, as he tried to estimate the distance. "Oh, I'd say a quarter of a mile. Not far."

"Which way?"

"Oh, you passed the road. It's on down by the crick. I can figger how you went on past it. Road's sort'a grown over right now."

"Well, thanks a lot, Mister."

"Got folks down there?"

"No, we just thought we might need to camp over a few days. Maybe pick up milk and eggs for the children."

"Well, friend, that'd be the place to do it. Them folks down there ain't got much, but they got milk and eggs. I got'a git on. GIT UP, THERE!" The horses struggled to move the hay on up the steep grade of the hill. The farmer tapped his line across the rumps of the mules, just to let them know they were being addressed, then he raised his voice.

"GIT UP, THERE!"

Nine

Hap watched the wagon creep slowly up the hill. So Peaceful Island would be their next stop. He could hardly imagine an island, peaceful or otherwise, anywhere in the Kentucky hills, but neither could he imagine having his ways directed by a stained glass window. Of late, he found his mind open to almost any event.

After breakfast, the stove was allowed to cool as they broke camp, and they headed back down the hill, sloshing through the shallow water. Sure enough, there was a small trail of a road that led off into the trees. The two-wagon caravan headed into the low tree limbs and vines that reached out onto and over the road.

At one point, the tiny creek divided around a massive outcropping of ancient volcanic stone and flowed along as two streams. The road followed one of them, and suddenly there was a cluster of four houses facing the creek. Farther down the road were two more. Hardly an eighth of a mile on down stream, the two halves of the creek re-joined and disappeared into the distance.

That was the island! What is an island if it is not a body of land surrounded by water? Several more houses were located farther down the road, and then there was nothing but trees and vines and piles of boulders.

A man was drawing water from a well in the yard as Hap approached.

"Friend, would you know of a place for rent, or maybe a place where a family could camp for a little while?"

"They's lots'a places to camp, but the Jones place's empty agin."

"Jones place?"

"Yeah, that house ya can see yonder. Folks comes and goes, and some'd pay rent if there was a body to pay it to. Don't know what happened to the Jones', and chances are, their youngens don't even know it's out here."

"So people just live in it…?"

""If'n it's up to your likin', move on in. Worse that could happen'd be the owners'd show up, and then you'd know who to pay rent to. Last folks was ungrateful and took the furniture, even the cookstove. We allowed that wasn't called for. Seemed to be a lot like stealin', we was thinkin'.. Reckon you'd be able to get a stove over to Compton, or… maybe…" The man struggled to be helpful.

"We have a stove," Hap assured him. "If you think it'd be all right, we'll go over and look at the house."

"Sure, and I'll take this water inside, and come with you. You go on, and I'll walk."

The caravan moved up the street and turned in at the weedy gate. The man from the well was right behind them.

"Name's Cecil Redfern. My folks named this little place Peaceful Island after the way the creek goes. Back when I was a youngen, they took to lettin' folks come and build houses and live awhile, or longer. Some stayed on, and others left. They's been a sight'a comin' and goin' around here."

Hap extended his hand. "My name's Palmer, Hap Palmer. My wife, Kathleen, and our four children. We'd like to stay a while. Is there a way to mail a letter?"

Cecil Redfern smiled widely. "You know, there wasn't, till about twenty years back! Now we got good service. Out where you turned off the main road, they's a mailbox, and the carrier comes by every week. He leaves what's ours and takes whatever's there. Works right good."

Well, that was taken care of. "How about a church? You folks have a church right close?"

"Yeah, but half the time we got no preacher. We go sing songs and sometimes… well..?" What more was there to say?

"Wonderful! We'd like to sing with you, come Sunday."

"Come, and welcome."

The house was old and would be drafty in the winter, but it had four large rooms and a lean-to kitchen (minus the stove). It had a ladder that led to a roomy loft, and there was a large building in the back that must have served as a barn, chicken house or shed, as the needs required.

The garden spot must have been very fertile judging from the size of the weeds occupying it. If the window liked it here, come spring they'd test it for growing a few other things.

The stream of water behind the house was rimmed with a dense thicket of willow sprouts, standing like so many ferns waving in the breeze. The Palmers stayed at Peaceful Island for a year.

Happy turned seven and became proficient with his toy gun, eventually graduating to one that would really shoot wild game. It was on the island that he brought down his first squirrel. The toy gun was passed to Charity, and he was given a real one.

It was also here that Charity and Mercy learned to tie bow knots and to brush the tangles from each other's curly heads. So daily, a cluster of red-gold curls crowned their heads, gathered and arranged by a sister, then tied by a ribbon bow. They learned to rub the soil from small garments on the washboard.

Happy also learned to wash sox on the washboard and to hang them on the line. He learned to catch turtles and small fish for the table. He took his turn in the garden and learned how to pull weeds from the vegetables.

Faith learned to walk over the rough ground without falling on her face.

Kathleen walked the hills and found the wild plants for her tea, cooked the vegetables from the garden, and tended a flock of laying hens. Contentment settled over her like honey over a warm rock.

Hap set up his workshop in the out building and created furniture from the willow whips, soaking them in the creek to bend into the twists and curves for the arms of chairs and settees. When he had a load of finished furniture, he took it to Compton, seven miles away, and he had excellent luck selling them.

Hap also preached. It was Acorn all over again, but with a bigger house to live in. In his studies, he remembered something that was said about the island…what was it? Ah, this was it. 'Isaiah 41:1 Keep silence before me, O islands, and let the people renew their strength.'

Thrill bumps of recognition rippled down his arms. Yes, that was it! Tired and discouraged, they had started out and were willing to continue their search, but God (the window?) had other plans. They were to rest a while. It would be easy to settle in, here in this lovely place, but there was no room for the window so, with a sigh, they knew they would eventually journey on.

The willow wicker furniture also sold surprisingly well. Was that also in the plan? Were they to be allowed to accumulate money for something that was coming later? It would be nice to know, but if they knew for certain, it would not require the use of faith… now would it?

It was in the comfortable house on Peaceful Creek that the twins were born. Girls. Round faced, rosy pink cupid's bow mouths, sky blue eyes and a crown (halo?) of red-gold fuzz on their heads. They came at a blissful and wonderful time of peace and joy in their parent's lives. After a short deliberation, they were named Joyful and Peaceful.

After a thorough search, the parents found something about them that was not identical. On one plump rear end, there was a tiny mole.

It was decided that it would not be practical to perform a "bottoms up" just to determine which girl was which, so from then on Joyful wore a red string around her ankle.

One day a package was hanging over the mailbox, and one of the neighbors delivered it. A dozen and a half flannel gowns in a range of sizes from Kathleen's mother, and there were four pairs of knitted bootees from the Palmers. Hap's sister, Lydia, now sixteen, sent a storybook for the other children so they wouldn't feel slighted.

Hap used the book of rhymes and stories to teach his children to read. Happy and Charity did well, but Mercy was still struggling with the alphabet.

The garden produced with such abundance that Kathleen fairly ached to fill hundreds of canning jars, but she knew it was not the thing to do. The window could decide to leave the island at any time. She stocked up on dried tea leaves, wild seasoning herbs, peppergrass, garlic, and medicinal roots, and even the hard-to-find salty, spicy colt's foot herb. She started each day with the decision to enjoy every minute before they must leave again.

Hap created a swinging cradle from a box big enough to hold both baby girls. Ropes attached to the corners allowed it to be hung from a tree limb and swung by the breeze. It would work well until the weather turned cold.

It was September of 1888 when the stained glass window once more began to assert itself. Nothing overt, this time, just a subtle nagging reminder that it still had a way to go. At this point, they had no trouble in understanding its language.

Hap worked over the wagons, greasing axels, strengthening joints and planning down splinters. The next trip to Compton, he'd get paint.

In October, they hitched up the horses, tied the two new colts to the endgate to be sold in the next city. Tools were packed into the workshop wagon, and all other portable goods went into the larger vehicle. The window crate was bolted carefully and securely to the bottom of the wagon once more.

With tears in their eyes, they pulled onto the road, and the people of Peaceful Island, also with tears, waved until the wagons were hidden by the trees along the road.

Hap had no clear idea of where he was going, but he was sure there would be opportunities in the river towns and that would be a place to start. He had gone north and had been stopped. Perhaps it was time to start south. As soon as he had an address, he would notify the parents back in Lafette.

They camped for the night in a deep valley beside a rushing stream. Ahead of them the mountain extended on and on, a seemingly endless climb.

When the stove was cooled after breakfast, it was hoisted aboard the workshop wagon, strongly secured, and they were on their way. The new blue paint had improved the looks of both wagons.

As they climbed into the sky, the road became more rocky, seeming to have been blasted from solid stone. The sloping stone sheets of the road made it hard for the horses to gain footing as their hoofs slipped and slid around. Finally, Hap was forced to rely on the chock block or risk loosing a whole wagon, plus horses, by rolling back down the hill.

Instructing Happy to pull over to the side and wait, he handed the reins over to Kathleen, and walked beside the wagon with the block, ready to wedge it behind a wheel as an additional brake if a horse began loose footing and slide. A loaded wagon that began to roll backward would be impossible to get stopped and would, doubtless, end up a pile of splinters in the valley.

When the first wagon moved ahead several hundred feet, he would pull over and let the horses catch their breath while he walked beside the other one. Several times he had narrowly averted a slide, and he was beginning to be concerned over his decision to travel this road.

It was on one of these times that the surefooted old mare stepped on the edge of a sharp break in the rock, doubling her foot backward. Struggling to straighten her leg, she paused in her pulling, allowing her partner to pull on ahead. The tongue of the wagon twisted, letting the wagon roll backward a few feet. Sparks flew as the horses' metal shoes sought purchase on the slick surface of the rock, but they were not successful.

In a sudden movement the wagon jackknifed, a wheel sunk into a stone crevasse in the roadbed and laid over on the ground. The corner of the wagon lowered, and the screeching sound of twisting boards, breaking nails and shifting cargo was frightening… sickening.

The older girls, riding on piled quilts, were wrapped up in a sliding lump of fabric. They were tossed gently aside and landed safely on the roadside. The double crib box bounced along the splintered endgate, scooting out onto the rocks of the road.

The canvas canopy popped loose. The four corners of the wagon separated and splayed themselves open, pouring boxes and bags over the edges. Kathleen jumped free of the buckboard and scrambled through the plunder toward the crib box, but realized she was hearing two voices yelling with indignation. They were safe.

She turned toward the quilt pile and pulled one after another of her daughters free of the tangle, and inspected them. Nothing more major than a case of fright.

Over it all was Hap's yelling voice, trying to calm his excited horses and draw them to the edge of the road and onto grass without actually letting them fall over the bluff. Finally, the wild-eyed beasts settled down and were loosed from the traces and secured to a tree.

Then he stood, biting his lip with dismay, surveying the pile of wreckage. He was not an expert on wagons, and the wagon was not exactly new, but it was also not old, and wagons climbed over this hill every day.

With a sigh, he walked down the hill to bring Happy up to the wreckage. Blocking the small shop wagon securely, and losing the horses, he began to pile the wagon contents on the side of the road and set up the tent. They would obviously not be leaving the bluff today. The stove was lowered, and the children were set about gathering dry sticks.

When he reached the boards of the wagon bed, he examined the corners, the bolts and the braces. The endgate was splintered, several sideboards had separated. Nuts and bolts lay on the flat rock along with other items of household goods. He gathered them all, knowing they came from somewhere and would have to go back there, and he continued to look at the flattened wagon.

The strangest thing of it all was that he was unable to figure out what had happened. The wheels were not damaged, nor the axels, apparently. There was some damage to the boards, but not so bad they could not be used until something better was found.

Gathering his tools from the workshop, he began to bolt the wagon bed back together. Several times he thought of the crate he had attached to the underside of the wagon, but he was willing to wager the pane of stained glass had not been hurt. No use to waste time looking at it. Better use the time to get his family and the wagons and beasts back down the hill that he should have never attempt to climb until… well, until he was sure the window wanted to go that way.

Hap worked all that day and half the next. Bolting and bracing, hammering and finally using his best rope, he pulled the wagon together, turned it around and reloaded it. With the family aboard once more, he started down the hill. A hill that is too steep to climb, is also too steep to descend. He still had to walk along with the chock block, ready to help the horses catch hold on the steep places. It was a long way down the hill.

They camped in the same lovely campsite in the valley beside the rushing river. While the horses grazed on the deep grass, and the children played games in the woodland, Kathleen retrieved the zinger tea made from ginger and hibiscus. It was time.

"Hap, you looked in that crate?"

"Not yet."

"Wouldn't you think that window pane'd be a box full'a glass chips, with the whole wagon fallin' on it that'a'way?"

Hap held his teacup in both hands, letting the spicy steam rise up into his face and circle past his eyes. "I wouldn't think so, Lena. It didn't break when it flew out'a the barn loft or when it fell flat on the roadbed. I keep wonderin' how we're gonna deal with that window. It's a hard job doin' somethin' when you don't know what it is you got'a do, let alone how to do it. It'd be good to have a lot'a faith, but when somethin' pushes from behind, and it's too dark up ahead to see where to step, a body gets to feelin' closed in. Sort of." He sipped in silence.

Kathleen sought to get the words started again. "I reckon somethin's got'a be done with the wagon… do you think?"

"Yeah, but I don't know what. Never could see what made that one come apart, and I'm even more puzzled why the boards didn't all splinter, heavy as it was loaded. I'm beginning to reckon we shouldn't'a gone up that hill, but we just about run out'a directions to go."

"We keep goin' back to Lafette every time somethin' happens."

"Yeah, and I reckon that'll happen agin, but it's just a step backward. It ain't a retreat. We know we got'a go agin, and knowin' that makes me restless. They's a lot'a strange things gone on in our lives, Lena, baby. We keep knowin' we got'a do somethin', and we're willin' to do it, but it don't never come clear how we got'a get it done. You reckon we can stand forty years'a this?"

Kathleen's rounded, dimpled chin became firm as carved ivory. "If we have to."

He smiled at her through the mist of steam. Lena, his lovely Lena! Six children, and she was barely twenty-eight. Lovely as the day she married him. Same bright hair, lovely mouth, changeable eyes. The same capable hands taking care of everything, never complaining. God may be trying his patience, now, but he did let him have Kathleen O'Keen to help him through it. Surely, she deserved better than this.

He sighed, bringing himself back to reality. "Wagon seems strong, but I thought it seemed strong when we started up the hill…."

"Was it that slick patch'a rock?"

"Lena, we know what it was. Maybe the rock was the 'where' but not the 'why.' We got'a think this thing through a little better. There's more of us, now, to be thinkin' on, and some of us aren't very big."

Kathleen warmed up the tea and settled beside him once more. He sighed and leaned his shoulder toward her.

"We ain't too far from Lafette, and the folks haven't seen the latest girls. It'd be the thing to do now… I'm thinkin.' Just go back for a while, tend to the wagon, and try to get a better idea'a what we're doin'."

Kathleen pursed her lips and blew back the steam, so she could take a sip. Hap turned to watch her, and the sky blue eyes caught the last of the evening light and turned to a deep, murky blue. She stared, unseeingly, into the trees around their camp.

"What're you thinkin'?" Hap asked, hopefully. Any idea should be a plus, at this point.

She made no answer, but just shook her head, tiredly, wearily. She needed to call the children to come and wash, but they were having fun, running and squealing, and they had been cooped up most of the day. Maybe another few minutes.

"You had an idea. Tell me."

"No, it wasn't no idea, only a remembrance."

"Tell me." Hap was desperate for a new thought.

"Well, it was back when you was studyin' in the mountain cabin. There was a time the Israelites let their ark get stolen, and the enemy thought that if they stole the ark, they would also have the blessing of Israel's God. But it didn't work that way, and all kinds of bad things happened, so they wanted to get that ark back to Israel fast as they could, so maybe the Israelite God would let them alone."

She paused, and Hap waited, hopefully.

"They put that ark in a cart pulled by two cows that had baby calves. They penned up the calves and let the cows go, and those cows started running toward Israel and away from their babies. It didn't seem like a natural thing to do."

Hap still waited. Surely there was something else behind those slate blue eyes.

She began again, "When we leave agin, would it be askin' too much to let the horses pick the way?"

"Our horses?"

"Yeah. Horses ain't no dumber'n cows."

Hap set his empty cup on the grass beside him and nodded. "The horses couldn't do no worse'n me. We'll remember that when we have to go on. I'm thinkin' we'll head into Lafette first thing tomorrow. Get there by mid afternoon."

Ten

The road through Kentucky tended to follow the valley as far as possible, twisting and turning until it was absolutely imperative to climb the mountain in order to go farther in that direction. When it reached the mountaintop, it tended to stay up there as far as possible before descending again into the valley. These efforts to avoid the climb created many turns and twists that made ideal places for small towns to develop.

The two-wagon caravan crawled slowly through these small towns, and the occupants of the front wagon gazed hopefully from the right to the left. Could one of these be the destination for the window? If so, the window was keeping quiet about it. The second wagon followed along with its serious seven year old at the reins and the large redbone hound by his side.

"Hap, we're doin' the right thing....ain't we?"

"You mean...?"

"Goin' back after it seemed like we was to...?"

"Lena, honey, I don't know that else to do. This wagon gonna take some attention, and I thought it'd be only right to let the grandparents see the twins 'afore we took 'em off to where only God and the window know fer sure."

Kathleen nodded. It had seemed right to her, but she could not bring up the feeling that she was again going to stay a while with her parents and in her hometown. She seemed to have the feeling that she had started on a trip and forgotten something so important that she had to return to get it but would immediately be going on. But where? And why this feeling?

"Lena, this travelin', it ain't puttin' too much on you, is it?"

"On me?"

"Yeah, you havin' so much to do, the children and all…?" There was apprehension in his voice.

"I don't rightly know what you mean. Food's got'a be cooked and clothes washed no matter where we are. The youngens ain't missed no meals. Them three oldest, they help a lot. Way I see it is, if'n the Good Lord didn't want me and them youngens out here wanderin' around, He'd either take back his window or tell us, flat out, where He wants it to go. Neither'a them things has happened, so here we are."

Hap reached a free arm toward her, pulling her close. She continued.

"Hap, you got no call to be worryin' about me and them youngens. If'n it gets to be more'n I can do, I'll speak up. We're out here on account'a you and what you got'a do, and that'd be enough for you to worry about, seems to me."

Hap slowly and sadly nodded his head. She was right.

The little town of Lone Oak crept slowly past, and up ahead was a sign pointing to a tree-shaded lane leading to the town of Rocky Point. Little towns were attached to the winding road like beads on a string. Some a bit newer, and some others somewhat fancier, but each had grown to the size it could without houses actually falling over the bluff or climbing a hill.

The town of Locust Grove was just ahead. It might be time now to stop and let the children have a bite to eat. A cup of hot tea would be appreciated, maybe even needed. A little fire under the metal tripod would heat the water. The mood of the adults was sober and thoughtful.

Happy pulled over behind his parents.

"Pa, I want'a ask somethin'?"

"What, Son?"

"When we go again, can Charity ride with me?"

"Ride with you? Well, Son, I...,"

Charity stood beside her brother, raising herself on her tiptoes as she waited for the answer. "Please say yes, Pa. We been tryin' to talk, and the horse in 'tween us makes too much noise with his feet."

Happy nodded, watching his father intently and added, "Yeah, I could talk to someone then. I talk to Roscoe, and he wags his tail, but it ain't the same. We could have the book and she could... maybe...?" His eyes pled.

His sister tried to help. "I'd read and practice my words. Mercy and Faith get to playin' with their baby dolls and don't want to listen to me. You 'member, they can't read too good, yet?"

"Well, I... Let's talk to your Ma about it?"

The brother and sister grinned happily at each other. Permission was as good as granted when the request was handed off to their Ma. If Pa cared, he wouldn't trust Ma to say no.

Hap watched the two of them run off together, leaving the others to playing at their own games. Growing up, that's what was happening. It would be so nice to settle somewhere so they could have friends, and... yes, it would be nice for himself and for Kathleen as well.

Leftover biscuits were toasted over the small flame that heated the teakettle. Butter and jelly (from the lovely valley of Peaceful Island) were spread on the bread, and the babies were fed and allowed to exercise on a quilt spread on the ground.

"Hap, you checked on the window? To see, if it's maybe...?"

"It ain't broke, honey. What happened was our fault, us not knowin' the way to go. Why it happened, was to get my attention. I keep thinkin' we need to go back home one more time."

The caravan pulled out with Charity on the buckboard seat with Happy, and the large dog gracefully moved himself to the floorboard. By mid afternoon, they could look ahead and see the small city of Lafette spread out around the foot of the mountain like the magestic robe of a queen whose colorful skirts lined both sides of the little river. A prettier town was not likely to be found in the state, or maybe even in the nation... or possibly the world.

The O'Keen house would be reached first, and they finally pulled wearily into the driveway, totally startled at the welcome they received.

Mrs. O'Keen was first to reach them and hugged Hap…an unusual action, with her daughter standing beside him.

"Oh, honey, they found you! I'm so sorry, so sorry…"

Hap stared at her, puzzled. "Found us…?"

"We send word to Peaceful Valley and they said you just left, but they'd try to find you. We couldn't'a waited no longer'n today, and was gonna have to have it anyway."

"Ma, what're you a'sayin'?"

Then Mr. O'Keen was with them. He put his arms around Hap's shoulders and hugged him, sympathetically. "Son, we'd'a done anything we could'a to keep this from happenin'. It's a blow to the whole town."

Then Mrs. O'Keen, again. "And the worse thing is about your sister. We tried to get her to come to our house. You got'a go over there right away! That girl, she…"

Kathleen looked from one to the other of her parents and their totally uncharacteristic behavior.

"MA! PA! Hush up and tell us what's goin' on. We got no idea'a what your sayin' and can't make no sense'a nothin'.'

Her parents looked quickly at each other. "They don't know nothin'!"

Mr. O'Keen looked toward his wife, and her shoulders slumped in utter dejection. "Come inside, all of you. We got really bad news."

There were hugs for Happy and the girls, but the grandparents' attention was on the upcoming and necessary delivery of bad news.

Hap prompted them. "About Liddy, she sick or somethin'?"

"Son, it's your folks. There ain't no good way to say what I got'a say, so I pray you got the strength. It was the influenza, we think. We ain't had it here in town, and we still ain't got it, knock on wood. But your sister goin' over to Coleman to see her friend, that'd be the only way… is what we were thinkin'."

"Liddy's got the influenza?"

"No more. She got well, it's what happened… first."

"Ma, tell us what happened!"

"I'm a'tryin' to. Well, Liddy, they sent her home from Coleman to get her away from the spreadin' of it, but it was too late, and she come home sick. Her Ma nursed her and took care'a it, best she could, and then Liddy was getting' better, and she got up, was it four days ago? I think maybe....anyway, she got up and your Ma and Pa both come down. And her hardly able to stand, she took to takin' care'a the both of them without a thought'a askin' us to help."

"Ma and Pa both down?"

"Wait, Son. It gets worse. I reckon, them bein' older and all, it was quicker. By noon time, your Ma was out'a her head, and your Pa was not much better. Liddy was afraid to stay and afraid to go try to get help, though where she'd'a gone, who knows? Nothin' can be done for influenza, that I know of. Well, that girl, she was in that house and watched her Ma pass on, and she finally told the neighbor to come tell us, and by the time we got there, her Pa was gone, too. Both of 'em, in the space of a day!"

"Ma and Pa are dead!" The sound of the words were dreadful and unbelievable.

"Oh, Son, I wisht there'd'a been another way to tell you!"

Kathleen turned toward him, wrapping her arms around him, and her mother hugged them both and wept with them. Mr. O'Keen stood by with downcast, moisture-filled eyes.

"We was just now getting' ready to go to the funeral. I was torn up about that girl, her lockin' herself in that house and not talkin', nor lettin' anyone in. I was thinkin' on the rightness'a breakin' a window. She needs help, and I was thinkin', forgive me Lord, but I was thinkin' maybe she'd ... already..." At this point, the distraught woman issolved into tears and sobbing.

Her husband picked up the story. "We was wonderin' if she'd get it in her head to... maybe... to follow her folks, so to speak!"

Kathleen pulled away from Hap and stared at her father. "Pa, you thinkin' she'll try to kill herself?"

"Well, honey, we..."

"Be straight with me, Pa! That's what you're thinkin', ain't it?"

"Well..."

"Hap, you stay here. You got enough to deal with. I'll take care'a this. What you got that I can break a window with?"

"I got'a iron pipe here by the door, in case of a break in. You take it, and our buggy, it's all hitched and ready."

"I'm gone. Hap, I'm leavin' the babies..."

Mrs. O'Keen called after her. "If they cry...?"

"Sing to 'em. They'll suck their fingers for a while. They're used to one of 'em havin' to wait, anyway. I got'a go."

"GIT UP, THERE!" she screamed at the horses, and they bolted from the drive into the street. Yelling at the animals, and half standing up in her eagerness, she forced the pair to propel the buggy through the streets at breakneck speed.

"WHOA!" she yelled, and whipped the reins around the hitching post. Grabbing the piece of pipe, she ran to the window of the room she knew was Liddy's.

"LIDDY! Open up! It's me, Kathleen, and I got'a talk to you!"

No answer.

"Open up, Liddy, if you don't want me to bust this here window!"

No answer.

Kathleen lifted the length of pipe and drew it back, crashing it against the windowpane. Cracking away the broken glass, she reached inside for the locking catch and flipped it. Pushing up the window, she could barely see inside, but she saw enough to know the girl was on the bed.

Running to the shed, she came back with a chair with a broken back. Climbing onto the chair, then through the window, she ran to the bed.

The white of the bed sheet was red with blood and a shiny-sharp, paring knife lay on the bed. The girl lay on her side with her arms crossed and her hands over the side of the bed. Blood had puddled on the polished floorboards.

Feeling her throat, Kathleen detected a weak heartbeat. Still alive! She had cut a sizeable, though shallow, gash in her forearm, but in her weakness, her other arm had dropped over the gash, partially shutting down the flow. Still, a lot of blood was on the sheet. When Kathleen lifted the weak arm, the brilliant red again flowed freely.

What to do! Bandage the arm! Where were the bandage strips? She had no idea where to look. Yanking open a dresser drawer, she pulled out a pettislip and grabbing a mouthful of lace in her teeth, she ripped wide strips from the skirt of it.

Salve, to keep it from sticking! Where would it be? Wait, she knew where the butter was! Running to the kitchen, she grabbed a spoon and dipped it in the dish. Spreading the butter over the gash, she wrapped the cloth strip around and around the arm, securing it with a large safety pin.

Now to the next thing. Carefully, she lifted the girl's eyelid, as she had seen doctors do, but, not knowing what to look for, she lowered it.

The skin was pale and cool, but she could feel heart was still beating. Frantically, she looked around, as a voice sounded at the window.

"Kathleen... ?"

"Oh, Pa! I'm glad you came."

"Honey, I was a'gonna say to you I'd come along, but you was gone 'afore I had it out'a my mouth. How is...?"

"Alive, Pa. Go get the doctor, and hurry. She's passed out and I don't know what to do."

"I'll go, but see if you can find the smelling salts. That helps some kinds of faintin' spells." Then he was gone.

Smelling salts! Smelling salts! Where would it be! In her Ma's bedroom, likely. She ran to the room and yanked open a drawer. Comb, brush, lip salve....there! The small bottle of smelling salts!

Running back, she knelt by the bed and wafted the bottle beneath Liddy's nose. She immediately wished she hadn't. While she was in a faint, the girl had felt no pain, but when her eyes opened, Liddy began to scream.

Scream after terrified scream came from her mouth, and the agonized screams came from a voice that was already hoarse from screaming. Kathleen held the girl's head and gagged her with part of the torn pettislip to save her throat. Then she heard pounding on the door.

Rushing to open it, she led the doctor to the room. He had his case open, and was sorting through the bottles. "Out of her head, huh? Did she recognize you?"

"Not that I could tell."

"All right. Now, you hold her head up, and I'll remove the gag and get the laudanum down her throat, if we can. Mr. O'Keen, you hold her bandaged arm, so's she don't flail around and injure it."

In the midst of a scream of terror, the girl gulped and gagged, swallowing the pain-deadening drug. Within minutes, she was calm and breathing steadily, though weakly.

The doctor stood and looked around. "Looks like she was caught in time. A few more hours and we'd'a been buryin' her, too." He turned to Kathleen. "Now about you. I got a gargle here for you, and you're gonna do it right now. Your Pa is gonna fix soapy water, and you'll both wash your arms and dry off with a clean towel. It ain't well known how influenza moves, but we ain't takin' no chances, you bein' in this blood.

"Best we know is, if you'll lock this place up for a week or so, then scrub it down, you'll be safe. Now, Kathleen, come time you scrub it down, you'll wear a mask and use rubber gloves. They're thinkin' that'd give a little protection. I'll give you some gloves. This here girl, she needs rest and liquids. We ain't gonna be able to wait for her to wake up and help. It's got'a be poured down her throat. A spoonful at'a time.

"All of us are needin' to be gettin' on out'a here. Mr. O'Keen, you need help a'carryin' 'er to the buggy? Kathleen, you get a gown and whatever she needs for a week or so."

Mr. O'Keen. "Doctor, the catchin' of this…? We got babies over to the house, and if we take her…?" His voice cracked in fearful strain, thinking of his grandchildren.

"No danger there. She ain't got influenza. She's done had it. I saw her though it, myself. We just ain't knowin' for sure what we're up against."

Within the hour, Lydia Palmer was in bed in a small back room at the O'Keen house. Hap stood by the bed and looked at his pale-faced, barely breathing sister, all he had left of his family.

Kathleen took his hand. "Hap? You got'a go on to the funeral. It's expected, and they've waited two hours for you. Take Happy along and Charity, too. They're little, but sometimes they got'a face death, and they had a lot of good times with their grandpa and grandma."

"Well, I could…"

Kathleen nodded encouragement. "Go, now. Things got'a be faced. Duckin' aside don't make 'em go away. They're six and seven, and they need to go."

"But you…?"

"I got the babies to tend…and Liddy. You go on."

Hap went.

The covered pine boxes were side by side at the front of the church. As they were together in life, together they went on to their reward. In the church where they labored so faithfully, they were given their final farewell.

The church building contained no dry eyes. A choir had to be imported from a neighboring church, as no one felt they could sing the songs.

Strains of "Shall we Gather at the River," "When they Ring those Golden Bells," and "In the Sweet Bye and Bye," had never been more meaningful than when sung that day.

No preacher had been engaged, deciding instead, to open the floor for anyone who wished to do so, to come forward and speak about their loss. It was a lengthy service, as many people had words to say… words they hoped would salve their own grief.

Happy and Charity looked with round sober eyes at the remains of their grandma and grandpa, and tightly holding to each other's hands, they stood like small statues as the boxes were lowered into the ground.

The women of the church hugged the silent children, and the men put their hands on Hap's shoulders, attempting to sustain him, when they, themselves, were crumbling. Such a terrible loss… so sudden…and so irreversible.

"Brother Hap, it was good you could get here…."

"Brother Hap, now if there's anything….?"

"Brother Hap, we're all of us standin' here, ready to…."

"Brother Hap…..Brother Hap…"

And then the terrible hours had passed, and he could return to his wife and sister.

Day and night they sat with Liddy, hoping their presence and strength would somehow impart itself to her. Every hour they fed her liquids, Hap holding her head, and Kathleen spooning water, tea or chicken broth to slide somehow down her throat. Her blood loss must be replaced, and it could not do so without liquid.

On the third day, she opened her eyes and realized she was still alive. The disappointment it brought to her made her close them again for another day.

On the fourth day, she looked at her brother and sister-in-law. "Why didn't you let me go? It was all my fault."

"What was your fault?"

"The… sickness." She could not bring herself to state the truth.

"Ma and Pa's death? You think that was your fault?"

"It was my fault. I brought the sickness home to 'em. If I hadn't gone visitin,' it'd'a not happened."

Hap sat on the bed beside her, taking both her hands in his. "Liddy, sis, what gives you the idea you're in charge'a livin' and dyin'? I didn't know God put you in charge'a that."

"Huh?"

"Livin' and dyin.' I thought that was God's business. You got sick, and you didn't die. You even tried to die, and you still didn't die. That'd seem to tell you somethin.'"

"Yeah, but it was you and Lena…"

"Liddy, honey, when you get well, we'll have to tell you what God put us through just to get us home from where we was in time to get you bandaged up. When you hear that, you'll know you got nothin' to do with pickin' the time when you die. Just like you had nothin' to do with them other two deaths. Things happen. God could'a let them live, the way He let you live, but He didn't, and we don't know why. I figure it must be 'cause we don't need to know why."

"Hap?" Her tearful voice was faint.

"Yes, honey?"

"I can't go back to that house."

"You don't think so?"

Slowly, and with finality, her head moved back and forth.

"Honey, there's nothin wrong with the house, 'cept a broke window. Houses are just wood and shingles. It'll get better."

But it didn't. Kathleen bound up her face in a mask and donned the rubber gloves as instructed, and she attacked the house, disinfecting every surface. She trusted Hap only to bring her clean water, and empty the dirty water and to repair the broken window.

He was also allowed to fire up the flame under the wash pot to boil the bedding and garments of clothing that might have been worn. Her work periods were somewhat shortened, due to having to stop to feed the twins, but in another week, the house was clean enough to meet her requirements.

They moved in. It was a lovely, big house, and the children spread into every room, exploring and investigating. Liddy moved into her own room and shut the door firmly behind her. Only absolute necessities brought her from the room, and she did not consider food a necessity.

Kathleen visited her. "Liddy, you feelin' sick?"

She shook her head.

"Would there be a thing we could get that you'd like to eat?"

More head shaking. Her eyes were on her hands in her lap.

"Could you tell me anything about the way you feel?"

She looked up slowly from under her tangled, uncombed hair. "I told Hap I couldn't live in this house. I said it to 'im, plain."

'Well, we could… Liddy, are you plannin' to run away, or somethin'?"

A full two minutes of silence passed. "Yeah, somethin.'"

Kathleen's heart grabbed for breath within her chest at the ominous sound of Liddy's voice. She reached out and took her sister in law's hands in her own. "Liddy, we always been friends, you and me. I'm thinkin' you owe me one favor. You got'a say you'll make me a promise."

"Owe you…?"

"Yes, friendship 'tween two people can't be counted as nothin,' and they was times you and me, we took little Happy, and then Charity, and went walkin' and talkin' like friends. I know I been away a lot, and it wasn't any'a my doin', but I always thought about the good times we had, and how you sent that book when Happy and Charity was bad needin' somethin' to learn on. That's a thing friends do. Now I come back, and I did my best for you, though you didn't want me to. Still, I did it. Now I got'a have one thing from you."

"What'd that be?"

"You're gonna promise me you'll wait two weeks before you run away…or somethin'. Could be, I could figure on how to get you out'a here by that time. Can you wait that long?"

A minute passed, and a long sigh escaped her lungs, "I reckon."

Kathleen reached her hand to Liddy's drooping chin and lifted it up. Smiling, she said, "Now, it'll take a little eatin'a what's cooked to keep you alive to keep your promise. You don't eat nothin,' and that'll break your promise to me. Remember, I got two weeks to fix this here problem."

She noted with relief that she had been rewarded by a glimmer of interest and a faint smile. Closing the door softly, she left the room. She had thinking to do. Hap was not in the house, and it was just as well. What she had to think on… it was something that had to be done alone.

In the lovely, roomy kitchen, she pulled the teakettle over the burner and poked up the coals. Spooning ginger and hibiscus blossoms into her cup, she noted that the supply was low. Before they took off again, she must build up the quantity. It seemed they had needed its bracing effect oftener and oftener, of late, and it was best to be prepared.

As the steam curled around her face, she considered the options. Move? Possible, but rather drastic. Her parents house… ? Not enough room. What else?

So moving it would be. Now, how to approach Hap that he was going to have to leave his lovely home? She had a promise of two weeks, so she could afford a few days decide how to tell him.

Eleven

It was the next day after the promise that the family had just finished supper and a knock came at the door.

It had been a pure pleasure to cook on the lovely stove in the roomy kitchen, and Hap and Kathleen had lingered over dessert. Liddy refused to leave her room but agreed to eat what was brought. She was clearly waiting out her two weeks and keeping her promise.

A sound at the door. Hap went to answer it and admitted a half a dozen men from the church.

"Brother Hap, how are you?"

The spokesman. "Thought we'd drop by to see if there was a thing you needed?"

A deacon. "You and the family doin' all right?"

Kathleen brought fresh peppermint tea and excused herself. She and Hap both knew the men had not come to see about their wellbeing.

"Brother Hap? We was just thinkin', the men of the church, that is. We're knowin' it's too soon, and all, and likely we ought'a back off. Instead, we come on over to talk about somethin.'"

"Yeah, we wanted you to know what was on our minds and hearts. We'd not normally say what we're gonna say this here bold way, but some of us has knowd you since you was a baby, and others growed up with you and Kathleen. We saw how you helped your Pa at times, and the way you took on the missionary work, and we feel we should...." He paused.

Another began. "What we want to say is this. We don't want no answer now, knowin' you ain't had your time a'grievin.' It's just that we want you to know the way our minds is turnin.'"

Still more. "We been havin' talks with this one and that one, and if you was to see fit to come to the church in view of a call, they's every chance you'd be voted in. We ain't got no problems you don't know about, and we already know you'd be up to the job."

The deacon, again. "We was thinkin', now that you got a family, likely the missionary work'd be a trial to Kathleen, to be on the road that'a'way. The salary here'd keep you good, or if you was to need more...."

The spokesman summed it all up. "Now, mind, we didn't come for no answer right now, and we want to go and let you think on it. We can't think of a body we'd rather have than you, but if you can't see your way clear, then we got'a get busy to find someone... else... you understand?"

As a body, they set their empty cups on the little table and arose. Each shaking his hand, they filed out and left him alone in the parlor of his parent's house. He was still standing there when Kathleen returned.

She put her arms around him and looked up into his thoughtful face. "We got us a church, now?" He needed her words to help his own to be loosed.

"Well, I was a'thinkin'...."

She encouraged, "Thinkin' what?"

"I was a'thinkin' whereat would we put that stained glass window in that church made out'a stone. For sure there ain't no room for it in that church that's been build there for forty years. That'd mean it'd be here in the house. What're the chances the house'd fall down on one'a the youngens, or maybe it'd draw lightenin' again?"

Kathleen supplied her own thoughts. "Or take off down the road by itself and us a runnin' to get it back?"

Her ridiculous words seemed so likely that they hardly produced a smile. "We got thinkin' to do. Would you make some tea?"

Back to the spacious dining table and the singing tea-kettle they went. The zinger tea was spooned into the cups, and there was none left in the canister.

"I got'a get more tea, first thing tomorrow."

"Get a lot. Could be we'll need it."

They waited till the swirling water turned rosy pink, and the aroma was lifting into the room.

Kathleen was first. "You thinkin' you'll not take the church." It was not a question, rather, it was just a statement to get the words started.

Hap began with a sigh. "There's be nothin' I'd like better that to step into the pulpit of that church with its steady members, lack of problems, our friends, and the parents of our friends all around us. I'd really like to do it, and if there was a place for the window, I'd likely be on my knees askin' God to let me have it."

He sipped the tea in silence. In a far room, the children laughed and played. Kathleen waited and watched.

Finally, he nodded. "Yeah, askin' God for that church'd be like Mercy askin' to play with a yellow jacket wasp. She'd know I'd not let her have it. Same with the church. It boils down to one thing. There ain't no place for the window. Never will be."

Still Kathleen waited.

Hap reached for her hand across the table. "Lena, honey, you with me on this?"

Kathleen answered, without a trace of hesitation. "Has there ever been a time when I wasn't with you?"

"No, but one of the men gave me a spell'a guilt, talkin' like maybe I owed it to you to get us settled on account'a the youngens. I remember you sayin' when the time come to make a change 'cause you couldn't go no farther, you'd let me know, and you ain't said nothin'."

It was Kathleen's turn. Hap waited. She wished she had been farther along in her thinking, but what did it matter?

"Hap, it's good to hear you say what you said, because of another thing you don't know about. You know Liddy ain't doin' well, but you don't know how bad it is."

"Liddy? She sick?"

"Not that you could see. She's sick inside. She ain't gonna stay here where there's so much misery."

"Where'd she be goin'?"

"Same place she was headed when I wrapped up her arm to stop the blood."

With great care, Hap set the delicate teacup on the table and clenched his hands into white-knuckled fists. "She gonna…?"

Kathleen nodded. "But we got a few days. She promised me to wait to see if I could think of a way to get her out'a this house."

"That bad, huh?"

"Maybe worse. She ain't gonna be able to stay in this town and go to this church. She's got it in her heart that your folks' death was her fault, and that the whole town blames her for it."

"That ain't true! Why'd she think like that…?"

"The heart don't need no sensible reason to believe somethin'. It just believes. She's got nobody but you, and you got'a see her set up somewhere before we take off agin."

"Where?"

"I reckon that'll be a matter'a thought. Could be she'll be able to help."

"No way we could take her with us."

"Why'd that be?"

"Well, a girl like Liddy? She's always had this nice house, and things come easy to her. She'd not… be able…" He sought for words that made sense.

"Hap, look at the house I lived in. Then I went to the mountain cabin, I lived in one room shacks, two room cabins, three room houses, and four room drafty barns, like down at Peaceful Island. I even lived in a wagon out in the open."

"Yeah, well you…"

"I know. I agreed to it. You asked, and I agreed."

"And you think she'd…?"

"Reckon you'd not know if she'd agree till you ask her. I'd figure she had the right to say no for herself, without you sayin' it for her. That girl's sixteen, and she determined. If we don't help her find what she can stand to be around, she'll be gone… somewhere. If you don't help her, she'll help herself, and we'd not be likin' what she did."

"Got any more tea?"

"Nope. I dusted the last of it in our cups. Tea drinkin's over for right now."

"When you think I ought'a talk to her?"

"Well, I'd say it's too late to do it yesterday, so right now'd be the next best time."

"What'll I say? I don't know nothin' about girls…."

"Tell her you're gonna get her out'a this house that causin' her so much pain. Tell her it'll take a while, maybe a month, but you'll find her a place to stay, or she can go with us."

After a final weary sigh, he left the table and walked through the door. Kathleen folded her arms on the table and bowed her head. The first tears dropped silently onto her arms and dripped down onto the lovely table soaking into the lace cloth, but the next tears were wrung from the depth of her soul by tearing, ripping sobs.

She wept for the torment of the girl in the far room, and for the brother who felt inadequate to comfort her. She wept for her children who would be denied the comfort of growing up in their grandparents lovely home. She wept for the weariness she knew would soon be on her as she rode in the jiggly wagon over the rough and rocky roads. She wept for the loss of the wonderful cookstove and the spacious table where she could seat her entire family in comfort.

Then she wept for her parents who, once again, would lose their only daughter and her children. She wept for her little girls who would not have the pretty things they would have if she could stay in this house.

When she had wept for everything and every tear was gone from her soul, she raised her head, dried her eyes and her arms… and blotted the tear puddles from the table. She looked into the mirror over the washstand and practiced a bright smile.

Hap returned. His lovely wife sat at the table, waiting for him. Her beautiful eyes looked slate blue in the dim light of the lamp, and her red-gold curls shone like tiny flames of fire. Her cupid's bow mouth turned up a little, just at the corners. He loved her so much it made him want to cry.

Kathleen was first. "You talk to her?"

He nodded. "She says she'll go with us. I wanted to tell her what she was in for, but I didn't know how. Likely you'll be better at it than me."

"I'll tell her. She'll need to be prepared."

"That'd be good."

"You looked at that window pane lately?"

"Well, I was thinkin' I'd…."

Kathleen nodded. “Seems it might be tellin’ us to get ready.”

“Need to sell the house, I reckon. Keep what we can use out of it. The furniture…?”

“Sell it. No tellin’ where we’ll be goin’. You thought on it, Hap? We been to just about every place close. I got the feelin’ this’ll be a long trip.”

“You mean when we put the picture on the wagon and tell the horses to take it the right way?”

The cupid’s bow mouth turned its smile into a laugh. “Now we’re thinkin’ the right way.”

So the words had been said, and all that was left to do was get ready. It was now late November of 1888.

Kathleen’s mother begged for reasonableness. “You could maybe wait till spring? You takin’ the babies out in this weather… it don’t hardly seem sensible.”

“We ain’t gone yet, Ma. We got things to do, and we can’t go till we get ‘em done.”

“I know, darling, but I see the look about you two, restless like a flock’a orioles bunchin’ up, readyin’ themselves to take off on their migration. I know it ain’t your doin’, and it’s purely frustratin’ that there ain’t no one to blame. I know I’ll wake up some mornin’ and you’ll be gone.”

“I know, Ma. There’s no one to blame.”

“But now, I know you’re getting’ things ready, and I have somethin’ to give you.”

Kathleen followed her mother to the small back room where Liddy had recuperated. There on the bed, like a flock of spring butterflies, were stacks of little girl’s dresses, all trimmed in lace and ribbons. Beside them were piles of warm flannel pettislips. On the pillow was a stack of striped overalls and checked shirts.

“Oh, Ma, they’re too pretty! You don’t know how dirty they get on the road, and…”

“Let ‘em wear ‘em.”

“But the lace and ribbons, just for play…?” The gift seemed too precious.

“It won’t hurt them to know there’s pretty things in the world. Let’m wear ‘em.”

“Oh, Mama….I’m so sorry…”

"You got nothin to be sorry over. If the girls was close, I'd'a been makin' the dresses. I just made 'em a little earlier, so's you'd know what you had and not buy 'em. When you get where you're goin,' likely there'll be mail service or a freight depot. I can send you…."

"Oh, Mama!" Tears filled her eyes, and she wept on her mother's shoulder. She cried for the days she would not have with her mother, and she cried for her mother who would not see her only child. They shared their tears, dried their eyes, and smiled. Life moved on, and the people were required to move on with it.

Her mother looked at her through red eyes and told her, "I got one more thing for you. Somethin' I think'll be useful."

She opened the closet and slid out a large box. In it were stacks of colorful bags made of sturdy fabric. Small bags made for tiny items. Middle sized bags for many sizes of items. And most of all, large bags with draw-string tops and many button-down pockets.

Kathleen stared at the colorful stack, her mind stringing up the possibilities like a flock of birds on a limb. Traveling in the wagon had presented one constant and inescapable concern. Where were things to be put so they could be found later? Here was the perfect answer to that continuing problem. Imagine! Bags for everything! Why had she not thought of it herself?

She turned to her mother with open arms and a fresh supply of tears lubricated their emotions. No words were needed. The daughter knew her mother had given a lot of thought to this gift, and the mother was jubilant that her efforts were successful. Bags! Kathleen must leave a lovely home, all her friends, and the only family she had, but she could make it. She had bags!

Liddy now appeared at the dining table at mealtime and Kathleen handed her the large bowl of golden fried potatoes, rich with ham chunks and flavorful with onions. Liddy needed to build up her strength.

Hap began. "I been thinkin' on what we'd need to take. I'm lookin for a bigger wagon…"

Liddy cut in, "I ain't meanin' you don't know that you need, but I got'a mention you don't need a bigger wagon for me. I'm takin' the visitation buggy."

"The visitation buggy…?"

"Bein two seated and roomy, there'd be a place for all my stuff and it'd not crowd you. I measured, and there's room for all I need."

"But, to drive…?"

"I'll drive. If Happy can drive a wagon, I can drive a buggy."

Later, in her room, Liddy and Kathleen looked at her clothes. Pretty and delicate and totally impractical. It was time to go shopping for serviceable dresses, thick shawls and warm shoes. The dainty dress were boxed up and set back.

"Now, Liddy, there's things that belonged to your ma and pa, and you need to decide what you want to keep."

"Nothin'."

"Not even…?"

"Nothin'." Her voice was firm and unchanging.

"I ain't meanin' to pry, but can you tell me why you don't want nothin'?"

"I don't deserve nothin'. Not after what I did."

"But, Liddy, you didn't do nothin.' You had permission to go on your visit, and you came on home when you was told. You didn't have nothin' to do with that sickness… Oh, Liddy, my precious sister, what can I say to make you feel better?"

In the second week of December, the house sold. They had a month to give possession. Hap sat with Liddy as she practiced driving the buggy. He was amazed that his sister had been allowed to reach the age of sixteen without basic knowledge of how to drive a team of horses. Apparently Papa had driven her everywhere she needed to go. Such protection! And she was about to plunge into the wilderness with them. He instructed her to pull over into the schoolyard for a serious talk.

"Liddy, honey, has Kathleen been talkin' to you on how it is to ride all day and sleep wherever you can?"

Liddy nodded.

"Have you thought long and hard and still want to go?"

No answer. She ducked her head.

"Now, I'm wantin' you to know. There ain't no reason you need to feel you have to go along, just 'cause ma and pa aren't here. There'll be a place for you, and we'll just have to find it. We'll get quite a lot of money from the house, and half of it belongs to you."

No response.

"Now, they's places where girls can stay and be looked after until they get ready to move on, or till they get married. You're not the only girl to have somethin' bad happen. You'll see other girls like you, and you'll make friends. How does that sound?"

"All right."

"You don't think you want to go with us?"

She shook her head slowly. "I reckon not."

"Then we won't need to work on this anymore. I'll get a small buggy that'll be more convenient to handle, and a gentle horse, and it'll be a lot easier for you. Would you like that?"

She managed a small nod.

"Well, we'll take this on back and put it up for sale. It's well made and almost new, and it should be worth a lot of money."

Hap stepped down from the passenger's side and, circling around to the driver's side, he took the reins with experienced firmness. Expertly tapping the horses' rumps and calling to them, the team obediently stepped forward and clomped down the brick paved street.

Lydia Palmer leaned back on the expensive leather upholstery and gazed at the houses passing before her eyes. The fingers of her left hand absently traced the scar on her right arm, still red from the knife blade.

Silently she left the buggy. Entering her room and stretching out on her bed, she lay staring at the ceiling. It was warm and cozy in her room, and her cheeks still burned from the brisk wind on the street. She could smell the meat and onion aroma coming from the kitchen. Smelled like beef stew, but she wouldn't need any. She lay on the bed and allowed her mind to go blank.

Kathleen's mind raced down the track it had followed ever since the sale of the house. Things to be done. Days were passing. In large boxes, she packed things of value to store in her parents shed. They might be back for them or need them to be sent somewhere. Liddy's dainty dresses were packed away and marked. She might need that box soon. Liddy was accustomed to wearing pretty things and the window might end up in a place where they would be useful.

She looked at toys with a thought toward providing quiet amusement under the canvas cover of the wagon. Dolls, paper dolls and toy scissors, two sets of ball and jacks, and four boxes of dominos.

They would be good for learning to count and to add, and they made very good building blocks.

She found a set of toy wooden farm animals, and she bought four sets. There were tiny wagons with movable wheels. Small houses.

She bought a small toy stove and table. Tiny dishes. She bought three sets of them. She set aside a sturdy box for all the toys, and it would be carried in the workshop wagon to be opened when they were camped overnight.

Concurrent with her toy purchases was the care of her family. Food to be eaten. Another day to be completed so another could be begun.

The beef stew and a mammoth pan of cornbread was set on the beautiful kitchen table. A bubbling peach cobbler was left on the stove to keep warm.

"Where's Liddy?"

Charity looked up. "She went in her room and closed the door like she didn't want me to come in."

Kathleen looked at Hap, who shrugged. "Maybe she's tired. It was really windy out there today."

"How did she do on the driving?"

Hap shrugged, again, and was silent. He didn't want to get into that discussion. He wanted to eat his cornbread and stew.

"She do all right?" Kathleen was insistent.

Hap nodded, blowing his stew. "She needs a littler buggy. She had trouble on the corners."

"She'll learn. It's easier on the road. Hap, she'd never get her things in a buggy no littler."

Hap looked at his wife and blurted out the reason. "She ain't goin'."

"AIN'T A'GOIN'!"

He explained, "She thought about it and decided we'd find a place for young ladies where she could stay."

"YOU DID WHAT?"

"Well, we…" He sought for an answer, but it wasn't needed. Kathleen was gone.

Banging her knuckles on the door, Kathleen demanded to be let in. With relief she saw that nothing had happened….yet. Liddy lay listlessly on the bed, staring at the ceiling

"Listen here, young lady! I expect you out there at the table, getting yourself built up in strength so's you can have fun on our trip. It's not all bad. But you got'a eat."

"I don't want anything."

"I didn't ask you that. You got'a eat. It's a requirement."

"Not if I don't go."

"I'm not listenin' to no talk'a you not goin'. Look at this buyin' and packin' we already done. You want all our effort to be wasted?"

"It'll be easer if I don't go."

"Easier for who…you or me?"

After a hesitation, "You."

"That's what I thought. That brother of yours talked you out'a goin', just when we had things goin' our way. When he goes to sayin' something you don't want'a hear, just don't listen to 'im!"

A small sound at the door. Charity stood with a piece of cornbread in her hand, rubbing her knuckles in her eyes. Mercy joined her. "What're you cryin' for?"

Sniff. Sniff. "Liddy ain't a'goin' with us on our trip."

"Sure her is!" Mercy patted Charity's arm. "Her said she would."

But Charity insisted, "But now she says she ain't."

"Girls," their mother said, firmly. "Go to the kitchen with your food and stay there at the table. We'll be in there in a minute."

The two small figures obediently disappeared from the doorway.

"Now, Lydia Palmer, you listen to me. I'm not havin' any of this backin' out, just when I got used to knowin' I'd have you along. I don't like givin' up somethin' I've been lookin' forward to."

"You want me to go?"

"Of course, I want you to go. Somethin' wrong with your ears?"

"But Hap said…." She hesitated.

Kathleen leveled her gaze at her sister-in-law and demanded,"What did Hap say?"

"He said it'd be easier without me. I know you got your family, and you got enough to do without someone else along. Someone that don't know how to do anything. He said we could sell the big buggy and get another one for me, but I don't need one."

"He's gonna sell the...what...?" Her blue eyes were wide with the realization to the extent that her carefully laid plans had gone awry.

"To get money, I think. Lena, when Ma died, Pa saw what was comin', and he told me where the money was, and I put it in my dresser drawer. You'll need to take it... and, Lena? Pa said for Hap to keep all the books and don't let nothin' happen to 'em. He said if he couldn't take 'em now, he'd need to store 'em, 'cause likely Happy'd need 'em someday."

Kathleen raised both arms with spread fingers, above her head. "WHOA, GIRL! Wait a minute. I think we're getting' somewhere, now. You think Hap needs money? You think he wants you to stay here 'cause of the money?"

The girl's answer was a faint nod. "Pa said he didn't know how you two managed to feed everybody. He said it like a joke, but I think he meant it."

Kathleen sighed and sat down beside her sister-in-law. "Let me tell you a story. God takes care of people. Remember when Baby Jesus was born and the king wanted him killed? Well, his parents had to take off to another country to keep him safe. Now I don't know how much money they had with them, but after the wisemen brought gifts, they had lots of it.

"Now it ain't like we are Mary and Joseph, but money is one of the things we have. We sold the pig farm and got a lot of money for it. We still have most of that. Your brother has been working on the willow wicker furniture, and people want to pay a lot of money for what he makes because he does such a good job. God is taking care of us.

"Now, your ma and pa's house is sold, and we have a lot more money, so whatever your pa handed you, that's yours. To keep or spend, whatever you want to do with it.

"'Nuther thing. We never missed no meal on account'a no money. We ain't sure where we'll be goin,' but we are sure there'll be enough money to get us there.

"Now there's one more thing I have to say. I DON'T WANT TO HEAR ABOUT YOU NOT GOIN' WITH US! DO YOU UNDERSTAND THAT?" She raised her voice until it fairly echoed on the rafters.

Twelve

A slight smile decorated the pale face on the bed.

Kathleen cinched the ground she had won and pushed on a bit farther. "So now you will get up from that bed and come and eat stew and cornbread, and you will eat every crumb of your peach cobbler. And if you give me any lip, you'll have to eat an extra piece of cornbread!"

Lydia Palmer stood and followed Kathleen to the kitchen and sat down at her place. Kathleen handed her a bowl of stew. "Liddy just had'a rest a minute. Drivin' that big old buggy ain't easy, but it's got'a be done so she's got'a eat and keep her strength up. Hap, did you check the springs under that buggy? Could be they're stiff and ride hard. You'd know if they'd be right to make a long trip. And the storm flaps? Would you check and see are they in good shape? Likely so, no more'n that buggy was used and the care that was took of it." She cast a meaningful look in the direction of her husband.

"Now, who's ready for cobbler?"

After desert, Liddy gathered the dishes together, rinsing and drying after Kathleen washed. Kathleen commented, "It's a sight easier here than on the road, and us havin' to wash dishes in a bucket settin' on the stove."

Liddy returned to her room and began to sort among the clothing, counting items and packing them into boxes. There was limited room even in the huge buggy, and she had to provide herself with a place to sleep. It would be like having her own bedroom… almost.

Would she really have to sleep in two nightgowns as Kathleen had warned, or maybe more? Just to keep warm? A tickle of excitement crawled up and down her back.

And in another room. "Hap, how could you talk that girl out'a goin' with us?"

Hap sighed. Women were so hard to understand. "It seemed like she wasn't wantin' to. I was tryin' to help her decide and be happy with the decision."

Kathleen tried to be patient. "She's just scairt, that's what. She ain't got no one but you, and she thought you didn't want her. She thought it would cost us too much money to take her."

"MONEY! How did she ever get an idea like that?"

"What you said about selling the big buggy."

"Did you tell her….?"

"I said we had lots'a problems, but money wasn't one of 'em, and she wasn't one of 'em, neither."

Hap was still concerned. "It makes me a little scary, her not used to things bein' hard, and all."

"Listen at yourself, Hap. You're ready to take a passel'a youngens on the road, and two of 'em not yet a year old. You might say that they ain't really, what you'd say, used to it, neither."

"But God gave me the youngens, and…" He sought for a reason.

"True. Could also be true that God just give you a sixteen-year-old sister."

Thirteen

Christmas was spent at the O'Keen's. Small, easy to pack toys, books with their own special box, and four huge goosedown comforters, tacked and tied with bright colored yarn were added to the traveling gear.

"Law sakes, these comforters are so fluffy, we may not can get 'em in the wagon," Kathleen praised.But they managed to.

It was bright and sunshiny, and almost warm on the eighth of January when the O'Keen's stood in their yard and waved as the first wagon pulled out, then the buggy with Liddy's smooth, white hands at the reins, and lastly was Happy, sitting proud and erect, with Roscoe by his side.

The older folks smiled until the caravan was out of sight. It was an effort, but it would not be well for the children to see their grandparents crying.

Hap first, shaking his head. "I sure hope she works them wheel brakes when she needs to. We got hills a'comin' up."

"You showed her how, didn't you?"

"Yeah, but she…" Kathleen's questions had a way of getting to the root of a thought.

"You think she ain't no smarter'n Happy? He don't have no trouble."

"Yeah, well, he's..."

"For sure, once we get up this first long hill and get down the next'n, she'll know what she's doin'. Either that, or she'll run square into us and we'll stop 'er. Either way, she won't get hurt."

Hap didn't appreciate the joke. "You wouldn't want'a go ride with her, just for a…? Maybe a little…?"

"And make her think she can't do it?"

Hap sighed, yet one more time. "I reckon you're right."

Ten miles seemed like a good distance for a first day. Hap had carefully mapped out in his mind how it would go. Traveling with several small children put certain restraints on efficiency. Food had to be prepared, diapers rinsed, and time had to be spared for them to run and exercise.

Early afternoon stops would be best, and he'd depend on getting as early a start as possible in the mornings. The younger ones could nap on the road until they were ready to get up. He'd have to manage to get a system about it, because they were certain to be on the road for a week and a half, maybe two weeks. Or more.

He had decided on a half hour stop at noon, rather than eating lunch as they traveled. Being a caravan of three demanded a long stretch of roadside space and just ahead was a grassy meadow with sparse trees. He pulled his team over to the side, and Liddy, with the help of well-trained horses, managed to line up behind him. Happy brought up the rear.

Over toasted biscuit sandwiches and raspberry peppermint tea, he explained. "Now, there's gonna be come changes, come time we stop for the night. Charity, you're to be in charge'a the wood gatherin' for your ma. You take Mercy, and you two get sticks to make a hot fire. You know the kind. Another thing, you take the ash bucket and fill it with fine, dry kindlin' and put it in the wagon with the stove. That'll give your ma somethin' to start with on the next stop while you're findin' more. We'll be hungry, and that'll start the food quicker.

"Now, Mercy, you'll go with Charity. You have to pick up all the sticks we need before you can run and play or get out the dominos or any other toy."

Mercy had a question. "Does Faith get to play with the dominos first?"

Fair question. "No, she has to wait for the wood to be picked up. If she doesn't like it, she can help you and maybe be finished faster."

He turned to his son. "Happy, you no longer gather wood. We got us six horses to tend to, and you'll help me. We'll get 'em to water, and short-hobble 'em to graze where they can. We'll keep 'em curried and clean, and there'll be times we'll have to grain 'em."

The sturdy seven year old brushed his black hair off his forehead, where it promptly flopped back down. "Yeah, Pa." The dimples in his cheeks deepened from the small smile at being promoted to a job more worthy of his skills.

"Nuther thing, Happy. We got three vehicles to keep greased and looked over for loose bolts."

The seven year old nodded. "And, Pa?"

"Yes, Son"

"I could maybe help get the stove out. Like we practiced?"

"That you can." The new apparatus for setting the stove out of the workshop wagon was going to be a time-saver, but it was somewhat of a four handed problem. When they were preparing for this trip, Hap, with Happy's help, had installed an "I beam" to extend out past the end of the wagon 'I beam," and the entire stove was raised by means of a pulley. Then the sling was moved along a track so the small stove hung in space out the back of the wagon, and required four hands to settle it securely on the platform made for the purpose.

"Yes, Happy, you'll help me set it out, and then you'll pull up a ways before you unhook your team. That'll give you ma a chance to get at the stove quicker.

"Now, Charity, you and Mercy'll be ready to get at hangin' diapers up to dry in your ma's wagon. We've got'a get on the road, now, but it'll be a short afternoon. Quick as we get to a creek, we'll look for a good place to stop."

Then they were in the wagons again. For a January day, it was warm and balmy, the way Kentucky weather can be. Blizzard weather one week, and sunshine the next. Thank you, Lord, for the sunshine.

Three hours down the road, Hap saw the place he wanted to stop. The rushing creek followed along the valley, and last summer's dry grass made good fodder for the animals. A grove of cedars would provide a good windbreak if the breeze should strengthen.

He pulled over, and the other wagons came in behind him. Hap motioned Happy to bring the stove to a protected spot, and he opened the workshop doors. Happy slid out the platform, and unhooked the first pulley. By now, Charity and Mercy were scouring around under the nearby trees for dry sticks and twigs. Faith began to pick up acorns to put in her pocket, and Kathleen spread a canvas tarpaulin on the ground, covering it with an old pieced quilt. The twins were piled into it and they began to squirm on their stomachs and pat their hands at each other, giggling and crooning.

Liddy watched. Kathleen took two pails and headed for the creek, scooping up water before the animals were taken to drink. One bucket was set on the back of the stove, and she began to build a fire from Charity's wood offering. Liddy watched.

Hap and Happy unharnessed the horses and took them to water.

Kathleen set on a pan of water to heat and lifted out a skillet. When the water was hot, she sprinkled in the cornmeal and salt, stirring with one hand while she mixed flour for biscuits with the other hand.

After a certain amount of bubbling and plopping, the cornmeal was pushed aside, and the biscuit pan was moved up. The pan was full of biscuits in a minute and a half and was deftly slid into the oven. A small bowl of the cornmeal mush was dished up, and a liberal amount of cinnamon, butter, and molasses was added to the remaining mixture. Corn Pudding was created.

Potatoes and onions were sliced into the sizzling skillet, salted and peppered, and the first pan of biscuits came out of the small oven and were transferred to the warming oven. While forming the next pan of biscuits, she lifted the onions and potatoes with the spatula and turned them, bringing the golden crust to the top. Liddy watched.

Grabbing Joy, the closest twin, she planted the baby on her hip and fed her small bites of the cornmeal mush while stirring the potatoes and onions.

Charity brought more wood, and Kathleen managed to get some of it poked into the stove. The second pan of biscuits were ready, and they joined the first pan, totally filling the tiny warming oven. By now, Hap and Happy were hobbling the horses in the deep nutritious hay made from the valley's summer crop. Then they were on their way back to the campsite.

Joy was put on the quilt, and Peace took her place on her mother's hip. One hand slid the potatoes off the fire, and moved another skillet over the flame. Popping the top off a jar of green beans, she dumped them into the skillet and plopped a generous dollop of butter on top. In between each action, Peace was given a bite of the cornmeal mush. Liddy watched.

Hap took the bar of soap from the food box and proceeded to wash his hands and extended the washing to Faith, not yet three. The other children took care of themselves.

A small platform was put on the ground beside the quilt, and the food was set on the board. Charity set the stack of plates and forks on the end of the board. The second pail of water was put on the stove. Liddy watched.

Before picking up their plates, everyone paused.

"Dear Lord, we thank you…"

Kathleen mashed soft-fried potatoes in a bowl, and between bites to her own mouth, fed tastes to first one, then the other, of the babies. Liddy picked up a plate and put her food on it.

Kathleen looked at her sister-in-law with a cheery smile. "Well, how did your first day go?"

Liddy, with a bite of potatoes on the way to her mouth, startled and asked, "Why, did I do something wrong?"

Hap opened his mouth, but Kathleen filled it. "Seemed to me you did a right bang-up job. Handled them brakes like they was growed to your hand, seemed to me."

"Do you think so?"

"Sure do. Leastwise you didn't run into anything, or fall over the mountain."

This started the children to laughing. The laughter turned into games, and with a handful of buttered biscuits, they left the quilt and began a game of hide and seek.

In minutes, they were back for their corn pudding. When they finished eating, each of them lowered an empty plate into the bucket of soapy water on the back of the stove.

Hap called to his oldest daughter. "Charity, remember the diaper line."

"Sure, Papa." From the food box, the six year old took a wad of heavy cord and tied it between two trees, hanging the bag of clothespins on a low limb.

Kathleen re-diapered the twins and gathered the soiled clothes with others from the wagon, and dunked them into the second bucket. Hap put his plate in the first soapy bucket and took the drinking water jugs to the creek. The animals had been away from it long enough for it to run clear again.

Kathleen washed the dishes and skillets, tossing away the soapy water. She poured clean water into the bucket and rinsed the dishes, setting them on a towel to dry. Liddy watched.

Kathleen rinsed and rubbed the diapers, tossing them into the rinse pail in water left from the dishes, and twisted them to wring out the water.

"Charity! Diapers are ready."

Charity and Mercy came running and picked up the load of wet squares, clipping them to the cord with clothespins. By then, the sun was lowering behind the mountain, putting the little valley into darkness.

Hap lighted the lantern and hung it on the side of the wagon. A puddle of golden light enveloped the campsite and the pieced quilt on the ground. He sat down and began to play with the babies. The table-platform was now empty, and Mercy set out the dominos. Houses, animal pens, wagons, towers and many other shapes appeared on the board as many small hands played with the nice square little building blocks. Liddy watched.

Darkness fell, and yawns were seen here and there. The babies were droopy and ready to be put to bed.

Liddy followed Kathleen to the wagon, carrying one of the babies. "Lena, I got'a talk."

Kathleen felt her lungs squeeze out their air, and her heart grab for a beat. It had clearly been too much, and the silent Liddy had made a decision. Dear Lord, please! Give me the right words.... please! Her mind pled for power from above.

"Sure, Liddy. Just let me pat these babies to sleep. Then we can get Hap and we'll...."

"No. It's got nothin' to do with Hap. It's you and me."

"Just us...?"

"Yeah. I know I can't tend to them horses. Hap'll have to do it, at least for a while. What I want'a ask, do diapers have to have warm water to get clean?"

"Diapers? You mean the twin's diapers? Well, I…"

"Cause if they don't, I could be washin' 'em out while you're doin' ten other things, all at once. If I did that, they'd have longer to get dry, wouldn't they?"

"Well, yes, if they got on the line…."

"I could do that, and then when we ate, I could wash up the dishes, and maybe you could go for a walk and rest your legs, or maybe stretch out on the quilt with the babies, or… somethin'…?"

"Well, the dishes didn't hardly take a minute…."

"You thinkin' I couldn't do 'em right? Now, that's one thing my Ma let me do. I did wash the dishes."

"Sure, you can wash the dishes if you want to. It would be a very good help. I just didn't think to offer to let you."

"That's all right. I'm kind'a new at this."

Kathleen nodded in the darkness of the canvas canopy. She was beginning to understand a lot of things. She was rather new at this, herself.

"Your ma, she was… well, she didn't let…?" How should she say this?

"I think she didn't trust me. Like makin' up the bed and cleanin' the corners with the broom. She had someone that come over every week and did up the washin'. I heard 'em talkin' about how good Hap did, and the way he could make the willow furniture, and the grades he made in school, and they…." She sighed and could go no farther with her words.

"But, honey, Hap was so much older than you. Twelve years, ain't it? There'd be a reason why he could…."

"No. They thought he did better when he was my age. I reckon he did."

"Did they actual say the words? That he did better?"

"They didn't need to. They said it like if I worked hard, maybe I could do good."

They sat together in the dark wagon and patted diapered bottoms. The mild January night still held, and their heavy serviceable dresses and shawls were enough to keep them warm within the protection of the wagon. Liddy continued.

"They wanted me to be a good girl and obey, and I did, and that made them happy. Ma told me what to wear to make me look right, and what to say when we had company. She was really good to me, and when I was sick, she stayed with me every minute. If she hadn't'a done that, chance she wouldn't'a got the influenza and died." Liddy drew a long, ragged breath.

Hap must be getting concerned. Kathleen glanced at the quilt, and her husband had leaned back with his hands under his head… likely asleep. The children played with the blocks in the light of the lantern. It was about time to get them into the bed.

But first there were words to be said. "Liddy, honey, it ain't your fault, how your pa and ma treated you. They loved you so much, they'd'a breathed for you if they could'a. Look at all them years between Hap and you, and them thinkin' they'd likely not have a little girl. Then you come along. I remember how they was like two kids with a new toy. My pa and ma talked about it, and how lucky they was to get you. All my folks had was one skinny little girl… me!

"Now, I love everyone'a my youngens, but I ain't got the time to do for 'em like your ma did. If I had the time, chance I'd be worse'n her. Now what I can promise you is, I'll take all the help you want to give. Like you said, they's times I do ten things at once. Another pair'a hands, that'll help, and them hands bein' attached to my only sister-in-law, that'll be even better."

Leaving the sleeping twins, she began to crawl out from under the canvas. "I'd bet you got your bed all ready, and after what all you did today, you'll be ready to get in it."

"Yeah, you're right. But I was a'thinkin' I'd not be able to sleep till I said what I said, so you'd know I'll do better tomorrow."

Stepping to the ground, Kathleen patted the pale, smooth hand of her sister in law. "You do just fine. Hap, wake up, and go to bed. You youngens put the dominos in the boxes and get ready for bed. It's too cold for you to be there on the ground, that'a'way."

Fourteen

Soon it was quiet in the campsite. A meadow mouse hopped onto the quilt to lick up a few crumbs, and a masked furry animal crept into the campsite and twisted at the oven door with his tiny, black-fingered hand. The smell of the food inside the box was too tempting to resist. In the end, though, he decided to move on in favor of the coyote who sniffed at the wagon wheels for information before lifting his leg to leave a message of his own.

Then it was morning and the winter crows, squawking and flapping about the trees, took the place of a farm rooster's serenade.

Animals were watered and hitched to the wagons. Liddy retrieved the diapers from the line and folded them, stowing the clothesline in the food box with the pins.

Oatmeal bubbled, biscuits browned and eggs fell sizzling into the skillet. Liddy spooned cereal into tiny mouths while feeding herself. Happy skillfully backed the workshop wagon into place, and the stove was hoisted aboard the minute it had cooled enough.

Drinking water jugs were filled again, and Liddy rinsed the plates, stowing them away with the buckets. The children took one last run down to the creek before settling in for the morning's ride.

Today was decision day. Sometime before noon, they would reach the crossroads where the north-south road overlaid the east-west road. The decision on which way to go would be made by the horses.

Kathleen wrestled with her thoughts. Hap had no idea of the conversation in the wagon last night, nor of any difference his parents had made between him and his sister. His sister had always seemed like a baby to him, and it seemed natural that his parents would spoil her.

Hap had always been a forward, confident sort of a fellow, much like little Happy, but he wasn't really strong on noticing what people did and why they did it… not that it would have mattered if he did, in this case.

The twins spent more time awake now that they were older and began to whine and suck their fingers. Kathleen broke apart a hard biscuit and handed each of them a piece. If they bit hard enough, they might get some teeth punched through their gums.

Hap broke into her thoughts. "See what's up ahead?"

Kathleen looked ahead and sighed, groaning inwardly. Such a strange way to decide a future… on the whim of a pair of horses. North, west or south, which way would it be?

At the crossroads, Hap called, "Whoa up, there! WHOA!" The obedient animals stopped in the middle of the road and Liddy stopped behind them.

To Kathleen, Hap stated, "Well, here goes. Git up! Gee, Haw, Git up, there!" He rippled the rein gently to tap on the horses rumps. With a rattle of the harness, the horses heard the confusing left-right command and snorted their response.

Then, without a hesitation, the animals leaned into the traces and turned their faces toward the south. As one animal, their heads turned, and their steps matched as they straightened out on the road. Plodding along, they moved in the direction of Tennessee… and the impossible mountain of several months ago.

Hap bit his lip with concern. "Lena, honey, you thinkin' we ought to do this? You know what's down this road."

"I know, Hap. It's a thing you'll have to decide. You'd have to be rememberin' we haven't done too well when we decided, so maybe the horses…?" It was humbling to think the horses could make a better decision.

"But we been this way, before."

"I know, and we'll go this way agin, if'n you don't turn around. If you turn around, which way would you go, then?"

"You thinkin' I ought'a warn Liddy?"

Kathleen sighed. That was a tough decision. "Well, if you do, just say it'll be a little rough up ahead, and don't let her think she can't do it. After God made us go back after her, would you think he'd let her fall over the bluff?"

"Well, she hasn't…."

"Hap, after we go down the other side'a that mountain, there ain't nothin' that'll ever scare her again."

"I hope you're right."

"Hap, don't depend on me. If you think we don't need to go over that hill, you do what you need to do."

He pulled over, and Liddy pulled over behind him. "Now, Liddy, honey, I ain't wantin' to scare you. I'm just tellin' you there'll be some mighty big rocks, about a quarter'a mile up this hill. You just keep talkin' to the horses, and let 'em find their own way. And don't you worry, none. You'll be fine."

Liddy stared, sober faced, at her brother. "You think…?"

"You'll do fine. Just keep goin'. They's a couple'a places I'll have to chock block, you know, like I showed you? But you pay me no mind, less'n I yell to you to stop."

Liddy nodded and gripped the reins, squeezing her pale knuckles even whiter.

Hap stepped back to have a word with his son. "Now, Happy, we're gonna try it agin. You let Liddy get on up ahead, and if you have any trouble, turn 'em short and crimp the wheels, 'an I'll get back to you. Just wait till I come. Hear?"

Happy nodded, confidently, his mop of black hair bouncing.

Hap returned to the first wagon. "Here goes, Lord!"

The beginning of the hill was a gradual slope, gently turning around the shape of the mountain. It crawled toward a saddle within two small peaks and then turned south for some serious climbing. The road builders must have used an entire wagon load of blasting powder to clear away the boulders. The road was literally chunked out of the solid stone of the mountain.

The mares trudged ahead, pulling hard but not straining. "I'm thinkin' a rest 'afore we go on, that might help."

"Couldn't hurt."

Hap pulled over, and the others fell in behind him. "Gonna rest the horses for twenty minutes. Get out and stretch, and walk around a bit." Maybe a walk would relax Liddy's tension. She came toward them, smiling.

"Doin' all right?"

"Doin' good. I think…?" There was a tentative question at the end of her words.

"Sure you are!" her brother remembered to add.

Then they were climbing again. Around the curve to the flat rocks, on out to the bluff, circle back, and wheel out again. Just ahead were the slippery slopping rocks. Involuntarily, Hap's hands tightened on the lines. With his toe, he located the chock block and scooted it forward.

The first rock was fairly flat, and not very big, and the mares felt their way across, planting solid hooves in the grooves made by many previous equine climbers. Then they were on the dirt again. Another rock up ahead. That must be the bad one. He turned to see Liddy crossing the rock, moving easily around the bend.

He lost Happy in the turn, but if Liddy made it, certainly Happy was right behind. The next rock was just ahead, but it was not the big one, either. So far, so good. Thirty minutes later he was still climbing, the chock block held firmly between his feet. On a straight away, he could see both wagons behind him. A comforting sight.

He felt Kathleen's gaze on his face, burning in intensity. He turned to look at her eyes, a deep slate blue in the clear mountain air. The corners of her mouth turned up a little… a very little, and her trim shoulders shrugged, ever so slightly.

Hap turned his face away and rode along, dreading to put words on anything so utterly ridiculous. God did not put rocks in a mountain and take them out again just to get His point across! Or did He?

The first wagon climbed out of the saddle and turned onto the steeper climb. The roadbed was firm and free of rolling rocks. He yelled encouragement to his team, forcing his voice to speak louder, to remind Liddy.

Behind him, he heard her, "Git up there! Pull on out!"

Another turn and they were on the top. He pulled out on a grassy plateau at the top of the world and let the animals grab mouthfuls of the dry grass, chewing as best they could around the metal bit in their mouths. Liddy pulled over and wound the reins on the holder as she had been told.

"I did it! I did it!" And she smiled, crinkling her eyes with pleasure like she had not smiled since long before the funeral.

As instructed, Happy had fallen behind, but had now reached the top. "I'm hungry," he informed the waiting party.

"Let's eat! And then let's have a cup of tea and enjoy the view."

The air on the mountain was crystal clear, and lower mountaintops could be seen in every direction. There was a saying that for a mountain to be considered really tall, seven layers of blue peaks must be seen from its crown, and this one certainly qualified.

Toasted biscuits with butter and jam with cups of steaming tea, and then it was time to go down.

"Hap…?"

"Yeah, Liddy?"

"Will it…? I mean, is it gonna to be steep…?"

"Yes, but you ain't gonna have no trouble. Just drive with your hand on the brake, pullin' with both hands when you have to. The horses'll find the best stepping places. You'll do fine."

And she did.

Coming down the mountain on the other side and into Tennessee took most of the afternoon, and the valley seemed to be a good place to camp, even if it was a bit early. The tension caused by the mountain had taken its toll on the drivers.

The diapers were on the line before the stove was hot.

The biscuit dough was in the pan, applesauce bubbled, spicy and rich, waiting for the pastry topping, and into the oven it went. Ham slices popped and crackled and were shifted to the warming oven to make room for the speckled butter beans to heat.

The children raced across the soft dry grass, and the weather held. Only a light jacket was necessary to stay warm and snug.

The next day was Saturday. It was always good to find a small town before the Lord's day, so they could attend church with others.

It was shortly after noon that the caravan pulled into the small Tennessee town of Hilltop. The livery stable was the most prominent building on the street, and they were always a good source of information.

"Church? Sure we do. My brother's the preacher here. He'll want you to camp over to his place, but I can bring the horses back here to the stable. You folks goin' far?"

"Well, we…"

"Wouldn't be nosy, ordinarily, but if you ain't locals, you might not notice the snow clouds pilin' up in the northwest."

Hap turned and looked up to see the mountains of puffy 'white sheep' clouds. White sheep usually brought snow. The tops were climbing higher and higher into the sky. Well, it was about time for snow since it was, in fact, the middle of January.

Staring at the clouds, he thoughtfully stroked his chin. "You wouldn't be knowin' of a empty house we could rent for a week or two? I got my family, and we was lucky to get good weather up to now, but the babies…? You know?"

"Like I said, Mister. My brother'll expect you over there. He's got the house we put up to take care'a visitin' preachers. He'd see no reason for you not to use it."

"We wouldn't want to…." What could he say that was not a lie? He really did want to be in a house before dark.

"Mister, my brother'd have my hide if he thought I let you go on the road, this weather comin' in like it is. Now, what you do, you just follow this here road, and when it turns past the grove'a sweet gum trees, look to your left. Can't miss it."

Around the corner, Hap came face to face with a sizeable church, a well-kept house, and a small log cabin in the rear. Had to be the place.

He knocked on the door. "Name's Palmer, Hapgood Palmer. Your brother at the livery said you had a place you might let out till the storm's over."

"My name's Blake. Come in! Come in!"

"Well, I got my wife and…"

"Man, don't stand and let the winter in the house! Go get her and all the family. Get 'em on in here, and we can talk business."

By now, the wind was scouring across the mountaintops, whipping dry leaves against the buildings and shaking down broken twigs. A blue norther was heading in for sure.

"Bring them youngens on in here. I got four'a my own. You got here just in time to eat with us. The missus, she's got the bean's a'cookin.'"

"Oh, no, we couldn't. Just show us…" The aroma of the beans was an intoxication to the hungry man.

"Now look, I ain't had no company to speak of since back last fall. You folks don't need to get fidgety and in a hurry, 'cause you'll not leave this mountaintop for a week, from the look of that sky."

The children disappeared into the rear of the house, and the noise level increased considerably.

"So you're a preacher! Land sakes, if this ain't my lucky day! Company, and him a preacher! Now, you'll have a sermon ready for tomorrow. There'll be a good number to come on if they can get up the mountain. That little house, now, it's a mite small, but I'll say it's a tad bigger than all them wagons put together.

"First off, you and me, let's take your animals over to the livery. My brother'll take good care'a the bunch and feed 'em up for ya. Now, tell me what it is that got you out on the road in the dead'a winter with babies along?"

Fifteen

The story of the stained glass window occupied the afternoon.

"And you ain't looked in the crate since the time the wagon came apart? How do you know you ain't got a crate'a glass slivers all shakin' around in there."

Hap grinned and shrugged. "If I have, or if I haven't, it's gonna be took wherever it wants to go!"

The three-room cabin was snug, and the two wood stoves kept it that way. The cook stove worked, though not as well as the one on the wagon, but one can't have everything.

During the next days, there was time for hunting in the snowy hills, hours of visiting, and the children invented new games every hour.

"Say, preacher, I got'a thought. How do you know this here ain't the place for you to stop? I can tell you been in a pulpit before. They's several vacant pulpits I could name right now. Tennessee ain't a bad place to be, especially this part. What'd'ya say?"

Hap could only reply that the window had the final word. Like Jonah from the inside of the whale, he figured he had enough of going his own way. He would move on until he was told to stop. There he would stay until he was told to move on.

"Well, you know somethin,' friend, they's been some movin' on around here and a lot more talk'a movin' on, headin' for the Oklahoma territory."

"Oklahoma territory…?" Some foreign country?

"Yeah, a place called the Unassigned Lands. They's gonna be a land giveaway. Like when they was openin' up Kansas and such. Surprised you ain't heard tell of it. They been spreadin' the maps around."

The idea was incredulous. Hap asked, "Folks are goin' all the way from here, all the way across Arkansas? Ain't that where the Territory is?"

"So I hear. Folks as don't have land, they'll do a lot to get it. All that's got'a be done to get the free land is to build a place to live and dig somethin' to get water out of. That'd mean a lot to some folks."

It was an interesting subject, and it lasted for several hours. The Palmers attended the church for two weeks, but by the last of the next week, the sun was bright and warm, the snow was gone and it was time to go.

"Friend, you wouldn't want'a let me see that window, would you?"

Hap shrugged. Why not? Especially after all the hospitality he had been given. Crawling under the wagon, Hap removed the bolts that kept the crate closed, and eased out the window. The wood frame was as new and bright as if it had just been set together. The leaded strips between the shaped pieces of glass were firm and shiny, and the baby in the picture looked as if he could reach out his hand, and it would be smooth and warm.

Preacher Blake stared at the window, sober and quiet. "I think if I'd'a been handed that, I'd be on the road, too. Babies or no babies." He nodded slowly and reverently.

So, with that benediction and blessing, Hapgood Palmer clicked to his team, pulling them onto the road again. Stopping at the livery to pay his stable bill, Bill Blake, the owner jabbed at him, again. "Reckon you're gonna head out to Oklahoma Territory, to get you that free land!"

Hap grinned. "Could be," and he was off. Certainly not so far away as the territory, of course. It was what? Five hundred miles? Maybe more! There were plenty of places to serve the Lord that were a lot closer than that.

The sketchy map he had picked up showed the next place of interest to be Butkin's Corners. "Corners" generally meant a crossroad, which generally meant a town of sorts and that should be a good place to stock up on a few things.

The caravan camped at the edge of the town. A dozen houses, a grinding mill, a general store, and a church made up the town. A pretty church, and it obviously had all the windows it needed. The general store had flour, meal, butter, eggs, and slab bacon. It also had maps.

"Help yerself to a map, Mister."

"Map'a what?"

"They say it's a map'a the Oklahoma territory, that's gonna be up for grabs. The papers is full of it. Could be that's where you're goin'?"

"No, not me. I'm just…." He looked at the stack of hand-drawn sketches.

"Well, pick yerself up a map, anyway. Might change yer mind. Looks to be a good deal for them as has no land'a their own."

To please the proprietor, Hap took a map and folded it up small. Slipping it in his pocket, he selected two dozen peppermint sticks to put with the groceries, paid for them, and carried them to the wagon. It must be some deal, that free land in the territory. It had folks a'talkin,' but then folks didn't have much else to talk on, come winter in the mountains.

The horses moved west, and the weather held. It was a most unusual winter. February started with the weather almost shirt-sleeve warm. They moved along, camping early, stopping at farmhouses to buy staples, such as eggs and butter, and occasionally home canned fruit.

The housewife was usually very glad to get a bit of hard cash for her canned tomatoes, peaches and apples, and occasionally jams and jellies. It was especially appreciated that the travelers were able to leave empty glass jars with her, and they were the same jars that had been purchased full from some homestead a few days back.

And then Memphis was just ahead. Memphis, sitting there on the Mississippi River… that could be their destination. Had he not twice tried to go to the river, but found himself turned around? Apparently, now was the time to go to the river.

The city of Memphis was a bustling place, centered mainly around the mighty Mississippi, its crossings, and its cargo. For people heading west, Memphis and St. Louis seemed to be the best crossing points, and the southern city had its share. There was a lot of movement through the streets, but even more were staying, colonizing, building, starting businesses and obviously they would be needing churches for the strength and healing of the soul.

Where would be a better place than Memphis for a young preacher eager to go to work for the Lord, and even able to furnish a decorative window in the church that would be a product of his work.

He breathed deeply with internal satisfaction. Finally, he had managed to get his family where he could put down roots, give his growing children a nearer-normal life and still obey the call from above.

Certain the city was his destination, Hap found a place for the family, and for the animals, and began to wait for direction. He spent time on the docks with his testimony in the shacks along the river with his friendliness and help, and he spoke to gatherings when he had the opportunity.

After a month, it became clear to him that he was following his own path, and the window was not a part of it. It was so easy to do. There were many instances in the Bible where leaders had done that, and he was amazed to realize how easily he had fallen into the trap. That understandable "trap" of deciding to help God, and, at the same time, do what he thought was best for the family God had given him. When he allowed himself to think of his family, the responsibility weighed heavily on him.

In addition to that, the lowland around the river did not agree with the babies who spent the nights crying and gagging with the effects of the croup. The low lying, moist air fresh off the river, coupled with the chill of being near water, kept them hoarse and continuously irritable.

So, after four weeks, he packed his family again into the caravan and headed south along the river toward the state of Mississippi. Surely, going south would be the correct direction. Surely the air would be warmer and dryer, and the family could get a little sleep at night.

He had gone only two days out of Memphis when he saw the little town ahead. A hand-painted sign proclaimed it to be Carrigan's Flats. He needed to restock his grain supply, and called out to the animals, "Gee up, there! GEE! Git along!"

As the horses turned, in unison, toward the livery stable of the small town, there sounded a crack that rang out like a rifle shot in the hunting grounds. The sound came from just below Hap's feet. The crack was followed by a splintering, grinding sound, which terrified the horses. They bucked and danced, flinging their heads about, and Hap fought with the lines to calm them. Just as they settled, snorting and grinding their mouths on the bit, the right front of the wagon began to tip.

Before the amazed eyes of Hap and Kathleen, the front wheel laid itself over onto the roadbed, totally separated from the wagon, and the heavy wooden tongue split itself from end to end, just as if it had been hit with a lightening strike.

Hap stepped out of the wagon and went around, patting the horses' noses to calm them, and he stood beside the separated wheel. Shaking his head sadly, only Kathleen heard him say, "I say, Lord, look what happened to Your wagon. Busted a wheel and split the tongue."

By now, a gathering of the town's men surrounded the split tongue and separated wheel.

"Now look at that! Never saw a tongue split like that! Seen 'em break, but never seen 'em split like that. And there ain't no sign'a rot on it nowhere."

Hap was tempted to say 'You should have seen what happened on the mountain,' but he didn't. There were some things that one just had to be there to understand… or believe.

There were comments. "Look at that wheel! Lost all its bolts at once!There they lay not ten feet back. The rocky road must'a wobbled 'em off."

And head shaking. "I knowd the roads was bad, but I never seen the like'a this."

There were statements of incredulity. "Look at that wheel! Not broke nor nothin'. Just came off."

And damage assessments. "That tongue, it'll have to come off. Be no way to fix a split like that."

There were attempts at comforting words. "Good thing it happened here at the shop. Beau Blanchard, here, he'll be able to set you a new tongue, Mister. Got the stuff right out back's the shop."

And sympathy. "And that wheel, puttin' the bolts back on, that'll put it right."

Then there was the final summation. "Yessiirree, Mister. Good thing for you that didn't happen back on the mountain. Could'a come down it faster'n you aimed to."

By now, young Happy had pulled the shop wagon to the edge of the road and stood importantly beside his father. All of this was no surprise to him, and he knew, without a doubt, that it would be easily fixed, and they would turn around and retrace their steps. He was an observant seven year old.

Beau Blanchard came sauntering up, thumbs in the bib of his overalls. "Yep, that's the strangest split on a tongue I ever saw, and me bein' in this business, forty years, man and boy. Ain't nothin' that can't be put to right, though. You just take off your horses and turn 'em on the grass out back. I'll have you fixed up by suppertime."

Happy heard the verdict and walked back to Liddy. "I got'a get your horses and put 'em out in the pasture," he announced, importantly. "We're gonna be here till suppertime, likely all night."

Kathleen looked up and down the main street of the little town where interested faces peered at them from every window. What a place to camp! The girls, however, had slipped down from the wagon and were looking in all directions for children to play with. Being constantly on the move had taught them to make friends quickly, and one must take their fun when they could find it.

Liddy climbed onto the buckboard beside her sister-in-law. "Window pane talkin' to us agin, huh?"

Kathleen nodded. "Seems like it."

Liddy continued, "I been thinkin'. The way I got them storm flaps that snap down tight, how'd it be if I let the…I mean, maybe I could…well…"

Kathleen turned to Liddy with concern. "You not bein' warm enough at night? We can…" But the younger woman interrupted.

"No, it's not that. I was thinkin' on how the babies cough and gag, and cry till they got no voice, keepin' you up all night. If I was to button down tight and maybe make a tent out'a a sheet, it'd be dryer underneath, and maybe…?" Then she hesitated, unsure of her words.

"You're sayin' you want the babies to…?"

"Not if you don't think it'd be best. Only, ridin' alone, it gets me to thinkin.' If it's the damp air, well, maybe… do you think…?"

"Why, Liddy, that's the nicest offer anyone ever made to me! Only thing is, how could you get any sleep?"

"I'd manage. And I was thinkin' if they didn't cough so much, likely they'd sleep and we'd all get to rest."

"You think you could manage both of them?"

"I could try."

"How about you take Joy and see how it goes. She seems to be havin' the most trouble."

Sixteen

The evening meal was prepared just off Main Street in Culligan's Flats. The forced delay provided plenty of time to bake sweet potatoes and make a hasty pudding with peaches mixed through it.

By sundown the new tongue was shaped and put in place, bolted securely and greased liberally.

The livery stable manager spoke, "Friend, not meanin' to be nosey, nor nothin,' but there ain't a thing down the road that you'd get to by nightfall. You're welcome to leave yer animals in the pen back there till daylight."

"Thanks. I wasn't gonna go any farther, tonight. Found myself goin' the wrong way, anyway. Missed a turn somewhere back there."

"Oh, you'd be talkin' about the cutoff to Rippley. That'n, it's a easy turn to miss. Well, good luck on your journey."

"Thanks."

Charity had strung the diaper drying cord from the wagon to the buggy, and Liddy pinned on the white squares to dry in the night breeze.

The little cast iron stove was producing the smells of supper. Baked sweet potatoes, boiled eggs, cornbread, and peach flavored cornmeal pudding. Then, Kathleen put on the tea kettle and measured zinger tea into the cups.

Liddy watched, knowingly. "Zinger tea time, huh?"

Kathleen nodded. "The window pane talks, and we got no way to talk back or even answer, so we drink tea. You'll get used to it."

While the children played, the grownups held the steaming tea in their chilly hands and contemplated their situation.

Hap first. "We knowd we were right to go to Memphis. Then I took it on myself to leave there, thinkin'a the babies. Trouble is, I didn't give a lot'a thought to the direction I headed out in. Thought it was up to me to do the best for the babies and God had other plans. Seemed like, but it got ourselves stopped."

Kathleen nodded. "It gives a body reason to think, bein' talked to by a split wagon tongue."

Liddy sipped her tea and added, "Yeah, well I remember one fellow in the Bible, named Balim, that got talked to by a donkey. I'd heap rather it'd be a wagon tongue that talked to us."

Kathleen agreed. "Yeah, or get swallowed by a fish."

Hap, again. "So, tomorrow we head back, and when we get to Memphis, we'll see if the window pane can tell the horses which way it wants to go." In the silence that followed, it seemed perfectly sensible to the three adults that a window could talk to a horse.

The twins were droopy with sleep, but the raspy breathing had already begun. Kathleen looked at Liddy, who nodded and reached for baby Joy. She was a round, soft bundle in three nightgowns, a sweater, and knitted cap. Socks and wool bootees were tied to her chubby ankles. All this was bundled up in a small thick quilt. She was warm as breakfast toast but a heavy, rattley breath came from her tiny mouth and nose.

Liddy took her to the buggy and placed her on her tummy over a pillow and began to pat her backside, humming softly. The heavy storm flaps sealed the moist night air outside, and the tiny girl began to breathe smoothly.

Easing away from the baby, Liddy joined her brother at the tea pot.

Grinning at her, he commented, "Gonna sleep with the youngen, huh? Well, it couldn't hurt. She was better when we were in the house in Memphis."

The chill breeze began to pick up and the children were ready to put away their games and crawl into the quilts, but there was not a lot of sleep with Peace fussing and whining.

Liddy crawled in beside baby Joy, scooting her gently aside to make more room. Such a cuddly, warm little bundle, she wanted to hug her but thought better of it and decided to try to get some sleep while Joy slept. The next thing she heard was the crowing of the town roosters.

Kathleen was poking wood into the little stove, and Hap and Happy were bringing up the horses. Liddy slipped from the bed, leaving Joy asleep, and took the water buckets to the town well.

Peace fussed and complained, and Kathleen hurried with the cereal. "Seems like the warm mush helps their throats. A little. How did you sleep? We didn't hear nothin' out'a you."

"Slept like a log. I hear Joy a'wakin' up. If you want, I'll give them their cereal. That is if…?" Always a question at the end of her offers of help.

"Please do."

The stove was lifted aboard, and the wagons were turned around in the middle of Main Street, heading them back toward Memphis. Should be there in two days, easy.

They arrived back in Memphis on Sunday, the Lord's Day, and found a church to attend, but they entertained no hopes of staying. The church didn't need another window.

It was now the middle of March.

Monday morning they bought their breakfast at a grocery store. Sliced bread and ham, and milk for the babies, and then climbed aboard the wagons. Even the long-suffering redbone hound, Roscoe, got ham for breakfast. The horses chewed their grain from their feedbags and pulled onto the street.

Hap yelled, "Git up, there!" but he did not guide the horses in any particular way. They walked along the curb, turned at a corner and added themselves to a great, milling crowd of people and vehicles. A long, snake-like line stretched down the street and into an alley. The mares took their place at the end of the line and stopped, switching flies with their tails.

The line to the river ferry! The near future was clear and simple, the Palmers would be crossing the Mississippi River over into Arkansas. Hap stepped down from the wagon and walked forward in the line.

The ferryboats were lined up at the dock, and wagons, buggies and people were being funneled aboard, measured, and turned away when the floating platform was full. The paddle wheels churned up the mud from the river bottom creating brown foam as it pulled away from the bank and was replaced with the next platform.

Walking back, Hap greeted some of those in line, and the man in the wagon just before him, called out, "Headed for the territory?"

"No, we was just crossin' over."

"Oh. I'd'a thought, the way you was together and loaded with your family, you was goin' after the free land. 'Course, you'd be obliged to move fast to make it with youngens. Can't make much time with the little folks needin' this and that."

Hap continued the friendly interchange. "You headed out there?"

"Yeah. Got a brother meetin' me about twenty miles into Arkansas. We're gonna make a run for it on horseback and maybe get somethin.' If we don't, we'll likely look for work. The way we figger it, there'll be more work to do there than there'll be hands to do it."

"Likely you're right." Hap waved a salute and walked on.

"Now, Liddy, we're headed out onto a ferryboat. What you'll do is drive out onto the platform and stop where they tell you. They'll tie up the horses, and chain down your wheels. You just stay there, and say somethin' to the horses every little bit, so's they'll know you're there. That'll hold down the nervousness in 'em."

Liddy nodded and smiled, and only the whiteness of her knuckles indicated any fear. Hap pretended not to notice.

"Now, Happy, we're fixin' to cross the river on the ferry boat."

"Oh, goodie!"

"Now, don't get too excited. Just do what they tell you to do."

"Can I get out and look at the river?"

Hap wanted to say no, but when would the boy ever get another chance to see the Mississippi from the middle of it? The small boy that was still within himself, answered the question.

"I reckon. But only for a minute, and then get back to the horses. Hear?"

"Yeah, Pa." His dark eyes sparkled with excitement.

Hap returned to the first wagon.

Charity first. "Pa, I want'a ride with Happy. Can I?"

"No, I think you better stay with me."

"Can I ride with Liddy? I could help."

"Sorry, no. You just sit tight."

The line inched forward, as a boat full at a time was clipped off the front of it. Then they were on the dock. A cleated ramp led from the dock to the ferry, its crossboards spaced to help a horse get traction with its hooves and avoid slipping.

Eyes rolling and tail switching, the mares pulled the wagon forward. Down the sloping ramp and onto the floating platform they came. A deck hand held to the bridles of each horse, guiding them to their place. The wheels were chained down, so the wagon wouldn't roll with the motion of the boat and possibly collide with its neighbor.

Hap's wagon was the last one on that boat, and the paddle wheels began to turn, splashing into the water, inching the platform toward the middle of the wide ocean of a river. This made Liddy the first one to pull onto the next boat.

She had watched as Hap's wagon was tied down, and the ferry moved away leaving her next in line. The dock hand began to wave her forward. With a sigh, she picked up the reins, but the guide put up his hands, palms forward for her to stop. She did.

He came walking back to her. "Ma'am…uh, Miss? You want I should help get your buggy on board? I could…"

Liddy looked at him and then at the water on both sides of the ramp. What was wrong, was the buggy too wide? Or something?

"Well, I…"

"I wouldn't mind, Miss. If you'd just slide over, I'll take the reins, and we'll be on the boat in a minute."

While she hesitated, he stepped on the footrest and into the buggy beside her. Reaching for the reins, he smiled at her.

"Git up, there!" he called to the horses and they began to move forward. Another dock hand reached for the bridle of the left horse, and one reached for the right one. The horses agreeable allowed themselves to be led forward.

"You headed out west?" the young man asked Liddy.

"West? Yes, we are…." It seemed a safe answer. They truly were actually headed in the westerly direction.

"I wisht I was goin' there. I should'a been on the way to the free land in the Oklahoma territory. You'll not make it in time for the run, will you?"

Liddy wasn't sure. "Well, we weren't really…."

"Well, Miss, I got'a get down and leave you now, but you'll do good." And he was gone.

Happy was next. The dock hands came forward as he clicked his horses into motion. The animals stepped carefully down the cleated ramp to be met by the guiding hands and were led to a position directly behind the buggy. No one seemed to notice the wagon was driven by a seven-year-old boy, and no one offered to drive his wagon aboard. He was glad about that.

When he had been chained into place, he hooked his lines on the peg and slid down to the platform. "Come on, Liddy, let's go look at the water."

"No, thanks, Happy. I can see it well enough from here."

"All right." He squirmed his way through the crowd of standing people until he reached the rail. By then, the ferry was very near the middle of the river. Happy leaned out and looked to the east and then to the west, and the river banks looked far away teeming with people too small to identify. The noisy paddle wheels fought against the current that was trying to send the loaded platform down stream. It was all too exciting.

On the west bank, the wagons were loosed from their chains, and the horses were led from their positions in line and guided up the ramp on the other side. Hap waited to motion Liddy onward, and Happy followed behind.

"Oh, Pa, that was a lot'a fun! Let's do it again!"

Hap thought once was enough. As he led his caravan away from the river, someone called, "Map'a the west, Mister? Only a nickel."

Hap thought about it. Maybe a map would be a good thing since he really had no idea where he was going. Handing over his nickel, he took the map and handed it to Kathleen.

Through the crowded streets he went, past people walking, people in carriages and people seemingly standing still in the streets. Glancing back occasionally, he saw the rest of his caravan was following closely behind.

Finally through the narrow, dirty streets and onto the road again, he pulled over. "Let me take a look at that map, Lena."

Kathleen handed it over. "I'm wonderin' why you needed another map'a the Oklahoma territory."

"The Oklahoma territory? Did I…?"

"You sure did. You paid a nickel for a map just like the two in your pocket. So now you got three maps, just alike."

Hap turned to look knowingly at Kathleen, who was looking back at him with squinted, slate blue eyes. "Hap, it's the window talkin', ain't it?"

Hap nodded. "That'd be my guess. Seems like it's handin' me notes that look like a map. Course we'd not make it in time for the free land race."

"Do we need free land? We got money, and likely we could buy some. Come time we need it, that is."

"Well, free'd be…" He smiled sadly at his wife, "What am I talkin' about. I don't need to figure on what we'll do. The window'll take care'a that."

Both Liddy and Happy had left their vehicles and had come around to Hap's buckboard seat.

"Pa, Liddy didn't get to drive onto the ferry. Some fellow made her scoot over and let him drive."

Hap turned to his sister. "Did you have trouble, or… tell me, was it the young fellow who waves you on when your turn comes? Was he the one to drive your team?"

Liddy nodded. "I could'a done it. Really, I could'a."

Hap grinned. "Yeah, you could'a, but then he'd have not got to sit by a pretty lady for a few minutes. That's what happened."

Happy stared from his father to his aunt. "He just wanted to sit by her? Why'd he want to do that?"

"Son, if you still want to know the answer ten years from now, just ask me again, and I'll tell you."

"Aw, Pa, in ten years I'll be old, and I'll know everything. I won't have to ask you."

"I 'speck you're right, Son. Well, we put in a day on the crossin' and we'll head out till we find a good camp spot. The girls, they're getting' jumpy as a snake on an ant hill, and I'm getting' hungrier'n a bear."

Seventeen

It was now the first of March, and the wind blew gently from the south. The winter sun was gaining warmth from the coming spring.

Leaving the town behind, they found a place to camp for the night. A stream of water rushed by, and a grove of trees gave a small bit of protection.

The stove was lowered and blazing brightly as the soiled diapers were rinsed in cold water and hung to dry. The horses were tethered to trees and allowed to nibble the fresh green shoots of spring.

All along the bank of the little stream were small white balls, growing in clumps and drifts.

"Look, Ma, mushrooms!"

"Can we get some?"

"I'll carry the pail."

"Let's get two pails. Ma likes to get a lot!"

"Ma, shall we get all of 'em, or leave the little'ns?"

Kathleen interrupted the cacophony of childish voices.

"Charity, wad up your fist, and if they ain't no bigger'n that, leave 'em till morning."

The fat bacon strips sizzled in the pan, preparatory to the arrival of the mushrooms. Biscuits were in the oven, and blackberry dumplings simmered on the back of the stove, right beside the bucket of warm water for the dishes.

"Lena, I can feed the babies. What're you wantin' 'em to eat?"

Peace and Joy were crawling all over the quilt, sucking their fingers noisily. Kathleen thought about the question. Mushrooms were not exactly suitable for babies not quite a year old."Liddy, pour some milk in a bowl with a little honey. This first pan'a biscuits is ready, and you can crumb a couple of 'em up in the milk. They'll like that."

Spring mushrooms! They appeared along the banks of the creeks like magic! There was nothing, and then suddenly, they were there, like tasty balls of snow. Like heavenly drops of flavor. The roots were sliced away, and they were popped into the sizzling skillet where they melted down into soft dark globs of goodness.

Carefully, they were removed to another skillet and more were added to the flavorful grease. Finally, butter and flour were added to the bubbling grease, and then water with just a little milk. The rich gravy bubbled and rolled, spreading its delightful smell out over the little valley.

The simmering gravy was poured over the brown and tan globs and allowed to heat to bubbling point once more. Biscuits were split open, and the mushrooms and gravy were ladled over them. Tantalizing steam arose from the plates as they were set on the small platform that served as a table.

Heads were bowed. "Dear Lord, we thank You for…"

Long after the children had stuffed their biscuits with browned, cracklin' sidemeat and had run away to play, Kathleen sat with the plate of lovely mushrooms, leisurely savoring the taste.

Hap watched from the corner of his eye. "Cravin' mushrooms?"

"Hush up. I always crave mushrooms. I just can't always get 'em."

While Kathleen nibbled on the last of the mushrooms, Liddy fed tastes of the gravy to the twins, dipping the spoon into the skillet and letting them suck it.

"Lena, I got room for Peace in my buggy. You think maybe…?"

"Oh, Liddy, surely you don't want…." But Kathleen's weariness took over, and she waited for the second offer.

"It's all right if you don't want her to…?" Liddy was always so unsure.

"It isn't that. I know it's a trial to sleep with babies. I been doin' it for the last seven years. You got Joy, and she don't have the croup and that's a blessin'. I wouldn't want you to…."

"But I got room. If it's good for Joy to sleep in the drier air, likely it'd be good for Peace, too. I'm thinkin'…?"

Kathleen hesitated no longer. The temptation of a sleep-filled night was overpowering. "Well, it'd be a thoughtful thing to do."

So Peace and Joy both lay on their tummies over the pillow, being patted to sleep by their auntie.

Sunrise comes later in the valleys, and it was barely daylight when Happy and Charity took their buckets to the grove beside the creek to gather the night's crop of snow-white globes of flavor.

"Mushrooms for breakfast?"

"Why not? We can't always get 'em, and if they're good for supper, whyn't they be good for breakfast."

Hap nodded in agreement as he spooned the brown gravy over his biscuit. "I just can't help but notice…." His mouth was shaped into a sly grin.

"Hap, I told you. I always liked mushrooms, and there's the end of it."

Hap finished his breakfast in silence. If he was right, there would be plenty of time later for words and maybe a bit more teasing.

When they were on the road once more, a bucket of the mushrooms rode along. Chances were they would still be good by suppertime, cool and damp as the weather was.

And the weather still held. The roads were hard packed and solid for the most part, and the little streams in Arkansas generally had flat-rock bottoms. Rock bottoms were easily fjorded by the horses, and they generally stopped amid stream for a drink of the clear water.

The map leading to the territory took a main road due west, following a valley until finally a mountain must be crossed, and then staying on the mountain ridge until into a valley was the only way to go and continue to go west. At some point they would reach the Arkansas River, and it would guide them through the rest of the state.

The winter sun shone down, temping the travelers to remove their coats in the warm afternoon. Comments from the farmhouses told them a rain or maybe a cold spell had just passed, but the weather was good now. And weren't they fortunate to have missed the storm?

How long could it last? As he passed through each small town where protection could be had, Hap studied the sky and tried to determine from the breeze if bad weather was brewing, but the good weather held, so he rolled on.

Finally then, the Arkansas River stretched before them, as swift and rolling as the Mississippi, though not nearly so wide, or quite so muddy. The clear blue of the sky reflected on the surface of the water, and the sunshine sparkled and flashed as it shone on the current.

Thank you, Lord, for the good weather.

Another concern involved one of the mares. It was a problem to be faced, and though he tried to put it from his mind, it was there. Sometime before the Oklahoma territory, and likely very soon, she would be due, and there would be the foal to contend with. When that happened, he would prefer to have her out of the harness for a while.

The little map showed a town just ahead that seemed to be large enough to have the services he needed. A livery stable would be good, and he would need a place for the family for a few days. For the last two days, he had traveled late into the afternoon amid complaints of hunger and boredom.

Then the rain started. One more day, maybe less, would have seen them into the town of Dardanelle, Arkansas, but already the huge drops splashed noisily onto the canvas canopy, and the wind picked up, tossing dry leaves about and shaking the needles of the pines.

A storm was brewing, for certain, and if that was not enough, the mare was showing signs of distress. It was like the old folks used to say, there was nothing like a storm to bring on the birth of babies and small animals.

As he spurred the team on to greater speed, the road took a sudden turn that brought them against a large body of water. A lopsided sign told them they had reached Piney Lake. Just what he needed! Hurrying on, he fjorded through the small creeks that fell off the mountains and emptied into the lake. Most were shallow and easily crossed, and then, just ahead, was a deep, wide stream of water.

Across the stream a small ferry boat was moored, and beside him on the road, Hap saw the huge bell. The sign below it read, "FOR FERRY SERIVCE, RING THE BELL."

He certainly need ferry service, so he yanked the bell cord, sending the heavy clapper against the brass curve of the bell. The sound of it echoed through the valley and bounded back to them from the mountains.

Immediately, a man appeared from a shed, and he hurried to the ferry. Drawing it along a cable, he pulled up to the bank beside Hap.

"Three vehicles to cross, huh?" was the friendly greeting. "Well, we'll take the horses out of the harness and swim them across. We'll be hurryin' on account'a the rain. You'll be wantin' to pull on into the livery shed, here."

Livery shed? Thank you, Lord!

"Name's Ben Fry. I got this livery, and I run the ferry 'cause this is a right mean stretch'a water to get over. Folks was havin' to go two miles up stream, just to get across. The ferry saves a heap'a time."

Hap offered his hand. "Palmer's, my name. Hap Palmer. Yep, I was sure glad to see that ferry. I'm needin' to get into the first town quick as I can." Then he added, "'Afore the storm hits solid, if I can."

The first wagon was pulled onto the ferry, and the horses were loosed. They bounded into the water and pulled themselves up and out on the opposite bank.

"Say, Palmer, I reckon you know you got a horse in labor. I'm wantin' to say you ain't a'gonna get into Dardanelle today. Not with her the way she is."

"Yeah, I been pushin' agin the clock on account'a her."

"Well, let's get the others over, and we'll talk."

The wagons and the buggy were over the river, and the wet horses shook themselves and rippled their muscles to dry out.

Ben Fry. "We got'a get these horses in the shed, or they'll have a chill. Swimmin' exerts 'em, and that water's cold from the mountain springs. Here, get 'em under the roof, and we'll take care'a the family. Then, you and me, we'll put the curry brush to 'em."

Hap shook his head with relief. "You got a place for…?" It just couldn't be possible! Here in the "wilderness" a place was prepared for them. The window…?

Ben Fry assured him. "We got a place for everything. First off, get your women folk and youngens up to the house. My Mae, she'll be glad'a the company, and we'll talk on what's to be done."

Hap couldn't think of a better plan, and Ben seemed to have all the figuring done, so he followed orders. Tossing a quilt over his head to shield from the rain, he grabbed up the little girls and headed for the big house. Happy took out after him. Kathleen grabbed up Faith, and Charity and Mercy each took one of Liddy's hands. Splashing through the puddles, they arrived, dripping at the kitchen door.

Mae Fry stood holding the door open. "Come on in here where it's warm. Hurry with them little 'ens. Come on now. Don't you worry about the floor, we got rugs a'plenty."

Mae's massive kitchen smelled of soup with beef and onions and of fresh baked cookies, (cinnamon?).

"I'll be havin' tea ready in a minute. You youngens might want a glass'a milk? We got cookies over there. Here, let's slip off them wet coats and hang 'em up back'a the stove, here. Need to get 'em dried out."

Kathleen and Liddy stared, amazed, as Mae bustled here and there, removing coats and seating children at the large harvest table. Surely they had died and gone to heaven! The air was warm and dry and so sweet smelling!

"Palmer," Ben advised, "could be we better get at them horses. Need to get 'em dried out and fed, 'afore the labor gets harder. That mare, bein' on the road like she was, could be needin' help 'afore mornin'."

Hap followed Ben to the shed and helped to lead his animals into private stalls with mangers filled with hay.

"We'll let 'em fill up on the hay, and we'll grain 'em in the mornin.' That is, if it's good with you? Likely you'd'a had 'em on ground hay, if'n the rain hadn't come on."

After a rub down with the bristly currycomb, a horse blanket was tossed over their backs, holding in their body heat.

"Now, Palmer, that mare'a yours… what're you thinkin'? She usually give you trouble with a foal? Looks to be in good shape, to me. Think we're lookin' at a few hours, likely near midnight? What'd ya think?"

Hap agreed.

"Best we get on in and have some grub. Likely Mae'll have tea ready to warm our insides."

Hurrying from the shed to the house, Hap tried to imagine what it would have been like to be on the road in this storm. The huge raindrops splattered on the ground and on the men, and the low, dark clouds rolled and tumbled, and jagged forks of lightening shot down from them.

"FIXIN' TO HAVE US A GOOD OLD SPRING STORM, DON'T YA THINK?" Ben Fry shouted above the storm, just as they reached the dry of the porch roof.

"Looks like it. But we sure didn't want to run in on you folks like this. We was headed for...." Where had he been headed for? Only the window knew.

"I know, but you got here first. We got a better place for the animals than you'd find in town, and we got a lot'a room. Our youngens'll be more'n glad to see company comin' in to play with. I'd bet they're in the back room right now, squealin' and hollerin' and havin' fun."

And they were. The noise of children's voices echoed through the houses. Mae compensated for the racket by talking louder. "Bring 'im on in here, Ben. He's likely chilled to the bone, and soakin' wet. Here, sit down and have tea, and they's spice cookies, if you like 'em."

Kathleen and Liddy sat, like honored guests, at the long table, teacups in their hands.

Kathleen found her tongue. "Mae, let me...? Tell me what I can do to help. Here we are, runnin' in on you and puttin' you to all this... trouble...."

"It's nothin'," Mae insisted. "If it weren't for the storm, you'd'a likely rode on by the house, and the youngen's 'n me, we'd'a had no company a'tall. Stuck out here like we are, we don't get to half see the folks we'd like to. Now I'm gonna whip up cornbread to go with the soup. Your two littlest ones, they eat off the table... or...?

Kathleen managed to say, "They like most things. Cornbread 'n milk, that'd do 'em fine."

Ben Fry again. "Mae, these folks got 'em a mare in labor. Palmer and me, we'll likely be in the shed in a couple, three hours. Likely the young lady'd like to have the spare room, and the youngen's can sleep with ours. The cabin's empty. Palmer, you and the missus'll need to take the cabin I keep for my hired help when I need some. There's a stove, and dry wood. You'll be warm there. That is, after we see to that mare."

Mae nodded as she shoved two huge pans of batter into the oven of the massive iron cook stove. She poked more wood into the firebox, shaking down the ashes. Kathleen gazed at the stove with an intense, heartfelt longing from deep within her being. Oh, to work with such a stove!

The men ate and were gone, leaving Kathleen and Liddy with Mae in the big kitchen. "Oh, no, you sit there. I don't need no help with this little bit'a dirty dishes. Tell me, whereat did you come from, and how come was you travelin' in the winter, with little ones? Not tryin' to be nosey, but I wondered, are you goin' far? I'd'a said you was goin' to the Oklahoma territory, but you're a mite late for the run, and travelin' with youngens, that'd slow you down."

Weariness had set in now that they were warm and dry and fed, and words seemed to escape them, but Kathleen and Liddy found that they had only to answer questions briefly, and Mae carried the conversation.

"The babies, twins are they? I was wonderin' if they had beds in the wagon, or could we, maybe…?"

Liddy found words. "Don't bother, Mae. The babies sleep with me."

"Oh, I was just thinkin', them lookin' like the older ones. I wasn't thinkin' they'd be yours. Beggin' your pardon."

"Oh, they're not mine. They're my nieces, but they sleep with me. I like to keep 'em."

Mae looked at Liddy with interest. "Do ya ever find two to be a handful?"

Liddy grinned. "Yeah, but mostly I like to have my hands full."

Eighteen

The storm lasted two days, and for another two days, the bottom was out of the road. It would be totally unwise to try to go on with heavily loaded wagons until it dried up a little.

The mare had a darling spotted filly, and even after four days, it was not really best to put her on the road, and the foal would be hard put to keep up.

"I could swap out with you, Palmer. I got a pair'a young fillies I took in on a trade, that'd be just the thing for the trip you got ahead'a you. Them two mare's and the colt, I'd keep 'em, and let 'em go to someone over in the town. You think it over. I know you're needin' to get on the road, but tomorrow's Sunday, and I thought you might…." Mae interrupted her husband.

"Now, Mister Palmer, don't let Ben be talkin' you into havin' church service here just for us. We can get out, most Sundays, and you…. Well, we know you…." Her voice trailed off hopefully, after the polite invitation.

After explaining that, if they had been on the road, his congregation would have consisted of his own family, and so now the addition of the Fry family almost doubled the audience, Mae was comforted.

"We'll bring in quilts for the youngens to sit on, this here kitchen bein' the biggest room in the house. They'll like that, and we'll have us a Sunday dinner with ham and dumplings, and I'll make a cake, and we'll be like a regular family!"

Ben Fry grinned, indulgently. "Don't mind my Mae. She'd keep you here all summer, if you'd let 'er. Say, Palmer, the thing about that windowpane, you reckon this here could be the place you was to go? I was just thinkin', how it'd be, but I reckon not. You seem to think you're goin' the right way. But I'll say this, chance that window stops you somewhere down the road, you can turn around and come back here, and welcome. We'll find a place for that window if we have to build a church around it!"

It was a tempting offer, but the window didn't want to stay, and five days after the storm hit, the caravan pulled out. Two frisky fillies pulled the first wagon. Gifts of a cured ham, canned fruit and a box of snow-white perfumed homemade soap were in the wagon. They were finally obliged to pull away before Mae pressed more gifts on them.

As they began to roll, Ben stopped them. "Now when you ease on around the lake and get on the river road agin, you'll come to a fork in the road. You'll be wantin' to take the left hand one, the one that heads on west, but don't do it. It ain't been long enough since the rain. Take the right hand road that has a rock bottom, and you'll not be hung up in the mud. It's a mite farther, but you'll be ahead in the end. Good luck to ya!"

And then they were rolling. Kathleen settled comfortably onto the buckboard seat and thought of the past week. It had been a restful interlude, such as the year in Peaceful Island. No doubt it was another gift from God to refresh them for what was ahead.

Noticing the fresh green grass clumps sprouting in protected places gave her an intense craving for mushrooms. She'd watch along the way, and if she saw some, it would be worth their time to stop a few minutes… and then, too, there was a chance there'd be some at their night camp. Wherever it would be. Yes, it was a good time of the year for mushrooms.

Nineteen

In the northeast part of the Unassigned Lands, Oklahoma Territory, a deep-channeled river wound its way toward a much larger waterway. The river was small, as rivers go, but it's depth of channel gave it the name of Deep Fork.

Deep Fork was a river of the prairie, in every sense of the word. Rivers in the mountains rushed pell-mell down toward the valleys, making their noisy way in as short a distance as possible. They tumble in misty veils over the rock ledges, pause momentarily in grassy pools only to hurry on to their destination.

Most Oklahoma rivers were different. Having practically no drop in grade to hasten them on their journey, they meander along, circling around the rolling knolls and cutting into the sandy soil. Prairie floods fill the rivers quickly, widening the banks and the channels by carving down the loose soil on the banks on either side and then sending it flowing away.

Then, when the flood is past, they settle back into their channels, carving first this bank and then that bank, as accumulated wind-blown sand and tree roots dictate.

The slowness of the water allows for floating seeds to be lodged along the banks and for native grasses and flowers to sprout and pop up in the very water, itself. Seeds of trees, such as oak, cottonwood, and sycamore, lodge in the clumps of grass, and quickly sprout and gain height. If a flood did not come too soon after the seeds were rooted, the tree could become fastened into the soil, and it would be instrumental in the further carving of the channel of the stream.

So it was that the year of the redbud seeds began. The tight clusters of brown bean-like pods ripened over winter, and in the spring they dropped into the water and sprouted within their cluster. Many small shoots emerged from the cluster of pods to set root, and many were torn out by the roots and washed away, but a large number of them remained to grow into trees.

A cluster of redbud trees is a sight to behold. Being mainly a southern tree, they pick the climate they like unless man or fowl intervene. Those seeds that spout in the northern parts make attractive small trees, and they blossom in the late spring.

Those that sprout near the streams in central Oklahoma arise from the sandy soil in spreading bouquets of stems covered with heart-shaped leaves. The gracefully arching limbs sway with the movement of the wind, but their flexibility usually sustains them during the sometimes violent spring winds and storms.

There is a mix of varieties that blossom each spring, producing buds and blooms of lavender, to crimson, to rose, and they are sprinkled in among the other trees like raisins in a cookie. Or blackberries in a steaming, sweet supper cake.

When one variety of blooms has passed, another with a blossom shade of a small difference may pop into bloom, covering the dark limbs with clusters of jewel-like buds that seem to sprout from the vary bark itself, and this happens weeks before the leaves appear.

Humming birds are first to visit the blossoms, after that the honey bees, and in this way the blossoms of the redbud sustain life. The clusters of tiny bean pods left when the blossoms disappear attract the larva of butterflies. As the summer leaves enlarge themselves, the branches become so dense and private that they are a favorite nesting place for many birds.

Then comes the clusters of ripe, brown seeds. They are so prolific and accessible that they are a virtual cafeteria for birds, both native and migratory. The birds carry the seeds, as birds do, and the lively little tree can sprout anywhere there is a bit of moisture.

They can thrive at various heights, but for their true glory and magnificence, they should be permitted to sprout in the soil of Oklahoma. Towering into the sky and arching in every direction, they could be an alter piece on the creation of God.

One particular stream of water was a tributary of the small Deep Fork River, and it ambled quietly across the prairie for a dozen miles before it emptied into the larger stream. The redbud trees had taken over the banks of the small stream, weaving themselves in among the other trees, filling in the spaces between taller trees where they could discover a bit of sunshine, and producing a floral canopy for weeks each spring.

For many years, it had been only the animals that frequented the banks of the stream, but then, in the spring of the year 1889, human beings gathered on the banks of Deep Fork, very near to the mouth of the small creek that could justly be called Redbud Creek, if anyone had bothered to name it.

At the time of the land run for the Unassigned Lands, a young cavalry officer with a hatchet had blazed a stand of sycamores and blackjack oaks by removing a slice of bark. This would serve as a guide to a particular tract of good land. The blaze would be meant to guide a certain person, but others also followed the blaze, finding for themselves, good, level, and heavily-wooded land tracts along the creek. They staked their claims on its banks, grateful for its water until a well could be dug.

Due to the ambling habits of the creeks and rivers of Oklahoma, this small stream wound through many of the quarter sections staked out in the Unassigned Lands. The small stream grew steadily from a seeping spring in a pasture land until it became a small waterway.

It began on a claim staked by two young brothers from Nebraska, circled around to the south, then to the west, and finally north. It had begun to turn east when it reached the basin of the Deep Fork, and its identity was lost within larger waters.

Six months previous, in the midst of a Nebraska snowstorm, the inhabitants of a small town had decided to become part of the Land Run of Oklahoma, physically moving south the part of their town and its inhabitants who wanted to come along. More than a dozen families joined the migration together, settling a quarter section tract by dividing it, unofficially, into thirty-two lots of five acres each. The town was given the hopeful name of Prosper.

The new residents designated a lot for the school and another for the church, both structures yet to be built.

Construction proceeded at a furious rate, the major hold-up being the availability of dimension lumber. Some settlers built log cabins from the clearings of their timber, but the settlers of the town, with only five acres, did not have the trees available to use for building material, and acquiring lumber was absolutely essential.

In the way that answers follow questions and needs find a way to be filled, an enterprising owner of a sawmill heard of the town and knew instantly what the first need would be.

Acting in the pattern of many capitalists he hired a dray company to relocate his sawmill as close to the new town as possible. He then proceeded to furnish dimension lumber and jobs for cash money. He paid cash money to those with trees to remove, and he also made a sizeable profit for himself.

David Hill and Herbert Bentley, two young single men from Nebraska, found work at the sawmill as it was, working ten hour days to try to meet the demand for lumbar. They originally had hired on as drivers when the town had begun to move and now hesitated to leave the excitement and return to their Nebraska homes. Their wages of $2.50 a day was suddenly raised to $4.00 when the saw mill owner found them to be capable, and he left them in charge when he went to set up another mill a few miles away.

Twenty

The mill was a busy place. The screech and roar of the motor and the metal teeth ripping into the logs was a welcome sound to all ears. At first it had been necessary to ration the lumber, allowing each household only enough to build an outhouse and a covered pavilion to keep the rain off household goods. Each household took its place on the list and received the allotted small amount of board feet, with the promise of more later when the sawmill could catch up with the demand.

Clancy Harper, temporary Mayor of the new town of Prosper, took it on himself to add the church to the list of customers. It seemed not everyone agreed with him.

"How come ya to take lumber for a church when there ain't no one that has enough lumber for 'isself?"

"Yeah, how come the church can't be the one to wait?"

"Next thing we know, you'll be puttin' the school on that list, and here it is just comin' into summer. 'Sides, the youngens'll find plenty'a work to do without book learnin'."

Clancy decided it was time for a town meeting. He began, "Now I didn't go out to get this job, bein' mayor, and if there's a body out there that wants it, we'll put it to a vote, and he can have it with my blessing. But right now, it's me that's got the responsibility and has to make the decisions.

"Now when we platted our town, back last winter in the snowstorm, we set aside a place for the church. You know the school's got'a be done, and I'd expect them that has youngens to take the lead on that. I got one, myself. We'll get to that later on.

"Now the church, that's another thing, and everyone'a you'll just have to deal with his own conscience. In the Good Book, there's a way to get a church took care of, and bein' fairly good with numbers, myself, it was plain to me what to do. The Book says a tenth part'a what we got goes to God, and since we can't hardly get that money up to heaven to hand it to the Good Lord, Hisself, it seems to me the church'd be the place to start.

"With the bunch of us there is and the ones that live around that'll want to come to the church, it'll be no burden to pay the mill for the boards, and in a day's time, some of us men can get up a place out'a the weather. Figure we'll need a couple'a outhouses, too." He paused, poignantly, before continuing.

"Someone got a problem with what I said, so far?"

A voice from the rear of the group. "Clancy, you recall we got us no preacher yet?"

Clancy nodded with exaggerated vigor. "Yeah, I do seem to recall that we didn't bring no preacher along with us. I just want us to be ready when one comes by. Anybody else?"

"How much'll it be, that each of us has to give?"

Clancy signed with exasperation. "Nobody has to give nothin'. We're gonna pass the hat. Tullius, you got your hat there? Good. Pass on around in amongst the folks, Tull, and let's see what we get. It's my idea that God'll give us what we need."

The group broke up into small conversations as Steven Tullius, owner and operator of the local gristmill, passed his sweat-stained straw hat around. Clancy motioned for James Hewett, owner of the general store that had made the trip south and brought his store, complete with furniture and provisions.

"Hewett, you be ready to help Tull do the count, so's everybody'll be satisfied that everything was counted right and proper. All right, Tull, bring the hat on around here."

Small conversations again filled in the time as the counting was accomplished.

"Ready, fellows?"

Stephen Tullius stood beside Clancy. "What we got was $16.45. What else we got was a slip'a paper sayin' we could cut trees on the Dunbar land and on the tract the Kendall boys claimed. That'll cut down the price for the lumbar we'll need later. What we need to spend right now is $10.00 for the lumber for the outhouses and the pavilion. I know that don't seem like much of a start, but that mill's goin' day and night, tryin' to turn out what we need. We're mighty lucky to get any at all, ain't that right, Clancy?"

Clancy stepped back up on the stump that was his platform and grinned at the townsmen gathered around him. "See there! God's still got $6.45 against the next batch'a boards, and a couple'a IOU's for trees. You folks was just givin' me a bad time. There weren't no time you didn't support the church back in Providence Falls, and you're the same folks. Anything else?"

"What'll we do for benches? Sit on a pallet?"

"Won't do to pass the hat agin. Can't get no more lumber. Anyone ask Dave or Herb when we'll get more?"

"Yeah, it'll be two months 'afore anyone gets anymore, and that'll be only if the sawmill don't have no breakdowns."

Clancy nodded. "So anyone got a suggestion?"

Nettie Gunther, next door neighbor to the church lot, suggested in her practical way. "Till we get the lumber, whyn't everybody be responsible for his own family. Bring a pallet, bring a bench, or sit on the ground. Don't seem like no big problem to me."

"Yeah!" came a chorus of assent.

Clancy again, "Next question. How long till the church's name comes up to get lumber. Anyone know?"

"Three weeks, if there ain't no breakdowns. That's what I was told, 'cause I'm next on the list after the church."

Clancy again. "They's one more thing to talk on. The church'll need a name. Who's got any ideas?"

"Prosper Community Church?"

"Naw. That's the name'a the town."

"Then what?"

"Fourteen Mile Church."

"How come fourteen mile?"

"That's how far it is from Guthrie."

"Why'd we want to name it for someone else's town?"

"Then what?"

"I know. Deep Fork."

"No," announced Nettie Gunther. "Name it Redbud Creek Church. See how the creek kind'a circles around the town and heads out for Deep Fork? The whole of the bank is covered with them redbud trees. For the first ones of us here, it was a ways to go carryin' a pail, but it was good water. It starts there at the back'a the Kendall Brothers and weaves around by the Kelvey's, the Dunbar's, and the Allegretto's 'afore it heads down to Deep Fork. Seemed like it wanted to take care'a us all. Had a thought that the church could be named for it."

"Yeah, Redbud Creek Church, that'd be a good name."

Clancy stepped up on his stump once more. "Let's see hands on Redbud Creek Church. Now, those against. You youngens put your hands down and stop jokin.' Nobody against? That takes care'a it. When the church gets built, it's got itself a name."

Twenty-One

A three vehicle caravan left the waters of Piney Creek and headed west.

The frisky spotted fillies, new to the traces, danced and clowned for the better part of the day, then settled into the rhythm of pulling. They developed the necessary measured steps to work together and the slight lean forward to let the weight of their bodies carry part of the weight of the wagon when the road began to rise. They learned the leg stiffening and the hesitation when the road fell on the other side of the hill.

Good training, these girls had. Hap hoped Ben had meant it when he insisted the heavy mares would be worth more to him to sell as carriage horses in Dardanelle, than the young fillies. Then, too, the foal would be valuable to him. Ben had refused to take any money for the shelter, food, and good company, and Hap hoped it was not that he thought the preacher had not had any money.

The wagon seemed practically empty and quiet, except for the grinding of the wheels against the gravel of the road. Mercy was now riding with Happy, and Charity and the twins were with Liddy. His sister insisted the babies slept better in the buggy. Maybe they did. It had better springs.

Little Faith, still in the wagon with her parents, had tried to stay awake, but finally had to give it up, and was curled up on the soft quilt at her mother's feet.

Kathleen glanced into the bushes and small trees along both sides of the road.

Hap noticed. "Lookin' for mushrooms?"

Kathleen treated him to a very small smile. "I like mushrooms. Always have. They make good gravy, and the youngens like 'em. Noticed you helped yourself pretty well. I got'a cook somethin,' and if I can find mushrooms, that's what we'll have."

"Fine with me."

"Hap, you just get that look off your face."

"What look?"

"The look that says you think you know why I'm lookin' for mushrooms. We got Mae's potato salad and pickled beets. And all that ham. Maybe four dozen eggs. It'd'a been a good thing to stay there, with a friend like her."

"Yeah, I thought so, too, but I wasn't able to talk the window into it."

It was early May, and the sun shone through the fresh-washed air, its rays glistening off the new green of the leaves. Violets peeped over every woodland log and ferns decorated every shady nook.

It had been a long day on the road before Hap began to look for a campsite. It would take at least a week to get from Dardanelle to Fort Smith. They would need a day or two there to wash clothes and restock supplies. Who knew where the next provisions would be, and then they would be heading out into the Oklahoma territory. Unless the window told them to stop somewhere.

The road climbed a small hill and leveled off toward the west into a thick grove of pecan trees. Small catkins, forerunners of next year's crop, thickly decorated every limb, and squirrels raced about on the strong limbs.

"How about squirrel stew for supper?"

"Too late. The youngens are gonna be hungry. Likely hungry right now. But you could bring down a few, and we'll have the stew tomorrow. Or you can roast them on the coals, or both. Anyway, this looks like a good place."

A crystal clear spring flowed from a pool beside a rock. Water would be handy.

Hap pulled into the grove of pecan trees, followed by Liddy and Happy. Off in a distance, the ground was sprinkled with white balls. All the way from the size of a walnut to the size of a man's fist, they grew. They flowed in drifts all along the edge of the grove. They glistened like the drifts of snow in the sunshine after a snow storm.

"Hap!" came Kathleen's joyful cry.

"See there?" He responded with a trace of a smirk. "The Lord provided manna for your next meal. He knew we'd make it this far today."

"But Hap! Look how many!"

"The Lord knew you'd be hungry. He knew you'd be eating for t…?

"Hush your mouth. I've always loved mushrooms! You know that! But there's somethin' else. We're a'gonna dry some of these."

"Dry 'em? Where?"

"I'll string 'em up and swing the strings of 'em from the ribs of the wagon canopy where we hang the diaper lines. If they get enough air, they'll dry. I'll see if I can find a big needle and some yarn."

The stove was hoisted out of the workshop wagon and set down on its platform. The fire was started, but the last of the daylight was spent in the mushroom patch. Kathleen, Liddy, and Charity crawled along on the damp, earthy-smelling ground, picking the white globes. Mercy was kept busy carrying them back to the camp to spread on a quilt. The twins were left to occupy themselves.

It took almost no time at all to gather hundreds of the mushrooms, but by that time, four small squirrels were roasting on green twigs. The warm sun was beginning to slip away by the time the biscuits were brown and the mushroom gravy was rich and savory. A jar of Mae's canned peaches, cinnamon-spiced and thick with dumplings completed the preparation.

The lanterns were lighted, and the fragrant smoke of the roasted meat floated over the site when they were finally ready to eat. Six other squirrels simmered on the stove, and Charity helped Liddy hang the diapers, but Kathleen sat on the quilt and strung the mushrooms onto yarn with a darning needle. She hung them inside the canvas canopy suspended at the sides from the ribs holding the roof canvas.

Swinging scallops of mushroom festooned the roof, and there must easily have been more than five hundred of them. Dried mushrooms were not as tasty as fresh ones, but they were infinitely better than having none at all and they provided a welcome flavor to soups and other dishes.

Hap surveyed the overhead decoration. "Lena, honey, you think you got enough for a while?"

Without an indication that she had noticed the jab, she retorted,"You want'a stay over a day and let me get more?"

"I reckon not," he admitted. "We need to be movin' on, 'afore the window has to remind us in some way that we don't understand."

Then they were in Fort Smith, Arkansas. Soldiers were everywhere. The sound of men and horses and the clank of artillery rang out over the plains. The Cavalry garrisoned at the Fort practiced their formations along the stockade fences.

Outside the Fort, a sizeable town had sprung up, also bearing the name of the Fort. The town was complete with houses, stores and brick streets. The animals clomped noisily over the bricks, and people shouted, the sound being almost deafening to ears fresh from the quiet of the trail.

New provisions were stocked. Crackers and peanut butter... flour and cornmeal... salt and pepper... spices and soda. Then, hairpins and ribbons, elastic for repair to girl's bloomers. Shoes. A lot of the merchandise was new, but there were many used items. It was almost as though folks had reached this far, and carefully prioritized their possessions, trading luxury items for more practical ones. The occasional pair of slightly-worn shoes were offered for sale.

Beautiful glass vases and dishes were for sale. Decorated and monogrammed silverware and fancy tea services. Lace curtains and musical instruments. There were guitars, mandolins, banjos, and an accordion. The accordion appeared to be in good shape. All of the keys worked, and the bellows were in good repair.

Liddy's eyes fell on the instrument, and she could not take them away. Fingering the buttons and keys, she could tell the music was still in the box. Respectfully, she blew the dust from its bellows. Lifting it shyly to her shoulder, she put her arms through the straps.

A request from an on-looker, "Play us a tune, pretty lady?"

At the sound of the voice, she startled and quickly removed her arms from the straps.

She was instantly admonished, "Oh, no! Don't do that! You have to play us a tune, first. That thing's been layin' there for months with nobody a'touchin' it. I can tell by the look'a you, that you know how to get the music out of it."

Of course it was just a sales pitch, but it was a good one. Liddy pressed a note, and the sound of it spread out pleasantly under the tent roof of the store, intoxicatingly inviting, like the smoke from a roasted marshmallow. Heads turned and Kathleen, some few feet away from her, startled suddenly.

"Oh, Liddy! Look what you found! Does it work?"

Liddy pressed another note, drawing the bellows out to give more life to the sound. Another note, and another, and the customers in the store began to move toward her.

"Play something, Miss!" insisted the salesman.

After a few experimental moves, she began the well-known and haunting notes of "The Sun is Going Down, Lorena," a song made popular during the war between the states. Her music became the only sound in the huge tent.

Then, "The Battle Hymn of the Republic" was followed by "When the Saints go Marching in." Somewhere in the middle of that last song, hands began to clap in time with the music, as though helping the saints to march.

Kathleen watched Liddy's face become transformed as she played the songs. "Oh, Liddy, I forgot how your ma had you take music lessons. We was away so much of the time for a while there I sort'a lost track. You got'a buy that, you know."

"Oh, no, I was just seein' if I remembered anything." She began to pull the straps from her arms and then set it back onto the counter.

Kathleen watched with total disapproval, and her voice became harsh and determined. "Liddy, you got'a buy that, or I will. Think what it'd mean to the youngens to get to hear tunes and maybe learn some new songs."

Liddy stood looking at the instrument, and someone called out, "Don't stop playin.' I ain't heard decent music for months."

And, "Can you play Yankee Doodle?"

"How about, 'When the Roll is called up Yonder'?"

Hap had been in another tent store checking harness repair supplies and softening oil. He bought four pounds of the slender tacks he used in making willow wicker, feeling he would likely have to resort to his paying occupation for a while. He stowed his purchases into the wagon and heard what appeared to be a musical concert going on in the large merchandise tent.

Coming closer, he saw his shy sister wielding the bellows and expertly fingering the keyboard, playing song after song to an enrapt audience. As he came closer, he was intrigued by the look on her face.

For the past six months, his sister had been thrown into what must have been an alien world. Everything that happened was something new to her, often strange, scary and unreal.

She had quickly learned to adapt, and did the best she could, but here…? Now…? It was evident that she had something she truly understood. It was as though she had met an old friend in a strange and unexpected place and was now wrapped in comforting and familiar arms. Hap had actually forgotten the years of music lessons his parents had required of her.

He pushed his way through the crowd to reach Kathleen, he put his arm around her. "Lena, honey, she's got'a get that accordion. Liddy's got plenty'a money, and just take a look at her face!"

Kathleen nodded decisively. "I done told her she had to buy it."

Twenty-Two

They spent three days at Fort Smith, including a Sunday. As was their usual habit, Hap gathered his family beside the wagon to lead them in a church service. Today, their songs were accompanied by an instrument.

As the sound drifted out over the camp, one by one of the bystanders drifted near to stand and listened to the music. Hap invited everyone to sit down if they could find a place. Many sat on the bricks of the street, and some joined in the singing. Most stayed to hear the sermon, and Hap realized his audience was the largest crowd he had spoken to since he preached in his father's old church in Lafette, Kentucky. It was another comforting island moment of rest in his sea of apprehension.

But then it was time to move on. The musical instrument, priced in the tent store at $5.00 had been finally purchased for $3.75, and the store was glad to get it. When could they expect to see another person with money who could pull music from it as that young lady did? It had been surprising how few customers had registered any interest in it at all, and it had lain on the dusty shelf for months. It now rode in a place of honor in the buggy beside Liddy. Having no case for it, she assigned it a place in a large pillowcase to keep it from gathering debris from the road.

The shopkeeper smiled as it left the tent and was glad to get back any part of his investment.

Twenty-Three

It was a warm afternoon in May in the Oklahoma Territory. Eben Carlile, who had come from the hills of Tennessee, trekked across northern Arkansas and journeyed on to the Unassigned lands, left his garden and its crop of new weeds. He allowed he'd had enough for one day. One could always find weeds to pull in a garden, and there came a time for visiting a neighbor.

Clyde Kendall, whose sons had staked a fine claim on a quarter section adjoining the new town of Prosper, tapped a few shingles in place on the roof of his new wagon shed. It was smaller than the one he had left in Providence, Nebraska, but now that his three sons had their own freighting business and were doing so well, he did not need a business so large. There would be a lot of work for a wheelwright in this new land, but a man whose sons were grown and on their own, well, he didn't have to try to get all the business that was available. That gave him time for visiting a neighbor.

He came down from the roof and waited in the shade of the cottonwoods for his neighbor, Eben Carlile, who was coming to sit a spell with him.

The May sunshine spread its golden warmth like honey over the activity all around them, but the two older men drew themselves apart from it.

Clyde Kendall's three sons were now staying in the bustling new city of Guthrie, taking advantage of everyone's need for transportation. Their three wagons, each painted green and marked "KENDALL BROTHERS, We Haul" were going three ways, delivering new goods and merchandise as it came in on the Santa Fe Railway. It was good for young men to be busy.

Eben's son-in-law, Dan Dunbar, was busily clearing land for his farm. He could readily see that the nearby thriving city of Guthrie would be a demanding market for whatever food he chose to raise on the rich dirt of the Oklahoma territory. It was good for a young man with a wife and child to support to be busily taking care of his future.

The two older men met under the shade of the cottonwoods, and settled back with their shoulders against the solid trunks of the trees.

"How're things?"

"Pretty much the same."

Standard greeting being now out of the way, the subject of the last town meeting came up for discussion.

Eben began, "Clancy Harper managed to get the church started. Done a good job getting' the minds'a the folks on the same track."

"Sure enough did. Always admired Clancy and the way he took care'a his blacksmithin' business back in Nebraska. We had us a preacher back there, but he was old and didn't want no movin.' Besides, he had about the same number'a his church that stayed behind, as that left, so he stayed with 'em. Good preacher, he was, but I'd not wanted to move neither, if'n I was much older than I am and not havin's sons a'pullin' me on."

The man from Tennessee agreed. "Yeah, a fellow finds 'isself wantin' to trim down the workin' of his days when he gets on in his years. It's good to have the younger fellows to take over."

Clyde pulled a blade of grass and chewed it as he stretched his feet out into the warmth of the sun. "It'd be good to have the church built on up into a buildin,' but the only thing we've got to do it with is these here short logs. These here trees on the boys' place, they seem to run to limbs and not to tall, straight trunks. For the runnin' walls of a church, they need taller trees to make logs long enough."

Eben agreed. "These Oklahoma trees, they do seem to grow big around, and not so tall. It's a good thing for making sawed lumber, but it takes trees taller and littler for makin' logs."

"Littler? You mean littler around, don't you?"

"Yeah." The neighbor agreed, and then sat bolt-upright and looked his neighbor in the eye. "You know, Clyde, there'd be a way to put up the church walls if folks was to want to bother with the shorter lengths. We had a way to put 'em together back in the hill. We'd make bends in the walls to make places to notch the logs together. Folks liked to make bay winders in the bends. Workin' that way put right-smart of strength in the walls, too."

The neighbor looked on with interest. "You'd know how to make them walls?"

"Sure would. I done enough of 'em. Rather liked 'em myself. Shorter logs being easier to handle, a body don't get so tired. 'Nother thing, them bay winders, they put more light in the rooms, durin' the winter months. Seemed like."

"And the walls'd be strong, you say?"

"Stronger'n straight walls, to my thinkin'."

The Nebraska man considered the answer, "My boys, they said the trees on their land could be used. Buildin' walls'd not be somethin' them boys'd know about, but they said for us to be free about cuttin' what was needed."

Eden Carlile nodded. "My Dan, he's got trees to spare. Fact is, the back part'a his tract must'a had a burn-over, some years back. Got a thick grove'a young blackjack oaks, and them the exact size that'd be needed. He said he was plannin' to cut into it quick as he could and use the new growth for a woodlot."

"You thinkin' he'd want to let them logs go?"

"For the church, he'd be glad. That'd make the buildin' material ready right now, stead'a waitin' for the mill to cut it up. He'd have nearly enough of eight and ten foot lengths, hisself. Then, later when the milled lumber was had, it could be used to trim out the inside."

Eben certainly had Clyde Kendall's interest. "You sayin' you know for a fact how to put them walls together?"

"Know it well as I know the back'a my own hand."

Clyde Kendall chewed a grass stem and nodded, meditatively. "We could have Clancy call a meetin.' Say, how'd we get them trees felled and trimmed?"

"You and me, we'd be a start. I got a long-toothed, two-man saw I brung from the mountains. Ain't crazy about bendin' over the handle of a two-man saw again, but I can still do it. Wouldn't want to be put in no speed race, though."

"You figured on how much it'd take?"

"How big would you want the buildin' to be?"

"Well, it'd take a town meetin' to pin it down, but thirty feet by fifty feet'd be a good start to make figures. Bigger'd be better, but we got'a start with what we can do."

The mountain man stared at the treetops as he visualized numbers in his mind. "Figurin' fifty foot sides, that'd make three bays, and if there was to be winders in the bays, that'd take the buyin'a six winders, for both sides. If you'd be wantin' one in the back, for the light behind the pulpit, that'd mean seven winders, total."

"How about front winders… say, one on each side'a the front door?"

"Could do that. It'd look good. It'd be somethin' to think on, later. Now if it come down to actual doin' what we're talkin' about, I'd be up to chippin' in on the buyin' of store-bought windows, with panes and all. That'd look good, don't you reckon?"

"I could team up with you on the buyin'. You think they'd be for sale in Guthrie?"

"Maybe, maybe not, but I know they're for sale in the Monkey Ward catalog your boys brought me. We could order 'em and have 'em come in on the Santa Fe. Your boys'd bring 'em on in."

Clyde settled back comfortably, grinned and commented, "Well, Eben, we done got that church built and the winders put in, and we ain't moved our backsides an inch either way. This here's about the way the town of Prosper came down from Nebraska. We sat there in Hewett's store with our feet propped up on the warmin' rail, and one thing led to the other, and here we are."

Eden returned the smile. "But ya got here, didn't ya'? How strong are you on the idea'a puttin' up a log church?"

"Pretty strong. Everything that gets done, got'a have somethin' back of it, pushin' it on. I reckon you and me on the two-man saw, that'd be the start of it."

Eben remembered a difficulty. "I had me a sprung rib back up in April. I found myself slowed down a mite, but it's comin' on. We could use scraps'a time, here and there…?" An agreement was necessary.

Clyde heaved himself away from the tree trunk and stood up. "Let's meander down in the trees and see if there's somethin' you think'd work."

"Could do that."

Twenty-Four

Hap Palmer saw his three vehicles aboard the ferry and across the Arkansas River. The horses were tethered to the back of the ferryboat and obliged to swim to the sandy bank on the other side.

They rippled their muscles as they shed the water from their skin and climbed onto the bank and into Oklahoma.

The workshop wagon, driven by seven-year-old Happy, had been packed with purchases made at Fort Smith. They had been warned that the closer they came to the formerly unassigned lands, now a grid of newly staked homesteads, the more scarce all necessary goods would become. So, heavily loaded, the Palmers headed west.

The mountains of Arkansas had turned into small hills as they moved west, and these were further reduced to rolling knolls. The time spent riding in the wagon, facing the west, was spent in wondering and anticipating what would be faced when the window finally got as far as it wanted to go.

Hap had been mulling over in his mind a situation that had intrigued him for the past few days.

"Lena, honey, I been thinkin'…"

"Now, Hap, you know…?"

"It ain't about the window. It's about us. Your folks was afraid for us to start out in the dead'a winter, and I wasn't too happy about it, myself. I thought on it a lot, it seemin' to be a stupid thing, startin' out with babies and little children, exposin' 'em to the weather, not to mention you and Liddy."

"Yeah, it could'a been stupid. Might still be. We ain't there, yet."

"You're right, but we already come through the cold'a the winter, and here it is up into May. The main thing that'd bother us now, that'd be rainstorms. But we come through the winter months with sunshine comin' down on us, 'cept for two places. There was the snowstorm in Hilltop, Tennessee, and we was put up by the Blakes. Then there was the rainstorm in Dardanelle, Arkansas, and it happened just when we pulled up into the Fry's livery. The mare didn't have that foal out in some Arkansas valley with the water a'floodin' down on it. She was in the warm, dry livery stable."

Kathleen nodded. "Yeah, we've been took care of. Is that what you're sayin'?"

"More or less. Who'd think they'd have a mare come due within a mile of a livery stable, and it stuck miles out'a town like it was? And what'd be the chances'a the stable owner wantin' to trade out with young fillies like he did? Wouldn't take a penny'a money, sayin' the value of the mares and the colt, over the price's fillies we got, was enough to cover our bill."

"Likely them mares was worth more'n we thought."

"Could be. But the way things all worked out, after the peck'a trouble we had at the beginnin'... What do you think of it?"

Kathleeen smiled indulgently at her husband. "You bein' surprised that things worked out? Likely all that studyin' you done has drained the thinkin' out'a your brain. When the Israelites were on the move, they were fed, and their clothes and shoes didn't wear out. I been meanin' talk to God about that. Happy's shoes is showin' some wear. Don't hardly know how that happened, him all the time in the wagon."

Hap again, "But when ya get to thinkin,' things worked out too good to be natural... don't you think?"

"Yeah, and that cloud floatin' overhead and the fireball at night, that likely didn't seem too natural to the Israelites. Reckon it might'a seemed even more unnatural to their enemies. And you recall, they got to walk over the river on dry land, and we had to be ferried. God didn't even open up the Arkansas River to let us cross. We might need to talk to God about that, too."

Hap grinned at the teasing of his wife. "You may be right, but I took note that He sent the mushrooms when you needed 'em. You got over your cravin' yet? Oklahoma may not be as good for growin' mushrooms as Arkansas or Tennessee."

"Now, Hap, you know I always liked mushrooms. But since you mention it, it'll be good if the window lets us be in a house by fall. Takin' babies out in the weather don't seem to be as bad as maybe havin' one in a wagon. So far, that hasn't happened to us."

"Don't you worry none, Lena, baby. I got confidence we're on the right track now. Look how far we've come with no problems? The way I see it, all them troubles we had was just sent to let us know for sure we was on the right way, when we finally got on it. Them troubles was just to let us know Who was in charge. If we hadn't'a had all them problems, we might'a thought we just had a run'a good luck, comin' this far. As it is, we know for sure we was took care of."

A pause, and then Kathleen. "How you reckon we'll know when we get there? Likely we'll see a sign sayin' 'We're in need of a window pane, about three feet by four feet to be put in a church. You got one on you?' The way they was talkin,' back in Fort Smith, the territory finds itself needin' just about everything one could imagine except a stained glass window."

"I ain't worried about that. When the window gets to where it wants to be, it's likely to just drop right out'a the crate, right in front'a Liddy's horses. And them horses, they'll know not to step on it, like Happy's did."

The rolling knolls seemed strange to eyes accustomed to mountains. There were no more roads curling around in the valleys, or following mountain ridges. Roads were cut straight in the direction they intended to go. And there was a sameness about the scenery, making it seem that they had traveled no farther along the way, by nightfall, than they had been in the morning. They traveled the way the sun traveled, so it stayed behind them or overhead unless they were traveling a long day.

And the fair weather held. Rain could be seen in the west, far ahead of them, and sometimes it could be seen in the east, building up cloud layers and moving on toward Arkansas.

Sundays on the plains were wonderful days of rest and music. Liddy fingered the notes and expanded the bellows, and music flowed out over the little hills and valleys. Soft notes, slowly drawn out in their sweetness, hard sounds of march songs, or the twisty sounds of waltzes. Often there were the quick, bouncy notes of children's songs.

The children sang, "Skip to my Loo, My Darling," "London Bridge is Falling Down," "Cockles and Muscles, Alive Alive-oo," and "Yankee Doodle."

Liddy played through her mental inventory of songs and sighed because she could not remember more. "Should'a looked around and saw if there was a book to be had when we was back there in the tent store."

Kathleen agreed. "Here we was so excited to find the instrument, it plum took away any thought'a findin' music to go with it. But don't you worry. We'll get music from somewhere, and if we can't find a way to get books, I'll write my Ma, and she'll find some for us and send 'em along."

Then, after the Sunday songs, the children and the two women sat on quilts and listened to the sermon for the day. A congregation of eight was small, but it was always there, and Hap preached his

Sunday message as though he had hundreds. One could not say that his children were neglected in their religious education.

After the service, the children spent the day exploring the timbered woodland and running across the plains. They could enjoy a day of unfettered freedom from the cramped quarters of the wagons.

It was on the plains of eastern Oklahoma that little Joy Palmer clutched the spokes of the wagon wheel with her tiny hand and pulled herself to her feet. The wonder of that achievement impressed her so much that she crowed with glee. Peace Palmer watched her sister for a minute, then crawled to the wagon wheel and stood beside her.

Charity yelled, "Look, Ma! They're standin' up!"

Kathleen looked, smiled and sighed. It was a good thing to see normal development in a child, but she also remembered how much faster a child could toddle than it could crawl, and this pair would likely go two ways at once.

"Charity, you and Mercy got'a help me more, now. Them little girls'll be takin' off runnin,' and I'll not be able to catch 'em both. I'll need you to be helpin.'"

"Me, too?"

"Yes, Faith. I'll need you, too."

Twenty-Five

A town meeting once again seemed necessary. Clancy, former wagonmaster, now mayor, stepped up on his stump and called the meeting to order.

"You folks 'member how we decided to wait to get a church? Well, we got somethin' new to talk on. Eben Carlile, here, he's offered his son-in-law's timber to make logs, and Clyde Kendall, he's offered to help out, too. They say we can put up a log building out'a short lengths, if we put bay windows down the sides. Eben knows how it's done."

"We got the logs?" someone shouted.

"We're comin' to that. Eben and Clyde, they say they'll fell the logs fast as their strength holds out, but they'll need help with the trimmin.' Now they was a time I'd ask you to call a work day, and we'd all come and get somethin' done, but the way things are, with us all so busy, I was thinkin' it'd be better to let everyone do what he can, whenever he can.

"Then, come time the logs all get cut and brought to the church yard, that's when we'll have a church-raisin' day. We'll try to catch the Baker Brothers in town, and the Kendall boys and Dave and Herb, and all the young fellows we can get. Eben's sayin' he thinks two work days, workin' dawn to dark, that'd get the walls up past the windows. Of course, we can't expect to have the young fellows all the time, but likely they'll be able to help, some."

"How many windows we figurin' to get?" The question was directed toward the older men.

Clyde scratched his head. "I'm thinkin' it was six."

Eben shook his head. "No, it was seven if we was goin' to be needin' one for the back."

"What'll they cost?"

Clancy Harper, again, "Reckon we don't need to worry on that. Clyde and Eben say they'll foot the bill."

"No work day till everything gets cut, huh?"

Clancy nodded. "Seemed the best to me. Anyone that can give time, you see Clyde or Eben. Now we can use boys young as ten. Remember that. What they'll mainly do is trim off the limbs and pile 'em up."

It was the first of June before a workday could be called. Dragging the logs, even the small ones, took time and effort badly needed on every homestead, but the non-availability of sawed lumber worked to an advantage for the church building. Until lumber was available, a house couldn't be built, so the work on the church slowly progressed.

The logs were heaped on the lot that had been designated for the church. Teenage girls came to help. The two Kendall girls, two Gunther girls, a McGhee girl, and various others came to the workday, prepared to help skin the bark from the logs with a draw knife. This was necessary because bark on the logs of a log house harbors insects and makes a rough surface that's difficult to clean. Bark would eventually drop off, anyway, making a mess inside the building.

Hatchets trimmed back the knots and shaped the rough places, while measuring tapes marked exact lengths. The more skilled of the hatchet handlers, under the direction of Eben Carlile, made the notches in the logs. Young men rolled them to the sight and lifted them into place. A long workday brought the logs up to the windows, and Eben pronounced the effort to be well along. Likely two more days would see it to the roof line… that is if everyone could spare two more days.

It actually took three more days, spaced in and around other duties, before the walls reached roof height, but when it did, it was then the church's turn to receive a small allotment of lumber. They would receive enough for a pavilion and an outhouse.

Instead of the pavilion, the lumber was used on the roof to make a base for the shingles. When it was in place, there was not enough lumbar left for the outhouses.

"Make it out'a logs," someone decided.

"Why not?"

So a pair of log outhouses were constructed behind the log church building.

Enough large Oklahoma Red Cedars were found to make the shingles for the roof. Eben spent his days in the shade of an oak, hacking out the thin slabs of wood with his hatchet. Anyone who could swing a hatchet was welcome to join him, and if they didn't know how to shape shingles, they could soon learn.

It was mid June before the shingles were in place. The windows that had been ordered from the catalog came in and were brought out by the Kendall Brothers in one of their green wagons marked 'KENDALL BROTHERS We Haul'.

"Getting' the winders in, that'll help to keep out the flies and such, come time we find us a preacher," Eben commented.

"Yeah, about that preacher… you reckon we'll have to send one of our youngens off to school to learn how to preach?" Clyde wondered.

"I don't know… but it's been done before."

Sconce shelves were placed along each wall to set the lanterns up high for better light for evening services. Linseed oil was applied to the logs to preserve them and to discourage boring insects. The dirt floor was raked clean of leaves and grass clumps, and several loads of sawdust were brought from the sawmill by Dave and Herb, now operating the sawmill business. It would be a while before lumber would be available to put in a floor.

The crate containing the windows was opened, and the panes of sparkling glass were lifted out to be admired.

"Just look at them winders! Imagine how they'll look, all up and down the sides'a the church!"

"And the one in the back."

"Yeah, that one, too. See here, we've got… Huh?"

"What's the matter?"

"If I ain't wrong in my countin,' we got one winder shy of a load."

"One gone?"

"Appears to me it ain't been sent."

"You mean we ain't got seven?"

"Come count 'em."

"What went wrong?"

"Don't know. Let's look at these papers."

"Yeah, and here's the money sent back. Say they ain't got but six of this particular size and ask did we want to reorder and get a different size."

"Can't do that. We done got the hole cut."

"Could fill it in and get a smaller winder."

"Or we could likely get a pane'a glass over to Guthrie, and put it in, ourselves. It ain't like the one in the back'd be needin' to be opened like the rest of 'em."

"Could do that. Reckon there'd be glass available in Guthrie with all that buildin' that's goin' on? My boys say buildin' stuff 's still scarce."

"Well, let's get these here six put in, and we'll be that far along. Could have your boys put us down for a sheet'a glass when our turn comes."

"Seems that'd be the thing to do. Here, you lift on that side and we'll carry the first one and put it in place. It ain't that heavy, but I don't want'a risk droppin' it…nor nothin'..."

"Yeah, we'll get these in place and figger what to do with the space in the back when we get to it."

"Good figgerin.'" The two neighbors found it easy to agree with each other.

Twenty-Six

The Palmers passed into what the map said was Sac and Fox territory. The rolling plains had become flatter, and great forests of black jack oak, cottonwood and red cedar decorated the landscape.

Knitting together all the woodland vegetation was the understory of redbud trees. Some few of them were still full-blown with their crimson to purple clusters of dainty flowers. Others were wind-blown, their nectar taken, and their seeds maturing. Others had no blossoms, but were decorated with clusters still-flat miniature "bean" pods.

Along the shallow creeks and washes the redbuds grew. They were tall when there was room, or shorter when crowded. They swayed in graceful arches, and in maturity were tall and strong with their black bark contrasting attractively their shiny, emerald, heart-shaped leaves. Always, there were redbuds, and the Palmer caravan rolled past their glistening bouquets.

The terrain of Oklahoma was much different from that of Arkansas, but twice more the Good Lord favored them with manna in the form of snow-white mushrooms popping up in drifts among the dead leaves under the blackjack oaks.

"We must be on the right road, Lena, honey. The manna is still fallin' to keep you healthy and content!"

"Now, Hap…!"

Between the groves were stretches where lightening fires had brought down the trees, creating flower-covered meadows. Small streams cut their way south toward the river called the Canadian, but the travelers were too far north to see actually see the water.

In one such clearing, Hap called a rest day, and he and Happy followed deer tracks into the trees. In due time they brought back a young buck.

"Papa let me shoot at it!" Happy announced, excitedly. "But I missed. Papa brought 'im down. I know what I did wrong, and I won't miss next time."

It took two more days to cook down the meat to be packed in crock jars and sealed in fat. The little cast iron stove was fired constantly to fry down the meat, and the warming oven was used to dry jerky strips. It made a welcome change from rabbits and squirrels, and Roscoe, the hound, enjoyed the large bones.

Moving steadily through Sac and Fox land, they neared the Oklahoma territory. Well worn trails were seen running in many directions, and there were cleared places where camps had been set up to wait for the day of the land run that had happened over two months ago.

The Palmers followed along the Deep Fork River, with its high-banked channel. Small steams and rivulets joined it at frequent intervals. The stained glass window rode along peaceably and contented, seemingly approving of the direction taken.

Happy stood with his father, looking into the depth of the ditches that emptied into the river. "Papa, there ain't no bottom down there. It's all mushy."

"Yes, son, there's a bottom, it just ain't made out'a rock, like back east. But you see how the banks got wore down by wagons goin' across, so I don't see how we can have no trouble. Besides, the rivers are so little, the front wheels are up out of the mud 'afore the back ones go in."

Sure enough, the pairs of horses plunged stiff-legged down the banks of the ditches and pulled out on the other side, their feet on solid ground before the back wheels of the wagons plowed into the mud.

They came to a large space worn down by the feet of animals and a lot of people. All available dry wood had been gathered to build fires, and some of the smaller trees had been brought down to use in cooking.

Up ahead they could see the beginning of a log house being built beside a canopied wagon, and a buggy was parked alongside. A young man was busily peeling bark from small logs, and a young woman tended a cooking fire.

"Look, Lena, I'd be thinkin' we made it. Looks like homestead land up ahead, and we're likely drivin' up on somebody's private place."

"What'll you do?"

"Go talk to 'em and see if there's a problem with us a'comin'. Likely that trail there is the road, but that young fellow'd know. Hello, the camp," he called from a distance. It was certain these people would be well armed with weapons, and it was good to shout a warning. Also, it was only the polite thing to do.

"Hello! Come on in."

Hap walked in.

"Friend, we been lookin' for what would be the road into the territory. We wasn't wantin' to run on anybody's private...."

"No worry there! Ain't no privacy to be found anywhere here, my friend," came the friendly answer. "This here's my claim, and

I'm tryin' to get a place up and in the dry 'afore winter, along with a garden and everything else that's got'a be done. 'Course, that's what we expected, comin' in on the run like this."

"Got yourself a tract, huh?"

"Yeah, we was lucky. I reckon you come through the campsite back yonder? We waited there for a week, just for the start date, and when everyone was on their horses, headin' for the interior, I took the chance to get the one just over the line. I was cuttin' trees on my land before most'a the runners got to where their land was!" The young man leaned on his axe and smiled with pride at the way he had nabbed the first tract of the territory.

"Seemed a clever thing to do. Would that trail over there be the road, by any chance?"

"Near as you'll find. Seems like folks're usin' the section lines for roads, that bein' a way to get the road to every tract. 'Course, it'll be a bit of a while till it's made smooth, everybody havin' their own house to tend to."

"I can see that. Well, friend, I got my family, and we got a ways to go yet today. We'll just take that road and see how far we get."

"Good day to you."

Hap Palmer guided the horses onto the worn trail, not quite a road yet that had been cut by the surveyors who had mapped out the territory. It followed along the bank of the Deep Fork River for a short way and turned where a small tributary stream blocked the way. The stream was thickly lined with new-leafed redbud trees, tall and spreading. A clump of the sycamores had a freshly cut blaze sliced through the bark of several of the larger ones.

"Looks like someone went to the trouble to blaze a trail. Road turns, 'stead'a tryin' to get through the little creek."

He turned the horses to the south to follow the trail, and ahead of him, every hundred feet or so, another blaze had been cut from a tree, either from an oak or a cottonwood. Hap followed along the marked trail, having no better plan.

It was a Saturday, the third week in June. The weather had become somewhat warm, and everyone was tired, hoping for a place to stop soon. Maybe a place by a steam of water.

Another two miles went by, and a stream did not appear. In addition to that, small homesteads were rising every half a mile or so. Activity was everywhere. Fresh, raw buildings were going up in small spaces cut in among the trees. Brush fences enclosed the animals, both horses and cows. Occasionally small children called to each other.

The Palmer children began to look this way and that with great interest.

Kathleen Palmer also looked this way and that and began to be concerned. "Hap, it seems like all the land belongs to someone, and they might want'a take exception to us just stoppin' and parkin' on it. What'll we do?"

"Figured I'd turn west down here where the most wagon tracks turn and ask the first person I see."

"I hope there'll be water. Ridin' has got me all hot and tired, and the youngens are all in need of a bath."

"Well, where there's folks, there's got'a be water somewhere," he reasoned.

The caravan moved along for another mile, and the evidence of settlement became more obvious. Just ahead was a massive cottonwood tree, and two older men were relaxing against the base of it.

Hap stopped and walked toward them. "Hello!"

"Hello, yerself. Come on in, neighbor."

"Name's Palmer. Hap Palmer. I got my family here, and we was lookin' for who we'd see for permission to camp over. Bein' the Lord's day tomorrow, we was wantin' to stop over somewhere and rest, two days, maybe three, if it'd be all right."

One of the men heaved himself to his feet. "My name's Kendall, and this here fellow is Carlile. This here land you're on belongs to my sons who got themselves a haulin' business, over in Guthrie. They ain't here to ask, yet, but I know it'll be all right with them for you to stop over, leastwise for a few days. They'll be comin' on in sometime 'afore mornin'. They try to get home for Sunday when they can."

Hap nodded. "Much obliged. Any particular place we'd ought'a park, to be out'a the way?"

Clyde Kendall shrugged. "This here's a quarter section'a land. Don't see how you'd be a bother. Right where you are'd be good."

"Thanks. Nuther thing. I ain't wantin' to be a bother, but my missus was wonderin' about water. Where'd be the closest we'd find it?"

"Pretty close, Palmer. My boys, they got 'em a punched-out well, and its right over there where ya see the bucket a'hangin.' Help yerself to all you want."

"Thanks a lot. Be talkin' to ya, later," and he was gone.

Within the hour, the small cast iron stove was on its platform, and a crackling blaze heated venison stew and bath water. Before another hour was passed, the white squares of clean diapers flapped in the breeze, and the voices of children could be heard among the trees.

Clyde Kendall settled back on the ground by the cottonwood tree. "Reckon where he come from?"

"Could be lost?"

"Wouldn't see how. There ain't much way he could come into the tract, less'n that was where he was headed. Didn't want to seem nosey and ask."

"Could be he's the relative of someone on towards Guthrie. He's got women and youngens, and likely they got tired'a travelin'. A body don't make too good'a time with little 'ens. My son's little girl, that we brought from Tennessee, she'd get tired'a ridin,' and we couldn't stop just to let her walk around a while. Yessirree, travelin's hard on youngens."

"Likely you're right. From the sound of it, he's got a passel'a youngens."

"Peers that'a'way. The fellow's got good eats, though. Smells to me like venison, less'n my nose is playin' tricks on me. It's fair makin' me hungry, just the smell of it. Could be time for me to get on over to my place and see if my daughter's got somethin' on the stove."

"See ya, later."

Twenty-Seven

Liddy filled two water buckets and brought them to the campsite. Kathleen took a look at the water in the buckets and drew back in surprise.

"Land sakes, I'd done forgot how clean and sparkly well water was, but I didn't forget how it don't need to be strained and boiled to be ready to cook with. We ought'a maybe plan on getting' heads washed and maybe white shirtwaists and Hap's white shirts'n collars done up."

Liddy commented, "Water's easy to get, too. All I had to do was pull down on the rope and up it came. Easy as back in Lafette. I 'bout forgot how to get water that I didn't have to stand in the mud and lean over to dip up after I shooed back the water spiders. I like this place here. I hope the window doesn't want to go much farther."

Kathleen sighed wearily and nodded, not trusting herself to speak an opinion. The trip over from Fort Smith had been especially wearisome. Her increased girth slowed her activities seemingly more than it had before. It felt good just to hold back and let Liddy take the lead on most things.

The campsite was surrounded with climbable trees and with vines begging to be swung on. Violets grew in the shade, and Johnny Jump Ups grew in the sun. Grass grew everywhere, and the six horses were making their way around within the circle of their tether ropes.

Hap carried water to the animals, and as he sat down to the venison stew, he commented, "Got good tastin' water here. Don't seem to be too far down, neither."

Dusky dark had fallen, and the lanterns had been hung on the side of the wagon as heads of red-gold curls were washed and brushed dry. White things and diapers were swished out in the soapy water from the hair washings and hung on a line strung between two trees.

Charity filled her "dry wood" bucket for the breakfast fire, and the Palmers were settling into their sleeping quarters when a wagon pulled along beside them, passed them, and went to the shed behind the well.

Along the side of the wagon were the words, "KENDALL BROTHERS We Haul."

"Looks like the owners of the land come home. Likely they're surprised to see they got squatters on their property."

"Yeah, but their pa gave permission just like it was his right to give."

The green wagon pulled into the wagonshed, and the weary horses were loosed onto the grass where they whinnied and nickered at the strange animals tethered nearby.

Douglas Kendall, first out of the wagon, wondered. "What do we got, Pa? Squatters?"

Pa's answer, "Just folks needin' a camp for a day or two."

"Reckon we're safe they ain't claim jumpers. If they was claim jumpers, they'd not pick a place with so many folks around."

"They won't be no trouble, Son. The fellow's name's Palmer, and he's got his women and youngens with 'im."

Chester Kendall, the oldest of the three brothers, made his weary way to the well to draw water for the horses.

Darkness was falling fast, and Chester Kendall was bone tired from six days of fourteen to fifteen hour days spent delivering freight for the Santa Fe Railroad in Guthrie. After two months there had been no let up of the incoming merchandise hauled by the railroad. The instant city of Guthrie suddenly had a population of thousands and everyone needed everything.

Chester let down the bucket and listened for the gurgle that would tell him it was full and ready to be drawn up. He let his eyes wander wearily around the wooded quarter section of land that belonged to himself and his two brothers. What a good piece of ground it was and....

Then there in the distance, he saw a bobbing light that could only be someone walking through the trees carrying a lantern. Now who could that be? Oh, likely the squatters.

Nearer the light came, and when it was close enough, Chester saw a young lady (girl?) not more than five feet tall, with lovely pale skin and flowing black hair hanging down over her shoulders.

The soft breeze lifted the wavy ends of her hair, fanning them like the feathers of a blackbird's wing. She carried a water bucket in one hand, and a lantern in the other.

Blinking his eyes, Chester Kendall vowed his stint of six straight days of fifteen hours a day would have to be cut back. He was clearly hallucinating, as beings of such beauty as this did not walk toward him at the end of the day with smiles on their face. Clearly, he was working too hard. And he was certainly seeing things that were not there.

Though the gurgle at the end of the rope had told him the bucket was full, he stood motionless, holding the end of the rope and leaning against the stone curbing of the well.

"Hello."

Hmmm, the vision speaks. Then it should be answered, "Hello to you."

"I'm Lydia Palmer, from over there." Her lovely elbow pointed in the direction of the lantern lit camp. "We was thinkin' we'd get water for breakfast right now, and then we'd not disturb anyone in the mornin'."

'Oh, it wouldn't be no disturbance. You get water whenever you want it. Oh, yes, I should say I'm Chester Kendall."

"You must be part of Kendall Brothers, We Haul."

"Oh, you know about...."

"Your Pa seems right proud to talk about you. You must'a worked hard today, gettin' in so late like you did. You want I should pull that bucket up for you?"

Chester startled into reality and gripped the rope. "Oh, no, I was just...."

Darkness had fallen, and Liddy's lantern furnished the only light. She lifted it so Chester could see the horse trough where he was to pour the water.

"We can fill your bucket, now," he offered, gallantly.

"Oh, no. This water was just for mornin.' You and the horses are tired, you go on ahead. I'll just hold the light here so's you can see."

Douglas Kendall, from his position by his mother's stove and within the aroma of her cooking, peered into the darkness where his brother was watering the horses.

"Who's out there? Is that...?"

"Ellie Gunther? Nope, that's one of the squatters, wantin' to stay over the weekend. Your Ellie, she'll be along, I guarantee. Quick as you get a chance to get yerself cleaned up and fed."

The younger of the brothers, Manford, was deeply involved with a bowl of beans that had been simmered with ham chunks and the whole thing teamed up with slabs of cornbread. Between bites, he confided, "Danged if I ain't so wore out, I like to'a gone to sleep right there on the wagon bed, bouncin' along the section lines. I can't wait to hit the sack and get some sleep."

Douglas ate his beans, thinking of whether he had a clean shirt to put on. The sight of beautiful Ellie Gunther and her bright curls and up-turned-corner smile was what he needed to give himself a little pep after the long, hard week of work. He had looked forward to the sight of her, and he felt he well deserved it. Out of the corner of his eye, he watched the spot of lantern light beside the well. Chester should have had the water drawn by this time. He was bound to be hungry, so what was keeping him?

At the well site, Chester lowered his bucket into the water again, and seemed to forget it… again. "You folks headed to see relatives…. or somethin'?" He knew it was ill-mannered to ask personal questions, but, after all, they were on his land, weren't they? That should give him certain rights to be nosey.

She answered. "I'm with my brother and his family, over from Kentucky. He was headed…" Surely she could not tell this stranger the bizarre story about the windowpane that had directed them to the ends of the earth.

"I don't know much about travelin,'" she finally said. Well, that much was true. "I was just kind'a goin' along with him…."Her voice trailed off.

"That's all right. It weren't none of my business. Likely, you folks'll be tired, comin' that far. We come down from Nebraska, ourselves. Pretty near wore us out, too."

Finally, Chester was able to bring himself to draw up enough water for the horses, and he drew one more bucket for Liddy.

"You want… I could carry it for you…?"

"Oh, no. I do this all the time. You're tired. I'll just take this and go on over to the…" Why were words so difficult to remember?

"Well…. see you in the mornin'?" It was a direct question.

"I reckon so. We'll still be here… if it's all right."

"Sure thing. Good night."

Chester stood in the darkness beside the horse trough, listening to the swilling of the horses as they drank, to the Whip-will's-widow calling from a grove of trees, to the chorus of cicada crickets in the trees above him, and the occasional punctuation of yips from a family of foxes. No sound came from the campsite where the vision of beauty had disappeared with the bucket and the lantern.

Why hadn't he been more clever and thought of more things to say? He could likely have kept her a little longer. She hadn't seemed to be in a hurry, but there he had stood like a dummy with nothing to say, with not enough sense to draw up his pail of water when it was full. What must she think?

But then, there was tomorrow, and he must somehow manage to think up something clever to say to her. Maybe her brother would be tired enough to stay over another day. It could happen.

Sixteen-year-old Manford lay back on his pallet and was asleep before Douglas, eighteen, had his shirt changed and had headed out in the direction of the Gunther's camp.

Chester ate his food and his mind was on the camp not two hundred yards away. As he watched, the several lanterns began to go out, one by one, and then there was total darkness.

The large redbone hound, tied to a cottonwood tree, gave out a few territorial barks, but Pete and Pokey, the blue tick hounds from Tennessee, did not bother to answer. Perhaps they did not consider a tethered dog to be a threat. After eating, Chester stretched out, wearily, on his pallet. His little sisters played quietly some distance away, and his older sisters, ages 13 and 15, were somewhere, wherever it is that girls go. His parents talked softly in the distance. He knew he should be asleep, as exhausted as he was, instead, he remembered the pale skin, the shadows around her eyes, and the lovely flowing black hair. Was she really as beautiful as she seemed? Well, he'd know in the morning.

Then, hours later, Douglas came home, yawned, and stretched out on his own pallet, and finally Chester was able to get to sleep.

Twenty-Eight

The lonesome calls of the night birds finally changed to the chirps and trills of the day singers, and the bluebirds and mockingbirds called. The jays squawked and quarreled in the cottonwood trees. A soft breeze blew through the leafy limbs as six-year-old Charity slipped down from the buggy where she had spent the night beside her twin sisters.

Quietly, taking off her nightdress, she put on her day dress that Grandma O'Keen had made, the one she liked best, with pink ribbons on the neck and sleeve. She tiptoed past Roscoe, the hound, to where her other sisters slept. Five-year-old Mercy and Faith, a year younger, responded to her gentle touch and crawled away from their parents, slipping quietly down to the ground.

It had become their habit, ever since the weather became warm, to get up as early as possible in order to have some time to play before the wagons started to roll. Sleep could be done later when the wagon wheels were grinding along the road.

Moving quietly away from the camp, they inspected the violets and the Johnny Jump Ups the tiny cups made by the acorn shells and the scattering of sky blue eggshells that lay under the limb of a blackjack oak.

"Lookie, Mercy. Bird egg shells. They would be…?" It was big-sister quiz time.

"Robin's eggs, I'd think."

"Obin's eggs," mimicked Faith.

"Shhh! Don't wake up nobody. Member what Mama said! Huh?"

The startled Charity had found herself face to face with a girl no bigger than herself with big blue eyes and yellow hair. The girl smiled.

"Hi! I'm Sophie Kendall. I live over there." She jabbed her elbow toward the newly-dug well.

"Hello. I'm Charity, and she's Mercy, and she's Faith," Charity advised, importantly. "We don't know where we live."

The girls stared at each other for a few seconds, and then Mercy made the next move. "You got dolls or books to play with? We got books in the wagon."

"I got a book with poems. I can't read, but I know the words."

"Can we look at your book?" Their own books had been "looked at" until they were in tatters.

"Sure. I'll get it." With that, Sophie disappeared into the trees.

Daylight became brighter, and a few rays of sun pierced through between the leaves of the trees as Sophie came running back with a large book. The four girls gathered around the book, and Sophie recited,

"Mary had a little lamb, its fleece…."At the snapping of a twig, the girls looked up to see two large dogs approach with one small girl between them. Sophie advised. "That'll be Alecia. She lives through the trees, and she has a book that says the ABC's. Come on, Alecia."

As the sun popped over the tallest cottonwood, Alecia was "reading," "A is for apple that grows on a tree. Some are for piggy and some are for me. B is for ball, for…." By now, Sophie was reciting with her.

The smell of cooking ham began to drift among the trees, and the morning sounds of waking toddlers came from the direction of the camp.

"Charity? You girls come eat breakfast, now."

Charity sighed, sadly. "That's my mama. We got'a go. Come on, Mercy and Faith." As she walked away, she asked, hopefully, "You'll come back after while, won't you? We don't got'a go nowhere today."

Sophie and Alecia walked away, carrying their books.

The breakfast bowls were filled with oatmeal, and biscuits stuffed with ham were passed around. Liddy skillfully managed two bowls and two spoons, one to feed herself, and the other to feed the twins. When the oatmeal was gone, the toddlers were given a biscuit and allowed to walk around the wagon, holding to the wheels and the wagon tongue for support. But they didn't need much support.

Seven-year-old Happy went with his father to tend the animals. They didn't need grain, with so much good grass, but they did need to be watered and tethered in a new place so they could reach more grass.

It seemed the watering would have to wait, though, as the well was located in the direction of the tent belonging to their host, and some people slept in on a Sunday. It would not be right to disturb them, just because the Palmer camp held church services on the Lord's Day.

Breakfast was cleared away, hair was brushed, and ribbons were re-tied. Bedding was shook to remove sand and dust and then folded away. When the sun was well up in the sky, clearly time that everyone should be awake and would not be unduly disturbed by the sounds, the children gathered around.

Kathleen Palmer was moving slowly. Her over-extended abdomen seemed to be a greater weight this time. Weariness settled about her as she found her place as part of Hap's congregation.

Liddy strapped on the accordion and tested the bellows, softly. Giving the signal, she began a few notes as softly as the instrument would play,

The muted singing began. "When the roll is called up yonder, when the roll is called up yonder, when the roll is called up yonder….. when the roll is called up yonder, I'll be there."

Then, "Rock of Ages, cleft for me. Let me hide… myself…."

By now, attracted by the music, Sophie and Alecia had crept back, and seated themselves on the pallet beside Charity and her sisters. A few minutes later, small Marcie Banner joined them, and Sophie's older sisters watched from a distance.

Kathleen motioned to the two other Kendall girls behind the trees, and they came and listened to the music, singing when they knew the words.

Alecia Carlile's grandpa was the next to arrive, and he leaned against a tree, enjoying the sounds produced by Liddy's skillful fingers. His thoughts ran toward "if I just had my fiddle, here…."

Soon, others were coming toward them. Down the trail came children and couples, parents carrying babies and curious teenagers.

Inside his tent, Chester Kendall thought he was being favored by angels songs, straight from heaven. Had he worked so hard last week that he had completely done himself in? Surely not!

Opening his eyes, his mind sought for the pleasant thought he almost remembered from last night. What was it…? Oh yes, the girl! The impossibly beautiful girl... and he had been going to think of something captivating and clever to get her attention and was somehow going to persuade her brother to stay over another day.

But the music? Surely it was only the birds in the trees, but why did it sound so much like… well, music! Pulling on his clothes, he left the tent just as his parents were walking slowly toward the squatter's camp.

It WAS music! It was coming straight from the other side of the wagon. They must have a gramophone… or something.

Kathleen looked about her and was amazed. Seated on the pallet and standing among the trees was a sizeable congregation, and pleasant voices joined in on the words of well-known songs.

Grownups stood back in the trees, listening, and the children crept closer, finally gathering together with those seated on the pallets. Kathleen quietly spread another quilt when the first one was full. Where were they all coming from? People came from all sides, like ants to a picnic. Could they have accidently stopped close to a town… or something?

After the songs, Hap stood and introduced himself. "I'm Hapgood Palmer, and the young lady playing the music is my sister, Liddy. I'm hopin' we didn't wake nobody up with our singin.' We're more'n glad to have you gather 'round and help us, and we'll be singin' more songs later.

"This here bein' Sunday, we wanted to stop and have our church service, the way we always do while we were on the road. You're highly welcome to stay for that. I picked out a story for today found in the book of Samuel, about when David was a little boy.

"Bein' the littlest of his father's sons, he was the one that had to take care of the sheep, and one day...."

The story went on to tell how David, in the strength of his Lord, killed the lion that was trying to kill the sheep. But David knew his strength came from his Lord, and Hap went on to tell how the Lord never expected anything from anyone without giving that person the strength to get it done with.

Then they sang more songs. The congregation in the trees moved in closer, and some song requests came from the bolder members of the bunch. After a dozen or more songs, Hap decided to finally cut it off, as it was almost time for lunch.

"Now, folks, I've not got the words to tell you how pleased we were for you to join in our service. It's time to dismiss, now, but we'll be havin' another service this evenin'. If you'd find yerself with nothin' to do, we'd be more'n glad to...." His eyes searched the congregation, questioning his chances of assembling them again.

"Preacher, could I say somethin'?"

"Sure thing, Mister."

"I need to introduce myself. I'm Clancy Harper, mayor'a the town'a Prosper, located right through them trees. Now, I could hear the music, and the rest'a these folks, they lived close enough to hear, too, but we got other families back there, nigh onto a mile or so, and they didn't get a chance to come and sing and hear the sermon.

"Now, what I was thinkin,' if you was stayin' over, like you said, and was gonna have another service, I thought chances are that you'd agree to have it in our new-built church buildin', and give us time to let the rest'a the town know about it."

Hap looked around at the faces and at the man who had stepped forward. "Well, for certain, Mr. Harper...."

"Call me Clancy. You could come and look at our new building, and you'd know if it'd be all right. It's got no floor, yet, 'cause there's not been sawed lumber available, and we're one window shy'a havin' it closed in from the moths and June bugs, but it has good sawdust on the floor...."

Hap felt shivers play up and down his arms and back, and even the scalp on his head tightened at the word. A weakness settled around him, and he reached a hand toward the endgate of the wagon to steady himself.

With a weak and breathless voice he asked, "Wait, Brother. Back up to what you said about the window…"

Clancy obliged. "Uh, well, we ordered seven windows, and the order come in one window short. Wasn't no big thing. Ever since the territory opened up, everybody needs everything, and we find ourselves havin' to wait on this and that. We're getting' used to it. That window'd be just another thing we'll have to wait for."

Hap plunged in. "That window, friend, what was the size of it…? The one you needed and didn't get?"

Clancy grinned and chuckled as he explained. "To tell the truth, the size was the problem. We must'a picked the size everybody else picked. We ordered size three by four, to make 'em wide enough to let in light, and short enough to be easy to open. Seemed a good plan, but we'll likely have to settle for a smaller one, or maybe make one up from a pane'a glass when we …."

While Clancy was still talking, the preacher walked over to his wagon and crawled under it. What strange behavior for a preacher! Clancy followed and squatted down at the rear of the wagon as he talked. The preacher was removing bolts… or something… from a crate from under his wagon.

"Son," the preacher called to his boy, "hand me that other screwdriver." To Clancy he continued, "Could be we could help out on the problem you good folks got with your church."

Clancy leaned his head to look under the wagon. "You ain't sayin' you got a window under there?"

Other men gathered around. Ed Gunther, Clyde Kendall, Eben Carlile, Alvin Banner, and others. Even Chester Kendall and his brothers came closer and knelt on the ground. The small boy with the mop of black hair handed down the requested tool to his father.

With a few twists of his hand, the preacher handed the tool and the loose screws back to the boy and drew out the stained glass picture that had been so beautifully made into the glass of the window.

With his handkerchief, the preacher wiped away a bit of loose dust, and the radiant June sunshine shone down onto the picture.

The sun's rays shining through it made a colorful pattern on the ground.

Hap held it high and turned it for everyone to see. The glistening white of the angel band shone as a flutter of wings in the sky, and the gold and silver strips of the hay in the manger glowed as clearly as the precious metal they were meant to symbolize. The circle of the halo seemed to shed light on the face of the baby in the rough manger box.

The beauty of it seemed unreal in the woodland of the Oklahoma territory on this Sunday morning in June. Those who stood in the shade of the redbud trees came closer to get a better look.

Liddy Palmer looked at her sister-in-law and saw the tears in Kathleen's eyes. As she watched, Kathleen leaned her face forward into her hands. Liddy could read her sister-in-law's thoughts… could it be? Oh, please, Dear Lord… let it be!

The men of the town looked at each other, puzzled frowns on their faces. Hapgood Palmer looked from one to the other of the men, assessing their reaction.

"I know this looks strange to you, but I been nigh onto seven years and five hundred miles travelin' with this here window. You'll find it to be three feet by four feet, and you're welcome to fit it in the space you got in your church. If it stays, it's yours."

"If it stays…?" Could it actually be theirs?

"Yes, friends. This here window, it's got a story back of it, and if I'm still invited, like you said I was, to speak in your church this evenin,' I'd like to be tellin' you that story. It'll take a fair amount'a time. As of right now I've got it in my mind that I was likely bringin' this window to you folks. I ain't worried about bein' wrong about it, 'cause if that window don't belong here, it'll not stay…" Then he added, "And that the God's honest truth."

He looked around at the silent gathering. "Am I still invited?"

"Sure you are, brother. We find ourselves a mite eager to get to hear the story…."

Hap nodded his acceptance. "Now, if someone'll tell me where the church is, we'll see if this little old window fits."

Several of the men took the window from him and walked with him for the quarter of a mile distance to the log building with the new red-cedar shingled roof. Fresh sawdust covered the floor, and the June sun shone in through the opening at the back of the church, creating a trapizoid of light on the sawdust. The men carried the window to the opening and slid it in place.

Hap nodded with satisfaction. "Wouldn't have a couple'a finishin' nails to secure it in the hole, would ya?"

"Sure thing, but first we got'a talk price. We know by lookin' at it that it's a thing of value, and we'd never have thought to buy somethin' like this, 'cept now that we saw it in the window opening, I think we'd all agree it fits."

Another voice, "Yeah, and we ain't got a lot'a money, this bein' a new congregation, 'n all, and we know it's not likely we got enough, but we'd like to hear it from you. Good as it looks, we'd not want to tap it in place if it wasn't gonna be ours."

"We could maybe pass the plate… again?"

Nods all around. "Everybody'll be here, tonight. Likely…"

Hap looked from one to the other, puzzled. "Now look here, fellows. Seems you might'a got it a bit wrong. This here window, it ain't mine. Never was. You'll understand when you hear the story. We ain't talkin' no money, 'cept if the Good Lord puts a price on it, and then the payment of it'd go to Him, and not to me. And I'll say this, if this ain't the place for it, I got'a load it on my wagon agin and be on my way."

"Well, preacher…" Where were the right words to respond?

"We'd be wantin' to see…."

"Fact is, preacher, we ain't hardly got no words…."

Clancy seemed to understand, and as mayor he took charge. "Preacher Palmer, we're gonna let you get at your dinner, and we'll talk things over later. That'd likely be tomorrow or whenever it is we know what that window wants to do."

Hap nodded, smiled, shook hands all around, and went back to the campsite. His feet felt lighter than he ever remembered, and his shoulders squared themselves in his white Sunday shirt. His head felt so light, it likely would not stay on his shoulders if he had not been wearing his Sunday hat.

Liddy had watched the unveiling of the window and saw the men walk away with it. Just as her heart began to pound with anticipation, she turned back to Kathleen just in time to see her lean forward on her knees and burst into silent tears.

Glancing quickly toward the twins to check their location, she ran to her sister-in-law. "Lena, are you…? Can I do anything?"

Other women began to close in around them.

"Honey," one addressed Liddy, "My name's Nettie Gunther. Is your…I mean is there anything I can do? We been…all of us women, here... we come here and, well, we like to help. Is she…?"

"Ma'am, my sister-in-law, she's plum bone tired, travelin' so far and havin' to take care of, well, everyone. And, you see, we come a long ways with her doin' everything at once, and she's just too tired to go no farther. Been pushin' herself too much over the last two hundred miles. What I got'a do is get her to lay down in this buggy, and then I can take care'a the youngens."

"If there's anything…."

Liddy smiled at them, reassuringly, "Likely we'll need help and be thankful to get it, and thanks. Right now, though, I got'a do what I said, and then round up the youngens and get 'em fed.… I been doin' too much ridin' along, and it's past time I was doin' a bit'a the pullin'."

The one called Nettie, cut in, "Sure and we're gonna go. You know what you got'a do, but I'll step over after dinner, just to make sure…."

"I thank you, Ma'am."

They filed away in groups and pairs, leaving Liddy with Kathleen.

Liddy made her voice unaccustomedly stern. "Lena, you're gonna listen to me. I don't say much, but I'm sayin' this. You're gonna let me help you into my buggy, and we'll toss the bug net over the whole thing. Then you're gonna sleep till you can't sleep no more."

"Sure and I'll do that, right after I fix…."

Liddy's voice was louder and more stern and commanding as she said, "You ain't fixin' no dinner. My fixin' ain't like yours, but it won't kill 'em. Can you eat somethin' now? A buttered biscuit, or…?"

Kathleen wearily shook her head and allowed Liddy to lead her to the buggy. Stretched out comfortably, she allowed Liddy to untie her shoes and remove them and to spread the fine meshed mosquito net over the buggy to keep away the flies.

"Now you ain't to be worried over nothin.' I'll try to keep 'em quiet, but if you hear something said or yelled, it's got nothin' to do with you. I'll be over with a drink, quick as I draw up a bucket'a fresh water."

Stepping away from the buggy, Liddy began to assign duties. "Happy, you can start a fire. Charity, you keep both eyes on them twins and keep 'em together in the same place 'cause you can't run two ways. Mercy, you help me look for something for dinner, and Faith, you go help Charity with the twins."

Liddy and the four year old looked into the food box. Eggs. Oatmeal. Sliced venison (needs to be used up because of the warm weather). "Here, Mercy, set this pan over on the stove. Then count the biscuits and see if there's enough."

"One, two… looks like seven."

Another look into the box. Crackers and peanut butter. There was a small amount left over from the stop in Fort Smith, and the two treat items had been carefully rationed. Today was the day to eat them, and that would help out on the bread supply.

All right. Mushroom gravy over sliced venison, and the little ones could have the peanut butter. There were two jars of peaches left. She could open them both, or she could put them back for cobbler… which should she do? And there was cornmeal pancakes. She knew how to make them, and there was still a fair amount of honey. How in the world did Kathleen turn out all those meals, one after another, with nothing to work with?

"Charity, come spread up a cracker and peanut butter sandwich for each'a the twins. Faith, honey, do you want peanut butter? Charity, make one for Faith, too. They're needin' naps.

"Happy, you got that fire a'goin'? Go see if you can draw up some fresh water. If someone wants to help you, you let 'em."

The gravy finally thickened in the skillet, and Liddy added the sliced meat along with dried mushrooms.

Charity looked at the product in the skillet and asked, "Could I have my meat in a biscuit?"

Liddy nodded and realized she should have probably gone that way. Her gravy wasn't very… oh, well, they could make do with it one time. Charity waited for an answer.

"Eat it however you want it, honey."

After an eternity, Hap came back to the camp. He looked at Liddy standing behind the stove with a question in his raised eyebrows.

Liddy squared her shoulders and stated, "Lena's dead tired. I made her go to bed, and you'll just have to put up with what I can gather up to eat."

"You'll do fine," her brother encouraged, with a voice sounding more confident than he felt. He walked over to Liddy's buggy and peered through the netting. His beautiful wife lay with her head far back on the pillow and her hair flowing awry around her neck and ears. The usual rosy cheeks were pale as ivory, and the area around her closed eyes was gray as a shadow. He took a deep breath and stared. Dear Lord… Had he been too hard on her? But what could he do now? Staring another moment at her stillness, he turned and walked away.

The twins worked on the crackers with all the teeth they had, and smeared their faces liberally, but Charity cleaned them up, and somehow managed to haul them into the wagon for a long-past-time nap.

The creamed venison over biscuits was ladled onto the plates and they sat down to eat.

"Dear Lord, we thank you for…."

Twenty-Nine

After they ate, Hap took Happy, and they went walking into the timber.

Liddy went to take Kathleen a fresh drink, but she was asleep. She slept through the afternoon and on into the evening. As the sun began to fall behind the trees, Nettie Gunther returned with another young woman she called Roberta Dunbar.

"Liddy, is it? Liddy, honey, we all wanted to do somethin' and not knowin' what was best, we went to cookin.' Seems like when one of us women gets down, cookin' is the first trouble that pops up. So if that little stove's still warm, we'll just slip this in the oven till you get ready to eat. We wanted to bring it on over, so's it'd be here and you'd know about it 'afore you got somethin' else started."

The stunned Liddy watched the covered dishes being tucked into Kathleen's little oven and into the warming oven overhead. The aroma coming from them was almost heavenly.

"Thank you, so much…." She felt her eyes becoming moist.

"No need for thanks. We all been there, and now we'll run on and let you take care'a things."

Liddy watched as the women disappeared into the trees, and she hesitantly opened the oven to take a peek. The first dish contained a dressing made from cornbread and liberally seasoned with onions and other herbs. The savory smell of it came from the chunks of meat (stewed squirrel?) that dotted it, throughout.

Another dish contained small new potatoes swimming in a cream gravy. Real cream. There was a dish of mixed greens, such as Kathleen might have gathered along the way. In the warming oven was a cobbler made from wild blackberries, and beside it was a plate of spice cookies.

Liddy stood looking at the food, and thrill bumps played along her arms and neck. Surely she was dreaming. She felt a tug at her skirts and looked into the anxious eyes of Charity.

"Liddy?'

"What, darling?"

"You sick… or somethin'?"

"No, honey. Why would you think that?"

Charity bowed her head and sniffed, quietly. Liddy knelt beside her.

"Honey, what's wrong?"

"Nothin'."

"That's not true. Little girls don't cry when nothing is wrong."

"I was scared."

"Of the woodland? The people?" Somehow that didn't sound like Charity.

"Of you."

"Me?"

"I thought you was lookin' like mama did, and I thought you'd both die."

Liddy gathered her little neice close. "Oh, darling, your mama isn't gonna die. She's just very, very tired, and I'm not even sick. I was just happy to see all this good food. I was so happy I thought I might cry."

"My grandpa and grandma died, and we had to go away."

"No, little one. I reckon it seemed that way to you, but grandpa and grandma got a bad disease, and that's why they had to die, but they're in heaven now. We had to leave because of the window, remember? Your daddy had that window before grandpa and grandma got sick."

"You're not sick?" Charity's relief made a whisper of her voice.

"No, sweetheart. And your mama isn't sick, either. Like I told you, she's just very, very tired."

"Oh. I thought maybe I'd have to cook."

That brought an understanding smile to Liddy's face. "No, honey, but I'm sure I'll need some help until your mama gets some rest and feels better."

Charity brightened. "I'll help."

The neighborly gifts took care of supper with leftovers for the next day. At Kathleen's insistance, Liddy took the children and went to the evening service. They would need her instrument to furnish the music.

So, sitting in the new church with the others of the town, Liddy listened to an account of the pilgrimage she had just lived through and been an important part of. She remembered, with her brother, the times they had strayed, and the "window" had turned them around.

After a small meeting with the town's leaders, Hap was asked to stay.

"We ain't got no house for you, yet, but they's room for your plunder here in the church yard, and you'd get a good well. Come storms and such, the church'd be open for ya to use."

So the three-vehicle caravan was moved from the Kendall claim to the churchyard. Kathleen stayed down for two weeks, being up only long enough each day to cook breakfast. Charity leaned over the mixing pan as her mother made the bread. She decided that, in her own best interest, it might be well that she learn how it was done.

Late the following Saturday, the green KENDALL BROTHERS We Haul wagon pulled its weary way into the town. When the exhausted horses were taken care of, a bit of Saturday night cleaning up was done, it was only natural that Chester would find reason to amble over to the churchyard.

Liddy was at the well when she saw him coming toward her. After taking the water back to the camp kitchen, she met him under the trees. It was only natural that they would walk a ways together down the trail.

This one and that one of the town's residents looked up from their Saturday duties and saw them, and it seemed only natural for them to smile and nod.

It was late one evening during the third week at the Redbud Creek Church, when the children were bedded down, that Liddy approached her brother.

"Hap, I got'a have a talk with you."

Kathleen looked from Hap to Liddy, and decided, "Think I'll go bring up a pail'a water for the mornin,'" and she arose to leave.

"No, Lena, you got'a stay. I didn't mean I had to talk to Hap, alone. What I wanted was to say I made me a decision. I got that money, you know, that Pa told me to give to you, and you said 'no', that it was mine? Well, I know what I want'a do with it."

Hap's face clouded with a concerned frown. "Now, Liddy... we haven't had a chance to...?" Whatever could that girl have seen that she would want to buy?

But Liddy stopped him. "Wait. If it's my money, then I know what I want. I been walkin' around and lookin,' and I know this town is where I want'a live. I saw one of the lots that was left, and..."

"Now, Liddy, you know your place is with us. You don't need to be thinkin'a goin' off on your own, just 'cause you're goin' on seventeen. You know that my house'll always be...."

"I know that, Hap. But what if the window calls you out on the road agin? It was you that got spoke to by the window, not me. I'm more'n grateful to you and Lena for takin' me in when I was all mixed up, but this here is what I want to do. I've got the money to get the land and enough to get on the lumber list. I'd not be in a hurry to get moved, but I want'a get it started. Then you and the youngens could stay at my house as long as you stayed here. Or forever, if you wanted to."

"Well now, Liddy, that'd take some thinkin', and...."

"I know that, Hap, and I already done the thinkin.' I know you're of a mind that I'm still the helpless girl you started out with, but I'm different. I got done to myself in the last six months what I should'a been doin' in the last six years. I know this is what I want to do."

With a sly smile, Kathleen put in, "This wouldn't have nothin' to do with young Kendall, now would it?"

With a toss of her head, Liddy answered, "Oh, maybe him, or maybe others, or… I don't know, yet. Mostly just for me." Her answer was definite and well-thought-out, ignoring her sister in law's teasing smile.

Hap, again. "Well, if you're sure. Land always sells, if you get a change of mind. But you're not to use what Pa gave you. Remember, I sold the house, and half is yours. That half is a sight more than what you got, and with the price'a lumber right now, chances are you'll need it. Now, I could go with you and look at…"

"I know what I want, Hap. It's the one with the creek runnin' through. It ain't sold yet, on account'a the creek takes up a chunk'a the land, and most of the folks think five acres is little enough, as it is, without allowin' for the creek with all the redbud trees. It's enough for me, and I want the creek. I can show you the little willow trees along that creek, too, and you'll see the good furniture it'll make, once you get your shop set up."

Thirty

It was hardly two weeks later that Eben Carlile was found at Kendall's Wagonshed, talking with Clyde Kendall, when the blacksmith/mayor, Clancy Harper, came by. Basil Hamilton and Alvin Banner were in the vicinity, as well as Ed Gunther and Steven Tullius.

"Seems the preacher's settlin' in on his own lot."

"Ain't his. It's his sister's."

"The girl? Now, why'd…?"

"Says she likes it here. Seems there was some money from the sale of a place in Kentucky."

"Good thing for us, her settlin' in, here, and bein' so handy with that music."

Clyde Kendall, now. "Seems that girl wasn't patient to wait for sawed lumber, and she's getting' logs cut off my boys' land to get up a little cabin. I reckon they're wantin' to get the preacher's wife in a house, 'afore…"

"Likely that's the rush. Then, agin, logs makes a good, warm house. Thought about goin' that'a'way, myself, for a while."

"They'll be addin' onto it soon, I'd reckon. What's the preacher got now, six youngens?"

"Yeah, and that'd be houseful...."

"Reckon that sister comes in handy, takin' care'a the youngens. Seems like the youngens look to her like they would to another mother."

"Right good seemin' girl. Your boy appears to have a more'n passin' interest in 'er."

"Yeah, him and others. Noticed Dave and Herb takin' a second look. I told Chester he better watch and see if she gets deckin' lumber from the mill quicker'n she should, and if she does, he'd better step up his attention! It's Dave and Herb that let the dimension lumber go."

A round of chuckles passed through the gathering. "Yeah, and it puts him at a disadvantage, bein' gone all week."

The young man's father nodded and grinned. "Yeah, you'd think that, but ya got'a remember, he comes out from Guthrie, and they're beginnin' to get things there. Last week he brought home a box'a store-bought candy. Well, he really brought two boxes and give the other one to his sisters. It pays to stay on the good side'a sisters."

Someone else said, "And that other boy'a yours... he getting' anywhere with that Gunther girl?"

"Hard to tell. Seems that'a'way when he's at home, but then he's gone back to the city to work, and there ain't no knowin' what Ellie thinks about till he gets back agin. So far, she's saved her Saturdays for him."

"Well, her pa bein' right here, likely we'd get the straight word."

Ed Gunther smiled and shifted from one foot to the other, leaning back against the cottonwood tree. "Now I'm wonderin' whatever gave you fellows the idea that a Pa knows what goes on in the mind of his girl? It's my feelin' that a Pa'd be the last to know."

The chuckle again. "You'd likely be right on that!"

The first unit of Liddy's log house was finished the last of September. It was a two-room structure, fourteen by twenty eight, and her first lumber allotment came through just in time to put on the roof. Lean-tos were planed for each side of the cabin, but the children would continue to sleep in the wagon until they were built.

The first week in October, Kathleen took to the bed, and little Patience Palmer made her appearance. Round cheeked, she was, with heavenly blue eyes. When her newborn redness went away, she had the same pale creamy coloring of her sisters and a halo of red-gold curls over the top of her head.

Her big sister, Charity, had just turned seven and was convinced that the new sister had been produced expressly for her to play with.

On the warm fall days, before winter set in, Liddy took the baby, along with Charity, Mercy, and Faith and spent time along the bank of Redbud Creek. It was never long until company showed up, in the form of Sophie Kendall, Alicia Carlile, Marcie Banner, and a host of other small citizens of the town.

This one and that one brought books to look at or have Liddy read to them. Alicia always brought her ABC Book and was glad to recite:

"A is for apple that grows on a tree.
Some are for piggy, and some are for me.
'B is for ball for baby to play with.
B is for ball that the dog runs away with.
C is for chicken, with flappity wings……………"

Only the winter birds were left in the trees. The crows were in charge, squawking and cawing, but there was the call of the chicadee and the meadowlark. A few feathered strangers came down from the colder northern states to populate the dark branches of the redbud trees, feasting and fattening on the small, bean-like seeds that were born in clusters all along the limbs.

When they left in the spring, they would carry seeds with them and make room for the robins, the wrens and the bald eagle that soared over the treetops.

"D is for dog with the waggley tail.
See how he digs with a shovel and pail?
"E is for…

Sunlight

One

Her life moved along for decades in much the same way, and then came the time that her eyes were opened, and she was determined to be pushed no longer. From here on, for the rest of her life, she would set the direction that her mind and feet would take. Like a bird, she would rise and take flight. It happened like this.

At first, the incidents that were happening were just straws in the wind. Incidents that, taken separately, meant nothing, but taken together indicated a pattern of prevailing wind.

Sadie had noticed first this thing, and then that thing, and then a few other things that had happened, and when several similar things happened, they fell into a pattern like the thumbprint in the center of peanut butter cookies so that everyone could tell that they were, indeed, peanut butter.

These straws were somewhat different from the print left on cookies, however. These straws were not really what was seen, but more like something that wasn't seen. Only sensed. Or maybe should have been seen.

She first became aware of these straws as she mulled over a recent conversation. There had been the interesting discussion at the house belonging to Willie McClure, Sadie's nephew, about the

Oklahoma territory and the interesting parcel of land that was going to be available for settling.

Sadie's nephew, Willie, and his wife, Lily, had seen the descriptive flyers and had even received a letter from her other nephew, Willie's brother, Thomas, and it had set them to talking.

"Whereat is Oklahoma territory?" Willie's wife, Lily, had wondered. "Ain't it a long way off?"

Willie had shrugged, "Not so far. Not much farther'n Tommy went, when he moved over to Nebraska."

"But he went to a town," insisted Lily.

Willie chuckled, knowing his younger brother very well. "More'n likely, the town happened to be where he was when he got tired'a goin.' Headin' for California to see if there was any gold left at Sutter's Mill could'a been at the top'a the list'a the stupid things Tommy ever done."

"Seems he found 'im a good wife there."

"That was surprisin.'" Then Willie had added, "But I'm of the opinion that it was somethin' he was needin'."

For the last three years, Sadie had made her home with her nephew, Willie, and his wife and their two children. Sadie didn't usually join into the conversation between Willie and Lily, figuring their discussions were none of her business, but that didn't mean she didn't hear what was said.

Then another letter had come from Thomas, two years younger than Willie's 26 years. Tommy, it seemed, wanted to go down to the Oklahoma Territory.

It also seemed, from the letter, that a number of people from the small Nebraska town where Tommy lived would be moving to the territory as a group, and he was going with them. Tommy had always been open to change and excitement. It seemed that he planned to win himself a building lot in the new town and had offered to get a tract of land for Willie in the same town.

Sadie, herself, had read Tommy's letter, for hadn't it been left lying around, and wasn't Tommy her own nephew? And that's when the first straw in the wind had been bent, but it had not been noticeable until sometime later.

Whatever the response written back to Tommy, it was not discussed, at least not in Sadie's presence. Then after that, there were no more conversations about the territory as Willie and Lily sat around the fire of an evening. That was another straw. Actual news was rare out on the farms of Illinois, and every scrap of it was usually discussed and re-discussed at length. Information was treasured, added to, and exclaimed over for lengthy periods of time, usually until another interesting happening took its place.

Also, when Sadie had off-handedly mentioned something about it, creating an opening for discussion, Willie had down played the whole idea as not worth discussion. Another straw. Also bent. That was just not like Willie.

"Oh, that Tommy," he had said, offhandedly. "A body never knows what he'll do. You know Tommy…!"

Lily had done her part. She had added, "Not too good on writin,' neither."

So Sadie had let it go. Lily's statement did not seem to fit, but she had a right to say what she wanted to. It did, however, constitute another straw.

Actually, Tommy was likely better than most young men of his age at keeping in touch, and his letters were addressed with clear and careful penmanship, which was not surprising, as Sadie, herself, had taught him to write.

Straw in the wind, Number one… Tommy's letters were being hidden from her.

Straw in the wind, Number two, was the conversation that was kept from her. Not that she cared about their private conversation, it was more like why had the change come about? What was it that had suddenly become private, and if it concerned the family, why would it not concern her as well? So other straws followed, all of them bent.

There was a thing that was said about straws. One straw was an incident, two straws were a coincidence, but three were a pattern, and another bent straw was about to occur. The thumb was about to be pressed into the peanut butter cookie dough.

The next straw had roots that extended into the boyhood of her nephews, and it had been the most noticeable straw so far.

Willie and Tommy had both been apprenticed to a publisher-bookbinder when they were in their young teens, and seemingly both boys had learned well. Tommy had taken off for parts unknown as soon as he had completed the apprenticeship, and Willie had never quite gotten started with it, opting instead for the farm.

There were understandable and legitimate reasons. The bookbinding equipment was too expensive to invest in, and Willie had not liked working for someone else. So when his father's farm had become available, Willie had moved out of Springfield, Illinois and back to Northbend to try his luck at it. He had not been very lucky.

So here was straw number three about to appear. Suddenly, the purchase of bookbinding equipment seemed to be a possible option. Had a sum of money suddenly appeared?

As Sadie dusted and straightened the house, mainly for something to do with her time, she had come across the brochures and advertisements. There were pictures of this machine and that machine, all of them expensive, and definitely out of the range of Willie's income. Willie, however, continued to look at them and sensible Willie was not inclined to moon over what he could not have.

Also, her nephew and his wife seemed overly restless, though that could not be counted as a straw. The restlessness was not something that one could put their finger on, just more of a feeling, actually. More like the "spring fever" feeling of not being able to center on any one thing.

Then, when Sadie had a restless evening and decided a cup of tea would relax her, she reached for her robe and slipped into the dark kitchen. She knew where everything was, so who needed a light? There would be water in the stove reservoir, and the tea would be.... But there was a light in the parlor!

Now, who would have a left a light in there? The parlor was seldom used, and she'd just step in there and blow out the lamp.

Then she heard the low voices. Was this where the conversations were being hidden from her? Moving closer to the voices, she heard.

Willie's voice. "But she's fifty five years old."

Lily's response. "I know how old she is, but she ain't never sick."

At this point, wild horses could not have dragged Sadie from her listening place. She was the only fifty-five-year-old person in the house, so the conversation was surely about her.

Willie continued. "It ain't like I'd go off and leave her here alone. I'd find a place. I know there's places for ladies where they can stay."

"But the youngens, they'd miss her. She's like the grandma they ain't never gonna have. I don't think....?" Lily's voice lifted into a question.

Willie was quick to cut her off. "I don't mean forever! It's just that it'll be a long, hard trip. It'll for hard for you and me, and she's fifty...." Still the unfinished thought. She thought she had taught them better grammar than that.

Then Lily. "I know how old she is. You don't need to be tellin' me. It just seems to me she ought'a be told and let to decide for herself. You promised your pa...."

Willie's voice was stern and determined, not the usual tone he used with his reasonable, soft-spoken wife. "I remember that, too. When we get there, we can send for her, and she can come on the train. That'd be a heap easier on her."

Lily knew when she had lost the argument. "Well, she's your aunt and you get to decide about her, but it don't seem hardly fair."

Then, with an air of finality, Willie had stated, "I think it's for the best."

Then the conversation went on to other topics, and they discussed this and that.

So, now, all the straws made sense. Sadie put the bent straws into a row in her mind, and the curves of the bends were all in the same place. They were going to go to the Oklahoma territory, Tommy might be already there. They thought she was too old to make the trip with them. Willie was somehow going to get money to buy the bookbinding equipment he needed, and the brothers were going to set up a business in the new town.

Too old, was she? Huh? Actually, how old was too old, and for that matter, too old for what?

Tiptoeing quietly back to her room, she again stepped into the kitchen, closing the door noisily behind her and lighting the lamp. The loudness of her entry would cut off any conversation that she wasn't intended to hear, and now she really did need the tea. Also, they would not realize she had overheard their plans, and that would give her time to think about them.

Instead of taking hot water from the stove reservoir, she'd put on the teakettle. Its whistle, when it got hot, would add to the sounds, and it would let the family know she was awake and stirring around in the kitchen.

At the first piercing burst of the whistle, Lily appeared. "I was sure glad to hear that whistle. I was just sittin' in there thinkin' how good a cup'a tea'd be right now."

Setting two cups on the table, Lily measured out the tealeaves for herself and Willie. "I'm gettin' so tired'a winter. My hands don't hardly get warm from November to April, and a hot teacup feels so good. It'd be nice to live somewhere that'd be warmer in the winter, wouldn't it?"

...like the Oklahoma territory?... The thought flashed through Sadie's mind. Another straw, maybe? "Sound's good to me," she actually said.

Then Lily and the two cups were gone to the parlor, and Sadie picked up her own tea went back to her room. There was thinking to be done.

Settling herself into her sewing rocker, she lifted the bracing tea to her lips and, blowing back the fragrant steam, she took a sip. Never, during the three years she had lived with Willie, helping with his two children, had he ever made her feel that she was in the way. Still... the straws were unmistakably there.

Oklahoma territory. She knew her geography. It was at least two states away.

From Springfield, Illinois, the way would be to cross the Mississippi River at St. Louis, and then all the way over Missouri. Then cross over the border into Kansas and go all the way to Wichita, where the traveler would then head south to central Oklahoma. It was now late March.

Two

It had also been late in March, so many years ago, that she and her mother had left the farm in western Tennessee. She had been ten, and her brother William, father of Willie and Tommy, had been twelve when a sawmill accident had taken the life of her father.

Her devastated mother had done the only thing she could see to do, and after sending her son to relatives in Illinois, she had taken Sadie and gone to Memphis. Cleaning and cooking were all she had ever done, so that's what she turned toward, finally securing a job in a large house overlooking the banks of the Mississippi River.

It had not been a bad life for Sadie, and it was there she had been introduced to the world of books. A tutor came daily to conduct lessons for the two children of the family, Dorothea, also age ten, and Phillip, three years older.

At an invitation from the family, Sadie was permitted to attend the classes. It was thought that Dorothea's academic interest might be increased if she had another student in her class, and perhaps it did, though it was evident the girl would never excel in her studies.

The two girls got on well, but it was with Phillip that Sadie was challenged. Their young tutor was delighted to included Sadie in the advanced studies he prepared for Phillip, and their agile minds competed, urging each other on, until they were studying far ahead of what would be expected of a mere girl.

For the next three years, Sadie's mother worked in the kitchen preparing the meals and bending over the washboard with the dirty clothes. She did all that was expected of her, and more, and was glad to do it for the happiness the family brought to her daughter.

At Phillip's age of sixteen, it was deemed that he needed to advance beyond the abilities of the tutor and was sent east to further his education. This brought about a lot of changes in the classroom, and the time came that the tutor was released and replaced by a seamstress who came once a week. She would instruct Dorothea (and Sadie) in the art of fashion, fancy stitches, and bonnet trimming, and an art instructor also came once a week to instruct the young ladies in painting.

The years that Sadie was fourteen and fifteen seemed very dull to her agile mind compared to the earlier years, but she made the best of them. Her seams were straight, and her stitches were firm. Her embroidery was so neat that it was difficult to tell which was the wrong side of the colorfully stitched pictures.

Wielding the paintbrush and the pallet were not so great an accomplishment, but she performed satisfactorily, and everyone knew that an accomplished young lady need not be an artist. She need only to be conversant in color, style, and technique so she could verbally hold her own among her peers.

The only thing was, who were Sadie's peers?

Dorothea began to spend her time with other young ladies who were the daughters of her parents' friends, and she went places where Sadie, with her servant status, was not welcome. Sadie's only bright spots of interest were when Phillip came home on holidays.

The young man was so excited to see his former classmate that he insisted on spending time with her, much to the distress of his parents. Rather than go to parties with young people of his own class, here he was, preferring to be around the daughter of the household servant. The situation was unthinkable.

So it was, when Sadie was sixteen, that she and her mother answered a summons to meet with their mistress. It was time, the mistress said, that Sadie go on with her life, as she had reached the age when she could be put into service. The mistress had been gentle about it, but the command had been there, nevertheless. Sadie's mother should get her daughter out of the house, or she, the mother, would be dismissed.

Her mother's position in the house was a good one, and she was well liked. She had also reached an age when a change was not as easy as it had been some years earlier, and who knew if they would not meet the same problem at another place. The only other option was to hire on as a mother/daughter team, and Sadie's mother would not consider that solution.

So, it was definitely time for Sadie to take her place in the world. She was sixteen, and she was capable, so she would go.

It was with the help of the mistress that Sadie was placed in the home of an old minister and his frail wife, keeping house and cooking for the old couple. It was lonely and boring, but it paid well, and Sadie had taken a certain satisfaction in the knowledge that she did her work well and was able to care for herself. She had no expenses, so her entire salary was put away.

In addition, there was the knowledge that her mother was extremely happy with her. Housekeeping and cooking were respectable occupations for any girl until she married. Sadie had not the heart to tell her mother about the dullness she felt as she worked and the emptiness in her head as she went to her room at night.

But then there were the books. The old minister saw her looks of longing as she dusted his many books and invited her to take what she liked and read them during her free hours. He was extremely impressed at her selections and began to talk with her about what she had read. As time passed, they had many lively discussions on poetry, the classics, and books on theology.

It could almost be said that her education continued in the library of the minister's home, and for Sadie, it was like the lighting of a lamp in a dark room. She was there for a year and a half before the old wife took to her bed and passed on.

So Sadie was not yet eighteen, but on her own again. It would not be suitable for her to live alone in the house with the minister, unchaperoned as she would be. Besides that, the old man was going away to live with his daughter, but before he left, he advised Sadie to take the test for a teaching certificate. He wisely knew that, as it was, she was surely headed for another domestic position, and for certain, her very soul would shrivel into nothing if that happened.

The old minister further reasoned that, though the teaching of children was not the most exciting of jobs, perhaps it would save her until she was able to save herself. With such a fine mind as she had, it was necessary that she learn to stimulate herself with good literature and not allow herself to be dragged down by life's boring routines.

As a parting gift, Sadie was allowed to select twenty-five books from the old man's shelves. Even now, rocking gently in her room with a cup of tea to comfort her, she remembered that moment. Even now, thrill bumps moved along her arms and back, stimulated by the memory of those selections.

It was with sweet agony that she made her decisions, choosing carefully and thoughtfully, passing over some favorites in favor of those even more thrilling to her.

The soft light from her bedside lamp shed its rays on the spines of those very books, now proudly occupying a bookcase in her room. Along with the original twenty-five, there were another dozen that had been purchased from her wages over the years.

The tea was gone, and the cup was cooling. It was time to get back in the bed and under the warm quilts. A brisk breeze rattled a loose pane in the north window, and her drawn curtains moved slightly in the breeze. She had not mentioned the loose pane to Willie, as she considered the fresh air to be healthy.

Two of her cats, Esmeralda and Matilda, moved restlessly from her chair to the bed, to the floor and back to her chair. They were always restless until Leopold came in for the night and that was sometimes very late.

Essie and Tilda rubbed their thick furry bodies against the pieced quilts of the bed, putting a shine on the marmalade pattern of their coats. The cream, yellow, gold, brown and black splattered its patches on the fur of their bodies like summer flowers often splatter a country meadow.

Occasionally, one of the cats would leap to the window and growl deep in her throat as if to remind their brother it was time he came home. Leopold, if he heard them, did not bother to comply. He would come in at his own good time. He had a social life to keep up.

Sadie blew out the lamplight, and the room was dark, but her thoughts did not stop. Slipping between the warm blankets, her mental images went on, creating a parade made up of the events of her life.

After her time with the minister, she had secured a teaching position very quickly. Her proficiency on the test was so great that she was quickly placed in a school in a well-to-do neighborhood. If her mother had been proud of her in her employment with the minister, she was ecstatic over her placement at the school.

Imagine! Her daughter was a schoolteacher! Other than being the preacher, the position of schoolteacher carried just about the most prestige of any person in the community. Sadie greatly enjoyed her mother's pleasure.

It was a pleasure to Sadie, as well. Or it should have been had it not been for the incident.

Sadie was pleased with teaching. Teaching, in itself, also had its satisfying moments. Her memory went back to her three years in the little school in the country before her father died and how happily she had studied, and now she tried to make her own lessons exciting.

The school was located on the outskirts of Memphis and was a comfortable two rooms, grades one to three being hers. The upper grades of four through six were taught by an older spinster, a Miss Haggard, who had spent her life in the classroom.

A two-roomed cabin on the grounds had been provided for each of the teachers, and a close friendship developed between the two. Evenings often found them in discussion of this and that, as well as the progress of various students. Though not as well read as the minister, the old school teacher's mind was still sharp, and Sadie enjoyed the discussions.

At age eighteen, Sadie began to miss the social life enjoyed by other girls of her age. The mothers of her younger students were often not many years older than she, herself, and she was severely aware that as a school teacher, she had no access to social life at all.

As a matter of fact, marriage would mean the loss of her good position. And how would she meet a likely prospect, tied as she was to the respectability of her job?

So she had turned her thoughts to the children, like eight-year-old Billy, who would be passing on, grossly unprepared, or be retained to spend the next year with his younger sister in his class. Sadie would need to talk with Miss Haggard about that. Perhaps Billy would do better in the next grade.

There was Candice, a bright second grader who would profit by studying with the third grade. If Sadie let that happen, however, what would the girl do next year when she was actually in the third grade, hungering for the fourth?

There was five-year-old Abigail who had slipped in, underage. It would certainly be necessary to retain her. The concept of letters and numbers seemed to totally elude her. She was such a dear little thing, somewhat clinging, but that was likely due to her immaturity.

There was Michael White, and he was another matter, entirely. Young Michael was seven and had possibly been passed into the second before he was ready, though she was more of the opinion that he was lazy-minded and likely had not been challenged enough.

Sadie spent precious time considering what could be done for Michael and had finally come up with an idea. If he could be retained for a little while, perhaps even just fifteen or twenty minutes, after the other children had gone, she might give him the individual attention that would tip the scales in his direction.

Miss Haggard listened to the problem and the possible solution and gave tentative agreement. She explained that Sadie would, however, be forced to bring the boy's parents into the situation, making certain that what she was trying to do was understood by them. Miss Haggard also insisted that she must have a parent in attendance if possible.

First, she must devise a plan. Perhaps it could be a game, maybe a game like tic tac toe. She'd start by using two and three lettered words instead of symbols. It would cause him to dredge up words from his lazy mind in order to get to play. At first, he would think of two lettered words, and she would use three lettered ones. Later, she could change it to names of animals, or trees, or…something.

The details of the games would surely come to her as time went on. If she could just get him to think of the games as fun, perhaps it would carry over to the classroom.

She arranged for a meeting with Michael's parents and saw a further possible problem. Or maybe not. It needn't be a problem, really. Michael had a younger sister of two years, and there was a new baby, still being nursed. It would not be possible for his mother to attend the after school session.

That left Michael's father who thought he could make it.

The first session went well, and Michael seemed to consider it a special favor that he was allowed to stay and play games with the teacher. His father sat back by the door, leaning against the wall while he waited.

Three days later, the father had moved closer and finally seated himself directly behind his son, enthusiastically joining in. Michael became so excited he jumped up and down in his eagerness to win, and his father acting as a cheering section made him try even harder.

Progress was sweet, and Sadie could hardly wait to report it to her mentor, Miss Haggard.

The look on Miss Haggard's face should have been a warning. "Sadie, honey, you've got to watch out about that man. Bein' a teacher, that makes you stand out like a sign at the crossroads."

Sadie had been puzzled. "But Michael is there all the time."

The older teacher had nodded, knowingly. "That might not matter."

And it hadn't mattered. The fifteen minute sessions lengthened, with the encouragement and insistence of the father, and then he insisted on talking with her privately, even after his son went out in the schoolyard to play.

Would it be rude to tell him to go away? Just when Michael's progress seemed to be moving forward?

Then it had become necessary to cease the after-school tutoring or risk her reputation. Miss Haggard had told how she had the same type of problems when she was young. So the sessions were stopped. The excuse had been that Michael might no longer need them.

Two days later, as she was making preparation for the next day, the door opened and Mr. Michael White, senior, had come through the door. Alone. Approaching her, he wore his most handsome smile and began to tell her how he missed the after school sessions and how he missed spending time with someone as beautiful as she.

Moving away from him, Sadie had insisted he must leave because she had things to do, but he came even closer and had just reached for her hand to pull her toward him when the door opened. In came the mother of another student, who watched in astonishment as the man pulled Sadie into his arms.

The man hurriedly turned and left the classroom, but Sadie knew that he had taken her life with him. There was not a chance that she would be retained on her job, and how could she ever get another one without a recommendation? And how could she get a recommendation, having been fired because of the father of a student?

So it was with Miss Haggard's help that Sadie secured a position as a governess. The new employer did not care why she was released from her last employment as they did not intend to give her a chance to stray from her duties. She was treated well by her employers, just as the expensive Queen Anne furniture in her room was treated well by the maid. She was given a lovely room, the daintiest of food, and a salary beyond her highest hopes.

If her mother had been joyful over Sadie's job at the school, she was even happier now. Her daughter had been successful beyond all hope and now lived in a mansion and had anything she wanted to eat.

But, like the Queen Anne furniture that was carefully oiled and treated gently, Sadie occupied a room in the mansion and cared for the three children, ages three, five, and seven.

It was her responsibility to see that they were clean, entertained, taught manners and school lessons, as required. She occupied a room near them, and if they were ill, she was the one to stay up with them.

If it had not been for her private library of books, she might have shriveled up and blown away as a husk, drained, from the emptiness of it all. It was while she was here that she had added five more books to her library.

It was also while living at the mansion that she passed her 24th birthday. It had been spent in the classroom and in the park with the children, and with a sigh she marked another year off the calendar, settling into her comfortable room with one of her beloved books.

It had been the next day that she had received the letter from her brother, William, who lived in Northbend, Illinois. She had hardly seen him since the day they were parted, fourteen years ago. He was now twenty-six, married to Bertha Mae, and was the father of two small children.

His wife, never a healthy girl, had grown into a delicate woman. The children, two lively boys named William, Jr. and Thomas, were more than she could handle, and she was now in a family way once again. The letter said that, though he knew she had the most perfect position, it had been their mother's suggestion that he offer her the job of… what? Well, he hardly knew what to call it, but he definitely needed some help at his house.

If she could find it in her heart to come, he would pay her as much as he could, and she would be a welcome member of the family. If she felt she couldn't do it, he would certainly understand. When she read the last word of the letter, she picked up her pen to answer it.

She stayed in the mansion for the three weeks it took to find a replacement and wept as she pulled herself away from the three distraught children, and watched as her books, carefully boxed, were loaded aboard the dray and taken to the train station.

Three days after that, she reached her brother's house, was installed in his best room, and treated as though she was a queen, and not like Queen Anne furniture.

At that moment, the parade of Sadie's thoughts was interrupted by a scratch and a growl at the window, and a jiggle of the bed as Tilda leaped to the windowsill. Shivering, she pulled herself from under the warm quilts and went to the window to attend to Leopold's demands.

A shadowy form clung to the outside sill of the window, and as Sadie raised the window slightly, the large tomcat and a gust of wind whirled into the room. The orange and yellow striped cat settled himself onto the cushioned chair, and the marmalade girls re-settled themselves on the bed, now purring with contentment. Everyone was at home and all was well.

Thoughts, however, continued to parade through Sadie's mind.

When she had moved to her brother's house, Willie was four and Tommy was two. Within a month of her arrival, baby girl Sarah joined the family, and Bertha Mae was confined to the bed for the next six weeks. Sadie found plenty to do.

Life was easy at William's house, and she was secure in the knowledge that her presence was essential to her family. All of the housework and most of the childcare settled onto her capable shoulders, and Willie was introduced to the world of ABC's and numbers. Years passed, and Tommy moved into his aunt's schoolroom. The boys applied themselves well, likely more than if they went to a regular school.

Then when little Sarah was eight and doing well, the boys, now ten and twelve, were apprenticed to a bookbinder publisher in Springfield where they studied in the mornings and spent the afternoons learning the trade of bookbinding.

The local school in the little town of Northbend became without a teacher, and Sadie took the position, again spending her time in the classroom. Sarah was taken along.

Sadie was then thirty-two. Her life in Northbend was a pleasant one, and her position gave her access to community activities, but her social life was just as precarious as it had been when she was younger. The community leaders and school board members wanted their teachers unmarried and above reproach in every way.

Sarah looked in the mirror as she prepared for her day in the classroom, and she saw the ivory skin, the sky-blue eyes and wavy chestnut hair. She had to admit that she was as attractive as most women her age, and more so than many. She could tell from the lingering looks of men of all ages that she was found acceptable… even desirable, but was off limits.

Another situation existed. At thirty-two, most men of the right age to be interested in her were already married, happily or otherwise, and if one became eligible, there were girls available who were six and eight years younger.

And she saw the first gray hair as it tendrilled its way through her chestnut waves. She paused a full five minutes as she studied the way the light from the window had shown on it.

Then she pulled the comb through her hair once more before she gathered the bulk of it into her hands to twist it into the fashionable figure eight. Skillful hands drew the hairpins from her mouth and secured the bun to her head.

The single silver hair was promptly forgotten.

She had been teaching at the school for two years when five-year-old Anita Welmon was enrolled. Anita's mother had died, and she lived with her grandparents while her father attended his job as packet boat pilot on the Mississippi. Anita was a darling child, and her eyes, the blue of a summer sky, never left her teacher except to study her letters and numbers.

She was among the first to scramble to the recitation bench, and her hand shot into the air before the entire question could be asked. She was such a pleasure to teach that Sadie struggled to avoid being partial to her.

She found herself being forced to explain to the child that, even though her hand was first to be raised, a teacher must be fair and call on the other children. Anita had smiled and told her teacher that was all right. She would just put up her hand anyway, so the teacher would know she knew the answer.

Little Anita adored her father and looked forward to the times he would be home. She confided with Sadie the importance of her father to the riverboat captain, a fact Sadie could well believe. She had explained that, without a pilot, how would the boat captain know where the channel was, so his boat would be safe.

It was common knowledge that the unpredictable waters of the Mississippi River were highly changeable. Even a passage that had been mapped just last week would undoubtedly be different today. Sand bars appeared in a matter of hours. Large tributaries created eddies and currents that could drag a boat against the rocky bank of the river or suck it into the deep mud of its bottom. Storms and cross currents scoured holes in the river bottom, and they threatened to pull an unsuspecting boat to a watery grave.

The settling of the western part of the country had created so much traffic on the river that packet boats seemed to blanket the surface of the water and every one of them required a pilot.

The occupation of pilot was a skilled one. It required years on the river to learn to read the water surface, the herringbone pattern of crossed waves, and the whirling eddies of a sink hole scoured away where none had been just hours before. The captain, crew, and passengers, not to mention the cargo of freight, owed their very existence to the skill of the pilot.

Archibald Welmon was such a pilot. He had been a river man before he had married Anita's mother, and when she no longer lived, he returned to the water, coming home when possible to spend time with his daughter.

When he was at home, he brought her to school and came for her after class to be able to spend the time with her, and it was then he met her teacher.

"Miss McClure, I'm Anita's father. I've heard a lot about you. According to my daughter, you are the one who sets the world to spinnin' each day, and my ma and pa are inclined to agree with her."

Sadie had looked at the leathered face of the seaman and into the sky blue eyes, so like his daughter's, and had instantly fallen in love. She felt that her whole life had moved forward toward this moment, and she now stood poised on the brink of happiness. Her career forgotten, she turned her attention to this man.

She was a free woman, and so was he, and if the community did not agree with her actions, let them do as they pleased.

Archibald then spent much more time in the little community of Northbend, and being from such a respectable family, he helped to set aside the criticism that would normally be aimed against Sadie. It wouldn't have mattered, though, as he quickly asked her to marry him.

Three

At the wedding, Anita, now a spindly legged seven year old, danced on her toes around her father and Sadie as they said their vows. Anita, who knew all the answers, was finally speechless with joy at having her beloved teacher as her mother.

Archibald Welmon moved his family to St. Louis, so he could spend more time with them, and Sadie and her stepdaughter shopped the stores of St. Louis, attended plays, and learned sewing and painting. Being a class of one suited Anita well, and she sailed through her studies much faster than she would have in a school setting.

Sadie adored the girl, and together they watched the boats on the river, waiting for their special seaman to come home.

It was as though her mind flowed through those four blissful years, and it was with these thoughts in mind that Sadie was able to relax and drift into sleep. The clock at her bedside had just registered one o'clock.

At three o'clock in the morning, one golden ear on Leopold's head swiveled to catch the sound of another tomcat within his hearing. The other ear turned toward the window… waiting… and the sound came again. With a growl and a fierce snarl, he leaped from the chair and sprang toward the window, catching his claws in the thread of the damask curtain panel. Dropping to the sill, he raked his claws across the glass, screechingly demanding exit.

Essie and Tilda added their voices, humping their backs and lashing their tails in their excitement.

Sadie pushed back the warm covers and walked across the icy floor to the window. When she had raised it a mere six inches, the tomcat had ducked low and slithered through it and was gone in a symphony of screeches and howls, answered by the intruder.

Justice was swift and painful amid snarls and yowls, and the other animal screamed once more and fled, but Leopold chose not to return to the warm chair. Positioning himself on the sill, he made a black silhouette against the moonlit yard. After a few excited circles on the bedcovers, the girls finally curled into a warm ball and went back to sleep.

Not so, their owner.

Sadie's mind picked up where it had stopped two hours before. She allowed her thoughts to sort through the four years at St. Louis, savoring this incident and that moment of her life as a normal woman.

She had felt she was now alive as she had never been alive, and Anita grew into an alert and capable eleven year old. Her twelfth birthday seemed a special one, and Sadie and the girl had made their plans.

They would shop for new clothes that would make them beautiful for the special man in their life. Then, when he stepped through the door, they would transform themselves into creatures that would be-dazzle him. They would dine at St. Louis' best restaurant and attend a new play. What could go wrong? Did they not have reservations, and tickets for the play?

But the hours passed and he did not come home. Then they heard the news. When the river was at its most crowded condition, a stern-wheeler attempting to pull ashore had caught an errant tide that had whirled it around into the river traffic. Its size had so unnerved an inexperienced captain of a string of barges that he had allowed the tail of the barge string to also whip into the traffic of the channel.

Two heavily loaded packet boats had been in position to dock, and they were crushed into the wharfs and into each other, loosing all the cargo and most of the crew of both boats. Both pilots were among the lost.

Knowing sleep was now impossible, Sadie opened her eyes to the dark room, focusing them onto the outline of the cat against the waning moon. Tears formed in her eyes, and then coursed down her cheeks as she remembered the funeral.

She and the girl had sought comfort in each other as the service progressed. Sadie had not insisted on any say in how it was conducted, nor did she demand her rights as a wife. She allowed his grieving parents to make the arrangements. What did it matter, after all?

Then the box was taken to the cemetery. She watched, with her arm around Anita, as the box was lowered. She swallowed hard at the lump in her throat that would not go down, as she felt her heart sinking with the pine box.

The girl clung to her and wept, and when they would have turned away to leave and comfort themselves as best they could, they were confronted by Anita's other grandparents, the parents of her deceased mother.

They would take the girl, now, if you please. She would be going home with them. Before Sadie's horrified eyes, they unwrapped the girl's arms from around her stepmother's waist and pulled her away, screaming.

They had papers, they said. Papers that entitled them to the girl. What could those papers say that allowed them to do such a thing? Well, the papers had said plenty. They had cast blame on both Sadie and Archibald for choosing to work on the river, thus depriving Anita of a stable home. The papers said they had foolishly spent their time in the stores and the theatre, failing to care for her properly, and they had even refused to put her in the school classroom, thus depriving her of the chance to get an education.

Lies.....all lies, yet they were believed by the judge. Anita was not a blood relative, and the old couple that had cared for her were the parents of the uncaring father who had left her an orphan. It was the decision of the wise judge that she would be better off with the wealthy parents of her mother.

It had taken most the savings left by Anita's father to fight for her in court, and in the end she had lost. And then, when the end was unchangeable, she had refused to allow herself to think of Anita. The memory was too painful. The possibility of changing the status of the girl was too remote, so it was best she walk away and deal with life as best she could. Certainly, Anita would be obliged to do the same.

She did walk away. She selected this piece and that piece from the furniture in the St. Louis apartment. She took only what she knew she would use. A bed and a chair, which were in her room at this moment. A desk made of curly maple, with a chest and a highboy to match. And, of course, the bookcase with two new additions. Her library now totaled 42 books.

She had been 43 years old when she moved back to her brother's house in Northbend. She was welcomed and put in her old room, but it was not the same.

Willie now lived in Springfield and worked for a bookbinder. Tommy had restlessly taken off to the west, stopping in a small Nebraska town. Sarah was sixteen was engaged to be married and would soon move to St. Louis.

Her brother's wife's health was no better, and she required careful nursing. Sadie picked up household duties, and was soon again employed as a schoolteacher. It passed the time, but Sadie vowed never again to allow herself to become attached to a student. A child that was not hers was a child who belonged to another, and nothing would ever change that fact.

Sadie's jobs had paid well, and her expenses were few, so her accumulated funds increased gradually but steadily. Her library was expanded by another five books, bringing the total to 47. She read the new ones, and she re-read the old ones, her mind reveling in the works of the writers from the old country whose works were so relevant, even today.

She moved into the world of books and found it satisfactory and certainly not as painful as the real world had been. The sameness of the content of the books comforted her in the evenings. Her library was a closet in which she could tuck herself away and close the door.

She saw her brother's wife's health failing, and it bore in on her mind, reminding her of her own loss, so she hid more completely into the world of her books.

She was forced out for a short time, however, when Bertha Mae's life became more than she could bear. The exhausted invalid finally shut her eyes on life and gave it up.

Sadie stood beside her brother and his children and watched the box being lowered into the grave. She wept with them because of their sorrow, and as quickly as permitted, she returned to her brother's house to live, again, between the covers of her books.

For several months they lived together in the house, William in his room and Sadie in her room, nodding to each other when their ways crossed. William woodenly attended his farm animals, and Sadie went to her classes. What else was there to do?

Years ago, William had offered his home to their mother, but she had declined. The mansion that had been such a part of her life had grown to be a part of her heart, and she stayed on, serving as she had always served, until there came the day that she did not get up from the bed. When breakfast did not appear as usual, the family found her there, and her breath had long since left her body.

William and Sadie buried their mother with a heavy heart. They had been years away from her, and as her box was lowered, the grief her children felt the strongest was for the losses of their own mates. The scab of healing was momentarily scratched aside by their mother's funeral, but the blood that was shed from the wound was not for her, but for their own losses.

They returned to William's house and moved in their own small orbits, disrupted only when Willie or Sarah returned home for a brief visit. Tommy had married in the Nebraska town where he had settled, and all they had of him was a distant memory and his letters.

He was doing fine but not happy with the variety of jobs he had tried. He wished he could find a way to get into the bookbinding that he had liked, but it took too much money. Maybe someday…?

Then, through a friend of the family, William had met a widow of considerable means, and he began an active courtship. She lived in Springfield, some miles away, but made regular trips out to his farm.

Four

Sadie had been forty-five when her brother married the widow and moved to her house in town. Before he moved away, he had gathered his sister and his two available children together in a generous act and had given the house to his sons. Sarah had been amply taken care of at the time of her marriage.

William had been firm and definite that his beloved sister came with the house, and she would be entitled to have a home there for the rest of her life. For the services she had performed for the family, himself, Bertha May, and Willie and Tommy, as well as her own mother, that seemed little enough to offer her.

Further, the farm animals would be sold, as she certainly had no need for them, and she, Sadie, could teach school if she pleased, or she could quit and live in the house.

It was then that Willie's dissatisfaction became known. Working for another had not given him the satisfaction he sought. Willie would move back home, and he would take care of his aunt Sadie. It was something he had always intended to do, and now was the time. He would be a farmer as his father had been.

It had seemed to be an answer. When he moved back, he brought his lovely bride, Lily, with him. Lily, the beautiful. Lily, the practical. Lily, the sensible. If anything or anyone could keep Willie on the right track, it would surely be Lily. Willie was 23 and Lily was 21 when they moved in to the house, and Sadie had been forty-seven.

The silver hairs in the chestnut waves of her hair had increased, creating a wavy band of snowy white across her brow and it extended into the twisted figure eight. She continued to teach school until Willie's daughter was born.

Sadie had looked at the squirming red bundle they had named Ruthie and felt the old familiar pull and its warning. This child, however, was blood kin, and there was no one who could ever take her away. Was there… ?

She gave her notice and walked away from the school. It held a lot of memories for her, but it was time to go. So she went.

A year and two months later, Frankie had been born.

A scratch at the window told her that Leopold had given up his vigil outside the glass pane and was ready to be let back into the warm room. As Sadie lifted the window a few inches to let him in, she heard the rooster crow.

Morning. Her eyes burned a bit from lack of sleep, but a dash of cold water would fix that. She had thought her way through the entire night, and her mind was no clearer than it had been when she first went to bed.

Willie was taking his family to the Oklahoma territory, and she was being put "somewhere" until it would be "convenient" to send for her.

Five

Sadie stirred cream into the oatmeal for Ruthie and Frankie and spread their breakfast biscuits with butter and red jelly.

"Aunt Sadie, do we got wind?"

"Wind? I think so… yes, the tree leaves are blowing."

"Oh, goodie! We can make kites!"

"Goodie, goodie! Kites!"

Kites? Oh, yes. She remembered. She had read to the children a story about kite flying and had tried to describe how they were made. Finally, she had promised that if the sun shone, and if there was a wind, she would help them make a kite. They would take the kite to the playground in the park, and she would show them how to fly it.

Well, that would take them into the fresh air, and she might find herself needing the fresh air to stay awake. She needed to stay awake because she still had thinking and planning to do. If she was to be left behind, plans needed to be made by her before they became made by another.

After breakfast, she spread the sheets of tissue paper on the table, stirred up the glue and pasted it to the thin wooden strips. From a catalog, she cut bright pictures to paste on the kite.

And a tail. A kite needed a tail to give it balance against the downward pull of the string. How much tail? She couldn't remember, so she gave it a long tail, and they would take along the scissors. If the kite had too much tail, she could simply snip off what was not needed.

Bundled against the wind, Sadie took the five-year-old girl and the four year-old boy to the picnic park they called the playground.

"Now, first you have to let me get the kite in the air, and then you can hold the string."

A lot of older children were already in the park, and their kites were larger and floated on the breeze, dipping and soaring, their colors vivid against the pale blue sky.

The small kite finally lifted, but the tail pulled it back down. Sadie snipped off a section, and it again went aloft. Ruthie demanded to hold the string, and the tiny craft nose-dived and crashed into the grass.

Frankie begged to hold the string, so Sadie pushed the damaged sticks back in place and managed to get it in the air again. Same result. By this time, the children became attracted to the other kites, preferring to run about and watch, rather than fly their own.

Sadie sat down on the ground and watched them run here and there, laughing and squealing as the kites were tossed about and sometimes pitched down to the ground, as theirs had been. It took skill to combat the playful wind.

Sadie studied the scene. A kite was an interesting thing. It floated on the air, dipping and diving as though it had a life of its own, and as though it could sail away, if it tried. Not so, however. It had a string tightly attached to it that would tether it to the ground.

The person who held onto the string directed the movement of the kite, even though it was high in the sky. Some strings were longer than others, but every kite was attached to a string, and every string extended all the way to the ground. It was necessary that the string be held, or the kite would blow away.

She continued to reason. The kite had no life of its own. It was flown and brought down at the whim of the person on the end of the string. Very much like a puppet in a marionette show, it enjoyed its temporary life as it rode on the wind, and then it was hauled down and taken away.

The flock of kites in the sky was large and colorful and seemed to be alive, until a flock of geese flew overhead.

Far above the kites, the geese flapped their strong wings, lifting themselves above the air for an instant. Then another beat of the wings and another lift for another instant. Every beat of their wings took them farther in the direction they wished to go, and kept them on top of the air.

The skein of geese formed a ragged "V" and, as she watched, the lead bird dropped back to rest his wings, and another took his place. Each bird kept his place, riding on the tiny wake of air made by the bird ahead of it. In this way, they eased the burden on each other. They shared equally the burden of staying aloft.

The lead bird, the one at the point of the "V," had no one ahead of it to create a wake, so it forged out in front, creating a wake with both wings. It was very tiring for the lead bird, but when it could fly the point of the "V" no longer, there was always another bird to take over.

What a wonderful thing to watch! Each bird taking its turn at the lead, secure in the knowledge it would be backed up by the flock.

The "V" moved on toward the north and was finally only a blurred dot, and then there was nothing at all but blue sky. They were gone and where would they light? Perhaps in the Oklahoma territory. Perhaps not. They could be headed for the wheat lands.

Now where had that thought come from? She had never in the past had an independent thought about the Oklahoma Territory. Why now? An omen, perhaps?

Ruthie and Frankie had become bored with the kites and were running around a circle with several other smaller children. Around and around, the circle of children ran until in dizziness, they fell into a laughing heap. That would get them dirty, all right! But what did it matter.

The kites still flew. They were bigger than the geese, but the geese were now far away while the kites were still tethered to the ground. Sadie sighed deeply. She was already weary of thinking, and she had just begun. Her thoughts whirled around each other, very much like the kites overhead. Or the dizzy children running in their circles until they dropped.

She had come to the realization that what she finally decided, actually, would depend on what others decided. This time it would depend on what Willie decided.

Looking back on her life, she strung together the many incidents in which she had reacted only after someone else had first acted. Her mother took her to Memphis as a child, but her friendship with Phillip, the son of the mansion, had forced her to leave. His parents had made the decision.

She had taught school, and a student's father had caused the trouble. She had been totally innocent, but there had been no recourse. The school board and the city demanded her removal.

She had taught the precious Anita, and the death of the child's father had changed her life. But when the blood-link to the child had been broken by death, she was not even permitted to keep the girl she loved as her own. The decision had been made by others and enforced by a rented judge.

She came back to her brother, and his remarriage had affected her status. He had tried to leave her unaffected, but it was impossible.

When Willie, her nephew, returned, it had set her life on another course. His children had then become her life because she knew they would never be taken away....yet.... What, her reason wanted to know, had she done wrong?

Then it was suddenly as clear to her as the crystal March air!

She was a kite! She was allowed to soar around in her world of books, and she was allowed her own thoughts, but when something important happened to her life, it was the decision of another that determined her fate.

Often, the decision was made with love, but it was a decision, nevertheless. Just as the kites were treated with love, yet they were a possession to be hauled in from their activity in the sky and taken away by the person who held onto the end of the string. The realization that she was a kite was an exhausting experience, and she sighed deeply.

She was tired of being a kite. She was fifty-five years old, and the silver band across her brow was joined by silver in other places, giving her chestnut hair the appearance of frosting, rather like the film of frozen mist on the early morning grass.

The color of her hair, however, did not bother Sadie. Being a kite on the end of a string...? Now that was another matter. It bothered her terribly. She longed to be a bird, taking her place in the "V," and when her turn came to lead, she would stir up the strength within her and plunge ahead.

The March sunshine had passed overhead, and it was time to get the children home for their naps. Just as she would have stood and gone to them, another skein of geese appeared in the north, flapping their way south. Sadie stood in rapt admiration and watched them until they were out of sight.

It was at the moment the last bird disappeared that the idea, fully fledged with feathers and rising aloft, settled into the agile mind under the frosted chestnut hair. Now, this moment, she would cease to be a kite and become a bird, and her first action as a bird would be to go to the Oklahoma territory.

She had never thought of the place except as an unsettled area of the west and a spot on the map of her geography textbook. But now, she would buy a book on the west, if she could find one, and she would get a map. She understood books, and if one was available she would get it.

She would not get it as a place in her closet where she could hide away, but it would be a key that would wind her up, like the Christmas toys sold to children. When she read the book, it would be as the fingers that wound the key that would finally move her into the place where she should have always been.

Others made the trip to the Territory, and so would she, and Willie and his family could do whatever they wanted to do. That decision created the need for another long sigh. She wrenched her eyes away from the laughing children, lest she be tempted to revert to being a kite. For once, she would make the decision for her own future, and she would see that it came to pass.

Taking the children by the hand, she returned them to their mother. In her room, she re-combed her hair and put on her most solid hat as protection against the March wind. She changed into her best walking shoes, and a more presentable coat.

She had a trip to make.

Sadie walked into the small town of Northbend, Illinois with a purpose. Lily watched from behind the window curtain as she left. It was not strange that Sadie would go for a walk, but it was very strange that she did not mention where she was going and offer to pick up some item on the way, if it was needed.

Lily nodded her head with tolerant approval. Certainly, Willie's aunt had a right to do what she wanted to do. It was just that it was unusual for her to do so without an explanation. Habits of a lifetime and that sort of thing. Also, instead of the dignified stroll, Sadie left with a very purposeful and brisk stride. Hat pulled down and feet planted firmly. Hmmmm.

The town of Northbend was two miles from the McClure farm, and Sadie had often walked that distance, but never in such good time. Her mind had fairly raced as her shoes had clipped off the distance, and she soon found herself entering the tiny town of one main street and two side streets.

It had a number of business establishments geared to the surrounding farm community. It had several very nice churches, various stores with general merchandise, and farm stores with feed grains and farm implements.

Sadie's first stop was the farm store. At the door, she adjusted her hat that had been loosened by the wind and stepped inside the door. The man behind the counter made no move toward her, waiting instead for the man who must certainly be accompanying her. Naturally, she would be riding with someone, very likely her nephew.

But the door closed, and there was no nephew. Sadie McClure advanced toward the man behind the counter.

"I need to buy some things," she said by way of getting his attention.

Old Charles Connelly, whose hair had the same approximate frosted trimming as Sadie's, smiled jovially and jokingly replied, "Well, I hope you brought'a bushel of money." It was one of his standard responses.

Sadie could parry words with the best of them and replied, "Well, however much I have, you'll not see any of it till I see the worth of your merchandise."

At this, the man sobered. "Well, what can I do for you?"

Her voice was firm with resolve, and she began, "I'm about to tell you. First off, you got a place where I can sit down and rest? I just walked two miles at a fast clip, and I got'a rest up and be ready to walk back."

She was duly furnished with a chair.

"Now, Charles, what I want first is someone who can keep a secret."

The old man's eyes twinkled. He now knew the direction the conversation should go. He had spent a lifetime studying people. "Buyin' a surprise for someone? What'd it be?"

"I didn't hear no promise out'a you." Sadie could feel her speech dropping from the schoolteacher correctness and lapsing into the local dialect.

Charles Connelly was no dummy, and he knew when the conversation was about to turn serious. "I promise. I'll be just like the priest down at the confessional, and what I hear from you won't never leave my head."

She nodded with approval. "All right. Now when I came in, I noticed you had wagons out there in your yard, but I didn't see one that I'd want'a buy. I want a very strong wagon. A very, very strong one. I want the best and strongest wagon you got available. If you ain't got it here, you can order it made or brought in, but I want'a see a picture of it to be sure it's what I want."

The old man leaned forward and cupped his fingers behind his right ear. "Did I hear right? You want'a buy a wagon?"

"You heard right." Sadie kept her voice taut and firm to retain his attention.

"You don't mean a buggy… or a surrey?"

"Now look, Charles, I may be gettin' old, but I can still tell the difference between a wagon and any other means of conveyance. If I had wanted a buggy or a surrey, I think I would have said that. Now we got past that, I'll repeat my question. You got access to a really good wagon?"

The shopkeeper reached for a catalog and thumbed through it, stopping at a well-worn page.

"This'n here. It'd be about the best there is made, and if they's a better'n I ain't privy to the information."

"How big is it?" She demanded, without looking at the page.

"Well, now if I was to order one of them, it could be eight feet long, or ten feet. Either way, it'd be four feet wide."

"It'd come with a cover?"

"Could be. Either that, or I'd be able to get you a cover. You thinkin'on a cover just over the top, like a surrey?"

Sadie shook her head. "Like I said, if I was wantin' a surrey, I'd'a ordered a surrey. I mean a cover that comes up over the sides and top, and closes in at the ends."

Old Charley Connelly sighed, long and loud. "Miss Sadie, if this here wagon is to be a surprise gift for your nephew, and if I was to know it, likely I'd be able to steer you toward the kind he'd likely get the most use of."

Sadie sat silent, looking at her hands primly folded in her lap. She was totally unaccustomed to conducting business with male adults. It was part of being a kite. As a teacher, you tell a child a fact, and he either believes it or doesn't believe it. Either way, he does not negotiate the answer. She must quickly learn to be firm or to negotiate.

"Charlie," she said, finally, "it's in my mind that you don't want to sell me the wagon I want. I'm disappointed, because I figured you could use the money, and it'd be a trial for me to go over to Springfield and deal with a stranger." She paused as she gathered her handbag into her lap and began to slip on her gloves. "But I can do it if I need to."

"Oh, no, no! Miss Sadie, you don't need to be gettin' huffy. I can get you the wagon and anything else you want. You'd be wantin' horses?"

Sadie nodded. "Very likely."

Charlie tilted his head and moved closer. "Miss Sadie, do you, for certain, know how to drive a team and wagon, like this one you like the looks of?"

Sadie removed her gloves and settled back. Charlie had zoomed in on a facet of the negotiation she had dreaded to face. "Now, Charlie, that was a sensible question. I've thought on it, and I have reasonable ability, and I consider that I have at least average good use of my hands. I can put butter on a biscuit, hairpins in my hair, and I can write with chalk on a blackboard plainly enough for children to read.

"In view of this, I think I might be able to learn to drive, though I am aware that driving a team of horses is possibly not as easy as it may seem to be. It's in my mind to hire someone to teach me the fine points of the art. I just thought I'd get the wagon first. Then I'd have something to learn on."

Charlie was now warming to the conversation. It had been a long time since he had been so interested in anything, and he leaned back in his squeaky swivel rocker. "Now I could be of help to you on that. Drivin' a team and wagon, it ain't so different from drivin' a buggy. That'd be the place to start. When you get ready to want lessons, you let me know."

"Thank you, kindly. Now, the wagon. You can order it and get it here, I understand. How long would it take?"

"A week. Maybe less. How soon you wantin' it to be ready?"

"By the first week in April. That gives me three weeks. Now, that driving lesson, that'd be tomorrow if you can work it out."

"Tomorrow it is. I can drive out your way and save you a walk in. Now, to get the wagon, my nephew's boy, he'd be the one to go in to Springfield to bring it out. And, if you was to take my advice, you'd let that young man pick out your hoof stock. He's a right sharp judge'a horseflesh. If it was to meet with your approval, he could get the animals and the trappin's and bring 'em all out together."

Sadie nodded. There was only one problem to that. "Where'd they be kept till I wanted 'em?"

"Why, he'd bring 'em on out to Willie's house."

Sadie shook her head. "No. I don't want them to be delivered till the first week in April. Like I said. Would your nephew have a place to keep 'em till then?"

"Don't see why not."

Sadie began to feel sorry for old Charlie. He was trying to be polite, but he was being fairly eaten up with curiosity. In spite of her best resolve, she weakened.

"Charlie, I see I ain't bein' quite fair to you. I'm expectin' help and leavin' you with half a story. I promise that tomorrow when you come to give me a drivin' lesson, I'll tell you everything, but that don't mean it ain't no secret."

Charlie nodded. "I'd purely like to hear the story, Miss Sadie."

That taken care of, Sadie continued, "Now this young man you referred to, and I'm thinkin' it'd be young Chad, is he handy with a hammer and nails?"

"Fair to middlin.' He can make most things a body'd need."

"Well, I need to talk with him. I'm needin' a cat cage."

Charlie forced himself to show no surprise. "I speck he'd be good at that. Quick as he knew what it was you wanted. Now when we're drivin', we'll have to go in some direction, so I'll just take you out to see him."

Sadie sighed with relief. Things were coming together, but it was still scary. This way of forging out ahead of the skein and creating a wake of her own was a lot different from floating on the wind while being safely tethered to the earth. It was really taking a lot of strength.

"Now, Charlie, it's time for me to go, and I'll expect you to have the total bill on what you'll need for the wagon and how much the team'd be, and bring it on out, tomorrow. Ten o'clock, that'd be good for you?"

"Ten o'clock it is."

So Sadie strode purposefully out of the farm store and walked across the street to the general store. There were clothes to be considered. Stout, comfortable shoes and heavy stockings. A heavy coat. Dresses? She had plenty of them, and all were totally suited to a schoolroom.

Surely, there was something more serviceable… stouter and more rugged, that would be better for the trip. She was sure to be at least a month out in the open weather, withstanding rain, maybe snow, certainly wind and surely a lot of blowing moisture. Perhaps gumboots and a slicker, such as men wear in rainy weather. And sleeping clothing. How many flannel nightgowns would keep her warm under the goosedown comforters? It would take some thought.

New thoughts poured into her head as though a great funnel emptied a new world down inside her. It made her slightly dizzy, and it could easily mount into a headache.

Horses. What kind of care did horses need? Her first thought was that surely Willie would know that, but she caught herself. This trip was being planned without Willie. It would be nice to have Willie along, but not because she needed him. That would mean more questions to ask of Charlie. Or the nephew's son.

She wandered through the store looking at items that had never attracted her before. Salves for weathered skin, iodine and other antiseptics, extra hairpins, a bonnet designed for warmth rather than an appropriate appearance. Plenty of handkerchiefs. A very large kettle or bucket to wash small items. Food…..water…. The funnel continued to empty into her head. It was very exciting!

Six

By the time Sadie reached the farm in Northbend, she could barely drag herself to her room and shut herself in, leaving the bewildered Lily staring at the panels of the closed door. What was going on with Sadie?

Lily poked up the fire in the cast iron cook stove and moved the teakettle to the hottest place. While the water heated, she spooned tea into two cups and waited. Was it right to intrude? She and Sadie had an excellent working relationship, and she certainly didn't want to risk destroying it.

However, if there was something wrong… if there was a problem… then likely Willie should know about it. He was highly partial to his aunt, and he'd want to help. If he could.

The teakettle whistled, and Lily determinedly picked it up and poured the simmering water into the cups. Why not? Since when was there a problem with two ladies having a cup of tea, together?

Lily's knuckles tap-tapped on Sadie's door.

Sadie, having flung herself across the bed, sat up and pushed her disheveled hair into place. "Come in."

Lily's smile preceded the teacups. "Was about to have me a cup and remembered you bein' out in this March wind. Likely you could use a cup, too."

Steam curled enticingly up from the cup, as Sadie reached for it. "Thank you kindly, Lily, my friend. You're a thoughtful young lady. I hope my nephew has an inkling of how fortunate he is to have you."

Sadie sat on her bed and sipped the tea, while Lily occupied the chair where Leopold had spent part of the night.

Lily attempted a conversation. "Went shoppin,' did you?"

Sadie shrugged. "More like just lookin' around. Didn't buy a thing. Mostly, I think I needed to walk off a bit'a energy."

Lily nodded. "Spring does that to me, too. Makes me feel like puttin' seeds in the ground."

Sadie perked up at the words. "Getting' ready to plant your flowers?"

Lily saw she had been caught. "Could be. Still decidin' on what to grow."

Sadie suggested. "Getting' time, and past time for some things to be in the ground."

Lily nodded and gazed thoughtfully out the window. It was time for a subject change. "Wind kickin' up pretty bad out there? Noticed it rosied up your cheeks."

"More like chapped my whole face, I'd say. Ain't there somethin' that men use when they milk and do chores to keep their hands from getting' too roughed up and bad?"

"You talkin' about udder crème? Likely your face ain't that bad, maybe face crème'd be all it'd take to ease you."

"No, what I want is that udder crème. Where does a body get it?"

"Willie'd have it out in the barn. He'll bring some in, if it's what you really want."

Sadie shook her head. "No. I don't want his. I just wondered where he bought it when he needed it."

"Connelly's farm store, I'd reckon. That's where he gets most stuff. We could ask 'im."

Sadie sipped the last of her tea and stood to return the cup, but Lily took it from her. "I'll put it up. I was just gonna start supper, anyway. You might want'a rest after that long walk."

Sadie did want to rest. What did Lily call that preparation? Udder crème? She'd need to ask Charlie if he had it. Likely it'd be best to start a list of the things she need to do… and buy.

After a sleepless night last night, Sadie was determined to get some rest. She bathed, dressed warmly in a flannel gown (again the thought, how many would one sleep in when spending the night in a wagon?) and snuggled between the warm blankets.

Weariness settled in and almost melted her new resolve. She couldn't possibly do what she had in mind. She really couldn't do it. She was too old, and her life had been too different (soft?), and it was too late to change. How had she let herself become so carried away?

But close on the heels of that thought came the next one. She was going to be sent to a place (home for old ladies?) where she would wait until someone who held the string of her life (be it ever so lovingly and kindly!) decided to move her to another place.

NO! She would not be a kite! No longer!

Yesterday, in the play park, she had decided she would no longer be a kite floating on the end of someone's string, but she would become a bird, flying with its own power. It was a lot harder to be a bird than a kite.

The sleeplessness remained, and the marmalade girls restlessly leaped from bed to chair, occasionally taking time to rub against Sadie's face or hands, their purr rumbling within their furry chests.

Thoughts began to twist themselves together. The cat cage. It would need to be at least two feet square... maybe two and a half, because Leopold would have to share it with them. Cat food? Whatever she ate, likely. When would there be time for them to hunt?

What else? The livestock was Willie's concern… except perhaps the baby goats. Sadie had taken care of them for the past three weeks, bottle feeding them and keeping them clean. Poor little things, they lost their mama the night they were born. A wolf had leaped over the fence into the confining pen. King, the golden collie, grabbed its neck and choked it, but not before the nanny had died.

Sadie had put a lot of time and care into those two little goats… It would be foolish to think of taking them with her. She had enough to think of, still…

Thoughts raced each other around and through her weary brain. Whatever craziness had made her think she could plan a trip of this immensity? Was she out of her mind? Probably!

And the furniture. Reason told her she could not take the bed, the rocker or the highboy in the wagon. Maybe the books. No, not the books because they might be damaged. Yes, she'd take the books. She'd be too lonely without them. But there would be other things to be concerned with, and there'd not be time for books. Which?

If she stored what she couldn't take, someone here would have to be responsible for them and be ready to ship them on when she called for them. Charlie? Could she ask that much of old Charlie? Likely, she'd have to. Birds had to use whatever help they could find.

And a guide. It had finally settled into her head that she would be forced to team up with someone going that way, or else she would have to hire a guide. A lone woman, and an old one, at that, could not cover two and a half states alone. And if she had a guide, (a man, of course) where would he sleep? Certainly not in the wagon with her. So many things to think of.

Finally, a scratch at the window told her Leopold wanted in. Maybe he'd go to sleep tonight and not keep the girls awake.

Blankets. Did she have enough to stay warm on the trip and after she got there?

Money. She had a very comfortable amount of money she had earned over the years, and she seldom thought about it. She always had money for what she needed and wanted, and it had not been a concern. She had even failed to ask Charlie the price range of the wagon and team she had demanded. That was certainly a thing to be considered.

The harder she tried to sleep, the more concerned she became over the money. Finally, she slipped out of bed and lit the lamp (what does one do for light in a wagon, at night? A lantern?) And she removed the socks from under her mattress. There were three of them that were packed full and another that had a fair number of coins.

She poured the coins out on her bed blanket and began to sort them, piling them in stacks of the same denomination. The stacks were arranged on the nightstand with the tiny, very handy drawers (could she take it?), and the stacks covered the top of the stand.

Counting the piles as she returned them to the socks, she reached $823.00 and some change. Writing down the amount, she poked the socks back under her mattress (where does one keep money in a wagon?) and crawled back between the warm blankets.

Thoughts again poured in. This was March. She told Charlie she'd be ready by the first of April. Two and a half weeks. It would be warmer then, (wouldn't it?) and would keep on being warmer as May approached. Also, Oklahoma was south of Illinois, so summer should get there sooner. Anyway, she'd cope with whatever came, now that she was a bird. That's what birds did.

As there seemed to be no backyard disputes for him to settle, Leopold lay curled up on the chair, and the girls settled onto the quilt beside Sadie. Finally, she, herself was able to sleep.

She had slept so lightly that she heard the preparatory flap of wings as the roosters wound up for their morning serenade. Pulling herself from the covers, she disturbed the girls and received a glare for her effort. The marmalade girls were jealous of their own comfort. How could they possibly make the trip? After staring meaningfully at her for a few seconds, they again curled their noses into their front paws and closed their eyes.

Sadie slipped quietly through the kitchen door. She had an appointment at ten o'clock, and she intended to be ready with her list of questions. With tea before her, a pencil in her hand, and a note pad handy, she began. She noted all the things she had thought of yesterday. How would she prepare food? Did Charlie have some kind of a stove…? Or something? How much grain did horses need? What if horses got sick?

Question after question filled the paper.

At nine thirty, Sadie was ready. Ruthie and Frankie eyed her carefully. When Aunt Sadie dressed up, it usually meant they were to be taken somewhere, but nothing was said. She didn't even seem to notice them.

Lily refrained from asking questions. If Sadie wanted her to know something, then she would tell her. She occupied herself with busy work, waiting and watching.

Then old Charlie Connelly pulled into the drive. Willie had not said Charlie was to bring something out today. Now why…?

Sadie picked up her handbag and gloves and the pad of paper. "It'd be for me," she announced to the walls. "I'll be gone for several hours, likely."

"For…you…?"

Sadie nodded. "Yeah, Charlie and I, we have some business to discuss, and it'll take a while. I'll be back 'afore night."

With that, Sadie closed the door behind her, and Lily watched through the window until Charlie's buggy was out of sight.

When he pulled onto the main road, he turned to her. "Well, Miss Sadie, do you want your lesson first, or do you want to tell me what's goin' on?"

"Seein' how you look, I'd better talk first, so's you'll be able to put your mind to the lesson." Whereupon, Sadie told Charlie what she intended to do.

She respectfully omitted the part about the kite and the bird, feeling that Charlie's practical mind would not be able to grasp the significance. What she actually said, in effect, was that if she was ever going to do something for herself, once in her life, and at age fifty-five, she needed to get at it.

"But Oklahoma territory? All that way? And you don't even know what's down there."

"Folks, I think."

"But, Oklahoma…?" He said is as though she had suggested a tour of the moon and stars. "After livin' in Illinois and bein' used to what you been used to? I'm hatin' to think on you bein' in a wagon for more'n a month, the lady like you are."

Sadie sighed, meaningfully. "Charlie, I just told you what I was going to do. I did not ask you to explain the wisdom of it. I did not ask your permission or even your advice. Now, on the other hand, suggestions as to how I could make this trip easier, those are something I'd appreciate. I'm ready for the lesson, now."

As Sadie had explained, she knew she was average and above on most things, and the art of commanding horses was not too difficult. Charlie did admonish her about her voice timber. "Ya got'a talk loud. They got'a know you're a'talkin' to them, and not to someone in the wagon, or to yourself. Then they got'a be tapped on the rump, now and agin. A tap just 'afore you yell, that'd be a help to get their attention. It's like you, bein' a schoolteacher, would say to a youngen, 'Make that first letter a capital so's the sentence'd know it was bein' started.' Now, are you ready to go see that boy'a my nephew's?"

Sadie allowed she was. "How old is Chad now, anyway?"

"Oh, he's no youngen. The years fly on by. He crossed over twenty-one last summer. Right good youngen, he is. Never brought his ma and pa a speck'a trouble. We got'a go on out here a ways, and we'll be there."

Chad was in the corral when they arrived. A frisky yearling was circling him, held by a lead rope, and an empty saddle rode lightly on the animal's back. Seeing his great uncle approach, he hooked the horse lead over a fence post and approached.

"What'cha doin' out here with Miss Sadie, Uncle Charlie? You stole her away, and thinkin'a holdin' 'er for ransom?" Chad had always had a sense of humor.

But Uncle Charlie was serious. "Settle down, youngen. We got business to talk on."

"Pa ain't here. He's gone into Spring…."

"Ain't your pa we want. It's you."

"Me? What'd I do?" His eyes widened into a 'little boy' stare of innocence.

"It's what you're a'gonna do. Help the lady down, and we'll sit on that bench over there. She's got a payin' proposition to make to you."

With Charlie and Miss Sadie seated on the bench, Chad squatted on his heels in front of them. "Let's hear it." Money was always appreciated.

Charlie began. "This here lady is wantin' herself a strong wagon, Conestoga type, ten foot long, and a pair'a animals fit to take it across two states worth'a travelin.' She wants it right away, so's she can see for sure that she's got it, but you're to keep it here till April. That 'bout cover it, Miss Sadie?"

Sadie nodded. She allowed he'd stated it right well.

Charlie continued. "Now, she knows the price on the wagon, and a fair guess on what she'll pay for the horses. What you'll be doin' is settin' a price on your services for goin' and getting' it, for keepin' it here, and for furnishin' the harnesses and the keep, for the animals. You can think on it, and let us know."

"Wait, Uncle Charlie. Let me get this right. Ma'am, Miss Sadie, you're wantin', for sure, a heavy Conestoga type…."

Before Sadie could answer, Charlie advised him, "Now, Chad, I done been through that with the lady. She's got reasons for what she wants. If you can't get it, we'll just find… someone…?"

"Wait! I can get it. It's just that such a fine lady like her, drivin' the animals that it'd take to pull that wagon…"

"Chad. I told you…."

"Sure you did."

Sadie watched the banter between the two men and decided on a way to settle it quickly. "Charlie, I'm gonna tell him what I'm gonna do. He'll just have to promise to keep a secret, the same as you."

"Secret? You getting' a surprise for Willie…?"

Charlie raised his voice to his nephew. "Hush, Chad. She's done been down that'a'way."

Sadie began again, and when she finished, she saw Chad's eyes sparkle like a newly opened diamond mine.

"The territory! All the way to the territory! I been wantin' to go there ever since I seen them circulars. You wouldn't want me to drive the team for you, would you, Miss Sadie? Now, I could…."

"Wait, Chad. You're walkin' on thin ice, there. Miss Sadie knows what she wants, and if she wants somethin' else, she'll tell us. Your job is to talk money to her."

"Sure thing, Uncle Charlie. Doin' fast figurin' I'd say a five-dollar bill'd cover my part'a getting that wagon and the horses. Leastways, no more'n that. When'd you want it done?"

"Soon, she says. Tomorrow or the next day, how'd that be, Miss Sadie?"

Sadie thought it would be all right. She was a trifle frightened at the speed with which things were working out. But she must remember, she was now a bird. They continued to fly in all weather, or they fell to the earth.

As they pulled onto the road again, Sadie remembered the many things she needed from the general store, and how she was not going to bother Willie with her errand. "Charlie, bein' that I'm payin' you for the day, I want you to swing round to the village and let me get a few things at the general store. That'll save me time later."

"Sure thing. You want'a drive?"

Sadie was just a little bit tired, and she wanted to say no, but she remembered the entire days of driving that were just ahead of her.

"I'll drive."

It was considerably after dinner when Charlie dropped her off at Willie's farmhouse. He jumped out of the buggy and gallantly offered her his hand to descend, and he waited while she trudged, wearily, to the house and closed the door behind her.

Willie, working on the wheels of his buggy, stood and watched as his aunt came to the house, and old Charlie Connelly drove away. A sly smile curved the corner of his mouth.

"Well, I'll be a hog-tied toad-frog. I never seen that one a'comin'!"

Lily slipped out the back door and joined Willie. "Did you see that! It could be you ain't a'gonna have to find a place for her to stay. Do you reckon he's… serious ?"

"Come a courtin'? Well, it's hard to figure… a crusty old bachelor like him, never been to the alter. 'Course, if anyone could get 'im there, it'd be Aunt Sadie. But, after all these years…" His voice trailed away in puzzlement.

Lily had her own input. "Could be she's tired'a livin' with our noisy youngens, beggin' 'er for this and that, taggin' along after her all the time. Couldn't fault 'er for that."

But Willie thought that didn't sound like Aunt Sadie. "I don't know. That don't make sense. She had time and patience when she took care of me and Tommy and Sarah. 'Course, she was younger, then…."

"Guess we'll sit back and see how it goes."

"Might as well. Likely wouldn't get no straight answer out'a either of 'em, anyway. We'll know what's goin' on when they want us to know."

Sadie lay across the bed for an hour, absorbing the activity of the day. She was now committed, and her heart pounded against her chest as though it was trying to get out.

Is this the way a bird felt when it looked down to the ground, or the ocean, and knew it had to keep flapping, no matter how tired it got? There had been a solid comfort to being a kite, but then, a kite never went anywhere.

A small smile twitched at the corner of her eyes as she drew up the picture of young Chad, wanting to drive her down to the territory. A sharp, strong young man like that… of course, the excitement of the territory would be to him as a magnet to a carpet tack, attracting it with a sudden force before the matter was thought through.

It was a nice, well-kept farm that Charlie's nephew had. Large barns and sheds. Say, she was going to have to find a place for her heavy furniture to be stored, and someone to ship it on to her when the time came. Why not Chad? He certainly seemed eager and business like, setting a good price the way he did without a lot of pencil figuring.

That would certainly be something to check on when she went out to look at her purchases. And her books? Well, some of them could be fitted in the wagon with her. She'd decide which ones.

The evening meal was eaten in silence, except for the chatter of the children. Willie and Lily must have enjoyed the day, because they seemed to be sharing a secret. That was good. Young people need all the good times they could manage.

Sadie washed the supper dishes and retired to her room. She needed to think on what would be packed and how it would fit in the wagon.

On a sheet of paper, she drew a wagon bed, to scale four by ten. There would be cooking equipment, bedding… Suddenly, she was so tired, she stretched across the bed and closed her weary eyes. The marmalade girls cuddled warmly against her arm, and she drifted off to sleep.

When the idea hit her in the head, she sat bolt upright and stared around in the dark room. Of course! What took her so long to realize it?

Striking a match, she lit the bedside lamp and stared down at the clothes she had worn all day. Here it was, midnight, and she was not even ready for bed, but it didn't matter. She had planning to do.

That nice young man, Chad, he could, indeed, go with her. If she could buy one wagon, she could also buy two, and do it for the price of storage and train freight, and help on both ends of the line.

For that price, she could hire him to make the trip with her. A good wagon like hers would find a market in Oklahoma territory, and the young man could ride one of the horses back. She could sell the other one, or… whatever!

There it was, laid out plainly before her. She could take everything she owned, and she would have a companion and help if she needed it, and it was obvious the young man wanted to go. All that diamond sparkle in his eyes was not for nothing.

Being a bird, and continuously keeping herself in flight was not easy, but there came a time, like right now, that she could drop back and ride the wake from another's wings to take a rest. It was obvious that young Chad was a bird by nature. A capable young man like he was? He would never have been a kite.

There was one small problem, but she had all the rest of the night to figure out how to get around it. Chad must be told to get two of everything. It would be two miles to get to Charlie's, and then the time to drive out there to Chad's, and by then the young man would likely be gone to Springfield. She'd just have to get there first.

There was no sleep for Sadie that night. As near as she could recall, it had been at least four miles, maybe more, to Chad's house, and it would take her two hours to get there. And she needed to be there very early.

At four o'clock, Sadie put the note on the table under the saltshaker, handed King a biscuit to quiet him, and slipped out the back door. It was a mild morning, so she wore only light wraps, and she headed out briskly toward young Chad Connelly's house.

It was almost seven when she walked up the front drive, and she was not a moment too soon. The young man was adjusting the saddle and preparing to leap aboard. He happened to look down the lane, and he saw Miss Sadie coming toward him.

Leaving the horse, he came running to meet her. "Miss Sadie, you all right? Whereat is…? You didn't come a'walkin'…? I hope…."

Sadie was indeed slightly breathless, but she hid it. "Settle down, young fellow. I'm fine. I just had to catch you 'afore you left."

"You changed your mind? 'Cause if you…"

"Hold it, Chad. I got more of a bargain to make. I heard you offer to drive me down to the territory, and I come to make a deal. If you got the time, I'll have you get me two wagons, 'stead'a one, and pay you to make the trip with me. How does that sound."

The young man's face broke into a grin. "Miss Sadie, you and me, we think alike, sometimes. I done decided I was goin' along, however it was that you was goin.' I spent the night thinkin' which horse I'd take, and how I'd ride along side'a you. I ain't never been nowhere in my life, and I didn't aim for that to continue no longer. Why, I ain't even been past St. Louie. I think we got us a deal."

"Good, and you'll need more money. I brought what I think'll be enough, so you just do the best you can, and bring the horses back to your place. Remember, it's still a secret."

Chad frowned and admitted, "I'll be havin' to tell my ma. 'Course, I'll just tell her about me, not about you. She's got a right to know about where I go."

Chad dropped his eyes toward Sadie's dusty shoes. "Miss Sadie, I got'a get you home. You come, and I'll hitch on the buggy. I still got a lot'a time. You could wait inside with ma, or… it'll only take a minute."

"I've got a minute, Chad. I'll come with you." What a thoughtful young man, thinking of her old feet.

Seven

Willie and his wife sat in the parlor long after the rest of the family had retired. It was a business meeting.

"What're we gonna say when folks come to look at the house?" Lily asked, sensibly. "She's gonna suspect somethin.'"

Willie nodded, his face twisted into a serious frown. "Gonna have to say somethin,' but I dread it. I took on this place, aimin' to stay here forever, but me and farmin,' we just didn't take to each other the way I thought we might."

"So you decided it don't matter what Tommy's town does. We're gonna go."

"Seems that'a'way. Pa said the place was ours, Tommy's and mine, and we want the money to get into the business Pa made us learn. Pa agrees there'd be a lot'a demand for books in the territory. Just think of the schools that'll need books!"

"Yeah, but that brings us back to Aunt Sadie."

Willie was thoughtful. "I know. And I wonder if there's somethin' to her a'seein' old Charles Connelly. If I thought there was, it'd be good to wait as long as we can, lettin' it take its course. I wouldn't want'a make no sudden move that'd mess up what she got started."

Lily added, "The strangest thing, though, was her a comin' in with young Chad, after leavin' us the note sayin' not to worry about her. If she had a thing goin' with old man Connelly, why'd she be out so early, bein' brought back by Chad?"

"Could be somethin' we'll never know, less'n we ask."

"Yeah, and we've tried not to be nosey. Shame she's not a mite younger, and she'd be able to make the trip with us." Lily was still hopeful.

"But she's not. It'd be too hard on her, bein' more'n a month on the road."

"You thought to talk to her about it? Givin' her a chance… maybe?"

"Didn't want'a do that. It'd make her think it was what we wanted, and she always tries to do what we want. I'd rather have the plans made. Pa, he's lookin' around for a place for her. Says maybe even she could stay with them for that long. We'd be sendin' for her, of course."

But Lily knew Sadie. "She'd not like that. Even if his wife was polite, she'd know she wasn't a welcome guest. I don't think you'd want'a do that to her."

"No, but we got less'n a month to go. She's gonna see us makin' plans. I need to get the money out'a this place so's to put in the order for the equipment. The Santa Fe Railroad can bring it right on down into the territory."

"But she'd got'a be told," Lily continued to insist.

"I know, but thinkin' of a way to do it makes my thought go round and round in my head like a dog chasin' 'is tail. He don't ever catch it, and all it gets 'im is tired. And that's what I am, tired. I goin' to bed."

In her room, Sadie took no notice of the light in the parlor. She had her own tail-chasing to do, with her own thoughts going in circles the way they were.

She made lists, tore them up and made new lists. Was there anything that she was forgetting, something that was small enough to get into the wagons? Now that she was taking her highboy, she could pack the drawers full. She could put it and the rocker in one wagon and the bed, desk and quilt chest in the other one, and there would be room for one person to sleep in each wagon.

Tucked in between her circling thoughts was a slightly nagging curiosity as to when Willie was going to start packing and when he was going to tell her where she was to stay until she was sent for.

She also wondered about Tommy's Nebraska town and would it actually make it down to the territory. It would make it a lot easier to have a place to go to. Being a bird was fine, but she couldn't very well camp alone in the trees.

Two days later, old Charlie Connelly came to the door and asked for her. He took her to Chad's house to look at her purchases and admitted he was not surprised at the way things went. Young Chad had been bursting at the seams to be out on his own and had carried the circular about the territory around with him for the last few weeks.

Chad stood back and beamed with pride as Sadie circled the huge, chunky wagons, bright in their newness, and the even more gigantic-hoofed monsters that would pull them. Would those beasts obey a little old leather rein?

Charlie also looked at the animals.

"Clydesdales?" he asked, doubtfully.

"No, but almost. They been bred up and come to more'n a quarter thoroughbred. Fellow said to me that a mix'd be better for what we wanted. A full blood, it's built more for heavy pullin' of a heavy load and not long time pullin' of a medium load."

"Sounds sensible."

After the third circle round the wagons, studying the animals as she went, Sadie nodded her approval. If anything could pull her heavy furniture, it would surely be these beasts.

"All right, Charlie, we got'a settle up. Take me back to your store and let me get some of that udder crème."

"Udder crème! You takin' cows, too?"

"No, but I'm takin 3 cats and 2 baby goats."

"For a fact, now! Well, climb on in."

It was an expensive day for Sadie. By the time the day was over, she had spent somewhat over $300.00. It was a scary thing, handing over the money, but what was it good for just laying around making a lump under the mattress?

If she needed money when she got to the territory, she'd just get a job. If she was looking for a job, there'd surely be schools in the territory and remaining unmarried could not present a problem. Not at her age!

"Now, Miss Sadie, I know that sounds like a lot'a money, but you're a'goin' first class, and I didn't even charge no commission. I was happy enough to get that youngen a place to go, with regular folks along, else he'd be headin' out to goodness only knows where."

"Well, you didn't need to do that, but it was good of you." She'd graciously take the gift he offered in friendship.

And then it was the last week in March. Sadie knew a letter had come from Tommy, but it would not tell them anything important, because the land run had not happened. It would not be held until the 22nd of April, three weeks away. She was well aware of her facts.

It was, however, time for Willie to tell his aunt that something was going to happen. Or, possibly, the other way around.

After the supper dishes had been washed and put away, Willie asked her to come into the parlor. Lily was bringing tea, and they both wore a serious look.

Sadie had given a lot of thought to this moment. She wickedly devised ways of telling Willie, and then discarded them. He was her own dear nephew, and she sincerely hoped the family would be traveling together.

In fact, she was sure it would happen that way. Even birds migrated in family groups, didn't they? Family groups, making it easier on all of them? Of course they did?

Sadie did, however, want to tell him her news first.

They sat down, and Willie began. "We been thinkin', Lily and me, that it was time…"

Sadie cut in, "And you'd be right. You got the right to know what's goin' on with me, you bein' the two people closest to me. I been thinkin' and come to a decision. Wanted to wait till it was goin' good, for sure, before I told it to you. Well, it's a sure thing, now."

Sadie paused to sip her tea, and Willie and his wife watched her, their faces wreathed in smiles. Sadie looked from one to the other and then down toward her lap. Their faces were as smug as a Cheshire cat that ate the canary.

"Did I do somethin' strange, like spillin' tea on my dress?"

"Oh, no, but we know about your surprise. Or we think we do."

"You do? Who told you, Charlie Connelly?"

"No, but we could tell, and I want you to know we're happy for you both."

"Both?"

"Yeah, you and Connelly…."

"You mean young Chad?"

"Young Chad? What's he got to do with…."

"Well, I don't know what you're talkin' about. My news concerns young Chad Connelly. Him and me, we been workin' it out together, havin' aims to go in the same direction."

Willie sought to be certain of the subject. "We talkin' about Charlie Connelly's nephew's kid?"

"One and the same."

There was a long pause as Willie and his wife searched for answers in each other's face. Lily was first to break away.

"Sadie, we're gonna shut up and listen, like you wanted us to. Seems we don't know a thing about what you're sayin,' and we're just confusin' you by tryin' to help you talk. Didn't ever see that you had a need for help on that."

Sadie resettled herself on the uncomfortable settee in the parlor. She had no idea what Lily meant, but obviously they didn't know what they thought they knew. She began again.

"It's like this. I been all my life livin' comfortably and doin' what a spinster schoolteacher does. Then I noticed I got to be fifty-five years old the same year the government opened up a place called the Unassigned Lands. It's located in the Oklahoma territory. I know you know about it, 'cause it was talked about in one of Tommy's letters.

"Well, when I decided for sure to go, I had old Charlie point me to the kind'a wagon I'd need, and in the course of doin' that, I found me a guide. He's a strong young man, and he had hankerin's to be goin' in the same direction."

Sadie looked back and forth between her silent relatives.

"Well, I ain't actually set the date, but I'll not be waitin' for word from Tommy about where he is. Chad and me, we'll be settin' out in two weeks, maybe three, if there's a reason to hold up that long. Then we'll be on our way. I want to say to you two that I've never been treated better in my whole life, and you both made me feel like you wanted me to live here with you. I'll miss you both, and I don't know how I'll get along without Ruthie and Frankie, but it's time for me to get on with what's left of my life."

She drained her tea and smiled at them both.

"I think I'll go get another cup of tea. That just hit the spot."

It was time to move out of the room for a moment and let them recover from their surprise. Besides that, she really did want another cup of tea. (Did herb tea plants grow in Oklahoma territory? Surely they did. She'd take some roots of her favorites, just to be sure.)

She added more peppermint leaves and poured the steaming water over them, stirring briskly. Then, when she would have turned to go back to the parlor, she hesitated, stepping, instead, into her own room. She had not said to them she would be back in the parlor, and she often spent her evenings in her room. This would be better. Goodness only knew, she had plenty to think about. Likely they did, too.

Sadie had been virtually certain her favorite nephew was about to force himself to say something to her that he didn't want to say, and she had saved him from that. So now there were no hurtful words between them. It was now time to stay away and let them absorb the shock of her own words. If she was wrong about what he wanted to say, well, there would be another evening… and another cup of tea.

Safely in her room, she busied herself with her lists. What would be packed where? And what item would be needed the most? And how much plunder would the boy be bringing? She should be sure she had enough bedding for him.

On paper, her packing schemes seemed workable. She had measured carefully, packed knowledgeably, putting items most used in the most convenient places. Maybe. The whole thing made her practically dizzy, the way her thoughts chased each other around in her brain.

The girls were puzzled. Lying side by side on the top of the highboy, they followed her every move with their topaz eyes, moving only the tips of their tails. Leopold was asleep in the chair.

At one point in his life, she had used a yellow cushion in the chair, but after almost sitting on him several times, she had changed to a black one. His orange, cream and yellow stripes stood out nicely against the black velvet cover.

Down the hall and in the parlor, the two puzzled people sat and waited. When Sadie did not come back, Lily made a trip to the kitchen and saw, indeed, Sadie had gone to her room. Refilling the teacups, she returned.

"She's in her room," Lily reported.

After a pause, Willie summed up his feelings. "Well, I'll be a hog-tied toad-frog. That sure puts a new light on everything. I'll need to check in on the wagons, and see what Charlie told her. If she really wants to go… well, there's nothing we can do to stop it. Maybe…"

"Willie?" Lily made her voice gently but firm. Men could be so pig-headed at times, especially with those they loved. They could also be blind.

"But I would…"

"Think about this. Did your aunt say she wanted you to check about the wagons? Seemed to me she was tellin' us she took care of it, and if we wanted to go with her, we'd better get a move on."

"Oh, I don't think she'd…"

"I think you'd better go slow. There wouldn't be no reason not to talk to old Charlie…she didn't seem to have no secret about it. It's just that I think she's made her plans. How soon can we be ready?"

"Well, I… Really, I was wantin' to hear from Tommy, first."

"To tell you what?"

"Well, I'd like to know about them town lots. It'd help me to plan. Aunt Sadie, she's…well, bein' fifty-five, I'd like to see her took care of. Where'll she go when she gets there?"

Lily nodded. She agreed with him, but she still had the feeling they were being passed over, somehow, and before they made plans to help Aunt Sadie, they should see if Aunt Sadie wanted help. It was a fair possibility that she, Lily, knew Aunt Sadie much better than Willie did, being in the house with her while he was outside with the farm and animals.

"Willie, let's think over what she said. She said she had checked on the wagons and she was going. She had a guide, and traveling help in the form of a strong young man. That'd be Chad. He must'a been in her class in the fifth and sixth grades, I think. That'd mean they know each other. She said she was goin' to the territory. Maybe that meant Guthrie, Edmond or Oklahoma Station. That'd mean a city. She has money. I got no idea how much, but she never spends any so she must still have it. Now, lookin' at what she said, do you see where we fit into her plans…? Anywhere?'

Willie stubbornly refused to give up his idea. "No, but she'd need to wait for us, and we'd be waitin' for Tommy's telegraph."

"That's not what she said. She said she was leavin' in two weeks, less'n there was a good reason to stay over one more week. That's three weeks. Here it is the 3rd of April, and the run is the 21st. That's three weeks, but I don't know if she'd think that was a good enough reason."

Willie sighed miserably and leaned his elbows onto his knees, resting his chin in his hand. His sun-bleached chestnut hair tumbled across his furrowed brow, and his blue-green eyes drooped. Aunt Sadie had certainly pitched him a curve. And he hadn't even had a chance to shoulder his bat.

Lily studied his expression. He needed relief, somehow. "Willie, I say agin, when can you be ready?"

Willie responded by sitting up and fixing his gaze on the northeast corner of the parlor. "Oh, I'd say not too long. Got the wagon and the buggy ready, the stock goes with the place, you're not wantin' to take any furniture… Could decide on two wagons, 'stead'a takin' the buggy."

"I'm not wantin' nothin' 'cept the stove. The other stuff ain't worth the trip."

"Yeah, that stove'll be a pill to move. Even took apart, the pieces take up a lot'a space. I reckon we can pack boxes around it."

Lily was as insistant as a fly on a honeybun. "So, when can you be ready?"

"I'd say, well, if there ain't no troubles I don't know about, maybe ten days. Or, more likely two weeks."

"Then the time works out perfect. She goes in two weeks. We go in two weeks, and chances are she'll let us ride along beside her wagon." Lily grinned at his dilemma. It all seemed simple to her.

"But then if we ain't heard from Tommy, there'll be no place to get the telegraph. If'n he ain't gonna be at the town, I'd want'a know where he'd be. We could spend the rest'a our lives lookin' for one another. Oklahoma territory's a big place."

"No problem. We'll be goin' through St Louis, and you'd want to stop and see your sister, anyway. By the time we left out'a there, it'd be the 23rd or 24th, and he could send his telegraph to her house. You could write and tell 'im."

Willie thought about it and nodded. "That could work. I'd been thinkin' that'll mean we spent a few days on the road, and there's likely a thing or two we'll need that we didn't know about. We can get it in St Louis. They have everything, there."

Lily helped him finalize his plans. "You got the business equipment ordered, and it'll go to Guthrie." It was a statement, not a question.

"But not till the first'a June. They promised."

"So when do we leave? I'll want'a have everything washed up clean to start. You got the rack made to hold the cookin' kettle?"

"Almost. I reckon you could count on ten days, and if there's a change at the last, you'll know it. You sure you don't want nothin' in the house?"

"Only the stove and our personal stuff."

Willie nodded agreeably. "Sure makes the move simpler. Just wanted to be sure. There'll be a way to get more plunder once we get there."

"I ain't worried about it."

Eight

The next evening, the 4th of April, 1889, the family again met in the parlor. Willie McClure was in possession of much better information than he had been on the previous evening.

Old Charlie Connelly had leaned back in his squeaky swivel rocker and grinned from ear to ear. "I'm a'guessin', since you know what you do, I'd not be tellin' a customer's business if I fill you in. Miss Sadie, she come in here for advice about the best wagon and the best animals for a long trek. She even shared with me where the trek'd be leadin' to.

"And that there Chad, he was havin' a itchy heel to be out'a here, and his ma worryin' herself sick. I said to myself, 'Charlie, you can take care'a two problems right there together. What trouble can Chad get into with Miss Sadie along, and what bad thing could happen to Miss Sadie that Chad couldn't make right? That boy's plum handy with most things that need fixin.'

"So I got 'em together, and she gave 'im the go ahead to get them wagons and bring 'em back to his place. She said he was bein' paid to help, so he could just start out by takin' care'a the horses tilst they was ready to leave."

"Did you say 'wagons?"

"If I didn't, I meant to. Said she had some heavy furniture to take, and them books she's always readin.' And there's the three cats and them two baby goats…"

"Goats! The cats, maybe, but why'd she want to take the goats?"

"Now, Willie, I didn't ask 'er. I'm only relatin' what went on twixt her and me. You want to know more, you ask her. Back to what I was sayin.' And then she let me show 'er the fine points'a handlin' a team. Wasn't too concerned about that, though, after I knew Chad was gonna be there. Ain't nothin' he can't drive, and if them horses ain't been broke in right, he'll fix that, too. His pa's sure gonna miss that boy."

"So, what else went on?"

"She bought a few things. One of them things to cook on, for folks on the road. The one to hold the pot, and the one to bake in. She got metal buckets, oilskin tarps, and a jar'a Udder Crème."

"Udder Crème! Is she takin' the cows, too?"

Charlie chuckled loudly. "That's what I thought, but we was both wrong. She wanted it for smoothin' skin in bad weather. Said she heard it was good for human skin, and likely she'd have need of it on her own hands 'afore she got there."

"Is that all?"

"All I can think of right now. So you're gonna make the big move! Can't say I'm surprised. I been readin' over them flyers, and I'll swear, if'n I was fifty years younger, I'd be thinkin' on goin', myself."

"Yeah, well, I'll tell you one thing. I'm gonna buy two of them big tents, the ones with the canvas floor. Supposin' she got sick or somethin,' and we had to stop, and there wasn't no place for her to be? That's one thing I'll do and she can't stop me."

So the family gathered in the parlor, and Sadie was once again on the very uncomfortable settee. It was a good job that it was being left with the house. It was only good to look at.

Bracing himself with a sip of tea, Willie began, "I reckon things are comin' together for you, getting' ready to leave?"

Sadie nodded. "Pretty much on schedule."

"Well, I want to say, I'd'a been glad to take care'a getting' you outfitted, but…."

"I know you would'a, Willie. The thing was, you and your pa have been takin' care of me most all my life. It was time I took care of myself. You got enough to do, takin' care'a your own family. Come time I need help, you'll be the first one to hear it. That Chad's a good boy, and we'll do fine. You'll be along so he doesn't have to be stuck with an old woman all the time. That'll be good."

"Now, this thing about the goats…."

"They're goin' with me, Willie. If it wasn't for me, they wouldn't be alive. At least at the start'a their lives. So they're goin' with me."

And what could Willie say to that?

Willie was still concerned. "Now, Chad, he's takin' care'a horse feed, axel grease for the wagons, keepin' the tarps fixed, and…?

"Chad and I, we've worked it out. It was somethin' I didn't want to put on you. I'm bettin' he hasn't changed from when he was in school, and he always got his lessons turned in complete and on time. He didn't always want to, but he did it. That tells me he'll do fine. Now, it'll be good to get to see Sarah, and Chad and me, we'll be movin' on out'a St Louis on the 24th if it's not rainin.' If it is, we'll be crossin' the Mississippi River by the 25th, rain or shine."

Willie nodded. That just about took care of it.

Sadie looked at the two people who were most important to her in the whole world, and her heart ached for what she had just done. Her Willie, her sweet, loving Willie, who was so quick to offer her his home for the rest of her life. He looked so confused. Puzzled, was more like it.

How could she tell him this had nothing to do with him? It was purely that she had become tired of being a kite. But she knew he wouldn't understand.

It should have happened years ago, but it hadn't. She decided it was time to take leave of the parlor and work with her lists, again.

Willie watched her leave the room, and he shook his head, sadly. "She didn't have to do what she did. I'd'a took care'a…."

"Maybe she did, Willie."

"Did what?"

"Maybe she did have to do what she did. She seems rather pleased with herself, I'd say. There's something to knowing what you want to do and doin' it the way you want. Seems easy to understand."

Nine

It was the afternoon of the 18th of April that Chad Connelly drove the first of Sadie's wagons to Willie's house. His paint filly, Rosy, followed along on a tether.

Leaving the first wagon, he rode Rosy back for the second one. Sadie circled the wagon twice, gazing at it from all angles attempting to calm her rolling insides. Did she really buy something this big and fearsome, and if so, did she actually buy two of them?

The horses looked down their long noses at her, snorting conversationally and slowly blinking their large brown eyes. What massive beasts!

Willie circled the team and wagon twice, wearing an expression of mild envy and outright admiration. What a team of horses! They couldn't possibly put enough weight on that ten-foot wagon to wear out these animals!

Sadie watched him. "What do you think of 'em, Willie?"

"You got yourself a real pullin pair! Good coats, slick and shiny. Always liked a big, dark horse, and this here's a pretty pair of 'em. White hoof fringes just set 'em off."

"Willie, I was thinkin'…. Lily wants that monster of a stove hauled west, and I'm thinkin' these fellows could carry part of it. What do you think?"

"Well, now that'd be a plan. You sure you'll be havin' room?"

"We can make room. That base, with the legs attached, it could set at the back with the goat crate on it. I measured, and it'll fit."

"Well, now if you don't mind…"

So the head and footboards of the bed were taken apart. Springs and mattress stood on edge. The matching bookcase (without the books) was pushed up against it. The boxed books made a bed when piled with the quilts. Nearby, in the front of the wagon, was the quilt chest and a small food box. That took care of the large items. The cat crate would ride on the quilt chest.

When the second wagon arrived, the highboy chest, its drawers packed full, went in first. The small dresser, night stand, a wooden box containing the decorative oil lamps created the bed, and the rocker was fitted upsidedown with the horses feed box tucked underneath between the rockers. Chad's small amount of belongings and other odds and ends were tucked around it.

Ruthie and Frankie climbed in and over everything, giving opinions and asking questions.

"You gonna sleep here tonight, Aunt Sadie?"

"I sure am. I don't have a bed inside."

"You gonna sleep outside, sure enough?

Willie intervened. "Ruthie, you go back inside the yard. I keep thinkin' you're gonna step in front'a those horses, and they'll not see you!"

Whereupon Ruthie ran to the front of the horses. "Are they blind, Papa? They got eyes and they're lookin' at me."

"RUTHIE! Get inside the yard."

"Papa, can I sleep with Aunt Sadie?"

"RUTHIE, GET INSIDE THE YARD THIS MINUTE! YOU'RE SCARIN' THE BE-JABBERS OUT'A ME!"

"Sure, Papa."

As she passed Sadie, the little girl whispered, "Can I sleep with you in your outside bed?"

Sadie whispered back, "Not tonight. You do what your papa says, and maybe you can sleep in my bed tomorrow night."

"Oh, goodie! Oh, goodie!"

By evening, the two Conestoga type wagons were loaded, and Sadie's room in the house was empty, all the way down to the dust bunnies in the corner. She could have taken her nightdress and robe into the house to change, but it was a matter of principle that she did not.

Drawing the end flaps together for modesty, she put on the heavy underclothes topped by the thick flannel gown. A modest robe lay nearby in case it was needed. Crawling across the bed of quilts, she stretched out and drew the quilts up over her shoulders. Not bad.

The girls, not yet in their crate, stood on the headboard of the bed and watched, lashing their tails with excitement and curiosity. Leopold was making his evening rounds. It was a concern to Sadie that he might not take well to the confinement of the crate, but that was tomorrow's problem.

As darkness fell, there was no sound from the other wagon. Chad was likely wore out from the all the driving, moving, and lifting. Then Sadie noticed the other sound. Tree frogs trilled, night birds called their mating songs and screeched their territorial warnings.

Something walked with soft steps around the wheels of the wagon. Probably the collie. Finally, with a soft thud, the first of the marmalade cats leaped down onto her bed, followed immediately by the other one. Twisting their bodies together, they purred themselves to sleep.

Then another sound. A tapping against the sideboard of the wagon. Sadie sat up and whispered, "Whose there?"

"Sadie? It's just Lily."

"Lily? Anything wrong?"

"Yeah, it's about Willie. I saw he wasn't gonna get to sleep till I came out here and saw if you were warm enough… and everything. He can be such a worry-wart, sometimes. I'm sorry to bother you, and you likely just gettin' to sleep."

"That's all right, Lily. Tell worry-wort Willie I'm fine. Though it is a nice feeling to know someone cares. I'm warm and comfortable. I'll be fine."

"I'll tell 'im. Good night, now."

Then it was quiet again. Until Leopold came. Growling harshly, he leaped here and there and finally left the wagon with a parting, throaty growl of disapproval.

Sadie readjusted the quilts, and shutting her eyes, promptly went to sleep. The next sound she heard was the flapping of the roosters' wings as they prepared to crow.

If the morning went as scheduled, Willie's plunder would be loaded by mid morning, and they would be off. But now it was time for breakfast. Sadie had decided today would be only oatmeal, and she dressed quickly.

Making a fire in the yard, she set her four-legged rack over it and hung the kettle on the little hook provided.

Now, if she heated the water for the tea at the same time as the water for the oatmeal, it would be quicker. There was surely a best way to do this efficiently.

She was joined by Chad and later by Ruthie. "You got a bowl I can eat out of, Aunt Sadie?"

"I sure have, darling."

With a few quick bites, Chad was finished with his oatmeal and was helping Willie load boxes. Lily held her cereal bowl and ate with one hand, directing the loading with her elbow.

Chad filled the water jugs, stamped out the fire, hitched the horses and waited for the signal. Sadie climbed aboard the buckboard seat, picking up the reins with trembling hands. Surely, she had completely gone out of her mind. These monsters would never obey her.

Charlie had told her to yell (loud!) when she spoke to the horses. Her mouth was dry and no sound came out. She wanted more than anything to run into the house to her room and bury herself under the cozy bedding on her bed, but she had neither bedding nor bed. Neither had she any room.

Ahead of her, Chad yelled to the team. "GIT UP, THERE! GIT ON OUT!" The black horses lifted their large solid feet and leaned into the traces. The wagon rolled out.

The two horses in front of her swiveled their ears and blew through their rubbery lips. They knew it was time.

"GIT UP, THERE! GIT ON OUT!" She tapped the leather reins lightly on their rounded rumps, and their feet magically lifted. They took steps. The wagon began to move into the road. She was on the way.

Tension twitched in her shoulders and up her neck. She realized she was sitting bolt upright on the seat, and she forced herself to relax. A little. The horses moved on, steadily and capably, and finally Sadie felt her breathing even out.

Behind her, she heard Lily's voice call out to her team. Willie brought up the rear, but she couldn't hear his voice for the jingle of harness loops, the crunch of gravel beneath the wheels, and the snorts of the animals.

The first quick stop was to leave King with the neighbors until the new owner of the house moved in. It was always good for a dog to go with a place. Pesky varmints needed to know that the boss was still around.

Now that she was moving, Sadie gave vent to the pang of loss. Leopold had decided not to come when she called. The girls sat comfortable inside the cage, watching her from between the wooden bars of it.

Well, she knew he would be fine. He was a big strong cat and would make his home with the new owners of the house.

By early afternoon they had reached Springfield. It had been decided that when prepared food was available, they would not take the time to cook, so a stop at a diner that provided sandwiches and hot coffee was next.

When they left the café, they saw sitting there, on the canvas cover of Chad's wagon, the cream and yellow cat, calmly straightening his whiskers.

"There's Leopold! I thought for sure he was left behind! Where was he all this time?"

"Why, Miss Sadie, he was ridin' with me. Last night he came in and crawled all over everything. Finally, he curled up on the bottom side'a that up-turned rocker. Right on the lid'a that feed box. That's where he stayed all night. I didn't know you wasn't knowin' where he was."

"Well, he always slept in that rocker. Guess it don't matter to him if it's rightsideup or upsidedown."

Sadie climbed wearily onto the buckboard seat and picked up the reins. Her shoulders and back hurt abominably, and her head ached from the tension of squinting at the road, the weather, the horses, and the two baby goats flouncing around in their pen.

The scenery moved past her with the speed of a sluggish snail, and she longed to be in a house with furniture and a comfortable routine. Whatever had gotten into her head to make her think of such a thing as an extended wagon trip? Willie had been right. Fifty-five was much too old to attempt what she was attempting, but it was too late to do anything about it now.

The realization of that fact flowed over her body, causing her to sag onto the buckboard seat like a candle in a summer-hot room.

But the horses plodded on and she stared ahead, tensing to keep her body straight against the wobble and jiggle of the wagon. Finally, the sun sank low in the sky, and Chad signaled for a stop. His signal was the question.

She waved back with the prearranged answer. Yes, stop as soon as you see a suitable place.

They made evening camp in a grove of trees that grew close to the road. The men took care of the animals, the children raced here and there, and Sadie and Lily undertook the preparation of supper.

"We got beans to heat up. Want'a try cornbread in the skillet oven?"

"Why not? I'm not sure how long it takes to get that little oven heated up. If you'd put the skillet down in the flame, that'd get it started quicker."

"What else do we eat? The fellow's, they're likely gonna be pretty hungry."

Canned peaches rounded out the meal, and anyone who was still hungry ate cornbread with molasses and butter. Frankie and Ruthie played tag and chase among the trees until it was too dark to see.

The lanterns were lit to make the camp cheery, but Sadie was not up to being cheered. She was totally and completely exhausted, and she crawled into her wagon and closed the end flaps. A few minutes later the girls poked their noses under the end flap, crawled in, and settled themselves onto the pieced quilt.

Sadie closed her eyes and tried not to feel her aching shoulders and arms. Outside the wagon, voices conversed, horses snorted as they continued to search the ground for new grass, and there was a faint sound of dishes and cookware being moved.

Sadie pushed it from her mind and sought to escape into sleep. Then a soft voice at the end flap called, "Sadie?"

"Yes, Lily?"

"I'm not wantin' to bother you, but Ruthie's runnin' me ragged, wantin' to come in there with you. She said you wanted her to sleep with you, but I knew she got it mixed up. She keeps on sayin' it, so I wanted to hear it from you so I can tell her. You ain't wantin' her in there, are you?"

At that moment, the last thing in the world Sadie wanted was a five-year-old in the bed with her.

"Sure. Let her come on. We'll see how she likes it."

"Well…" Lily replied, hesitantly. "I'll let her, but if she gets too much, you just make her come back…"

"She'll be fine."

The wagon jiggled lightly as the little girl was lifted over the buckboard. Crawling across the quilt, she lifted the edge of it and slid under. She still smelled of the soap from her bath, and the edges of her hair were slightly damp.

"Aunt Sadie, I didn't step on the kitties when I crawled across the bed."

"That's good. They'll appreciate that."

"What is 'appreciate'?"

"It means they'll be glad you didn't step on them."

"Oh. Kitty? Kitty? You kitties can come over here and sleep on my feet if you want to."

The girls did not move, but continued to clean their whiskers.

"My mama said for me to shut up, and not talk, and go to sleep."

"That's a good idea."

"Goodnight."

"Goodnight, honey."

The little girl turned to her side and within minutes her even breathing indicated she was asleep.

Sadie was not asleep. She thought through the day. Miles of sitting, holding the rein, watching the backsides of the horses. Today had been a short day. Tomorrow would be a lot longer. How in the world could she manage it? She must have been daft to even consider it.

It seemed she had hardly dropped off to sleep when nearby voices told her it was morning. It couldn't be morning.

Sadie moved to raise herself up on her elbow, and tons of rocks fell on her body. They crashed down on her arms, tearing the flesh from her bones, ripping it into bleeding ribbons. They cut into her neck with a force that seemed to sever her head from her shoulders.

Her lower back and legs were slashed with knives and pounded with sledge hammers. Surely, she was dying. Or worse.

She eased back onto the bed, and the pain lessened slightly. Very slightly! Of course. Why hadn't she known this would happen? She should have been exercising her muscles for the past month, getting ready for this! Her unaccustomed back screamed its protest with stinging bolts of fire extending from her neck down her arms and even into her fingers. Closing her fingers, she felt the cramp of the rein-holding muscles.

Surely she could not get up today, and possibly not tomorrow.

Beside her, the little girl stirred. Lily called softly at the end flap, "Ruthie? Slip out quietly, honey."

Ruthie sat up and crawled from the quilt, past the cats, and into her mother's arms. Sadie moved again, carefully, this time. Millions of nails punctured her with their points and remained stuck into her skin. She braced her hands against the bed and pushed herself to a sitting position, awaking a whole new set of protesting body parts. Drawing up her legs, she knelt on the bed and looked around.

She was four feet from the buckboard and after that, about three feet above the ground. Somehow, that distance must be covered. Clenching her teeth against the pain, she crawled forward to the buckboard seat and permitted herself a minute of rest.

Lifting her feet one at a time, she set them down in what was certainly a pail of fiery coals, and it shot its flames into her ankles and calves.

Positioning her feet over the sideboard, she rested them on the wagon tongue, summoning the courage to continue to move. Forcing her knife-slashed body forward, she stood on the ground and slipped her robe on over her flannel nightdress.

A fire had been built, and was crackling merrily. The morning air was filled with the smell of baking bread. A basket of eggs was setting on the ground beside Lily's kneeling body.

"Good morning! The oven makes good biscuits! I was just getting' ready to break the eggs in the skillet."

"Sounds good."

"You know, Sadie, I was so stiff and sore this morning, I couldn't hardly get out'a the bed. Who'd'a thought just sittin' on my backside, doin' nothin'd make me so sore! How're you doin'?"

"Not bad," Sadie lied. (A lie told in kindness was not really a lie. Was it?) "Morning stiffness'll work out in a few miles." Now, whatever made her say a thing like that?

She looked down at her robe, and realized it had been a mistake. It was time to get dressed, not lounge around in a dressing robe. Tottering through the fiery pain back into the wagon, she sat on the buckboard seat and put on her clothes, lacing her shoes snuggly and buttoning her dress with her aching, stick-like fingers. Lifting her feet over the endgate once more, she saw the goat pen was empty and the little goats were bouncing around on the green grass.

Bless you, Chad! How had he removed the little animals without disturbing her? Oh well…

"Breakfast's ready!" Lily ladled the fluffy yellow mound of eggs onto plates and set out the butter and jelly. Large, nicely browned biscuits were in the iron skillet. It was good to know the strange looking oven that had cost so much, actually worked so well.

Chad and Willie had fed the horses and the sound of their crunching and chewing was not unlike the sound of wheels on the gravel of the road. The road she would soon be traveling on… If she was still alive.

Willie looked toward her, concern showing in his eyes. "Sadie! You look bright and well after your first day! How'd you sleep?"

Sadie managed a smile. "Just fine. And you?"

"I did fine. I figured Ruthie'd keep you awake. Did the ridin' yesterday make you stiff and sore?"

"Oh, not so bad that I couldn't get up and at it again." She was amazed at the confident cheeriness of her own voice

"It sure looks like you're doin' good!"

Sadie smiled into her breakfast. If he only knew how her muscles were being shredded and sliced with a hundred knives. How her fingers rebelled at clutching the fork, and her elbow jerked away as she attempted to raise her arm. The pretense, however, must continue.

"Lily, you go ahead with what you got'a do after breakfast. I'll wash up these dishes and put up the stove."

"You sure? I can't see how you're not too stiff and sore to move! I sure am glad you ain't, 'cause I am!"

"I'm fine." A thought raced through her aching head. How many lies can I get away with before lightning strikes me?

Lily moved away from the camp. “Ruthie, you and Frankie come on back here and get cleaned up.”

The men left to hitch up the horses, and Sadie gathered the dishes and skillets to wash them. She gripped them with white-knuckled strength so the pain in her arms would not force her to drop them on the ground.

The tiny oven was not heavy… at least it hadn’t been heavy yesterday. When it had cooled she gripped the little side handles and lifted it. Flames of pain blazed up her arms and across her shoulders, but she held onto the stove until she could set in into Lily’s wagon.

Now her hair must be combed. Bravely, she reached into the little drawer and picked up the brush. Her arm, however, would not lift past her head. She leaned forward and stroked the front of her hair, tucking in the straying ends. Hiding the rest of her hair under her bonnet, she tied it securely under her chin and returned the brush to its drawer. Brushing her hair would have to wait until…? When... tomorrow? Perhaps longer…?

When it was time to get aboard and on the road, Ruthie climbed onto the wagon tongue and up over the endgate. Under her arm was a rag doll with a floppy neck, and in her hand was a color book with all the pictures colored. She seated herself beside Sadie and announced, “I’m ready.”

Within minutes, Lily appeared. “Now, Ruthie, honey, you got’a come with mama. Aunt Sadie don’t need you chatterin’ her ears off

Ruthie sat tight. “Aunt Sadie needs me to here.”

“Now, Ruthie, honey….”

It was time for Sadie to intervene. “Lily, she’s fine, unless you especially want her to ride with you.”

“Well, no, I don’t…” Lily paused a minute, shaking her head. “Sadie, I just don’t know what to think about you. I just can’t get over how you’re doin’ so good and lookin’ so rested. I had a time gettin’ to sleep, and I’m still sore as a boil. You sure it won’t be a bother to have Ruthie in here? ‘Course, we can start this way, and in a few miles…”

“Lily, she’ll be fine. She’s right. I need all the help I can get.”

And they were on the road. At Chad’s suggestion, the goats had been put on a tether behind his wagon.

He had said, “Them little fellers could use a mite’a exercise, and bein’ back where they are, you’ll see when they get to bein’ tired and yell at me to stop and get ’em aboard.”

Sadie was proud of Chad, and proud of herself for thinking of hiring someone like him. Willie had his own family and didn’t need to tend to her foolish notions of bringing two common goats on a trip of several hundred miles. This way, they were part of Chad’s job, so he took care of them.

The little girl beside her wrapped her doll carefully and put her on the floorboard so she wouldn’t be jiggled off the seat. The gravel rocks in the road were causing the wagons a lot of bumps and wobbles. Sadie’s inflamed muscles felt every one of them.

“Aunt Sadie?”

“What, dear?”

“Why do you got so many books?”

“Why? Well, the best answer would be that I like to read.”

“I can read.”

“You can?” Sadie answered, automatically. Then she realized what she had said. “No, Ruthie, darling. You can’t read yet. You remember stories about the pictures, but that isn’t quite the same as reading.”

“It isn’t?”

“No, sweetheart.” Now where in the world had Sadie been, that she let little Ruthie become five-years-old and not know what reading was? Why, when her father and Tommy were her age…? For shame!

“Aunt Sadie?”

“Yes?”

“When we stop, could we get one of your books so I could see how to read?”

“Ruthie, honey…” What could she say? What a time to realize the terrible omission she had made? She did not even have paper handy to print a word, even if the jiggle and jerk of the wagon would let her. “I’ll tell you what we’ll do, Ruthie. You know how cookies are made of raisins and nuts and other things? Well, words are made up of letters, and when we stop, I’ll find something to write the letters down for you.”

“Would this do?” Ruthie held up her favorite color book, with all the pictures colored.

"No, darling. We wouldn't want to mess up your book that you colored so prettily. We'll wait until we stop."

They rode along in silence. A flock of crows had been attracted by the activity of the four vehicles and flew back and forth across the road. Leopold sat on the top of the canopy of Chad's wagon and batted his yellow paw at the birds. Spitting in frustration, he clawed the air as they taunted him, squawking and cawing.

The little goats had quit frisking back and forth and had begun to walk sedately at the end of their tether. It would soon be time to call to Chad to stop and put them in their pen.

Where would she find paper? What she really needed was a slate and some chalk, but there was no place to get it until they reached St Louis.

Perhaps numbers should be first. There were fingers and toes to count, and she could deal with writing them down when she had the paper.

"Aunt Sadie?"

"Yes, dear?"

"Frankie gets to ride with papa."

"Yes, he does. He's a lucky boy, isn't he?"

Ruthie nodded. "It's fun to ride with Papa, isn't it?"

"I'm sure he thinks so. I think Papa would let you ride with him, too, if you asked him."

Ruthie shook her head, decisively.

"You don't think so?"

"No, and I won't ask him."

"Would you like me to ask him?"

Ruthie looked up, her blue eyes round with concern. "You mustn't ask him 'cause he might let me."

"But...."

"I wanted you to know it was fun to ride with Papa so when Frankie asks can he ride with you, you can say it ain't no fun."

"Are you tried of riding with me?"

"No. I'm tired of being with Frankie all the time. He likes to run and chase me, and sometimes he makes me fall down. I like for him to ride with Papa and have fun in another place and not where I am."

"Oh." Something new began to seep into Sadie's head. The little girl was tired of being treated as half of a pair. Strange, though.

She had never objected when Sadie had drawn them both into a game, or taken them both to the park. Well, now she knew.

"Will you?" the little girl asked, pleading with her eyes.

"Will I...?"

"Will you tell Frankie he's havin' more fun somewhere else?"

Hmmmm, this could take some thought. "Maybe he won't ask."

Ruthie sighed a long, meaningful sigh. "He will. He always does. He always wants what I got first."

"Perhaps you should tell your mama what you want." Sadie had always tried to stay far away from the children's relationship with their parents.

"Mama'll say I got'a be nice and play with him. She always does."

Inwardly, Sadie nodded to herself. Ruthie was right. Lily always encouraged them to play together, which was a good thing, but she had failed to notice, as had Sadie that Frankie was strong and strong willed, and the games always turned out to be Frankie's choice.

The little goats were stretching their necks, being practically pulled along by the rope tether. It was time.

'CHAD! I THINK IT'S TIME TO STOP!"

"Whoa, there! WHOA! WHOA!"

The wagon ahead of her pulled to the right of the road and halted. Her team did the same. By the time Lily' waagon reached them, the little goats were in their pen, and both front wagons were again rolling.

The miles crept by, and Ruthie nodded, her eyes half closed from boredom. Sadie would have suggest she lie down, except it was so close to time for the lunch stop, she would just get to sleep and have to be aroused.

Sadie straightened her back, painfully, and flexed her shoulders, sending fiery arrows in all directions. A stop would be greatly appreciated, and all she would have to do was say the word, and they would be stopped.

Never! She had made it this far without admitting her weariness. It was much too late to start now. She had done many things in her life that were hard.

Leaving her mother had been very hard, but it had been the right thing to do. Losing her husband had been hard, but she guessed it had just made her stronger. Losing the girl she considered her own left her with a broken heart and a resolve never to be that close to anyone… ever… again…!

Ruthie nodded her head, jerked upright and nodded again, her eyes tightly closed. Gently Sadie pulled the little girl's head into her lap. So what, if she had to be woke up in a half an hour?

They stopped by a clear running stream and refilled the water jugs before the animals were taken to drink. An inviting stand of willows were nearby to provide further relief.

Lily instructed Willie, "Would you hand down that kettle rack? I got'a heat water and make me a cup'a tea. That jigglin' wagon's 'bout got my insides shook loose. I got chamomile and rosemary. Sadie, which do you think'd be best for relaxin' sore muscles?"

Sadie sincerely wished she knew! "Maybe rosemary. It's got that strong flavor, and maybe we'll feel like it's helpin,' whether it is or not?"

"Rosemary, it is." She soon had the fire crackling hot under the hanging teakettle, and Sadie had split the leftover biscuits from breakfast and was warming the sliced ham by holding it in the flame on a toasting fork. The hot tea would certainly be welcome.

Ruthie sat silently on a rock, watching the proceedings. Frankie skipped noisily through the campsite, teasing the goats and the cats. He ran circles around the camp and bumped against Sadie, causing a slice of ham to fall in the ashes.

Sadie quickly retrieved the meat with the long fork.

"Aunt Sadie, I want'a ride in your wagon with you."

Sadie ignored the request. Glancing from the corner or her eye, she saw Ruthie was staring at her, meaningfully. The little girl had known it was coming. What could she say, now?

Lily was occupied at the wagon.

"Aunt Sadie, I want…."

"Well, Frankie, it's not much fun, riding with me."

"I don't care…."

Think fast! "I'll tell you what, Frankie. If you get to ride with me, then Ruthie gets to ride with your papa. She just told me how much fun it would be. She'll like that."

Sadie glanced quickly at the little girl, and her tiny chin quivered with disappointment. Sadie winked quickly and put her finger to her lips, conspiratorially. Ruthie sniffed and forced a smile.

Frankie looked from Sadie to his sister and back. "I'm hungry," he announced.

"It's about ready," his mother called. "Frankie, come here and carry the jelly over to Aunt Sadie. Be careful and don't drop it."

The teakettle's whistle announced its readiness, and a handful of tealeaves was dumped in, and then it was taken from the fire. It had become one of Lily's new rules of the road. No individual cups of tea. Tea was made in the kettle, and if anyone was not pleased with the choice of it, they could drink water, or whatever!

Ruthie left her rock and came to sit on the ground beside Sadie. Her eyes pled with Sadie to solve the crisis she saw looming ahead. Sadie gave her what she hoped was an encouraging look.

Frankie took his ham and biscuit sandwich and zoomed back and forth among the willow trees. Ruthie nibbled dejectedly at the edges of her food.

"Eat up, Ruthie." Lily encouraged. "It'll be a long time till we stop again."

"Mama, could I have tea?"

"Ruthie, honey, we don't have any milk to put in it. Maybe we can get some before tonight."

"I don't care. I want tea."

Lily poured a third of a cup of the steaming greenish brown liquid into a cup and handed it to her. "Careful, honey. It's hot."

Ruthie blew the steam away and noisily sipped the tea.

"Ruthie, don't forget your sandwich."

"I ain't hungry."

"But… well…?" So many new decisions.

Then they had all eaten. "Lily, I'll clear away the things. You rest a bit or straighten out your legs. Did the tea help?"

"Maybe. Thanks for…."

"Sure thing."

Lily walked away toward the stream of water, and Frankie, pretending to be a butterfly, flitted along ahead of her. The men were busy with the animals.

"Aunt Sadie?"

"What, darling?"

"How come you said I couldn't ride with you?"

Sadie left the suds bucket full of forks and cups. "Ruthie, honey, I didn't say that. But this is what I think. Frankie wants to ride with me because of you. If you are with your Papa, he'll be quick to get tired of me, and you can change back. Don't you think that might happen?"

Ruthie began to smile, creasing the dimples in her pink cheeks. The blue eyes twinkled with relief and anticipation.

Sadie watched, and breathed, Dear Lord, could you please let it happen that way?

Lily and her son walked a ways downstream and circled back. It was time to get on the road.

Frankie approached Sadie. "I don't wanna ride with you."

Sadie appeared to be puzzled. "You don't? Why not?"

"Cause it's more fun to ride with Papa."

Sadie nodded. "You're probably right. But if you do that, Ruthie will have to ride with me again."

Then Sadie decided to be brave and push her luck. "Do you think that's fair, for you to have all the fun?"

Whereupon Frankie tipped back his head and laughed uproariously. He grabbed a jelly biscuit and ran to the rear wagon. Sadie picked up Ruthie's uneaten lunch and watched as the little girl climbed up the wheel spokes and onto the buckboard. Thank you, Lord.

Hardly a mile down the road, the biscuit had been eaten and Ruthie was curled up contentedly in the bed of quilts, fast asleep. Sadie was alone with her thoughts.

Books for the children. Ruthie needed them now. Why…? Why hadn't she already gotten them? What in the world was she thinking?

The best would be the McGuffey series, strong on phonics and early word identification. St Louis was two days ahead, and that town had everything. She could even remember the names of the stores where the books would be carried. And numbers? Perhaps she should look around for what she would need for the next few years. Who could know what they would run into in the territory?

On to pleasanter things. It would be so good to see Sarah again. What had it been? Two years? …Three?

…Several years, anyway. And her baby girl… hardly a month old.

Then, after that, she could look forward to seeing Tommy again. It had been over six years since she had seen him. He now had a wife and a little boy. How old was he? About two… maybe? Time was flying past her like a blue-norther Illinois storm, one with a solid wall of snowflakes blowing parallel to the ground.

Here she was, fifty-five. Up until her marriage, time had simply dragged past her on leaden feet. Then there were the glorious years with the girl and her father, all taken away in a few minutes time. After that, one day melted into the next with no thought on her part.

Looking back, they seemed to be like the pattern on a pieced quilt, one block following the other with continuous monotony. There were different colors and designs, but they all fit together, somehow.

Her days in the classroom held no more challenge. Her days with Willie and Lily lay in a sweetly comfortable pattern… and still no challenge. More like a twig or a leaf floating down stream with the scenery passing beside them.

Fifty-five. That was a lot of years spent being a kite. A lot of years of being taken out and allowed to soar on the wind, briefly, but only on the whim of another.

She shifted her position on the buckboard and moved to the other end. That would bring another set of muscles into action. Her shoulders ached dully, and she pulled her bonnet forward to shield her eyes from the afternoon sun.

Looking from side to side, she saw the expanses of Illinois farmland, and its houses and barns dotted here and there. Then there would be a church and a school with a number of houses clustered nearby. A small town.

The wagon moved along, juggling her painful muscles, and Sadie smiled a wide smile. Pain! Perhaps she could think of it as a thing to be relished! The only pain she had suffered up to a month ago had been the pain of a broken spirit. The pain caused by another and not within her own power to heal.

But this pain! Now this pain was of her own making! It would have been an easy thing to ride the train to the new land, and no one would have thought she should have done otherwise. It was her own choice to sit on this impossible bench with the sun in her face and fiery pains darting about inside her.

Now a kite, for instance… it would never feel pain. It was tossed about on the wind, and sometimes it was dashed to the ground where it might lay torn and broken. (She certainly knew what that was like!) It had not caused its own damage, nor could it repair it. Fifty-five years was a long time to be a kite. Much too long.

On the other hand, a bird most definitely felt pain, weariness, and hunger. It, also, might be dashed to the ground by wind, storms, or another bird, but it could often rise again. On sore and painful wings, it could flap its way back into the sky.

Carefully extending one leg out before her, then the other leg, she savored the pain it caused, as a reminder that she was no longer within the control of another. She had a mental skill that would allow her to live well and stay in control. She could not imagine what would be waiting at the territory, but she was not afraid.

Small threads of excitement traveled down her arms and into her fingers. Perhaps her life would be with Willie and Tommy, and that would be good. However, if not… it would be somewhere else, and that would also be good.

The sun lowered and finally hit her full in the face. It was time to wake Ruthie, so she would be able to sleep tonight.

"Ruthie? Wake up! RUTHIE, HONEY?"

Ten

The smoke of the St Louis industry was visible when they made camp two nights later. The air held the dampness of the river valley, the dampness of familiarity of her life with her other family.

Look past it, Sadie, she chided herself, sternly. Put it far from your mind. This is no time to be nostalgic. Look ahead. So she looked ahead, noting the many and vast changes that had been made to the city she had known so well. And then they pulled the wagons into the yard of the house where her only niece lived. Sarah, sweet Sarah. Such a darling baby and such pleasure she had brought Sadie. Those were the things to think on.

Sarah was jubilant. Her beautiful face was wet with tears as she hugged everyone, even the very surprised Chad. Her words tumbled from her mouth like the sound of a mountain waterfall. Happy, excited and free. Sadie found herself being happy for her beloved niece.

"Oh, hurry and come in. I've been waiting and waiting. I have so much to say, and you must see my baby. She's beautiful."

And she was. Her newborn redness had changed to ivory and rose petals, and she looked just as Sarah had at that age. Sadie looked at the baby and a startling realization shook her. What was the baby's name?

Had they told her, and had she forgotten? Was her memory that bad? Why hadn't she asked? Sarah's baby had been referred to simply as Sarah's baby. Why had that been? Usually the name is the first and most important fact to be known

Sadie held the little girl and smelled the warm sweetness of her. "She's too small for a whole name. What do you call her?"

A silence fell thickly into the room, and all eyes turned toward her.

"Did I say something stupid? Or thoughtless?"

Sarah shook her head. "I'm so sorry, Aunt Sadie. I didn't want to hurt you for nothin'. It was just that I…Well, I knew how you felt about her and…."

"What is it? Tell me," she demanded. Was there a problem with the baby? Was she not well? She certainly appeared to be the very picture of health.

"It was just… well, I loved her, too, you know, and I thought it was a beautiful name."

"What? Tell me what!" Fear for her grandniece clutched as her chest.

"My baby's name is Anita. I just wanted…." and Sarah was at loss for words. Sarah's beautiful head hung with sadness.

Sadie felt her throat tighten and her chin tremble at the sound of the name of her stepdaughter. In spite of great effort, her eyes filled with moisture. "Sarah, you have made me very happy."

Sarah's chest heaved with relief. "I did?"

"You gave this beautiful baby a suitably beautiful name, and you cared so greatly about my feelings. That is more than I would have had the right to expect."

"You don't…?"

"Care? I think it's a wonderful name for a wonderful baby. But more than that, you are a most wonderful niece." She held her arms open, and Sarah walked into them.

"I just didn't want you to be hurt at the remembrance of her," she whispered into Sadie's shoulder. "…but I liked hearing about her, and I liked the name and…" Sarah repeated, helplessly.

Sadie's arm wrapped around the shoulder of her only niece. "Shhhhh! It's all right, darling."

St. Louis was a wonderful place. Anything a person could dream of could be found in St. Louis. Sadie visited the bookstores and picked up a set of McGuffey textbooks, from primer to grade six, also the eclectic speller, and the several books of numbers. Might as well be prepared.

While she was there, she looked at the classics and at some of the newer titles, ultimately adding six new books to her collection. Was it possible to read while driving a team? Why not? Where could the horses go except right along behind Chad's wagon?

They had hardly arrived at Sarah's house when the telegraph came from Tommy.

"SUCCESS stop TOWN NAME PROSPER stop FOURTEEN MILES SOUTHEAST OF GUTHRIE stop BRING EVERYTHING stop WE LEAVE HERE 3 MAY stop"

Willie was jubilant. "Whoopee! He got the building lots! Fourteen miles from the city! Perfect!"

"What does 'bring everything' mean?"

"I don't know."

"We got'a wire 'im back."

"HAPPY ABOUT GOOD NEWS stop EXPLAIN BRING EVERYTHING stop"

It was later that that day that the second telegraph came.

"BRING EVERYTHING YOU NEED stop GUTHRIE SHORT OF EVERYTHING EXCEPT MONEY stop COOKED BEANS A NICKEL A CUP stop"

"Beans a nickel a cup? Why'd we be buyin' beans? What does that mean?"

"Well, he says Guthrie's short of everything, and that could mean there isn't anything to buy, yet. Even food. Town ain't even a week old, yet, but folks still got'a eat."

"So we take everything we're likely to need right away. Figured to do that anyway. Don't reckon we'll be buyin' any beans in Guthrie."

"Could be that we'll have to give better attention to last minute shoppin'. There's a town on the border called Arkansas City. Likely that'd be a good stocking-up place."

Despite protests, Chad moved out of Sarah's house to stay in the livery stable with the animals and the wagons. The family needed their time together, and he needed to be where he could see to the welfare of Miss Sadie's four horses and two goats, as well as Rosy, his own paint filly. He could watch out for Willie's hoof stock while he was there. Making sure they were fed properly, and such.

The 22nd and 23rd went by quickly with so much to see and so many things to be said, and then the storm came in. Late in the day on the 23rd, the wind arose, whipping the dark clouds into a pile of black and bending the small trees before it.

In the night the rain began to come down. Huge drops pounded on roofs and on umbrellas and, as the next day progressed, the wet wind blew even harder. Thick moisture seemed to seep through the very walls and through clothing. Skin became clammy and sticky. Well, so much for the wonderful memories of the perfection of St Louis! A storm blowing off the mighty river was a thing of misery.

The evening of the 24th was chilly with remnants of showers skirting across the river, ripped into ribbons before the last puffs of wind. Sadie stood before the window watching the rivulets stream down the panes.

Her own words printed themselves on her mind. "I leave the 25th, rain or shine." Why didn't she have the good sense to keep her mouth shut?

Willie watched her, concern in his eyes. It would be stupid to start out in the rain with small children when a dry house was available. Of course, weather was fickle, and who knew what tomorrow would be?

But when the day dawned, it was drizzly and cloudy. Chad showed up for orders and reported that the west looked clear. Could be, by the time they got loaded up…?

Sarah quickly fried two chickens to go with the potato salad she had made for their lunch. The leftover slices from yesterday's baked ham were wrapped in waxed paper and tucked into the basket. Sadie and the children had made cookies to pass away the rainy indoor day, and the cookies were packed in a cracker tin to keep them crisp.

Preparations continued to be made. Chad went back to the livery and brought back one wagon to take the family back to the other wagons. The mist had stopped, and the day was brighter. By the time they crossed the Mississippi on the stern-wheeler ferryboat, a ray of sunshine stabbed through the last of the black clouds.

As Sadie rode through the streets of St Louis for, perhaps, the last time in her life, she refused to allow her mind to think back. It was only a town, and she was going forward. Birds did not moon about the nice forests they had remembered or the good feeding grounds. They looked ahead.

The pull she had felt since she left Northbend was now focused. She had a destination name, "Prosper," and it beckoned her forward. Like a bird, feeling the pull of the migration instinct, so the unknown town in the Oklahoma Territory pulled her onward.

Tommy and his town would not be leaving for another nine days, but he did not have to cross the rugged width of Missouri. It would take them a long time to cross the state of Missouri and a good part of Kansas going the route they planned. No effort had been made to meet the wagon train, and it was best that way.

How hard could it be to find a town once they got there?

Tommy McClure, age twenty-four, had paid the fifty dollars for two five-acre building lots in the new town of Prosper, Oklahoma Territory, and had wired his brother in Illinois.

Nancy McClure, Tommy's wife, raked her thoughts through her brain, trying to uncover the answer as to what should be packed. How could she put her life into two little wagons?

Clothes, of course, then what…? Tommy said he didn't have to take anything, because the book binding equipment, whatever that was, would be shipped on the Santa Fe Railroad, and after he put the little garden plow into the wagon, the rest of the space was for her and little Thomas Joseph, age two. Little Thomas' name had quickly melted into Teejay.

Toys? Teejay didn't have all that many, the money shortage being what it was. Tommy was a wonderful man, but nothing had come easy to him. Farming, repairs on the house, raising animals… he'd tried them all. Her father had said to her, what did she expect, marrying a fly-by-night on his way to the gold fields in California? He'd only stopped over in Providence Falls to escape the worst of a winter storm.

If she, Nancy Littletree, hadn't been in Hewett's store that day when he came in to get warm and to ask was there a boarding house or a place to stay for a week or so, she'd have missed him completely and would not at this moment be trying to pare her belongings down to fit into two wagons.

Her aunt had given her a large trunk that she said would make a good bed for Teejay on the trip and for a while after that. That was good…

Her wedding-present dishes, those she had been afraid to use lest they break, she would leave with her aunt to be shipped later. Ditto with all the embroidered scarves and ruffled lace curtains.

Excitement sent a shiver of thrill bumps up her arms and onto her neck. It was a little scary, but terribly exciting. There was Tommy's brother, Willie, who had two children, and it seemed an older aunt was coming with them. She would have a sister-in-law named Lily. It was so doubly exciting!

Two wagons. That is what she would call home for a while. For one month, at least, and maybe two. So she'd take the iron bedstead, the mattresses and quilts. A tall highboy chest of drawers, lamps (remember to pour out the oil and clean them up), and the small iron parlor stove.

She had a little three-legged stand that held a soup kettle, or it could hold a skillet on its little swinging platform. All she'd have to do was build a fire under it. She would cook on it until… when? She had been told that the building to house the machinery would be first, and living quarter would come later. It had made sense, the way Tommy had explained it. Having money coming in would, of course, have priority over their comfort in living.

Working with his brother on something they had studied in school (how does one study how to make a book?), surely it would be something Tommy liked and would do well at.

Making books. Interesting thought. Printing words on paper and binding the stiff backs onto the books. It all sounded very important.

Two wagons, and they were leaving in a week. She'd better get on with it and decide. Enough of this wondering about the future, she was now a part of it!

Outside the houses, Tommy restlessly moved about, unable to settle on anything, and trying to remember all he had studied about book-binding. He could hardly wait to finally see the equipment. He had not actually worked at it, as he had left soon after he had completed his apprentiship. But Willie had. He had worked for a while, but not as his own boss, and that was what he wanted. Willie would remember the things they had learned.

Willie had ordered everything they could afford. He said he had ordered printing equipment for brochures, thinking there would be print orders for new business establishments, auctions, price lists, and such.

Tommy was good at brochure printing, at least he had been a few years ago. That was one thing he could do.

He tried to stay out of the house. Nancy was walking in circles, trying to make up her mind, and it was best he stay away. Eventually, she would decide, and it would happen all in a minute. Then he would need to be there to get everything in the wagons.

All he would need to do then would be to take orders. Nancy was much better than he at something like packing. At a lot of other things, too.

Now, those brochures, for instance. If he could make up a packet of samples showing what they could do, he could go into Guthrie, or maybe even down to Oklahoma Station, and he would pick up a lot of orders. New businesses would have all kinds of things they needed to say on colorful handout sheets.

Feeling light hunger pangs, he picked up Teejay who was playing in the dirt at his feet and headed for the pump. Nancy appreciated cleanliness, and it was no trouble to swab down the boy. It was time for his nap, anyway.

Entering the kitchen, he saw Nancy still circling the rooms. He was not concerned, because when she made up her mind, things would start to happen. Suddenly. And she was never late.

When he stepped through the door, she pointed, wordlessly, toward the table.Thick-sliced, fresh-baked bread lay beside a slab of roast beef. A crock of butter, a jar of jelly, and a knife completed what was going to be lunch. It seemed to be a 'do it yourself' day, and Tommy liked that.

Slathering the bread thickly with butter, he carved succulent slices from the roast. Would there be food like this on the trip? Likely not. However, Nancy had often surprised him.

"How are things?"

"Still figurin'."

"That's good." He handed Teejay a bread and jelly sandwich for one hand and a small chunk of the meat for the other.

Nancy knelt to the kitchen floor and began to set pans and kettles out of the cupboard. Then sitting down on the floor, cross-legged as a tailor, she contemplated the mess. Separating out two skillets and two pans, she announced.

"I'm ready for a barrel. Just put it on the porch."

Teejay's head drooped sideways and he dropped the bread and jelly on the floor. Tommy picked up his son. "I'll put him down for a nap."

No answer.

Back in the kitchen, Tommy sat down at the table to better attack his massive roast beef sandwich. His eyes automatically focused on Nancy, beautiful, dark-skin, with the brownest eyes he had ever seen. He could look into her eyes and seemingly loose himself.

His Nancy had never lowered her eyes in shyness, or looked away in deference, as some girls do to tease. When Nancy looked at you, she saw you, and you had the feeling that you had no secrets. Tommy quickly got the feeling that she knew all about him, inside and out, and loved him anyway. What more could he want?

He watched her as she continued to circle the room, opening and closing doors and drawers. Apparently she had begun to make up her mind, having asked for a barrel. He'd go get it for her now. The sooner things were packed….

Nancy continued to circle the room the way a firefly on a summer night circles the honeysuckle vine.

Eleven

Sadie McClure again faced the west seated on the buckboard bench behind the powerful team of horses.

St Louis disappeared in the distance behind them, and the sun came out. The world, however, had been drenched with the two days of rain, and the trees still dripped water from their leaves. There'd be no fire to heat water for tea at lunch. Certainly, all the wood would be soaked and drenched.

It had been good to see Sarah and her so happy with her marriage and her new little Anita. Somewhere out ahead of her, Tommy was preparing his family to head south.

Such a clever little boy Tommy had been, but only when challenged. He lost interest when his lessons were too easy, so she must always search for something new for his quick mind. Thinking back, she remembered how he had liked the book binding apprenticeship but was not content start at the bottom with another firm.

Willie, having more patience, tried it with an established firm but gave it up. Surely the newness of the territory ahead would be a challenging backdrop for the both of them.

Ruthie sat beside her, carefully selecting crayons to color the pictures in her new book. Tomorrow Sadie would start her lessons in the McGuffey Primer.

The time of rest at Sarah's house had removed all the stiffness and soreness, and Sadie had climbed easily into the wagon. After the lunch stop, the little goats had been tethered where they could run along behind Chad's wagon. Sadie shook her head and smiled as she watched them. What a foolish thing to do… insisting on bring two worthless little goats along on such a trip. But Chad took it in stride.

When they made their night camp, the kindling wood was still wet. Chad scouted around, finally bringing some cedar branches that smelled good when burned and eventually caught a smoky fire under the kettle.

He watched the attempt, and decided, "I need to be gatherin' up wood to start the next fire. I could put it by the feedbox, and if we run into where there's been a rain, we'll have our wood right with us."

Sadie contemplated his statement. "Yes, Chad, that would be good, but that is a job for Frankie. Come along with me, Frankie, and we'll find sticks to make a fire for breakfast, and we'll take it along with us."

"Me, too!" announced Ruthie, brightly.

"No, Ruthie. This is a better job for Frankie. You're bigger, and you can help your mama. I'll go with Frankie."

The little boy grinned with pride, and looked at his sister. This was something new. He had the attention, and she didn't. Joyfully, he bounded along with Sadie, grabbing up twigs and small sticks.

"Frankie, I think we need a bucket to put these sticks in. Go ask Chad to give you a bucket."

Away he ran, eager to prove himself worthy of his responsibility.

The next day dawned bright and clear and road ahead of them made its way around the knobbed hills and white chalky bluffs of Missouri. Sadie had a lot of time to think.

Fifty-five years old was a strange age. She should clearly be settled in her own home with a husband to grow old with and have grandchildren who came to visit her.

Of course, no son could be better loved than Willie, and she easily filled the grandmother status with Willie's children. Surely it would be the same with Tommy's little Teejay, however… she'd just have to wait and see.

Looking back, she knew had done wrong to withdraw into the safety of her inner self when she had lost her husband. She should have made herself more available. There were surely other men, those who had lost their wife or their family. Tucked as she had been inside the safety of her family, she could not be found, and now she was alone.

So what was next…? Trekking across the rolling hills of Missouri, it was time to take stock. Here she was, in reasonably good health, she had never considered herself pretty, but she was neat, and that had seemed enough. Her wavy chestnut hair was bordered widely in silvery white, framing and softening her face and its skein of small wrinkles beside her eyes and mouth.

She had always stood and walked straight, as she had continuously encouraged her students to do. She could speak correct English when she pleased, but it seemed better to drop into the dialect of the locality. Their heavy Scottish heritage had given an inverted syntax to sentences, which may not be textbook correct, but they were easily understood.

In fact, the invertedness of sentence structure gave a softness to speech that seemed comfortable, even desirable.

She had received an education far above what she could have expected if her father had lived. It tended to isolate her, but it also gave her the confidence that a marketable skill can give to a person.

Could that be what pulled Willie and Tommy toward the skill their father had insisted they learn? Did they have an inward confidence that this was the place for them? Please, Dear Lord, let it be!

And Oklahoma was a new land. From the time she had watched the kites in the park with the children, seeing them passed by a flock of migrating birds, she had decided what kind of person she was, deep inside. The kind of a person she must, always, have been.

She was a strong woman when strength in a woman was not particularly admired. Looking back, she saw she had used her strength to stay hidden, as she had thought was becoming to her gender and age. She had pulled the closet doors snuggly around her and relaxed in their safety.

Well, she had been wrong. Totally and abysmally wrong, and it was time to correct the situation. She was who she was.

From here on, and for the rest of her life, she would consider all moves in the light of her newfound inner person. She would determine if an action was in the direction she wanted to go, and if it was not, she would turn aside.

She might not be able to do exactly what she wanted to do, but she certainly didn't have to do what she didn't want to do. There was not a big difference between the two..

There was a good chance she would live her life alone, but it would not be because that was her only option. It would be because she chose aloneness. There were certainly many things worse than being alone.

The thought of the bright bindings on her books brought her comfort. There they were, packed in boxes under what she now considered her bed. With new additions from St. Louis, she now had forty-eight books.

With an appreciation for round numbers, she wondered why she had not bought two more to make her library contain a rounded fifty. But, there was time.

The cool mornings with the sun on her back melted into warm days with the sun shining on her knitted shawl, warming her shoulders. Shoulders that no longer ached from sitting on the buckboard.

The sun shone on her hands, the hands that were no longer raw and stiff from holding the reins. The udder crème she had bought from Charlie Connelly brought out a softness that was not possible with the standard hand crème of the day.

Then, after lunch, she must adjust her bonnet to keep the sun from her face. Its warmth relaxed her feet and took away the soreness from her knees. The sparkling rays of it bounced shiningly off the rounded rumps of the large black horses as they easily pulled her heavy wagon.

All in all, she felt a strange happiness pour over her. Like warm honey, it flowed and covered her as she moved west. Its sweetness seeped into every pore, removing worry and concern.

Was this the way the bird felt? What was behind was gone forever, and it looked only to what was ahead?

Twelve

After all of the careful packing, the day came for the town of Providence Falls, Nebraska to move itself (or at least, part of it) to the Oklahoma Territory and a new life. Old things were behind, and all attention was on what was ahead.

On the third of May, Tommy McClure pulled his team into the wagon train in his assigned position directly behind Nancy's wagon. Her lovely black hair was tucked into the bright red bonnet, apparently one of her favorites. Her smooth, tanned hands confidently held the reins that commanded the horses.

Of course, she was much too far away for him to actually see her, but he knew exactly how she looked. He often drew from his memory and created a picture of her for himself. Sometimes she looked this way, and other times that way but always uniquely beautiful.

Maybe it had been stupid for him to take off by himself toward the California gold field, but if he had not done that, he would never have found his Nancy.

Nancy could count many generations of her family who had lived and died on the Nebraska soil, but she had turned away from them and excitedly faced the new land with him. Yes, she would go with him to the territory. Had she not promised him before the preacher that she would go where he went? But still he marveled over the wonder of it all.

Young Teejay, still asleep, lay in the big trunk given to them by Nancy's aunt. It had been a clever idea, and a trunk could always be used later when he became too tall for it.

Ahead of Tommy, Nancy McClure was filled with her own thoughts. What had she forgotten that they would desperately need? Tommy had left it all up to her, and now she was concerned. Food…? That was first and most important, and she was sure there was enough. Perhaps not what they would prefer, but cooking time and spoilage had limited her choices.

As she had packed, placing her choices into the barrel among the linens, the excitement of all had settled upon here. She fleetingly wondered if her excitement was akin to that of her ancestors as they took down their tipi houses and rolled up the skins. As they tied the rolls to the dragging travois sleds behind their horses, had they felt this same sense of adventure? She was glad for wheels instead of feet to make her journey, and she liked pottery and metal for her food and water, rather than animal skins, but the feeling must have been about the same.

She had hummed in monotone to an internal beat as she went about necessary duties. She had been born to survivors, and she was a survivor. Tommy would be proud of her as she traveled.

Just sitting on the buckboard was a thing she looked forward to. The last two days were so busy, and she was so tired, she was almost sick. Breakfast yesterday morning was more than she could stomach. Just a severe attack of nerves.

Tommy had told her she shouldn't worry so much. If she forgot something, they'd just do without for the next two weeks, and they'd get it in Arkansas City. His words didn't help a lot, though, because getting something in Arkansas City would mean spending money they might need later.

They finally got everything aboard, and as there was no furniture in the house to keep them there, they had driven to the south edge of town where they were to gather for the trip. Clancy Harper had told them the train would leave at dawn, with or without all its wagons. It was a sure bet he would not leave without the McClure wagons.

The beds had been made in Tommy's wagon, and Teejay loved his private bed. The horses spent the night on short hobble, grazing on the clumps of new grass. It all seemed so romantic.... the cozy canvas tarp that covered the wagon, the sounds of the night birds.... She should have slept like a log, but tension had upset her stomach.

She was still upset when she cooked the oatmeal for their breakfast. She was really looking forward to getting on the road. It would then be too late to get whatever she forgot, so she could just quit thinking about it and ride along and get some rest.

As the day wore on, she began to feel better, as she had been sure she would. She thought ahead, planning the food. The lunch stop, Clancy had told them, would be too short to make a fire, so she had decided on cold cornbread. She had the last of the buttermilk in a Mason jar, and she could shake it up frothy, season it with salt and pepper, and serve it with the cornbread.

And then supper…? Well, it would give her something to think about during the afternoon.

She had sausages that had been fried down and packed in jars with grease so they wouldn't spoil. They kept that way for weeks, and she had put in a lot of sausage. Tommy liked it with his beans… or fried potatoes… or baked sweet potatoes. And the packing grease around the sausages would be very important. Tommy was easy to cook for.

However, the more she thought of the sausage, the more upset she got. How could something she hadn't yet eaten yet be upsetting to her stomach? Well, she didn't have to eat the sausage. She could toast some bread over the cooking fire. That sounded a lot better, and her queasy stomach began to relax.

The crunch and grind of the wheels against the gravel also relaxed her, and she allowed her head to droop sleepily forward. The horses knew what to do. They walked ahead, keeping an even distance behind the wagon in front of them. It would be so nice to just go to sleep and get over this bellyache. Of course, she couldn't. There was Teejay to think of, and there was no knowing what he would decide to do if she was not watching him.

This was a rather strange bellyache. Not so much pain, as it was the intense desire to upchuck. Oh, dear! Could the oatmeal have been bad? Or what? Could oatmeal spoil before it was cooked? Surely not. It was still warm when they ate it.

Searching behind her, she found a small container and set it by her feet, just in case. She couldn't ask the whole train to stop, just for her to upchuck.

She sternly chided her body. Very poor timing, getting an upset. She had no time to be sick.

Then she felt the rolling deep inside herself… the gagging bitterness… the heaving, which brought nothing up. As she bent over to put the container back on the floor of the wagon, the answer came to her, clear as a birdsong at dawn. There had been another time she had this same sickness, and it had ended with the birth of Teejay.

Now, she really chided her body. Such very, very poor timing! With all there was to do, what business did she have being pregnant? Of course, it was what they wanted, but why couldn't it have waited until they were settled?

At the lunch stop, Nancy said nothing. She kept the newness of it to herself, and was able to eat some of the cornbread. The heaviness of the cornbread had somewhat of a settling effect, and she spent the afternoon in relative comfort.

At supper, sausage was out of the question. She could hardly stand to smell it.

Tommy commented, "You cookin' cornbread again?"

"Yeah. Seemed to have a cravin' for it."

Tommy took care of the animals, brought water and played with Teejay. Nancy forced her mind away from her condition.

She dished up the fried potatoes and sausage and allowed Tommy to feed Teejay from his plate. She slit open a piece of cornbread and buttered it lightly, pouring on a drizzle of honey. Moving across the cook fire from him, she settled down to nibble it.

Now, Tommy was nobody's dummy. He might not be as swift as an arrow on some things, but in matters pertaining to Nancy, he was an expert. He looked from the cornbread to the honey jar and to his wife, sitting apart and not eating heartily as she normally could.

He felt a catch in his stomach, and a trill of fear ran down his arms, causing the hair on them to stand out. What could he do, now?

With Teejay, she had suffered an upset stomach for months. How was she going to be able to drive the wagon? Surely, she was not… really…? But, if not, why was she acting the way she was?

Later, under the cozy canvas cover, he could stand it no longer.

"We got'a find a driver, somewhere."

No answer.

"Nancy, there's no need to pretend to me. I know you got a bellyache you can't put right and it's got nothin' to do with the sausage. I been thinkin'. We're only a day out on the road. We'll go back in the mornin' and get us a driver to take our wagon, or we can wait till…"

"Can't."

"Sure we can. You can't be drivin', bein' the way…"

"Can't go back. I don't drive with my stomach, and I don't know how it'd help, not to be drivin'. We got plenty'a cornmeal, and I'd bet anything that the Hewett's got crackers somewhere in all them wagons. I'll make it."

"But, Nancy, baby, I can't let you…."

"Tommy, it ain't your decision to make. Our family's my family, same as it's yours, and I say we'll go on. You'n your brother got things to do, and we can't wait around for our baby."

There… she had said it.

The horses snorted and stomped about and prairie night birds called to each other. In the wooden chest, little Teejay breathed softly. The moon gave just enough light to dimly see around inside the wagon.

Tommy sat upright in the cramped quarters of their bed and looked at his beautiful wife. Her dark hair blended with the darkness of the interior of the wagon, but the moonlight outlined her smooth face and put a sparkle in her dark eyes.

His thoughts raced as he whispered to her. "Oh, my Nancy! What a woman you are! You'll never know how much I love you, but I'll keep tryin' to tell you. I'm a bit restless, so I'm gonna sit up on the buckboard, so my fidgetin' don't keep you awake. You sleep now."

And Tommy sat on the buckboard seat and watched the horses graze in the dark, feeling for the grass clumps with their muzzles. The moon gave a dusty outline to the groves of cottonwood trees beside them, and the lacy fingers of the willows bordered the small stream that provided water for their camp.

Another child.

Excitement boiled up inside him. A new land, a new child, seeing his brother again… with the wonderful young woman that was his. How could one man be so fortunate? He looked up into the starry sky, and he knew from whence his gifts came. He knew he did not deserve them, but that did not keep him from being humbly grateful.

He glanced back into the wagon but could not tell if she was asleep. Rather than risk disturbing her, he stretched out as best he could on the bare board floor in front of the buckboard seat and finally slept.

Thirteen

The rounded hillocks of Missouri passed by in pleasing monotony. Sadie felt herself relaxing into the nothingness of her day. She sincerely wished she could say the same about her nephew's wife.

Lily seemed to be weary of the trip. Sadie had noticed a listlessness about her, so different from her usual bright and cheery consistency. She noticed it even before the evening at the Kaw River in Kansas.

On the western border of Missouri, just before crossing into Kansas, the marked road came upon a sizeable river. Even at non-flood stage, it would have been impossible to cross without a ferry, and this river was definitely at spring flood.

The men, Willie and Chad, walked down to the bank, contemplating the river. It was early to make camp, and the ferry crossing was only a short distance away. However, if they attempted crossing today, they would reach the other side very late, and who knew where they would find a campsite as good as this one?

In addition to that, it was obvious that the flood had brought down a lot of fish, and the pools and eddies were fairly alive and splashing with them.

After three weeks on the road, the wealth of fish and the change of activity tempted the men beyond their ability to withstand it. Besides that, the children, especially little Frankie, had not been initiated into the predominately male pleasures of the fishing pole. Canes grew along the bank, and the hooks and lines were within easy reach in the plunder.

Sadie watched their eyes dance with pleasure as they suggested an early camp and possibly a fish fry in the evening. Why not? They had no set schedule, and the trek across Missouri had been long and tedious. Sadie had said nothing, but she thought it was a good idea. She, herself, could use a change.

And there was another reason Sadie was in favor of a stopover. That reason was Lily. Perhaps an extra afternoon and evening of rest would do her good.

The children were dancing on their toes in anticipation as the men cut the tall, limber canes and attached the lines. Sadie went about making the fire and preparing for night camp, after persuading Lily to lie down and rest.

Lily had protested. “I feel all right. It ain’t like I’m tired. I been restin’ all day sittin’ on that buckboard.”

“It’s not the same,” Sadie had insisted, and finally Lily disappeared into the quiet of her bed.

Squeals of delight came from the river’s edge as the children dipped their poles in the water. Excited screams followed the bouncing of the corks and the landing of yet another fish.

The marmalade ladies, Essie and Tilda, sat on their haunches and waited until a fish was tossed their way. Leopold growled and paced the bank, as though supervising the operation. The gift of a whole fish settled him down, and he tore into the succulent, white flesh.

From the sound of it, Sadie decided she’d better prepare to be cooking a lot of it. Maybe a good, fresh fish dinner would help Lily. Sadie seemed to remember that for the past few days, Lily had been doing more picking at her food than eating it. While the fishing was going on, Sadie gathered a pan of fresh greens, stewing them while the fire was building itself up.

The sun was still fairly high in the sky when the girls joined Sadie at the wagon, sitting on their haunches and cleaning their paws and faces. Their rounded abdomens advertised the size of their lunch, and when they were clean enough to suit their particular selves, they would likely sleep for hours.

Leopold was not with them. Who knew where he was, or where he went, but he always showed up to ride in Chad’s wagon, either on the rocker bottom, or on top of the canvas canopy.

Scaled and cut up, the fish finally appeared at the camp. The grease was popping and crackling in the skillet, and Sadie set the first batch on to cook.

At the wagon tongue, she called to Lily, “Supper’s on the stove. Thought you might want to get up and eat.”

“Well, I don’t… think…?”

“Smells good. Maybe a good fish dinner’ll do you good.”

With a sigh, Lily pulled herself from her bed and washed her face. The greens were steamed and buttered, the cornbread crisp and brown. The pieces of fish lay on the platter, steaming and crisply succulent.

Sitting on the ground, the men piled their plates full of the fish, bemoaning the fact that they would leave this wonderful river the first thing in the morning. The children ran and played, coming back for more fish. Lily put fish and greens on her plate, and Sadie was relieved to see her eat a fair amount of it.

Poor girl, the trip was beginning to wear on her. Likely she was worrying herself down, thinking about how life would be in the territory. That would be something a good mother like Lily would be concerned with, that and bringing two small children into a totally unknown land.

Lily offered her last bite of fish to Esmeralda, who sniffed it and turned away. "Looks like someone finally got full of fish for once," she commented.

Sadie nodded. "Now you got'a get back in the bed and get some rest. I'll clean up here and wash the children. Getting' to bed early may put some life in you."

"Well, I could…" It was within her to object, but the offer was more than she could resist.

"No, you couldn't," Sadie was quick to say. "When I said for you to go to bed, it wasn't a suggestion. We can't have you gettin' down."

Lily smiled her appreciation and crawled back onto the pieced quilts.

Sadie cleaned up the camp and the children and used part of the long evening to read a story to them. The lantern, hanging on a low limb of an oak tree, shed a pool of golden light around the campsite, and the coals from the cooking fire sent a fragrant smoke in the air.

The children became droopy, so Sadie put them to bed in her own wagon, rather than disturb Lily with the rambunctious Frankie. With two children and two cats, there was very little room left for her, but that was only a small concern.

Even after the men retired, it seemed pleasant to sit on the buckboard and enjoy the bright moonlight as it spread over the campsite, sparkling on the water in the river and seeming to warm the earth with its golden rays.

A small sound in the nearby grove of trees announced the arrival of Leopold. He must have had a pleasant evening, because he stalked up to Sadie, rubbing against her and purring in a most un-Leopold-like way. Then he left her and jumped to the top of Chad's wagon and stretched out, watching her.

Of the many books she had read, none, to her knowledge, had been written about a beautiful evening of moonlight and pleasantness. Strange that she had never read about it. But then, there were a lot of things she had never read about, and those things were not likely to be found in books.

A small sound in the trees attracted her, and she saw the moonlight reflected in two pairs of eyes. Rabbit? Possum? Leopold also noticed the shining pairs of eyes, and growled deep in his throat. He did not move, however, except for the twitching in the tip of his tail.

His bellyful of fish had no doubt robbed him of his fierceness. He lowered his golden head to his cream colored paws, and the tip of his tail became motionless.

Everyone in the camp was asleep except Sadie. It would be nice to have a lighted lamp and a book to read, but that was out of the question. She allowed the titles of her many books to parade through her mind, halting as she examined this one and that one…special favorites. The titles of her books were to her as jewels on a chain, a treasured necklace of pleasure.

There was no book about watching a baby girl turn into a person with words worth listening to. Or the excitement of a little boy, when he lands his first fish, even if it turns out to be a crawdad. She had no book about the plunging of a family into the wilderness of a new territory.

Perhaps one had to be there to know how it really was. And how many people were there who knew how it was to be there and also had the properly descriptive words to commit it to paper? That could be a clue as to why there was no such book.

A dark object moved between Sadie and the moon, a pair of flapping silent wings beat softly overhead and disappeared into the grove. Then a squeal of terror as the talons closed on a warm furry body, and there followed a rustle of leaves and broken twigs as the remaining animal fled for its life.

The panorama of life went on… the hunter and the hunted. Grass for the rabbit, rabbit for the owl, and the owl whose body would nourish the grass. The cycle of life, such a deep subject for this time of the night. Shouldn't she be sleeping?

Sadie sighed, knowing she should find a place to lie down, so she could get some sleep, but she seemed to be not quite ready. Was the water from the supper tea still warm? Stepping softly down from the buckboard, she moved toward the glow of the coals and tipped the teapot toward her cup. A small amount of liquid poured out.

Not really very hot, but not bad. Leaning against the canvas of her wagon, she looked out across the shining surface of the water. As many books as she had read, she knew just how they should start. The first sentence should set the mood. A sentence like….

At that moment, she heard a sound behind her in the direction of Lily's wagon. Turning, she saw Lily appear, struggling to find a place for her foot and being somewhat tangled in her long sleeping gown.

"Lily!" Sadie whispered, hurrying to help.

"Thanks. I got'a get down!" Her voice was urgent.

"Are you…?

"I'm gettin' sick. Hurry and untangle me."

Sadie hurried, and Lily made it to the edge of the camp before she was sick. Poor Lily, trying to be quiet and not wake the camp, but she needn't have bothered. Full stomachs and weariness prevailed, and her heaving and gagging went unnoticed by anyone except Sadie.

Sadie struck a match to the lantern and hung it on the tree limb. Finding Lily's cup, she poured the last of the tea into it and waited. Finally, the heaving stopped, and Lily sat on a rock beside the coals.

Accepting the cup, she reasoned, "I don't know where that came from. Fish never made me sick, before."

Sadie asked, "Have you got a pain anywhere?"

"I don't think so. I'm just dizzy and my stomach hurts. I keep tryin' to think what that'd mean, and I keep thinkin'a cholera."

"Oh, Lily, surely not that!" It was a thought too horrible for words.

"I sure am sick. First town that's got a doctor, I think I need to get somethin' to help me feel better."

"Well, there's a town somewhere around the ferry. Don't know how big. How long you been feelin' like this?"

"Two, maybe three days… off and on. Maybe, longer. Found myself bein' glad the youngens weren't ridin' with me, in case what I got is catchin'."

"Lily, you want me to make more tea?"

“No, I don’t think so. I got’a get back in bed, my head’s so swimmy and whirly.”

Sadie nodded, taking Lily’s cup. She helped Lily back into the wagon bed, and carefully washed her cup in the soapy dishwashing bucket. Likely, it was just a stomach upset, but it paid to be safe if it indeed happened to be something that was catching.

Sadie’s moonlight mood had dissolved into the reality of night in the campsite, so she blew out the lantern and climbed into the wagon. Moving small sleeping bodies aside, she made room to stretch out. Tiredness flowed over her and the comfort of the quilts drew her into sleep.

It was hardly daylight, when the sound of Lily’s distress woke her. Easing herself past the sleeping children, Sadie crawled from her bed and piled sticks onto the gray coals. Tea had eased Lily last night, so tea needed to be steeped again as quickly as possible.

The water had just begun to steam as Lily returned, holding to the wagon edge to keep her balance. Settling herself on the rock, she stared at the fire blazing under the kettle.

“I sure must’a caught somethin’ bad. I told Willie he had to find a doctor or a midwife or someone to get me somethin’ to settle my stomach.”

Sadie had no words to reply. Everything had gone so well on this trip, she had begun to expect that it would continue. The grayness of the dawn was disappearing, and the animals began to snort and blow, ready for their morning grain, and the goats were tuning up, baaaing plaintively.

The remaining members of the camp were waking up.

Sadie oiled the skillet and put in the last of the fish. Fried and set back, it would make a good lunch, especially for the men. The oatmeal kettle bubbled and steamed, and Sadie stirred in raisins, cinnamon and butter, setting it off the fire to plump the fruit and absorb the spices.

Lily climbed back into the wagon.

Animals taken care of, the men appeared for breakfast. In addition to the oatmeal and biscuits, several pieces of the browned fish disappeared.

Still no Lily.

Willie shook his head sadly. “She was sick in the night. Likely caught somethin’ a day or two back. We’ll find her a doctor and get somethin' to get her feelin' better." His voice betrayed strained hopefulness.

Sadie wished she could be so confident. With Lily sick and unable to drive, some important decisions needed to be made. They were Willie's decisions, however. Certainly not her own. Yet…?

She cleaned up the morning camp, and Lily finally appeared. She poured herself a cup of tea, and Sadie brought her a bowl of cereal. Lily shook her head and turned away. Not good.

"You're not doin' no better?"

Lily shook her head. "But I can drive to the town. If I can get somethin,' I'll be all right."

Lily spoke with no more confidence than Sadie felt. At least it wasn't cholera, not that she had thought it was. If it had been cholera, Lily would not be able to stand up, much less offer to drive. That was one good thing to be grateful for. Thank you, Lord.

It was a late start, but finally they were on the road. It was near noon by the time the four wagons had been ferried across the river. The horses were obliged to swim the muddy water, and they climbed up the bank dripping and shivering.

While the men tended to the animals, Sadie and Lily looked for a doctor. Luck was with them, and Sadie sat in the waiting room in a state of tense apprehension. A half an hour passed, then forty-five minutes. Sadie began to wonder if she should check on her, but forced the thought from her mind. Lily was with a doctor, wasn't she?

After an hour and ten minutes, Lily emerged, followed by the stooped, gray haired old doctor.

Sadie looked from one to the other. Lily grinned a lopsided grin.

"I'm all right, and it ain't catchin'."

The old doctor nodded. "It wouldn't'a took so long, in there, if I'd'a known she didn't know she was in a family way. Here I was, lookin' for all kinds'a bad things she could'a picked up out on the road. Tried to think where there was influenza or cholera or even small pox or somethin' that started with upchuckin'."

"But it was different, this time," defended Lily.

"Sure it was," the doctor agreed. "The other times you weren't strung out along the road all day, sleepin' out, and eatin' whatever was handy. I'm givin' you a half a dozen pills, but you ain't to take 'em unless you just can't stand it if you don't. Most times, pills that are swallowed ain't so good for the little tike in your belly.

"What I want you to do is get you some crackers first chance you get and eat 'em for breakfast when you feel sick. A young healthy woman like you, missin' a few meals'll not hurt you. You'll make up for 'em in no time. There's folks all over in these mountains whose mother's had 'em in a wagon bed or a tent along the way. Didn't hurt 'em none."

Lily took the pills and paid the doctor his fee.

He admitted, "I almost feel bad about takin' a fee, you not even bein' sick with anything."

Lily shook her head. "Oh, no. You spent more'n an hour with me. At least I know I've got nothin' else wrong with me. That's somethin'."

The doctor had more to say. "The thing is, not knowin' what your situation is and how fast you got'a go to get where you're goin,' I hate to mention it, but if it was possible, mornin' sleep'd do you good. Seems like early mornin's are the worse, so if you could… maybe wait around…?"

It was time for Sadie's decision. "We're not in no hurry at all. Gettin' a late start'll be good for the youngens and the animals, givin' 'em more time on the ground. We'll manage. Thank you, doctor."

Back in the wagon and heading toward camp, Lily ducked her head in embarrassment.

"What'll I tell Willie, after getting' 'im so upset?"

"He needed to be upset. Whatever affects you needs to affect him. The thing is, he'll be so happy and relieved, we may not get started till noon!"

"No, I been thinkin.' Gettin' it off my mind that there's somethin' bad wrong, that'll help. If I stay in camp, I feel sick anyway, so we might as well keep goin'."

"Well, we'll have to see how it goes…" She'd make sure Willie knew what the doctor had advised.

It was early afternoon before they were headed out again, and three hours later they found a good campsite. One too good to pass over.

The last of the live fish, swimming circles in the buckets, provided the evening meal. Lily ate left over oatmeal.

It was an early evening, and the family was soon asleep in bed, but Sadie again sat on her buckboard in the moonlight, savoring the magic of the night. If she was to ever write a book, not that she ever would, but if she did… it would start in a way that drew a picture in the mind of the reader.

"………Moonlight. Threads of it filtered through the new green leaves of spring. As the evening cooled, dew formed on the grass creating diamonds in the moonlight. First there was darkness, then a sparkling jewel rising in the east……."

Her thoughts continued. Spring was a time for newness. New animals, new babies in the family, and new thoughts. Even the roundness of the marmalade girls promised two families of kittens for the new territory.

She must pull her thoughts together and put words to fit exactly the way she felt. The book should continue, "The family turned their faces to the west, filled with fresh ideas and hopes. The newness of the land, the rivers and the farms along the way had stripped from them everything that was old. Even their old thoughts were gone. The old things were left in the ashbin of the old house…"

She sighed with contentment and completed the sentence. "…in the ashbin of the old house that was fast becoming only a memory."

Why, there must be dozens of families with a story to tell. Stories that were not written down were stories that were wasted. They were left in the memory to mold and fester and dry up into dust. When the memory was gone, the stories were gone, and it was such a waste.

Like spring flowers pressed between the pages of a book, the stories of this wonderful exodus must be written down for those to read who would come later.

Willie's children and Tommy's little Teejay must be made to know how it felt, for they would remember it only through the screen of immaturity. Even Sarah's little Anita must know. It was part of her family, hence a part of her life.

Sadie knew she must get to bed, and she forced her thoughts away from her mind, promising them she would bring them up again. When she crawled between the quilts, Ruthie sighed and turned, and the marmalade girls nestled themselves again into the folds and hollows of the quilt.

Lily was slow leaving her bed, and the family tried to be quiet and let her have a few more minutes. Chad was tending to the animals, and Willie sat beside Sadie, savoring the comfort of the tea.

"Willie, the equipment you ordered, what all can you do with it?"

Willie turned toward her, his eyes brightened. "A lot of things. We'll have all the cutters, vices and forms. We'll have the machine to sew the sections of a book together. The clamps we got, they'll hold several books at a time, dependin' on the size of 'em."

Sadie tried to picture what he had described. Why hadn't she paid more attention when the brochures were spread about the house?

"Will you be doin' a lot of book printin'?"

Willie sighed. "Not like we wanted. Tommy thought makin' brochures and handouts for customers in Guthrie'd be a good thing for a start. Thinks he can drum up business, and I'm thinkin' he can. You know how he's always been… forward and talkative with strangers. Me… I'd rather work in the shop."

Sadie pressed forward with her questions. "So you'll be able to print up posters, but not pages of a book. The books you bind, they'll be done by someone else. Is that right?"

Willie nodded. "Likely, at least at first. Later, it'd be nice to have everything. We was thinkin,' Tommy and me, that what we ordered was all we'd be able to say grace over till we remembered what we learned and then forgot. Typesettin,' that's sort'a special, and takes a lot'a time. It takes a lot more time than settin' up for posters."

"But when you can afford it, you'll know how to operate everything?"

"We ought to. We spent long enough doin' it."

"If you could make a book from start to finish, you'd get a lot more of the money for it, wouldn't you?"

"Sure would. That'd be a thing we'd want to look into, quick as we could."

She had said enough and learned what she wanted to know. The boys had wisely invested in what they could do the quickest, leaving room to move up as the business was available.

Tommy would likely be very good as drumming business. He had an openness that appealed to people, and he loved to talk.

Whereas, Willie was quieter, more serious and careful with details. It could be a very good partnership.

Finally, Lily was able to get up and eat a few crackers. She insisted they get on the way. So they did.

Fourteen

It took almost two weeks for the wagon train from Nebraska to reach Arkansas City, Kansas, and that was the last town before entering the Cherokee Outlet of Oklahoma.

Nancy had made a list of things to look for. An all-day rain during which the wagons had come to a complete standstill, had reminded her how muddy the ground can get. She had never used gumboots, as Tommy had always taken care of outside things, but situations were different, now. She needed boots.

Also, she needed medicated salve. She had some, somewhere in the packing, but Teejay was in a clumsy stage of growth, and she'd had been forced to borrow salve two times to treat his skinned knees. Also, one of the neighboring wagons had a box of dominos and their children used them for toy blocks. If Teejay had dominos, he should have a lot of fun with them while he was confined to the wagon.

Clancy Harper, the wagonmaster, ordered the train to skirt around Arkansas City to avoid damage to the city's roads with their 35 wagons. They were allowed to camp in a huge field and given a day to go into town.

One of the women who had a very large iron and steel stove had insisted it be taken down so she could bake a supply of bread. She kindly offered the use of her stove to anyone who had yeast dough ready, and Nancy had quickly taken advantage of that… though cornbread still sat the best on her delicate stomach.

After a day at Arkansas City, the 35-wagon train pulled across the border into Oklahoma. Clancy had playfully fired his gun into the air, and a cheer went up. They were finally in Oklahoma, though still at least a week away from their destination.

It was on the first night in the territory that the twister struck. Seemingly out of nowhere, the black clouds piled up overhead with rope-like funnels dropping down to the ground. Clancy had stopped the train and made everyone crawl under their wagon and lay face to the ground.

It was the closest Nancy had ever been to a tornado, and she and Tommy had lain close together with Teejay wedged, squirming, between them. As the roar of the storm neared them, the sound was so loud, she had clamped her hands over the little boy's ears, as he screamed in terror.

The deadly rope of swirling wind looped and twisted, breaking apart and rejoining into a double-tailed funnel that moved along the ground, pulling up trees, dust and clods of grass. She and Tommy had watched with horror as it swept across the plains toward them.

A drenching downpour of water emptied out of the cloud, hiding the deadly rope for a few minutes, then the roar of it was gone. Quickly as it had come, it was gone, and the rain pounded against the ground and flowed under the wagon where they lay.

Tommy grabbed Teejay and held his face up from the layer of water, and the roar of the twister was replaced with the whipping and cracking of canvas against the wooden stays.

They could feel the shivering and shaking of the wagon above them, and the whinnies and cries of fright of the horses could be heard from the grove where they were tied.

Then the rain stopped. Suddenly as a sneeze, the lightning was gone, taking with it the clouds and rain. Tommy squirmed out from under the wagon, pulling Teejay after him, and Nancy gathered her sodden skirts in her hand and crawled on hands and knees. Her soaked hair streamed in rivulets down her face, and the wet layers of cloth were stiff and cold against her skin.

Then she saw what had caused a lot of the popping and cracking of canvas. Like the bare ribs of a picked carcass, the stays of her wagon lifted themselves up from the wooden bed. The canvass cover was completely gone. Everything in the wagon was soaked and dripping, but the wind that took the tarp had thoughtfully left all the wagon contents.

While they stared at their loss, the news came to them that one of the Hewett wagons had been completely lost. Blown away. Gone. It had contained a lot of items destined for the new store in Prosper, but the loss of it meant nothing to the storekeeper when stacked against the lives of the two girls who had crouched under it and remained unharmed.

The storm took some things and left others, and no one had been hurt. It gave everyone a reason to look up and be thankful for help from above.

The blown away tarp was seen in the top of a cottonwood tree, wedged among the limbs. Several teenage boys considered it a lark to climb up and get it. Back in position on the staves, they found several holes open to the sky, but they could be patched.

It took a day for the travelers to get themselves together again. Nancy and others had water damage and were glad to get to dry things out. It had been a hard day, and dry wood was impossible to find. Nancy opened a jar of sausage and scraped away the grease it had been packed in. Slicing her fresh-baked bread thickly, she made sausage sandwiches for herself and Tommy, and Teejay had bread and peanut butter.

The sandwiches were hearty and strengthening, even if there would be nothing hot to go with them.

Grateful for a dry bed in the other wagon, Nancy had gone to sleep immediately. She awoke to the wonderful smell of wood smoke. Tommy had somehow gotten a fire to burn, and she quickly had the kettle over it. Buttered oatmeal and hot tea made the world look better. Tommy watched her eat with the vigor of a field hand.

He said nothing. Maybe she forgot…? Can one forget to be sick?

Nancy put away the breakfast things. Today would be a slow day, as the road was so muddy, and everything seemed to take twice as long. She had reason to be grateful for the purchase of the gumboots.

Before crawling into her wagon, she set a pan of beans to soak. Likely she'd get a chance to cook them at the supper stop. Tommy watched as she sorted and washed the beans, but he said nothing.

It was truly a short day of traveling and an early stop. The new night camp had not been in the range of the storm, so all the twigs, broken limbs and buffalo chips were powder dry and a good fire simmered the beans. An hour past midnight they were cooked to perfection.

It was later, in the tight quarters of their bed, that Tommy found the courage to ask,

"How're you feelin'?"

"Good," came the hoped for response.

"No feelin' like you got'a …"

"Upchuck? No. I made up my mind not to."

"You what?"

"While we was layin' face down under that wagon with the water runnin' in, I was too scared to be sick. When I saw we didn't have anything that blowed away, I was too relieved to be sick. So I made up my mind. If bein' scared and bein' relieved can chase away the feelin,' then why wouldn't bein' mad at it, do the same thing. So I just said, I'm mad at bein' sick."

"And it works?"

She nodded in the dimness of the wagon canopy. "Up to now, anyway. I got too much to do to waste time bein' sick."

Tommy watched her face in the dim light. She was wearing her tiny smile that meant 'see there! I won that argument!' Just the tip of one side of her mouth turned up. The darkness made a smudgy blackness of her hair and her eyes, all except for the twinkle of reflected moonlight.

What a woman! She makes up her mind she isn't sick, and it works… maybe. At least, she was smart enough to try it.

The cramped quarters of their bed forced them to lie closely, but he could not resist pulling her even closer. What other woman would leave her family and head out into the unknown with a scatterbrain like himself? She might be the only one in the world like herself, and wasn't he lucky to have found her!

Interesting, though. It had been a Nebraska snow-storm that had stopped him a few years ago. When the snow became too deep to travel in, he was forced to take refuge in the town, and he had gone to the general store (Hewett's) to ask directions to the nearest house that would in take overnight travelers. That was where he first saw her.

It was another snow-storm that spawned the idea for the move he was now on. Interesting, that one's life could be so easily influenced by the weather.

It was the next day that they approached the Cimarron River. They had been following the Santa Fe Railroad for some distance and when they reached the bank of the river, only a tiny ferryboat was there to take them across. Clearly, the boat was not big enough for even one wagon on board.

The railroad had a good bridge over the river. Thick bridge timbers held the stringers for the cross ties which were spaced fourteen inches apart. The train shot, rumbling, across the bridge, and rattled on down its track. When it had passed over, planks were strung out along the outside of the rails for the travelers.

Wagons were detached from the horses and pulled by hand across the rolling river, deep and brown with mud and sand from a storm up-river. Horses were swum across, tethered to the ferry, and people had the choice of riding the small, dangerous and tipsy ferryboat, or walking the rails over the train bridge.

Tommy walked onto the bridge and looked down. A fourteen-inch window looked down between each cross tie. Muddy, rolling water was below. He could make it fine, and he could carry Teejay, but strong-mindedness notwithstanding, Nancy could not walk the length of the bridge. Why, no bigger than she was, she could slip down between the cross ties and be gone in an instant.

The ferry was no better a choice, tipsy as it was. There was no way she could swim against the current.

Tommy watched as the wagons were towed across by those who had a contract to do it, and who charged a dollar and a quarter for the service. They had trouble with one wagon. It was loaded with heavy milling machinery, and they were more than an hour getting it moved along. During that time, Tommy made up his mind.

Drawing aside one of the pullers, he showed him the dollar in his hand. "Man, I'm askin' for help. My missus, she's in a family way and ain't walkin' too steady on 'er feet. She'll be on the bed in that wagon over there, and she don't weigh enough that you'd notice it."

The greedy puller pocketed the money and nodded.

Not so easy to do was the persuading of Nancy, herself. "I can walk! You think I'm maybe too weak to get across this little old river?"

"No, likely you could. Then, again, if you had a sick spell and fell through, where'd I be? I can't afford the loss'a nothin' I have, least of all you, and this here thing that I'm sayin' ain't no suggestion. You're gonna go get in that wagon, and get under the quilt, and I don't want'a see or hear nothin' out'a you till I come and get you on the other side."

Nancy watched Tommy's soft blue eyes turn fiery and his voice harsh and firm. That was not like Tommy. She looked at the bridge, and the women who were gingerly stepping from one cross tie to the other, holding to each other for balance. She looked at the rolling river, whirling sticks, twigs and leaves along its current.

She looked back at Tommy, and the fire still burned in his eyes.

Without a word, she slipped away from him and crawled into the wagon, settling into their bed. Pulling the quilt she had pieced in the bright prairie flower pattern, up over her face, she lay motionless.

Tommy. Her Tommy. So soft and loving, but when something was very important to him, his softness had turned to the hardness of steel and the brittleness of glass. When it didn't matter, he let her have her own way. But when it really mattered to him, he put up with no nonsense out of her. Wasn't she lucky to have gone to Hewett's store during that snowstorm?

Sounds and motion were all around her, and finally she felt the movement of the wagon tongue. Up the graveled grade it went and over the hump of the rails.

It was tapped into place on the planks and moved smoothly along. Voices around her spoke of keeping the wheels straight, of waiting until a plank was adjusted. They halted and proceeded several times, and then the wheels bumped over the rails again and she felt the wagon being rolled down off the grade.

Then it stopped. She drew the quilt down from her face and started to get up, but then she remembered Tommy's command. Lying back, she waited.

There were footsteps, and Teejay was lifted to the buckboard. "Mama! Water, mama!"

Tommy stood by Teejay, holding him. "Nan? You can get up, now,"

She grinned, playfully. "No. You can come and get me!"

Tommy lifted Teejay into his wooden chest bed, and crawled up over the buckboard seat, and then on into the bed. The quarters were very cramped, but Tommy managed to get his arms around her shoulders. He looked into her laughing dark eyes and her 'see there expression? And her 'I won that argument!' smile.

Teejay watched from his perch, laughing and crowing. "Mama! Papa!"

"Tommy, we got'a to get up. Folks'll talk!"

"Yeah? Well…they got'a talk about someone. Why not us?"

They camped on the south side of the river and were back on the trail at first light the next morning.

Two days later they passed through the edge of the new city of Guthrie, startled at the number of people who still lived in their wagons, or even in shelters made of wood strips and cardboard boxes. The streets teemed with horses and dogs, and billowed with dust.

Rough streets were marked out and were packed with people. Noises of talking, yelling, barking and bell ringing were periodically overpowered by the whistle of the train and the clickity-clack of its drivers on the metal track. There was the Santa Fe depot where their machinery would come in.

It was late in the afternoon when they headed out to their own town, and dusky darkness had fallen when Clancy rode by and told them, "Pull in anywhere, folks! You might be campin' on your own land!"

Nancy looked around at the thick grove of tall trees, their dark fingers outlined against the starry sky. The men took care of the animals, but Nancy curled up in the cramped bed, not even bothering to change into her nightgown.

Teejay slept peacefully in his box, and Tommy? Likely he didn't go to sleep at all, but spent all night talking with the other men!

Fifteen

Tommy McClure had been in the new town of Prosper for a week when his Illinois relatives reached Wichita, Kansas and headed south. Starting late and early stopping had used up a lot of time, but it had helped Lily.

By an hour after sunup, she was able to sit up without discomfort. By mid-morning each day, she was able to take her place, rein in hand.

Sadie was no longer sore after a day of driving. The sun shining warmly on her bonnet seemed to pour strength into her mind and body.

Her wagon wheels crawled steadily across the flat Kansas prairies, through the small towns that had cropped up along the road, and beside the isolated homesteads, hopefully fenced and farmed. There was a stop, now and then, to purchase eggs or milk from a farm site and transfer a bit of hard cash into welcome hands.

Sadie looked this way and that, saving, in her mind, the sights she saw. She would need them when the perfect idea formed in her mind. She would write a story, a book, actually, and Willie and

Tommy would print it. She would write it down, and wait. When the right time came, that is what she would do.

The book would contain the whole of the trip, all her thoughts and fears, the antics of the children and the concerns of the adults. It would not contain just her own story. There would be many stories like hers, and she would ask many questions. She would pull minute details from others she would meet in the town, and she would add their stories to hers.

This settlement, she realized, was unique to America and also to the Oklahoma territory. Many places were assigned, others squatted on, and some were requested through a platted mat. But here, the place she was headed, it had been settled by a gunshot, and she would meet many who participated in the "run," and each would have his story. She could not know that later another parcel of land would be settled by lottery, the new settler not knowing what he had until he found it by map coordinates.

As she rumbled and rolled along, her mind projected into the book. It was obvious that there would be many books, just as there were many stories. She would collect stories from everyone who would talk with her, and her Willie and Tommy would set it (or them) into print. The whole of the project made interesting speculation as the wagon rolled along.

At Wichita, Chad led them out of town, following the roads to the south, and the others followed. From now on, the sun would be over her shoulders and not in her face. Arkansas City was ahead, and that was where she would buy the notebooks that would hold her story. Many notebooks.

Arkansas City was a beehive of activity. Throngs walked the streets, crowded into stores offering plow points and pitchforks, hammers and nails, boots and shoes, and miles of yard goods for dresses. Sadie watched the faces of the people, and all about her was an air of excitement, a feeling of movement and transition.

Faces, eager and tense. What would they face and would they be ready? She could say this for Arkansas City, they were prepared for the activity. There was no attempt to display articles for sale, and they were sold from the packing boxes. Woodstoves and matches. Mattresses and pillows. A few toys. Some books, but none of the caliber Sadie would have added to her hoard.

And finally there were the notebooks and pencils. The question, now, was how many should she buy? She picked up three of the thickest… no, get six. At least. She paused to consider and glanced down at Ruthie staring up at her with apprehension akin to fear.

Back to the tablets. When would she find them in Guthrie? She had been warned to "bring everything." She lifted the notebooks from the packing crate and counted, seventeen, eighteen, nineteen… there, twenty of them. No, get four more and make it an even two dozen. That number meshed well with Sadie's sense of balance and completeness.

Hugging the tablets against her with one arm, she began to count out the pencils. She felt a tug at her skirt and looked down into the worried face of Ruthie. What could be wrong? Was it time to look for an outhouse for her?

Another tug and a tentative, "Aunt Sadie?"

"What, darling? Do you need to find…."

The little girl cut her off. "Aunt Sadie, I can't do it. Please don't make me do it?"

Sadie balanced on her heels and lowered her face to Ruthie's. What could possibly be causing her pain."Darling, tell me? What's wrong?"

"It's the tablets, Aunt Sadie

"What about the tablets, sweetheart?"

"You got too many?" she wailed.

"Too many? Why do you say that? You don't have to carry them."

"It's not that! I just can't do it!"

"Do what, sweetie?" Sadie made her voice as gentle as possible.

The tears flowed and Ruthie swabbed her sleeve across her face to wipe them away. "I can't write words to fill up all of them tablets. I'm too little!"

Oh, yes, then Sadie remembered. She had been away from the classroom for so long she had forgotten the mind of a child and its workings. Events are clear to a child only as it affects them, personally. She had learned to fully explain any new action from their viewpoint.

And here was Ruthie. She had never seen Sadie putting her notes in the tablets because it was late at night or when the little girl was occupied. Tablets, in Ruthie's presence, meant she would be writing her numbers or practicing the shape of her letters.

Ruthie was agreeable to tablet work, but there was not the eagerness she had seen in small Anita Welmon. And there didn't need to be. There was only one Anita, just as there was only one Ruthie.

"Ruthie, darling, these tablets are not for you. They're for me. But look what's in this box? These are for you, and Frankie, and maybe some other little girl we don't know, yet. Besides, tablets can hide in my drawer until we need them

A sniff, and another swipe of the sleeve. "Not for me?" she asked, hopefully, still needing reassurance.

"Not for you, sweetheart." Her words brought a smile to the little girl's face.

Other purchases were made, packed away in the recesses of the crowded wagons, and they were again on their way. Ruthie drowsed, and finally gave it up, crawling back into the quilts with the marmalade girls.

Sadie reached under the buckboard seat and drew out her tablets to put down the thoughts when they came. To put them down before they were lost within the new thoughts that crowded into her head to be mulled over.

Cocoons. That's what the wagons were like. Life, as they had known it, had been halted and encased within the canvas-covered boxes with wheels. There they stayed, being towed along by the horses. The wagon cocoons had become comfortable, and after more than a month, it was difficult to think of another life.

The cocoons moved south out of Arkansas City and into the Cherokee Outlet. The activities of life were defined and shaped by the contours of the wagon and the 4 foot by 10 foot size of the box bed. At first, it had seemed impossibly small. Later, it had seemed almost roomy.

At the Cimarron River, they lost most of a day waiting to be towed across the river on the train bridge. Three days later they passed through the edge of Guthrie, amazed at the noise and the people.

Over his tea, Willie observed, "I'm more'n glad I don't have to buy nothin' in that town. Could be, though, that our machinery is over there in the depot, right now, a'waitin' for us."

Following the compass needle east by south east, they traveled the last fourteen miles. All along the way, every half-mile or so, small camps were set up with sheds, small log cabins and tents. Children played and dogs roamed among the trees sniffing the scent of varmints.

The trail was bumpy with grass clumps and roots and stumps from sawed trees. Somewhere in the distance, a sawmill screeched its way through a tree trunk. Life and activity were everywhere.

Sadie, within her cocoon, felt the stirring of life. She soaked up the sounds and sights, taking them inside her being. She ingested them with her breath. The team of huge black horses pulled steadily forward, and Sadie pushed her frivolous thoughts away.

There was no magic, here. Only trees and people, miles and weariness, a pocket of noise in the quiet woodland. And yet, she looked from side to side, printing her mind with the sights and sounds.

It was late afternoon as the black horses pulled the first wagon past Leon Baxter's claim, then past the claims of the Kelvey brothers. Roberta Dunbar hung the last of the washing on the line that was stretched between two trees.

Willie stopped his wagon and called out, "Ma'am?"

Roberta came toward him. "Can I help you?"

"Could be. We're lookin' for the town of Prosper."

Roberta smiled a welcome. "Well, you found it!"

"Do you know a fellow by the name'a Tommy McClure?"

"Sure do. See right through the trees, there? That's where they are."

"Thanks a lot, ma'am."

Willie turned a wide circle and headed into the trees, following a trail of crushed grass and trimmed bushes and limbs. Lily followed. Sadie ordered her team to 'gee around,' and Chad was behind her. The four wagons filled the entire lane.

Glancing around, Sadie saw people coming through the trees. Young people, some older people and laughing groups of children. It was like a scene from a storybook with a whole town gathering to witness an important event.

From the beginnings of a log building, Sadie saw Tommy. It was certainly and unmistakably Tommy, running toward the first wagon and his brother. Careful, deliberate Willie stood and waited, his arms outspread.

At the moment of their embrace, someone clapped their hands in appreciation, and the applause spread around the circle of faces. Smiles and laughter were everywhere.

Sadie, from her cocoon, watched the unfolding. It was as though those who surrounded them were welcoming one of their own. As though they were embracing one who had been gone and had now returned. But these people had never met Willie. It was an amazing thing to witness.

When the brothers finally pulled apart, Tommy reached behind him and drew Nancy forward. Teejay peeked from behind her skirts. It had to be Teejay. Sadie saw Tommy's laughing eyes and smile look out from the small dark-tanned face of Teejay, who had eyes of shoe-button black.

Lily was helped down, and Frankie followed her. Ruthie… where was Ruthie? Sadie looked around and saw the little girl huddled under the quilts, peeking shyly around the edge.

Like Sadie, Ruthie was still in her cocoon, not quite ready to emerge. Wait a minute, and they'd both be ready to join the family. They would join the huge family of more than a hundred people who stood around them. This family who surrounded them with smiles.

One of the women came toward Sadie. She was an attractive woman with light hair, delicately touched with silver. Her eyes were bright with interest and her smile was genuine.

"You must be Miss Sadie. I'm Nettie Gunther, your neighbor to the north. We been waitin' and hopin' you'd make it in today. We've had a party ready for three days and all of us in a hurry to get to celebrate."

Party? Waiting for them? For three days? What sort of a world had she woke up in, for surely she must have been asleep?

Sadie stepped down from the wagon and turned to see Ruthie crawl toward her. Ruthie, who never wanted to be picked up and held. Ruthie, who always wanted to do things for herself. This Ruthie held her arms to Sadie to be helped down. It was difficult to wriggle out of one's cocoon.

Sadie lifted her from the wagon and held her a minute before setting her on the ground. Closing in on them was a tiny dimpled black-haired angel, another with chestnut hair like Ruthie's and several others.

Nettie Gunther watched as Ruthie backed into Sadie's skirts, and she attempted to explain. "You must be Ruthie! This girl is Marcie, that one is Alecia, and those are Sophie, Charity, and Mercy. I know that's a lot of names to remember, but they know all about you. I think they want you to come and play."

Whereupon the girl identified as Alecia stepped forward and reached for Ruthie's hand. Tentatively, Ruthie extended it, and she was led away.

Watching it, Sadie felt a thrill of excitement crawl along her arms. Ruthie had also come home to a place where she had never been before.

Nettie again. "Now, I know you folks are tired and got things to do, so we're all gonna clear out. But come late evenin', we got a party goin' over in the schoolyard. If you're not too tired? Sure and you'll be there. For a little while, anyway?" Eyebrows lifted hopefully and with encouragement.

School yard? This brand new town had a school? Surely not!

The wagons were pulled into a more workable position under the trees, and Chad took over the care of the hoof stock. The little goats ran rambunctiously through the trees followed by laughing little boys. The horses were grained and tethered.

A cook fire blazed on Tommy's lot, side by side with the one he had picked for Willie. A stew (squirrel?) simmered in the pot. The smell of baking sweet potatoes flavored the smoke from the coals of the fire. Lily and Nancy eyed each other for a few minutes, and then began chattering like long separated sisters.

Sadie seemed to be at a cinema, watching the actors play their parts. Movement went on about her, but it did not involve her. She opened her mind to absorb every detail, as this would be a part of the book.

They had been promised a place in the town, and this was undoubtedly the Promised Land. The Promised Land! What a name for a book!

And then it was evening. Through the trees Sadie could see the lanterns being lit and hung in the trees. Pools of yellow light shown down on the newly trampled grass. Someone had a fiddle, and someone else had a harmonica. Sounds of their turning up competed with the singing of the insects in the trees.

Faces washed and refreshed, and hair re-combed, the family walked toward the hanging lanterns. Where was the school? That was the missing piece of the puzzle.

Talking, singing, and dancing (more like the circling games of the school children) and a lot more talking and laughing. So many young people! A few older people, and hordes of children!

Ruthie and another little girl came running toward her, flushed and excited.

"Is she your grandma?"

"No. I don't have no grandma. She's my Aunt Sadie."

The other girl contemplated Sadie. "I don't have no Aunt Sadie, but I have a Big Papa. He's my grandpa." The girl pointed to the man standing somewhat in the shadows behind her.

The man looked like a grandpa. The right number of wrinkles, the very slight stoop and a pleasant smile of acknowledgement. These things were highly desirable in a grandpa.

"Let's go play." And they were gone. Formalities over, they sought better excitement.

Sadie was left standing alone once more. She should be helping somewhere, but she couldn't see where. Someone was stirring a kettle (vat?) of hot chocolate, spicy with cinnamon and nutmeg. Another was setting out cookies. Where would they get cookies, and, wherever they came from, what an honor it was to have such a fancy party for their arrival.

Another smell. Coffee? Without a doubt, that was the aroma of coffee! It had been weeks (months?) since she had tasted coffee, and the very smell of it was intoxicating.

The man behind her moved forward. "Miss Sadie, I presume? My name is Eben."

Sadie turned to smile at the grandpa. "Yes, I'm Sadie…."

"Could I bring you something? I remember our first day here. Seemed I wanted nothin' more'n a hot drink and a chance to catch my breath.

Well put. "Do I smell coffee?"

"Sure thing, you do. Someone still had some, and it's been saved for when you folks got here."

"Us? Who could know….?"

"Well, to be truthful, everyone was tired and hankerin' for excitement. If there hadn't been no one comin', likely they'd'a thought of another thing to have the party for. Turned out, you folks came in handy! So many of these folks, the ones from the town in Nebraska, they know each other, and a brother'a Tommy's was considered one of the bunch, even before he got here. Now let me get you that coffee."

Sadie watched as the man stepped sprightly along, making his way through the excited crowd. Presently, he returned with two mugs of steaming black brew.

"Them young men, they made this a mite strong. If it's too strong for you we can…."

Sadie took a sip. The rich flavor of it woke up taste buds that had been unused for weeks. "No, no. It's just right."

"Now, Miss Sadie, we can stand here, or we can find ourselves a tree to lean against, or there's flat rocks to sit on. I can help you sit…."

"Thanks and I been sittin' on rocks all the way from here back to Illinois. I can manage rocks, all right."

"I can imagine."

They sat on the low rocks and watched the mingling crowd. A "Mrs. Grandpa" should be showing up soon. Sadie looked around her, and saw several older persons.

A tiny woman, with snow-white hair knotted on her head, leaned heavily on her cane, but her eyes were turned toward the activity. Another woman, aproned and smiling, approached them with two cups of something, but she turned aside and handed the drink to the man with the neatly ironed overalls and shirt with a starched collar.

"Neighbors," explained grandpa. "Clyde and Maude Kendall, folks that come down from the town."

Sadie nodded and sipped, as the man made this comment and that statement about the town and its people.

Sadie. "You're not from the town, I suspect?"

"Oh, no. We come from across Arkansas, dodging storms and high water. 'Speck you had better weather."

"Only a storm at St. Louis, and we were at my niece's house at the time. All in all, we had a good trip." The cocoon had held them adequately until the time came for them to emerge into this glorious throng. Full fledged with wings strengthening they were poised for flight.

And the conversation continued, but "Mrs. Grandpa" did not appear.

Two hours later, the party was still going strong, but Sadie began to feel the tiredness settle over her despite the bracing effect of the coffee. Even in the semi darkness of the edge of the lantern light, the man seemed to notice (sense?) that she had experienced all the day that she was up to.

"Could be, you'd be wantin' to rest? These young folks, they'll be at this till all hours. I don't try to keep up with 'em, myself."

"Well, I…."

"Now, these trees can be confusin.' I could walk you back to your wagon, and see you don't stumble in the dark. They's tree stumps and rocks and…."

"Mr… uh, Eben? I got'a ask a question."

"Shoot."

"They said the party was to be in the school yard. I know it's dark, and all, but I think I'd'a seen a schoolhouse if there'd'a been one."

Grandpa's chuckle was laced with merriment. "Yeah, there's a schoolhouse, all right. Only trouble is, that school is still in the minds'a the parents that has youngens needin' to go. A lot'a the folks used up a lot'a what they had, just to get here. Anything else they got, its got'a last till they get a crop up, or till they get on with whatever they do to earn cash money. They's not been too much'a what you'd say was hard cash a'floatin' around.

"There'll be a schoolhouse, though. Don't you never think there won't. Youngens like these, bein' either brave enough or desperate enough to cross the country and start a new life, they'll find a way. Now, me and Clyde Kendall, we had the plans to help get a church up and goin' That's a start. But the time'll come when that schoolhouse'll be standin' there on that lot, and there's no doubt about that."

They had moved into the darkness, walking carefully on the grass. The wagons were darker shapes outlined under the trees.

Sadie recognized her cocoon. "This is mine. Thank you for walkin' me home. Good night."

"Good night, to you. We'll be seein' more of you tomorrow."

Carefully, Sadie placed her feet on the well-known stepping places learned over the last six weeks. Step on the wagon tongue, adjust her skirt out of the way, bring up the other her foot. Hold to the handle of the wheel brake, raise her skirt and step into the wagon. Sit on the buckboard, re-gather her skirt, then step over the back of the buckboard.

Then she was home. What would it be like to, once again, step into her home standing upright? To be able to change her clothes while standing? To again sit on the edge of a bed while she untied her shoes?

Well, Sadie, don't get too eager. The shed for the machinery… that'll come first. Just get used to the idea of this wagon being home for a while longer.

Dressed in her sleeping gown, with a dressing robe handy (it seemed strange to be going to bed with the sound of a party so close), Sadie stretched out on her quilts, sighing tiredly. It had been a long day.

Pleasant thoughts. Willie and Tommy together again. Lily and Nancy so quickly finding common ground. Frankie with a bright faced little cousin. Shy Ruthie with so many friends waiting for her to come. The friendly man, Eben… what did he say his last name was? Well, it didn't matter. Likely she'd meet his wife tomorrow, along with more of the older folks.

His smile. The twinkle in his eyes, even in the dim light of the hanging lanterns she could see it. The pleasantness of conversation, if only for a moment, seemed so comforting to be with someone near her own age. It was something to savor.

Nettie… what did she say her last name was? There was the big fellow called Ed, who kept his eye on her. The loving looks that flashed between them as they passed. More for her book.

Maude Kendall, with the steaming cups and the confident and loving smile toward the man in the starched and crisply ironed shirt. A starched and ironed shirt in this wilderness of trees? Truly, a woman's love took on many forms of expression.

The pleasant familiarity of the hard bed and the pieced quilts pulled her into a light and drifting sleep. And dreams.

She was at the little schoolhouse in Northbend with the precious Anita. Anita's father… her loving husband. Where was he now? Surely he should be there any minute. Her loneliness drew her from the depth of sleep into a reluctant reality. She felt the bed beside her, and her hand rested on the hard wood of the wagon bed. Startled, she pulled her hand away and sat up.

Sounds of laughing and singing were nearby, and she looked through the trunks of the trees at the bright lights and happy sounds. The party!

Slipping on her dressing robe, she moved toward the buckboard, sitting behind it with her arms resting on the backrest. As she watched the moving shapes in the lantern light and smelled the aroma of the coffee and the chocolate, a tear oozed from the corner of her eye and slid over the delicate crow's foot of wrinkles below her eyes.

Sadie lifted her hand and impatiently brushed it away. Nonsense! Tears, for goodness sake! When there was so much happiness everywhere? When her beloved nephews were together again and both seemingly doing so well with their lives? Steady Willie had always made solid decisions but was ready and willing to change if another path seemed better. Free spirited Tommy, but he made a choice of a girl who might provide an anchor for him, but not a cage to capture his spirit. He was here, wasn't he, and the lovely young lady was with him.

Tears? For shame, Sadie! It was a time for joy and laughing. Either that, or it was time to get back in the bed where she belonged and go to sleep. But still she sat behind the buckboard and watched, fascinated.

There was so much life, here. The cocoons of the wagons had broken open, and new life was everywhere. New life was wonderful, with its sights and sounds, its colors and feelings. The only trouble was, with new life, came new pain.

When she lost her husband, and then the daughter of her heart, she had left St. Louis, even leaving her new name in the city that had taken everything else from her.

When she walked away, the city had kept a chunk of her life… the part with the pain. She shut it away as in a closet, as one would an outgrown jacket. She became, once more, Sadie McClure with the books, the quiet thoughts, and the ability to teach children.

Now, how did that chunk of pain escape from the closet and finally catch up with her? Why was it still alive, when she was certain she had dealt with it? Or had it been following her, all along? Lurking in the shadows, ducking behind the shrubbery, ready to leap out and claim her once more. How much grief was enough?

Then she made no attempt to stop the tears but let them flood down her cheeks. The coolness of the night breeze chilled their wetness, but she savored the feeling after the years of numbness.

How long she sat there, she did not know, but finally the lights were taken down from the tree limbs. People and lanterns moved away until a light came toward her, and she could hear the voices of her nephews and their families.

Scrubbing the moisture from her face, she moved back into the shadows of the wagon (cocoon) and stretched out. Lily would see to Ruthie.

The girls, purring and round, settled into the hollows of the quilt, their noses buried in their marmalade patterned fur. The little goats? They were wherever Chad had put them.

Chad. What a solid young man he had become. He had fitted himself into the fringe of the family, loosely becoming a part of it, yet knowing he was hired to drive and tend the stock. He was, without doubt, the result of good training, and she hoped she had been a tiny part of it. There were surely many 'Chad's' within this joyful and lively group. Those who were weak and timid would have stayed at home… in the east, or wherever home was. The brave were here, their happy sound still fresh in her ears.

Sleep. Get to sleep. Now that she was alive, there were plans to be made tomorrow. She was fifty-five years old, and she needed her rest. Didn't she?

Sixteen

There were no more dreams that night.

The raucous screeches of the crows in the trees over her head roused Sadie from her sleep. The girls yawned and stretched and resettled onto the quilt, but Sadie heard sounds outside the wagon. There was no Ruthie beside her, but little girls voices, high-pitched and excited, were all around.

Sadie changed into her dress and took her shoes to the buckboard to put them on. A short distance away (on Tommy's lot?) was a plume of smoke and a chatter of voices. The business of breakfast was going on without her. Lily, the morning sleepyhead, was up and about.

Sadie reached in the drawer of her little nightstand, the one with the many small drawers, and took out her notebook. With a sharpened pencil, she wrote, "June 5, 1889. This is a day of decisions. Life brings happiness, and it brings pain, but it also brings the necessity of decisions."

Closing the notebook, she slipped it back into the drawer. It was time to get up and join the family.

"Aunt Sadie!" Ruthie squealed. "You woke up!"

A greeting from Lily. "Good morning, Sadie."

"Did you sleep well?"

Willie's concerned voice. "I looked for you at the party but I didn't see you. Someone said you came back to the wagon, and I was worried you might trip on all those stumps, so I came part way and didn't find you. Seemed like you made it."

Kind and thoughtful Willie. Statements kept coming and apparently no response was required.

"Did you meet a lot of people? The youngens practically went wild."

"We're gonna put up the tent and move you into it today. That'll free up the heavy wagons to bring in the machinery. Chad's gonna help."

"You could look around and see where you'd like the tent to be put, if you want to."

"Aunt Sadie, this girl is Marcie. She has new pigs at her house."

Sadie sighed and looked about her. This new land… it was for young people. But there were older ones here. What was their part in all of this? What would be her part? What did the older birds do when the flock migrated?

She ate oatmeal and biscuits with sausage. Nancy had apparently brought a supply with her. There was milk for the children. Someone had made a deal for a herd of cows that were, at the moment, considered community property. Their mooing in the distance gave a feeling of settledness. She could even hear the oink of the pigs.

Sadie chose a massive oak as shade for her tent.

"Only thing is, you're likely to get acorns droppin' down on you and maybe even a squirrel. This place is alive with squirrels."

There was room in the large tent for her bed with its solid maple panels and for the roomy highboy. Wedged in beside it was her desk and chair. The rocker, of course, and her little night stand beside the bed. It was all there, though there was hardly space to walk around it.

It looked good. Almost civilized. She walked over to the sweating Willie and put her arm around him, and calling Tommy to her, she enclosed him with her other arm.

"Such a pleasure you give me, you'll never know. You're not even my sons, but you take such good care of me. I couldn't be happier with you if you were my own flesh and blood. I just want you to know that."

The young men had no words but stood beside her. Willie sniffed softly, and Tommy lifted his hand to the corner of his eye.

"Well, we…"

Sadie, again. "All right, you youngens. You get on out of here and let me get straightened up. I know you got somethin' important that needs doin.'"

"Yeah, sure. We got'a get on over to Guthrie."

And they were gone.

Sadie took the notebook from the nightstand and, scooping Leopold from the rocker, she sat down. The curves and shapes of the rocker cushions molded themselves comfortably to her back, as they always had, and she wrote:

NEEDS:

1. Old friends. Old enough to remember what I remember.
2. Schoolhouse. There must be at least 25 children between 6 and 12.
3. Much paper. How much paper does it take to write a book?
4. ...

At item number four, she paused, as no further needs came to mind, and she slipped the notebook back into its drawer.

Among the items set out of her wagon was the large bucket containing the damp roots of the garden herbs. It had been a last moment thought as she was preparing to leave Northbend. Sprigs of rosemary, comfrey and peppermint were trying to green up in the dark dampness of the paper around them. Roots of the hollyhock, cannas and rose (a pink Seven Sisters) were trying to grow.

Pale green snippets sprang from the stalks and bulbs, just as they would have back in Northbend, Illinois. Plants were programmed to bloom where they were put, and so, possibly, were people.

Finding a bright spot in the yard, she dug with her small trowel. It was not a good tool to use among the network of tree roots, but she didn't want to bother anyone for a shovel.

Her mind was on the packets of seed for annual flowers that she would have already planted if it had not been for the trip. They would be late, but would still bloom and provide seed for next year.

While she knelt on the ground, the June sun warm on her back, she sensed someone close by. Ruthie? Or…

A shadow passed over the plants in the bucket.

A voice. "I'm thinkin' you need somethin' with a bit more push than that little old trowel. This Oklahoma sod, it's got'a tough mat'a roots…."

Sadie turned and looked up into the face of the grandpa. Eben…what was his last name? It didn't matter.

"I suspect I do, but I didn't…."

"You didn't want to bother the young folks to get it for you. I can understand that. Now I got me a little slim shovel that I don't hardly use no more. If you'd just wait, I'll bring it on over and help you with them holes."

"Oh, you needn't… I can do it..." But she hesitated. Strangers began conversations and offered help. She must get used to it.

"Sure you can, but it'll be easier if I help."

His last words were from a distance, as he hurried away through the tree. Politeness dictated that she wait for the help. Sitting in the ground, she felt the warmness of it through her skirts, and the damp rich smell of it was everywhere.

In minutes he reappeared with the shovel. It was, indeed, a small one, the kind sometimes referred to as a "lady's shovel."

"This'll work good in around them roots. Reckon there's never been a shovel point in this ground since the Good Lord spoke it into being. Now where'd it be you want them holes?"

"Well, I thought along here in a row, just to keep 'em alive till the boys got things goin', and decided where the garden'd be."

"That sounds like a plan."

Small holes appeared in a line, and Sadie carefully spread the roots in the damp soil and tamped them into place with the trowel."I'll have to say, that little shovel does make things easier, especially when someone else is on the handle of it."

Eben chuckled at the weak joke. "Yeah, I wondered why I brought along such a dinky little thing."

"Your wife doesn't get out in the garden?"

There was a pause while several more holes were made. "Didn't bring my wife along. Left 'er in the churchyard."

Sadie's hands stopped as she reached into the bucket. Drawing them back empty, she allowed her eyes to follow the handle of the shovel up past the man's hands and onto his face.

The pleasant smile was gone, and his eyes looked out past the trees. She sat motionless on the ground until he moved again, and another hole appeared.

He cleared his throat. "Been some time ago, but they's times that it don't seem all that long."

Sadie lined up the roots of the peppermint plant at the edge of the hole. The tiny pale green shoots would be popping up in time to make a lot of peppermint tea. Small things helped to make a rounded life, and it would be a dull life without peppermint tea.

Eben again. "Brought lots'a peppermint, I see. So did I. My daughter, that I brought out here with me, she remembered everything from inside the house, but I brought the garden. Got it up several inches high already. Brought a few sprouts from the peach and apple trees, hopin' to keep 'em goin' till I get a place for 'em."

Say something, Sadie. "I know what you mean. I brought hollyhocks and roses, and likely they'll be in the way wherever I put them and hafta be moved."

They moved along side by side, and then the big wooden bucket was empty.

"Miss Sadie?"

She looked up, and a hand was extended to her. What young person would know that she needed a hand to help her stand, after being on her knees for so long? He clasped her dirty hand and held firm while she straightened her knees.

"Thank you."

"Miss Sadie, I'm not knowin' if you're still wore out from the trip, or if you might want to stretch out your legs and look around at the town. I find myself at loose ends, today…."

Loose ends. What a wonderful old expression, and it covered so much. It was clearly an invitation without obligation.

"Eben, I'd love to walk around and get my knees limbered up. And I'm just plain Sadie to my friends."

"Sadie, it is. Now if you'll just walk with me to return this shovel, I'll show you where you can wash your hands. I'd leave the shovel here in case you'd need it agin, but if you need it, then you need me, too. I'm good on the end of a tool."

Eben also lived in a tent, a small one. His big, husky son-in-law was laying the foundation for a cabin. The young man smiled and waved at the introduction but did not pause in his work. Roberta, his daughter, made a polite invitation to tea, but Eben turned her down. Later, perhaps.

The stroll took them down the road, up the east easement of the town, along what would be Main Street, and on to the marked out foundation for the new church.

"Decided to make it like in the mountains. I always liked bay windows along the sides. Seemed to be a necessity with the way the trees grow here. Time they get enough length, they get too big around to be useful."

Next to the churchyard was the grove of trees where the lanterns had been hung last night. Not a sign of a building.

"The mountains, you said. Where in the mountains did you live?"

"Nowhere, really. Just a little place outside of a small town. It was a good place till things happened to make it necessary to leave."

Yes, things had happened in the little place in the mountains. And then it had become necessary to leave. For him and also for her. Recognition was settling gently in her memory, and her breath became short with excitement.

Eben again. "But this is a good place. I wanted my daughter in a new place. It was gettin' to where she was needin' a new start."

Sadie nodded in acknowledgement. Yes, it was a good place. Willie and Tommy were needing a new start.

Eben again. "You're not talkin.' Am I getting' you too tired?"

"Oh, no. I was just thinkin' while you were talkin'. The mountains were a good place for a child, but I'm sure this place will be just as good... perhaps even better."

"You came from the mountains? I thought you were from Illinois...?"

"That was later. Circumstances took me from my home when I was very young. Ten years old, actually. I remember a mountain schoolhouse and a lot of the names from there. There was a boy at the school they called Eben."

"Really? I haven't ever met anyone with my name. Where was that school?"

"You wouldn't know it. It was just a mountain school in Tennessee, and the closest place with a name was Hilltop."

Eben sighed a long sigh and looked out in the distance.

"Hilltop, Tennessee, northeast of Memphis. Had a church and a big harness shop on the main street. Had a little store where peppermint sticks and licorice ropes could be bought, if one had a penny."

Sadie turned to look at the man, his mind seeing a distant place.

With misty eyes, he said. "And the church. 'Course it wouldn't'a been there when you were ten. And how is your brother, William?"

Sadie watched his eyes fill, and his chin quiver. "My brother's fine, Eben. Tommy and Willie are his little boys. You're Eben Carlile."

The enormity of it all was too much to bear, and the man and woman sat down on the logs of the church foundation.Words would come later, but for now it was enough to stare at each other, each reliving a picture from the past.

The boy in the patched overalls, doing his sums on the blackboard, fishing in the stream with William, sharing a precious licorice whip that made their teeth black when they chewed it.

The girl with the light brown wavy hair that would not stay in the braid. The missing teeth in the freckled face. The way she could read the words in the McGuffey reader with no hesitation.

The boy who lived up the hill... the girl from the bench farm on the side of the hill.

The boy who was so brave he could smile when his knee was skinned and bleeding, and the girl who had disappeared from sight and no one knew where she had gone. There was the funeral and then the empty McClure house.

"Sadie? They were calling you "Miss" Sadie. Surely, there was....?"

"Yes, and too quickly I left him in the churchyard."

"No... children...?"

A short pause. "No... no children. But William's wife was in poor health, and he needed me to help with his...."

Eben nodded. "I knew you would be special. Tommy could hardly wait for you to get here."

There were many things Sadie could have said at this point. Yes, she was special, but now Tommy had Nancy... the darling girl who was pregnant with his next child. Surely, he loved his aunt, but....

She needed to move onto a safer subject. This was not a time for the strange tears that often surprised her.

"Eben, the schoolhouse. How could a body get it started?"

"You mean the labor of it? It could take a while. All the young fellows, they got all on their plate that they can say grace over, and more. And money. Most of 'em used what all they had to get here. And another thing. Buildin' material is scarce as hen's teeth."

"No lumber to buy? For no amount'a money?"

"Not yet. Got a sawmill down the road, and they're lettin' everyone have lumber for a outhouse and a shed to keep their plunder dry. Then they don't get no more lumber till everyone gets some. Seems fair, but I don't see getting' no dimension lumber till fall, and then it'll cost a pretty penny."

Sadie's mind drew up the picture of the notebook notation.

1. Lumber
2. Schoolhouse. There must be at least 25 children between 6 and 12.
3.

"Eben, how'd a person get in line for lumber?"

"Well, you'd need to get on the list...."

Two little girls came racing by, stopping suddenly at the edge of the trees.

"There they are. Both in the same place."

"We was lookin' for you. Mama said maybe you got lost, or somethin'."

"And Bertie said see where you were, Big Papa. I see you're here. You ain't lost. Let's go, Ruthie."

Suddenly as they had come, they were gone.

"Guess we could wander on back. Wouldn't want the youngens to be concerned about us, and we got lots'a time to talk…."

"And lots to say. That lumber, would you…."

"I'll check on it."

Sadie settled into the comfortable curves of the rocker and moved back and forth. The lumps and clumps of the ground made a bumpy motion. From the third drawer of the nightstand, Sadie drew out the bulging stocking and removed $60.00.

Chad should be paid and released.

Seventeen

It was time for the evening meal, and Sadie presented herself to help but when she looked for something to do, there was nothing. Lily and Nancy had planned together and combined their skills. The meal appeared without any help from her.

When evening came, Ruthie no longer occupied her bed. She was tucked in with Frankie and made no complaint.

The maple bed in the tent seemed to Sadie to be impossibly large and soft, and when she turned over in her sleep, the movement woke her up. The bed belonged to another life… the caterpillar life she had led for so many years.

A caterpillar. Crawling along, attentive to only what was in front of her and closing herself off from the world. The maple bed belonged in her room in Northbend. She would, of course, get used to it again, as one gets used to anything new.

The hard wagon bed of the cocoon had become appropriate. Hard, flat, and unyielding, spread over her boxes of books. It had been appropriate for the weeks of her change from caterpillar to butterfly. She had been passed from her mother to tutors, to the husband, and then her brother. Finally to Willie.

The resolve was firm in her mind. She would be passed no more.

The cocoon life ended as the Conestoga pulled by the black horses had entered the town of Prosper. She was set free by the songs and laughter of the party, and now she was a different person.

What would that person do? Whatever was done must be done quickly, before Willie tucked her back into his life again. Sweet, caring and adorable Willie. He would lovingly care for her as he would have cared for the mother he no longer had, but she must move quickly. She must escape while she still could.

One thing she knew already. She would buy the lumber for the schoolhouse as soon as it was available. Eben would see to it. A place must be built for the schoolteacher, and there was a lot of room to do it. Such a far-thinking thing for the town to do, setting aside the place for the school and the church.

She had not been here to be a part of that, but the schoolhouse, now that was one thing she could do. She could furnish the cash.

Perhaps they had a teacher in mind, and that was good. Perhaps they would need someone until that teacher came, and that was also good, and she would teach, if needed, but only until no longer needed.

For this new life, teaching was no longer enough. Teaching in the school was a part of her old life, and it contained no new challenge. A teacher should be charged and fired from within with zeal, and she had no more fire for that purpose.

Twenty-four hours ago, she would have turned her thoughts toward the city of Guthrie… new, noisy, bold and boisterous. Somewhere in that city would be a place for her. But that was twenty-four hours ago.

The thought for tonight was that she would buy her own lot, separate from her nephews, and live her own life. It would be hard but no harder than the life in the wagon had been. Eben would know what was available.

Finally, she slept.

It was midmorning of the next day that Sadie walked the row of new plants she had set yesterday. Droopy, they were, needing water. Taking the wooden bucket to the well, she drew water and would have carried it to the plants, but the strong, calloused hand of Chad picked it up.

"Where you wantin' it to go, Miss Sadie?"

"Over here, Chad. I need to water my plants, but first I want to pay you."

"There ain't no hurry, Miss Sadie."

"But it's yours, and you need to take it. You may be wanting to head on back."

"Miss Sadie?"

"Yes?"

"You're not really set up good, are you?"

"Uh… well… I'm not sure what you mean." Did he consider her to be a lifetime job?

"I mean, you ain't in no solid house, yet."

"No, but that'll be taken care of."

"Well, you might need… me?" His eyes pled to be understood.

"I'm fine, Chad. You did a wonderful job, and your parents can be very proud of you. You did everything I wanted you to do, and more, and I thank you very much."

"But you ain't really set up, like you'll be later."

"Well, no, but that's no reason…." Her voice trailed away searching for words that would reassure him.

But the young man interrupted, "Cause my ma and pa both said to me that I wasn't to leave here till you was set up safe and proper, like a lady should be. And I was thinkin,' that'd likely not be till late fall, or more likely in the spring. I know I been paid off, and all, but I can do things for you on my own."

Sadie's thoughts might be slow, but they finally got there.

"Chad, you're wantin' to hang around here and get in on the excitement, aren't you? Things going on… pretty girls everywhere. Well, you know, Chad, it could very well be spring before I get really set up, and if you need me to write to your ma and pa to that effect, I can do it. Chances are, I'll need more hired help, time and again."

A wide smile creased Chad's sunburned face. "Thank you, Miss Sadie! I can do whatever you want. I'm gonna be gone for a little while, though, but I'll do what you want quick as I get back."

"Gone? Do you mind tellin' me where you'll be going?"

"Oh, no, Miss Sadie." Excitement hurried his words and widened his smile. "There's these two fellows that come down with the town? They dig wells, you see, and they got so much to do, they say they can use hired help for a year, maybe more. On top'a that, they heard how I took care'a you and your wagons and horses, they want me to go up to Nebraska and bring back their families. They say they ain't got the time to do it, themselves, and they'll pay me for both ways."

Sadie looked into the happy face. Old Charlie Connelly would be proud of his grand nephew. The young man was as ambitious and enterprising as the old man himself.

"And, Miss Sadie, I'll write to my ma and pa, but if you'd send off a letter, too, it'd ease their minds. They set a great store by you and the way you taught me in school. Likely not the easiest thing you ever did."

Sadie could only smile at his eager enthusiasm. "I'll do that, Chad."

"And there's a nuther thing, Miss Sadie."

"What is that?"

"Them big heavy wagons. Them fellows, name'a Hamp and Bart Baker, they're brothers. Well, they asked me did you aim to keep both'a the wagons, cause they're short'a somethin' strong to haul their machinery in. They was hopin' you'd set a price on a wagon and the team to pull it."

Sadie nodded with understanding. Hmmm, well, why not? Of course, she would first make sure Willie or Tommy didn't need it.

"I'll think about it Chad. I'll have an answer tomorrow. You come see me, and I'll pay you then."

"Sure thing, Miss Sadie." And he was gone.

Sadie watched his long legs carry him away into the trees and she felt a pang of sadness for his parents. If they ever saw him again, it would be only on a visit, and they would never, really, know what gift they had given to the new land of the territory.

She dipped a cup into the water and poured it on the roots of the drooping plants. The Oklahoma sun in June was bright and hot, and she felt the sweat beads on her forehead. She moved into the shade of a tree where the breeze was cool.

She had more flowers to plant, and she would need the shovel again. Now, where was Eden's house? Which direction had they gone yesterday? There were trees everywhere, and all the directions all looked alike. Maybe this way, she decided, she started out.

Eben saw her coming. "You need the shovel, don't you?"

Sadie's mind saw the boy in the cutoff overalls with hair flopping over his forehead. The words formed in her mouth, "What

I need is you." Then startled at the sound of her words, she amended, "I need help getting' some seeds in the ground."

"I'll get the shovel," and he walked toward a small shed.

"Sadie," she told herself. "You told the truth. Your mouth sneaked the truth right past your brain. You need this man, and he needs you."

As he came toward her, she pushed the frightening words from her mind. Whatever would he think of her, talking bold that way? What did they know of each other, except a few years as children? Watch your words, Miss Sadie!

As Eben dug the shovel into the rich soil, he commented. "Good sized tent you got there. Likely big enough to get stretched out in, after bein' cramped up in the wagon so long."

Sadie nodded. "It's good. No room for my books, though."

"You got lots'a books?"

"Fair amount. Around sixty, at last count. Some I got on the way and haven't really got to read."

"That's a good amount. Readin's somethin' I miss. Didn't do much for years, bein' busy most'a the time. Lately, though…" and his words trailed off, meaningfully.

"Now, Eben, quick as I figure how to get these books in the bookcase where they can be seen, I'll want you to look 'em over and take what you want. Likely, we'd like the same kind'a readin'."

"You needin' a place to live? I mean… your nephews, have they…?"

"We've not got so far as that on our talkin'."

"Now, Sadie, I had no business askin' that. It's none'a my…"

"Sure it's your business. I had it in my mind to ask you how to go about gettin' a spot'a this ground. I need to start thinkin'a what I'm gonna do. There's another thing. You know a couple'a fellows named Baker?"

"Hamp and Bart? Sure. They're the fellows that dug all the wells around here. I hear tell they're busier'n a cranberry merchant in the fall."

"Well diggin', huh? Seems they offered a job to that young fellow that drove for me. What'd you think?"

"It'd be a good deal. Everybody wants a well, first thing right off. Good business for a young fella' to be in."

"They want'a buy one'a my wagons, too."

"Really? You'll want'a charge plenty. You got good strong wagons, and they got good money a'comin' in."

"So, about that spot'a land...."

"You mean you're wantin' a buildin' place, just for you. Like a cabin, or somethin'?"

Sadie nodded. "I got'a put some thought to it. This tent'll be cold, come winter." Her smile added humor, but he got the point.

"Let me think on it a while. I hear some new land is openin' up to smaller lots, and there might be another place. Let me think on it."

That point made, Sadie moved on to other topics. The Eben she remembered would follow through to the best of his ability. It may not be immediate, but, for a fact, he would get there. She could have, of course, looked into the matter herself, but it often paid to have a partner.

Sadie had been in Prosper for a week. The bookbinding equipment had come and was set up in the Willie's other large tent. Willie and Tommy were bent over the pages of instructions as they worked to get it put together.

Both nephews still lived in the wagons. Maybe they would get lumber for a house before the summer was over, and if they did, who would build it? But they didn't ask her, so she tried to look away. It was often good for young people to go through hard times. At least, it seldom inflicted permanent damage

From the second drawer of her nightstand, she took the notebook titled, The Promised Land. She made notes to be expanded later. Plants (they must be brought along) Wells (to be dug) Work everywhere and the young men were busy from daylight to dark. School nonexistent (children were everywhere)

Her plans began to come together. When she actually started the book, she would pick up a family from the east. Tennessee? Likely!

There would be children... a girl about ten years old. That was a good age for wondering about things. Yes, the book would be written, and Willie and Tommy would have their equipment put together in time to print it. She had money to pay for it, and it would be their first book.

She put the notebook away and blew out her oil lamp. The soft bed moved and jiggled alarmingly, but she would get used to it again. Her thoughts whirled around in her head and came again to the same place.

Eben. He had commented that he knew a "Miss" Sadie was coming. He had come to her at the party, that first night. He helped with her planting. He was interested in her books. And maybe most important of all, he was old enough to remember the same things she did, and they had done some of them together. That was certainly a desirable attribute in a friend.

She smiled into the dark as she remembered catching the tiny spring crawdads and making them close their pinchers on a string. They could often get a dozen or more of them hanging by their claws before the first ones dropped off.

Then there were the persimmons. They looked so sweet and juicy, but were puckery with acid until the first frost. The children knew what would happen if they tried to eat them, looking so much like tiny peaches, as they did. The temptation, however, was irresistible. Then they tried to whistle with their puckery mouths. The experience always ended with gales of exuberant laughter.

Then there were the persimmon trees. They grew in groves, tall, slender and springy and if you were big enough and the tree was small enough, you could pull the top over and hold to top limbs and the tree would bounce you up and down. Great fun.

But, of course, if you were too light, the tree would try to straighten up, and it left you hanging high off the ground. It was then you hoped for a friend to add his weight to the tree and bring it down to the ground by pulling on your feet. It was a marvelously fun way to spend an afternoon!

And the leaves. As they fell, they floated down to the valleys and made heaps many feet deep. Hiding in the leaves and searching for each other was great excitement.

And caves. There were always rock ledges to be dug under them to make hidey holes. What child can resist the lure of a hidey hole?

Eben was there. William and young Sadie were there. A million memories were there, and certainly they would fill a multitude of books.

Eighteen

The log walls of the church rose steadily, accomplished with precious labor stolen from each homestead. A lumber allotment provided the roof decking, and Eben was busy splitting shingles, hacking them from the numerous Oklahoma Red Cedars.

Willie and Tommy worked from dawn until late, and then gathered around the cook fire and ate whatever was served, their faces creased with frowns of concern. They ate hurriedly and returned to the tent, continuing to work by lantern light.

It was far after dark one night when a ka-clank, ka-clank sound came from the tent. Again, ka-clank. A pause, a silence, and then a whoop of glee. Sadie left her tent, and Lily and Nancy, carrying a lantern, ran ahead of her, sober with concern.

Like two small boys, Willie and Tommy danced around the pile of metal and grease, and a fair amount of spilled ink. Tommy triumphantly waved a sheet of yellow paper, clearly printed with an announcement of a sample sale.

The bold black letters were clear and bright, and the two ink-stained, work weary faces were wreathed with excitement. Two small boys in an ice cream store in August could not have registered that much excitement.

"It works!" Willie's face was amazed at the wonder of it.

"We did it! Now we got'a make more samples." Tommy's agile brain projected to the next requirement.

"Let's set up another one and print some copies." Cautious Willie, wanting to be sure before they went ahead.

Abject relief showed on the faces of Lily and Nancy.

"Finally workin', huh?"

"You quittin' for the night?"

"Shucks, no! We got'a make up samples. I'm headin' out for Guthrie come daylight." Tommy was fairly dancing with eagerness. How could prospective customers resist his enthusiasm? He would be a wondrous success at selling.

"Yeah, it'll take all night. You girls go on to sleep. We got'a get this done." Willie, thinking ahead and making plans. Willie, ready to back up his brother's enthusiasm with concrete samples.

Sadie sighed deeply and with great relief. *William, if you could only see your boys this instant!*

She had become concerned, trying to tell herself it was no business of hers that it was taking so long. Yet, of course, it was. Willie and Tommy were her's, sons of her heart if not her body, so what affected them was definitely her business.

She turned back to the shelter of her tent and went to sleep to the magical sound of the ka-clank, ka-clank of the wheel being turned and the inky print blocks being pressed against the paper.

Morning came, and when she finally left her tent, Tommy had been long gone. A jubilant Willie sorted among his type blocks, ink and paper, getting ready for the business Tommy would surely bring home.

Thank you, Lord.

Sadie, in her comfortable life, had not often felt the need to plead for Help from on high, but from the time she had ridden out of St. Louis, she had seen many times when her own strength seemed to need a bit of bolstering. There seemed to be nothing like a pressing need to force one look up, hoping for help from a Higher Power.

The brochure printing could now be done. Bookbinding would be next, and after that, could typesetting be far behind? From drawer number two, she took out the notebook. It was time for notes to refresh her memory.

She made her notes. Small things were important. (Lily and Nancy had giggled like young girls as they had returned from the blackberry thicket with overflowing saucepans full of the juicy fruit.) The only cost had been precious time, a few scratches and various stains on clothes and fingers. A small price to pay, certainly!

Self-reliance was absolutely necessary. (In St. Louis, or even Springfield, Willie would certainly have called for expert and experienced help in assembling his equipment. He was not particularly mechanically minded when it came to putting things together, but between them, he and Tommy had succeeded. A wonderful boost of confidencs for whatever lay ahead.)

Church. (Time and skills, so badly needed at each homestead, were freely given so the walls would continue to rise.)

Basic skills were valuable. (Eben aimed his hatchet at the cedar chunk, flaking shingles with each stroke. Young men watched and learned. Skills were passed on.)

Horses were essential. (No place was close enough to get there without them.)

Slipping the notebook back into the drawer, Sadie stepped out to her impromptu garden. It looked good.

She strolled back through the trees toward the schoolyard, where there was no schoolhouse. Someday the state would provide a school, but that might be years away. The Unassigned Lands, filling suddenly as they had, created an urgent need for many schoolhouses, but the state would not have to be concerned about a school in the lovely Redbud Valley.

Sitting on a flat rock, she looked about her. In her mind, she could see the school, its shingled roof, sidewalls lined with windows, and a bell tower to call the children in to study.

Eben, with his persuasive powers, had successfully negotiated enough lumber to complete the school, also a cabin for the teacher. They did not feel it was necessary to mention it to anyone else how it was done. There would be time enough when the actual lumber was available. Often, one learned tricks along with their years, and he had been successful.

The promise of the lumber was early September. Classes might need to be started under the shade of the many trees.

School under the trees! That would go well in the book.

Nineteen

It was time to go back to the tent. It was late afternoon, and there might be something for her to do, though the family seemed to be doing well without her. She walked into the clearing of the camp just as Tommy rode in, his tired horse heaving for breath.

Sadie, herself was the nearest person to him as he leaped from the horse. In his exuberance, he wrapped his arms around her, practically lifting her off her feet.

"It worked, Aunt Sadie! We got orders and more orders! We're gonna be busy for a month! Only thing to hold us up is paper, and I ordered more to come in on the train!"

He loosed his breathless hug on and shouted, "Hey, everyone! We're in business!"

Willie heard, and his and total relief made him lower his tired body to the high stool and hang his ink-stained arms toward the Oklahoma soil. Only the small smile (a 'finally we made it' kind of smile) indicated that he had heard his brother's victory yell.

The McClure's had their own party. Blackberry cobbler, fresh greens, and the last of Nancy's canned sausages made into a gravy with their share of the community milk. Sadie sat in the shadows and basked in the glow of their happiness. Another note for her book.

Happiness. It must be enjoyed for its own sake, and don't think too far ahead. Parties were important. They could become the punctuation of their otherwise work-weary life.

Frankie chased the excited Teejay, letting the younger boy outrun him. Then he let Teejay catch him. A small grown-up, give and take step for the somewhat spoiled Frankie.

The two young families were laughing and happy. Time must be taken away from the business to build a house of some kind for the equipment, but that was tomorrow's problem.

Twenty

The church came together, piece by piece, and finally the windows were in, except for the one that wasn't shipped. It was on the next Saturday that a family came into the town, looking for a place to camp over the weekend. Eben's friend, Clyde Kendall, was quick to offer his son's land as a stopover.

The transient family settled in quietly, but on mid-morning of the next day, Sunday, strains of music (accordion?) floated through the trees. Sadie left her tent to hear it better and saw this one and that one also attracted by the sound. They were gathering under the trees to hear better.

Old songs. Songs from the little church in the Tennessee mountains. Songs written when the people were in the old country, with ancient, melodious tunes. Songs with softness and feeling.

The keys of the instrument set the notes, and the bellows expanded the tones into exquisite sweetness, as thin and sweet as spun sugar cake frosting. The sound seemed to float among the groves and clumps of redbud and blackjack oak, rounding them out better than the pipes in a cathedral organ. Or perhaps it was just that it was so unexpected in this place.

As they drew closer, they saw the young lady who made the music, lovely with her pink and white skin, and her black, black hair piled in attractive rolls about her head. She fingered the keys with practiced confidence and smiled at the children gathered around her.

Some of the children, Sadie could recognize, but others were new. Little girls with creamy strawberry-blossom complexions and cheeks, the delicate shade of the flower buds on her Seven Sisters rosebush. Little girls with red-gold curls clustered about their heads and pretty, lace-trimmed "Sunday" dresses.

The children, those she knew and the newcomers, gathered around the musician and sang, and Sadie felt the tears forming in her eyes from the sweetness of the sound. She knew she was not alone, and turned to smile at Eben.

After the concert, a young man, pale-skinned with unruly black hair, invited everyone to come closer and join his family in their Sunday service. Then he began to talk. His voice had the solid force of one who was confident of his words.

He read words from a worn Bible and then finished with a story about the young shepherd, David, who pleased God so well that he was promised that he and his descendants would always occupy a throne.

Eben and the other men were quick to offer the pulpit of their new church to this young man, who was obviously a preacher, if he would stay over for an evening service.

There was also the interesting fact that this preacher had a window, a fancy stained glass one that just fit the last window opening of the new church. The wonder of it was in every conversation for days.

The young minister and his family moved onto the lot behind the church, and the whole town breathed a sigh of relief at the completeness his arrival made.

More notes for the book. Clearly, a Higher Power was in control of this place.

Twenty-One

It was now the middle of June, and Sadie knew it was time to solidify her own plans. She had spent wakeful nights in thought, but now it was the time for action. A bird may consider the options, but eventually it must fly… or die.

"The land, Eben. Tell me about what you've found, and I want to talk with you about a buggy. With Clyde Kendall's boys buying one of my wagons, and the well diggers taking the other one, I find myself without means of transportation."

"You needin' to go somewhere?" He was quick to offer, as she had known he would.

Sadie nodded. "I'm thinkin' on a trip in to the city. Maybe…" At times it was best to leave one's options open.

"Guthrie?" Eben suggested. "There's not much to be had there. Wouldn't hurt to go and look around a mite, though. Have to admit, there's quiet a lot to see."

And Sadie reiterated her request. "And that's why I'll be needin' a buggy. A small one, of course, and there'll be a time I'll need a pony."

Eben nodded. "I can hitch up my buggy and take you where you want to go. I'd like a time to get away, myself, bein' so tied up with the finishin' of the church. When would you be wantin'…?"

"Soon. I got things to talk to you about. Seems my nephews got a full plate, gettin' their business started. They weren't quite expectin' the success to happen right off."

The older man nodded. "I got time, Sadie. We can go when you want to. Maybe tomorrow?"

"That'd be good, Eben." At her age, there was no time to waste with conventions and the thoughts people may have had about decorum.

It was during the evening meal that Sadie mentioned her plans. "So's you'll know ahead'a time, I want'a say I'm gonna be takin' a little trip tomorrow. Likely be leavin' early and might not be back till late."

"A trip? Someplace you're needin' to go?" Willie was quick to feel his responsibility for her.

"Just goin' into the city."

Willie looked quickly at Tommy, who was quick with the right words.

"Well, now, you know, I'll be goin' in after the print paper that's comin' in on the Santa Fe. Won't be goin' till the day after tomorrow, but I'd be glad to have you ride along, and we…."

Sadie felt the need to stop Tommy's hesitant words. "No, Tommy. I thank you kindly, but I wasn't askin' for nothin.' I was tellin' you that I was goin' tomorrow, and I was ridin' along with Eben Carlile from down the road. You know him… the fellow who loaned me his shovel?"

Forks moved between plates and mouths, and nothing was said for a minute.

"Uh, Sadie? You just been here two weeks, and…."

Sadie cut in. "That's right, and ain't it a handy thing, him makin' a trip, just when I needed a way to go. Worked out about perfect, I'd say." She smiled happily at her family. Words that might cause concern must not be spoken unless they were needed. When it was time to fly, birds need not wait until the day after tomorrow or to take away precious time from their busy nephews.

More silence and finally the meal was over. Sadie took her teacup to her tent and left the family to sort sense out of her words.

Tommy, first. "Well, for what it means, old Eben Carlile, he's a good fellow and a big help. Can't really nothin' happen to her, bein' with him."

"Yeah, but she…" Tommy wasn't sure, and something just didn't seem right. She should have taken him up on his offer, even though his time was… Well, she had certainly had time for him when he was little, so it was only right that he…?

Now Lily. "You know, we ain't seen too much'a her lately, come to think on it. She's likely tired'a the inside'a that tent."

Willie felt concern and a little guilt. "Don't know what else we could'a done, bein' busy. Once we get the business a'goin'…."

Tommy's voice filled in. "And get a place to live…."

Willie, again. "I still say, can't much happen to 'er. Everybody in the territory is too busy and too tired to stir up mischief. Even old Eben, the way he's been tied up with the church buildin'…"

"Still, it seems strange…"

Lily had been silent, contemplating the situation. "Willie, you remember old Charlie Connelly and how we got to thinkin' things was one way, and you remember how wrong we were?"

Willie nodded, and Tommy and Nancy looked from one to the other, puzzled.

Willie explained, "There was a day, just before we left Illinois, that old Charlie Connelly, a storekeeper in Northbend, come by in his buggy and took Sadie out for the whole day. Lily and me, we got to thinkin' maybe old Charlie was finally gettin' hisself led to the alter, after all these years. We were wrong. Sadie was just conductin' a bit of business on her own, namely, hirin' wagons and horses, and a driver to bring 'er here."

Lily nodded. "Sure surprised us."

Tommy narrowed his eyes thoughtfully. "Now, what kind'a business would she be conductin' here?"

"You think she might be thinkin' on movin' into the city?"

"Never thought'a that. Could be."

Willie, again. "She gettin' tired'a the tent, likely. I was afraid'a this. That was why I was thinkin' to bring 'er in on the train, after we got things settled and more comfortable for her. You know, she's fifty five years old, and…."

Now, Lily. "But she made the trip better'n I did, and no one's heard a word'a complaint out'a her."

Again there was a short silence, and Lily continued, "But I'm a'sayin' one thing. If she's got it in her head to move into Guthrie, there ain't nothin' you two can say that'll change her mind. She's stubborner'n than the two'a you put together."

Then Tommy, still frowning. "I didn't know there was a place to stay in Guthrie. What I saw was packin' crates and cardboard boxes. Even the tents there wasn't as good as the one she's got."

Then Willie. "Well, if it comes to that, Tommy and me can keep check on her, goin' in town as often as we're gonna have to."

A pause, and then Lily. "Well, she's not my aunt, and I ain't rightly got no say in what goes, but I'll just remind everyone of you that I've spent more actual time, as a grownup, with her, than any of you. My best words'd be for us to go to bed and get some sleep, and when she comes back home from Guthrie… and if she wants to tell us… we'll know why it was she wanted to go to the city."

Then Nancy. "I put my vote with Lily. I've hardly known her more'n a week, but it seems to me when she wants you boys to worry about her, she'll tell you. Till then, you got worries enough on your own to keep you busy."

Twenty-Two

Faced with such logic, the family disbanded to their separate beds, and Sadie lay in her tent on the strangely soft and jiggly bed and contemplated her next moves.

In nature, after the progression from caterpillar to cocoon, another metamorphous must follow. The butterfly.

Sadie had never in her life felt such a freedom from concern as she did at this moment. She could close her eyes and feel that she was hearing the beautiful strains of music from the accordion from deep within her head. Maybe she was. The church was hardly more than an eighth of a mile away....

The butterfly... there must be a pause, of course. The instant the creature broke through the crust of the cocoon, it did not stretch its crumbled and wrinkled wings and soar away on a breeze. Cramped as it had been, there were bends and creases that must be exercised and stretched with the newly made blood supply. Wings that had never touched the air must now be drenched and overflowed in it.

All of this took time. As she lay on the softness of her retrieved bed, the thoughts that flowed over her felt like the air, and she thought she felt strength coming into her hands... feet... legs... Her inactivity was part of her exercise as though she must wait for her body, and the rest of the world to catch up with the soaring within her own head.

Back to her plans.

A bird, as it headed south or went about its nest building, and a butterfly, moving from flower to flower, what, really, was the great difference? They were both in control because of their wings. They knew what they wanted, and they proceed to go after it.

Sadie knew what she wanted. All her life, she had waited for things to come to her, but now, finally, she would go after what she wanted. The new Sadie had no time to wait.

What would she tell Eben that she wanted to get in the city? Maybe she'd just look around, and see where the nephews business would come from. That was it, she just wanted to look around.So then, having answered her own question, she slept.

It was early when Eben Carlile hitched his filly, Dancer, to the buggy. She sidled and tossed her head, prancing excitedly and lifting her shapely hooves. Then she finally settled into pulling straight ahead. She had not been named Dancer for no reason.

Twenty-Three

Sadie was ready to go. A white lace bonnet crowned her head, revealing only the silvery fringe of her waves.Her dress was charcoal gray with white polka dots, and the skirt of it swung jauntily above the shiny black buttons of her soft leather dress shoes.

With a smile that deepened the dimple embedded in the delicate wrinkles of her chin, she tossed a shawl of brilliant blue over her shoulders and picked up her black leather purse.

She walked beside Eben to his buggy and allowed him to hand her up to the bench seat. Glancing back toward her tent, she saw Lily and Nancy staring in her direction. Lifting her hand, she fluttered her blue lace handkerchief in a cheery farewell and turned her face toward the backside of the horse.

Eben circled around the buggy and climbed in beside her. Tapping the reins on Dancer's rump, he clicked her into motion. As she pulled the buggy out of sight, Lily and Nancy looked at each other, and neither had words of comment. This would take some thinking about.

A half a mile down the rough trail, Eben turned to Sadie. "You look totally lovely, my dear."

Sadie turned toward him in time to see the fleeting redness of a blush pass over his face. It had been a long time since he had used those words. She answered his compliment with a smile.

Another half a mile. "I wasn't sure about what'd be able to be bought to eat, so I had my Bertie make up a lunch basket. Fried squirrel, potato salad, and cinnamon buns. Thought it might come in handy."

"Sounds like a picnic. I love picnics."

The buggy rolled along, past the growing homesteads she had seen two weeks earlier as she drove in behind the team of monster black horses. At that time she had been wearing one of her black dresses and black knit shawl. The dark, serviceable bonnet had shielded her from the sun. She had still been in her cocoon.

After the heaviness of the wagon, the lightness of the buggy reminded her of butterfly wings. The cool breeze of the June morning fanned her cheeks and encouraged her to be brave.

"Eben, I'm thinkin' I'd mostly like to just drive. I don't even have to go to the city. I'm thinkin' I don't really want to."

"You don't? You're not needin' to look for somethin' to buy? 'Cause, if you're not…" He hesitated, his bravery faltering.

"What…? She wanted to encourage him.

He continued, "If you're not, then we can just go here or there. It's a good day for talkin.' It's a good thing to have someone to talk to about other times. My lass, she's a good girl, and there ain't none better. The only thing is, I remember what she remembers, but she don't remember what I remember."

Sadie nodded, encouragingly.

He continued. "That's natural though. And she'd got her Dan. He's a fine young man… Their memories match."

"I know. William and I, we lived for a while together, but we were both in the pain of our losses and didn't have much to say. Then William, he headed out to change his life."

"Found someone, did he?"

"He did and moved away to be with her."

"That was good."

"But I didn't.

"You…uh…?"

"I said, I didn't do nothin' to change. Willie came home and brought his sweet wife. I stayed. Things just moved on."

Eben nodded. "I know."

"Folks hadn't ought to do that. There isn't a good place to stop, unless you're ready to say your life is over."

A pause, and Eden sighed. "But change… it's hard to hold onto. The young ones, it's easier for them 'cause it's their world."

Sadie nodded, knowing the thoughts behind his words. Eben understood. He knew she must have similar thoughts.

A small stream crossed the road, and Dancer paused and lowered her head to drink. Margarette daisies grew on the bank of the stream and swayed in the breeze, bowing beneath the weight of a bumble bee, and bouncing back when the bee flew away.

Blue-pagoda Monarda plants lined the road, attracting a flock of miniature yellow butterflies. A scissortail flycatcher swooped into the flock of butterflies, beak opened wide. The disturbed air of its wake disbursed the golden wings in all directions.

Dancer was satisfied with the water and lifted her head, drooling streams from her chin. Eben left her to her own decision, and finally she stepped her dainty hooves out of the water and back onto the road.

Eben. "Sadie, when I realized who you were, it brought me a pleasure like I hadn't had in years. It was like just seein' you reminded me that what I remembered was real and actual, and not a dream I was gonna wake up from."

Sadie nodded, knowingly. "Eben, how come you to make this trip?"

"It was the wee lassie. The coal mine took my sons, and the Dougherty's would'a took my son's lassie if I'd'a stayed."

"Dougherty's! I remember…."

"Then you know… why…"

"I know."

"We made a promise to her ma, and this was the only way to keep it that I could see. So we headed out in the dark'a the night, leavin' a blind trail to hold 'em off till we got away."

"You did good."

"Strange ain't it. Folks get pushed around by things. The coal mine made me leave the hills, and for you it was the sawmill."

"Yeah, folks tend to wait till somethin' outside'a themselves moves 'em… on…"

There were a lot of long silences. Some shared memories were too painful for words, and others were so strong, they did not require words.

Then the warm June sun was overhead, and Eben pulled the buggy aside and under a large oak tree.

"We can eat in the buggy, or under the tree, which would you…."

"The buggy's fine. Not so many bugs."

"My thoughts, too." He relaxed the reins, and Dancer turned her head looking around at the meadow. A fat doe stepped from a grove of sumac, and a pair of fawns shyly followed her. They picked at this and that, nibbling with their dainty noses and then moved out of sight.

"Your Bertie packs a good lunch."

"Pretty much. She's took good care'a me since…" More memories just too painful for the bright light of the June sun.

"I know. My Willie, he's the same way. A blood son couldn't'a done better." She hoped her words said it all.

Eben was not ready to let it go. "But I keep thinkin,' over the past week or so, it's like… Well, I keep on thinkin.'"

Sadie nodded and waited. They had a lot of time.

"This new place, it gives me new thoughts. It seems like…."

Still, Sadie forced herself to wait, picking small flaky, sugary strips from the cinnamon bun. They were so delicate they melted on her tongue.

"More times than not, I think it'd be good…." What made words so hard to say?

Dancer became restless and pulled the buggy a few feet forward to get a better look at something.

"Sadie, when I talked with you at the party, that first night…."

Eben turned to look at Sadie then looked back toward the meadow.

Sadie finished the cinnamon bun and cleaned her fingers on the damp napkin Eben's Bertie had thoughtfully included in the basket.

Eben sighed, and turned back to Sadie. He opened his mouth, but nothing came out. She could see he needed help.

"Eben?"

He closed his mouth and turned his attention to her.

"You remember that day we raced down the hill to the crawdad stream, and when we ran under the thorny locust trees, you stepped on that long thorn? And it stuck in the back'a your heel?"

Her words tweaked at his memory, and he smiled slightly, shaking his head. "Them thorns. Some of 'em was two inches long as I seem to recall."

Sadie smiled and nodded. "That'n was. You remember how it broke off in your heel, and we stopped playin' to let you pull it out. And you couldn't twist your heel around far enough to get at it."

Eben nodded, smiling a small smile, reliving the incident.

Sadie continued. "Them thorns hurt like bein' cut with a knife, but you didn't cry nor nothin.' You worked at it, but couldn't get at it, and William, he couldn't help. He didn't never have no fingernails, chewin' 'em like he always did."

Eben nodded again.

"Well, it was then that you needed me to help. You held out your heel, and I grabbed onto that thorn and pulled. The blood came out behind it, but you didn't act like it hurt at all."

Eben waited. He sensed that Sadie was not through talking.

"Well, that was a time you needed me, and I was able to help you. It's been a few years, but I think you're needin' me agin."

"Needin'…?"

"You're havin' trouble with somethin' you want'a say, and you can't quite get out the words. I can help you."

"Well, I..."

"Eben, it only makes sense for you and me to get married. It'd need to be right now, so's our youngens can get on with what they have to do. It'd happen sooner or later, so it ought'a be now. You're in a tent. I'm in a tent, we need to be in a house, together."

A wide smile and a sigh. "Well, sure and that makes sense." He had a fleeting memory of young Sadie's quickness in thought and action, and how she added to the fun of any group.

"Will you?" She smiled her special smile.

"Huh?"

"Eben Carlile, will you marry me?"

He said he would. In fact, he'd be glad to.

Twenty-Four

There were plans to be made, and it was midafternoon before Dancer's path was turned toward Prosper.

It seemed that the McClure's names had come up for their allotment of lumber. Willie and Tommy stood by the small pile of boards, measuring and figuring. If they combined the two allotments, there would be enough to box in a shed, maybe just big enough to house the printing equipment.

From the tent came the ka-klunk, ka-klunk, and Nancy's shiny black hair could be seen at the lever that released the press onto the inky print. Lily was on her knees preparing the paper to fit into the feeder.

Sadie slipped quietly into her tent and changed into her serviceable black dress. As busy as they were, she could surely find a way to help with the evening meal. There were beans to heat, and she could gather some sticks of wood for the fire.

Finally, the young people could tear themselves away from their work and were gathered around the food.

Willie was first. "Sadie, how's the city? Was there a way to find what you wanted?"

Four pairs of eyes focused on Sadie as she spread butter on her cornbread and smiled. "I'd say, we had a most satisfying day. Accomplished everything I set out to do."

A moment of silence.

Then Lily. "That's good. I was hopin' you'd not be disappointed."

More silence.

Sadie drew in a deep breath. Now was the time.

"There's more I need to say, so's you'll know my plans. I wouldn't want to keep you wonderin' about me, as good as you've been to me. That'd not be fair.

"First off, I see you makin' a place for the machinery, and that'll free up a tent. I'll have to ask for two more weeks, and then my tent'll be free. That'll get both'a you in a place where you can stand up to put your clothes on."

"Oh, Sadie, there's no hurry…"

"I know it, but it'll happen soon. I'm announcin' that I'm gonna get married."

Spoons paused between plate and mouth, and eyes stared at her, stunned and unblinking.

"Married?"

"Did you say…?"

"But, who…?"

Sadie nodded. "I'm gettin' married to Eben Carlile. It'll be in two days at the church house. I've spoken to the preacher."

"But you don't even know 'im!"

"You only seen 'im two weeks ago. You sure…?"

Sadie chewed the bite of cornbread and swallowed. "Didn't see fit to tell you sooner, all of you bein' busy like you are, but me and Eben, we've known each other for more'n fifty years. You boys' papa played chase with him, and him and me, we shared licorice whips and skinned knees."

"For a fact?"

"But it's been so long…."

"That, it has! And that'd be why I ain't a'wastin' no more time. Eben, he's been busy gettin' the church in the dry, but he says he'll have a starter log house for us in two weeks. That's why I'm askin' for the use'a the tent for that length'a time. Now, don't you be concerned at the movin' of it. You got work to so. Him and me, we'll tend to the movin'."

"Well, Sadie, if you're sure…" What else could Willie say?

Sadie nodded. "I'm sure. That's why I sayin' to you what I'll do. Time comes there's sometime I ain't sure of… well… and that's likely to happen… I'll say to you boys, 'I need me some advice.' When I say that, I know I'll get the best advice you got to give.

"Now, I see I'm keepin' you from eatin' and that ain't good. You need your strength for what's up ahead'a you. So I'm gonna take my bowl and my cup and go to my tent and rest."

Whereupon, she did just that.

Lily dipped from the kettle and filled Willie's bowl, and then her own, and sat down. Smiling, she looked around. "Now, I wouldn't go so far and be so tacky as to say I told you so, but didn't it happen just like I said it would? I always knew there was more to your aunt than you boys were seein'."

A sigh and a nod from Willie. "Gonna hafta say you were right."

Lily again. "It's like…you know those soft quilted gloves men wear to be able to do hard work in the cold? Them gloves, they're soft and smooth, and they wad up easy. But when a fellow puts his hand inside them, they become as strong and hard as his hand. Sadie's like that. She looked soft, but there was always somethin' inside. We just didn't know what it was."

Practical minded Nancy was next. "I think it's a wonderful thing. There wasn't no way, nor nothin' we could do, that would keep her from bein' lonely. And I, for one, can say I'll be glad to get myself in a tent."

Twenty-Five

And that was the night that Tilda nosed around the tent and finally settled on the braided rug beside the bed. Circling it to be certain it was a suitable place, she settled onto the edge of it and produced five small mewling copies of herself, and two yellow and orange creatures with squinted eyes and tiny impatient mouths.

Essie sat beside her on the rug during the travail, awaiting her turn, that was surely not more than a week away.

As Tilda's tongue cleaned one small face, Essie's tongue worked on another one.

Eben had dropped Sadie off and turned Dancer toward the Dunbar tract. Heads turned and watched with interest. Not much happens in a small town that isn't noticed by all and discussed to infinity.

Dan Dunbar had left his work, coming to the well for a fresh drink, and Roberta was changing the drinking water in her baby chicken pen when Dancer turned her face toward her home.

Eben pulled her up to the well and drew a pail of water for her trough. He leaned against the curb of the well.

Roberta waited a respectful minute, then, "Good day for a drive. How did it go?"

Eben nodded, as if to reassure himself. "It went well, Bertie, lass. It was good to talk with someone who remembers what I remember. Sadie does that. I liked her fifty years ago, and there don't seem to'a been no changes."

"She feel the same way?"

"Seems to."

The pause that followed found the father and the daughter looking meaningfully and seriously into each other's face, fully understanding everything.

"Well, when'll it be?"

"Two days from now. Next Saturday. Done spoke to the preacher."

Dan had joined them, and Eben looked from one to the other of the two smiling faces. "Looks like we may have the first weddin' in the new church."

Roberta wrapped her arms around him. "Oh, Papa, I'm so glad. It's been so long since Mama… and me and Danny, bein' busy like we are…?" Unspoken words begged to be understood.

"Bertie, lass, there's no fault goin' your way, nor Danny's way. I just needed to get on…."

"And you will, Papa."

Twenty-Six

It was midafternoon on the last Saturday of June that Redbud Creek Church was aired out and freshened with Margarette daisies in vases in front of the pulpit.

There were no benches, as yet, on the sawdust floor, but planks had been stretched out, held up by rocks at each end. They were a mite low, but the people of Prosper were accustomed low seats.

The loaned planks would later become part of McCLURE PRINTING AND BOOKBINDING after they had served their purpose on this day.

It had been a busy morning. Danny, Roberta and Eben joined with the McClure brothers, and the heavy maple bedroom was moved to the new location, and it was once more covered with a large canvas tent vacated by the young Dunbar couple. The bookcase was set in the smaller tent, the one that had been Eben's home, and the boxes of books were opened and set on the shelves.

But there were not enough shelves. Not a problem, as there was plenty of room for another bookcase.

Then it was afternoon.

Sadie dressed carefully in her baby pink, Swiss-dotted Sunday-best summer dress. The wide white collar was of hand crocheted lace, and the white buttons marched primly down the dress front, from collar to waist to hem. A white knit shawl would complete the outfit.

Sadie brushed and combed her hair, examining it in the mirror. A band of silvery white waves framed her face, but the color beneath the silver was the light chestnut brown. Gathering the length of it in her hand, she twisted and pinned, and the perfect figure eight lay against the back of her head.

She turned her head to examine her work in the two-way mirror that had been packed away, but was now unpacked. She smiled with satisfaction. She had not lost her touch.

She nodded her head in acknowledgement. She looked like a lady who had lived for fifty-five years, and not all of them had been easy ones. She looked like just what she was, and that was enough.

Eben, came for her. He was dressed in gray pants and white shirt, with a jaunty black bow tie beneath his chin. His Sunday shoes were shinned to mirror brightness, and his fingernails had been trimmed with his pocketknife.

Prosper had no barber, but most women were fairly adept with clippers and scissors, and Roberta had trimmed here and there, and pronounced him handsome, indeed.

The church was full, with all the plank benches occupied, when Eben's buggy arrived. It was such a short distance, they could easily have walked, except the buggy seemed so appropriate. Dancer tossed her head gaily and lifted her feet high as she pulled it into the churchyard. She had always had a special pride when she thought she was being watched.

Except for the birds and insects in the trees outside, the church was pindrop quiet as they stepped through the door. The soft sawdust whispered beneath their feet as they walked forward toward the vases of daisies.

Rev. Hapgood Palmer waited at the front, as the strains of "Golden Bells" filled the church, issuing forth from the talented and trained fingers of Lydia Palmer, sister to the minister. The notes of the song melted into "Rock of Ages, Clef for Me," and Eben Carlile and Sadie McClure stood side by side.

When the sound died away, Rev. Hap Palmer opened his blue leather wedding book, and began:

"Dearly Beloved, we are gathered here before God and these people to join in holy matrimony, two of God's beloved children. Miss Sadie McClure and Mr. Ebenezer Carlile are not recent acquaintances. Miss Sadie, after many years of teaching and caring for children, comes to Prosper to share her life with us. Mr. Ebenezer Carlile, when his family was in danger, fled to our town for safety, and contributed his skill toward this fine church building. We are honored by the presence of them both.

"As children, these two people played together and studied together, and then they were parted by circumstances not of their making. Now they are together again, and we rejoice that they are a part of our town."

Someone clapped lightly, and the applause grew until the sound reverberated against the oak rafters beneath the hand-shaped cedar shingles. When the applause finally died away, Rev. Palmer continued.

"So, today, we ask, Miss Sadie McClure, do you take this man…"

Soft strains of "Sweet Bye and Bye" arose from the accordion, and, as the required questions were asked and answered, the sound became louder, and with the words, "I now pronounce you man and wife," waves of music drowned out all other sounds.

Mr. and Mrs. Carlile turned to face the people of the town as they came forward with their congratulations and best wishes.

Cakes and cookies, pies and cinnamon buns were served. Smiles and words, music and laughter filled the little church. It was so good to have a happy occasion tucked in among the days of hard work.

Dancer waited in the shade of a tree, switching her tail and rippling her skin against the flies.The newly joined couple left the church, and Eben handed his bride up into the buggy. With a wave of her white lace handkerchief, they were gone.

Much later....

Mockingbirds were noisy in the trees. Sadie and Eben were awake early, as older people sometimes were. Hot tea steamed in their cups as they sat in the yard and listened to the morning bird songs. It was another warm June day, and it would soon be time to dress for church.

A small sound caused them to turn and see the two small girls coming toward them.

"Aunt Sadie?"

"Yes, Ruthie?"

"You got that little book?"

"Which book, darling?"

"The one with ABC in it."

"Oh, you mean the McGuffey reader. You'll find it in the bookcase."

The two little girls disappeared inside the small tent and came back with the book. Sitting on the ground, they opened it to the first page. The other girl opened another, larger book, filled with brightly colored pictures.

Ruthie pointed, "See, they're the same."

Alecia looked in her book, then in the small one on the ground, and nodded. "The same," she pronounced. "Let's read my book. I'll point to the words.

"A" is for apple that grows on the tree
Some are for piggie, and some are for me.
"B" is for ball, for baby to play with.
"B" is for ball that the dog runs away with.
"C" is for chicken, with flappity wings.
He scratches for worms...."

Together, the two small voices recited the twenty-six poems of Alecia Carlile's book... which exactly matched the letters in Ruthie McClure's book. Such a wonderful coincidence, to find that they matched, and such a compliment to the young minds to have noticed it.

It was a Sunday in June, and the two small white goats nibbled on the leaves of scrubby brush, and leaped and bounced about.

It was just a Sunday morning in the town of Prosper, and it was certain there would be many more.

- Bonus Excerpt -

The Sheltering Stones Series

Book 5

Golden Gift from the Meadow

Golden Gift from the Meadow

THE HAYSTACK

She had gone as far as she could go. Not even one step more.

It was late in September that the first cutting of hay had been piled in the sheep pasture, and it had now turned golden in the early fall sunshine. The second cutting of the rich prairie grass would be soon, and then the present stacks would be hauled to the barn for storage, or tarp-covered in the field. It happened that way on the prairie.

The young woman had traveled as far as her strength permitted. Total exhaustion had teamed with the infected gunshot wound in her leg and she knew she could go no farther, even though the church steeple she saw before her was within what should be easy walking distance. The sight of the cross on its tip had pulled her along for the last mile.

Beside her was the haystack. Tempting. She stopped and rested beside it, for the small protection it gave, and she tucked the basket of her most precious possession under the edge of the hay. She must shut her eyes and rest, and if she awoke, she might be able to reach the steeple and certain help.

Easing back against the fragrant hay, she heard the music.

The melody seemed to fill her entire being. So relaxing. Her exhaustion, hunger, pain and fright just floated away. She was no longer uneasy about the baby's future. There, in the warm sunshine on the sheep pasture, she sighed her final breath and permitted herself to be pulled upward toward the voices. Toward the music that seemed so close it had become a part of her.

So loving and enticing were those angel voices…and then she was among them. They were all around her…seeking ways to comfort her. She sighed, and drifted…floating….

The little dog was sniffing bushes and grass clumps for messages from other four-footed residents of the area, and he sniffed a message he could not read. Best he call for help, so he barked. And barked and barked.

The woman at the piano heard the bark and when it seemed to continue, she called the dog to the house. "Biskit! Come on, Biskit!" But Biskit did not come.

Eventually she realized she would have to go after him or listen to his yips and barks for who knew how long. Pressing a bonnet down on her hair, she walked out to the haystack.

Seeing the woman before she reached her, she called back to the house, "Daniel! Come please. Looks like trouble."

It was when Biskit finally hushed and bounded toward her that she heard the baby cry. What terrible thing had occurred to cause a baby to be under their haystack?

Momentarily ignoring the body of the young woman, she pushed aside the hay and was greeted with a red face and open mouth. And a lot of screaming from a set of healthy lungs.

Baby well clothed but soaking wet. Also obviously hungry… and for how long?

It was a known fact that babies were occasionally found on doorsteps of homes and churches, but under a haystack? And what had happened with the mother?

The field from which the hay had been cut was a large one. It was currently rented to a sheep farmer who grew special sheep for a certain kind of long fibered wool…merino, it was called. Great demand for it, actually.

There were at least two cuttings of the rich, prairie hay to be harvested each year in the sheep pasture, and sometimes three. These golden piles fed the sheep during the winter.

The field was also the playground of the community's children. Backing up, as it did, to the tract of land owned by Miss Josie, the originator of the Prairie Academy, groups of children tended to spill over into the sheep meadow with their games.

It bothered the sheep not one bit, and if they were occasionally hit by a flying ball, their luxuriant wool absorbed the blow. They continued their nibble and chew, and the production of small ones to carry on their work of producing wool.

The wool was highly prized, even before the government began to buy it up for uniforms. There was always a war to be expected, and nothing was better than wool for the clothing that got such hard use.

This sheep meadow was a favorite with the children. The fluid and intermingled ages of groups lent interest as they laughed and played their way through the summer. Any child who could slip away from duties at home could be sure of a welcome. Miss Josie's children had been among them.

Summers on the prairie of the Oklahoma Territory were a happy interlude of sun, fun and games tucked in between the beginning of fall, the inclement winter and the budding spring days that were filled with work. Everybody had a job.

What these children could look forward to were bowed heads over books, cramped fingers from chalk and slate, and hours with bent elbows, lesson books and lamplight on their family supper tables.

Miss Josie had been firm about schoolwork and home work, and her successors at the Prairie Academy were even harder, if possible.

Miss Carmelita and Miss Rosalie were indeed firm task masters, having been taught by the best. The two ladies might be Mellie and Rosie during parties or in family gatherings, but they were properly addressed when present at the school. Respect for teachers and other elders was one of the lessons taught.

There was one summer that stood out above the rest during times when memories were reviewed. There was Daniel, age almost fourteen, and the oldest of that particular group…also the acknowledged leader on this special summer.

Then there were Aaron and Adam, age almost twelve. Then came the second set of Miss Josie's twins, John and James, age ten. Next was Josie's daughter, Mutt, who had just cleared eight. Daniel's younger sister, Prissy, came in at six and a half and was followed quickly by Sunny and Rainey Day, a year younger.

These last two were grandchildren of Nettie Wilson, the aunt who took in Josie when her parents were killed. The twin girls were actually Catherine and Carolyn, daughters of Esther Wilson Day, who gave up her life when her daughters were born. She just found no strength to go on.

There were these nine children, ten when Miss Josie's youngest son, Barney (actually Barnabas, after Miss Josie's beloved tutor) could slip away from his mother. With ten players, there was no end of the games to be invented. The wide sheep pasture welcomed all others who could slip away and join in.

Most of the games began with a few trips sliding down the haystacks. Dust, grass seeds and injuries from splintering hay stems were a small price to pay for exuberant squeals and heels-over-head tumbles.

Then came the struggle through the loose hay to climb to the top…and the shrieks and screams and unsuccessful ducks in avoidance of someone bigger who was determined to push you back.

Finally, there would be the ultimate joy of standing on top of the wobbly center of the pile deciding when to slide. Or waiting for someone to give a shove.

Miss Francine Canfield, the teacher of the school in the nearby town of Shady Ridge had made a rhyme about the haystack. Of course, Miss Francine had rhymes about a lot of subjects, many of which the students in Prairie Academy were required to learn to read with correct emphasis.

Miss Carmelita demanded perfection and Miss Rosalie was the enforcer. Hard task masters, though they were, some of Miss Francine's rhymes were fun. The one about "Under the Haystack" was one of those.

It had come about when she was collecting her own pony from being shod at the blacksmith's that she had overheard a group of gray-haired loungers recounting the fun they had as boys on a haystack. Miss Francine, herself, had enjoyed her share of the screaming fun, the hay straw down her neck and bruises when someone behind her was sliding faster. Tumbling and rolling together, landing finally on the soft grass and scattered hay.

Miss Francine always saw things from all sides, Miss Rosalie had explained, and she wanted the students to learn to see everything from many angles. It was the only way good decisions could be made…she explained. Miss Josie had insisted the two teachers learn the rhyme when they were the students, so it was therefore worthy to be taught to the next generation.

UNDER THE HAYSTACK

Green prairie grass cut with the scythe
Waves of emerald, scattered on the field.
Insects, wildflowers, seed pods, all
The sharp scythe slays the prairie's yield.

Turned and raked and left in rows,
Moisture pulled by summer sun.
The hay is stacked with pitchforks high
For boys…a playground full of fun.

At this very moment, she could hear the shrieks and squeals from a nearby field. The sight and sounds of the fun tugged her back into her memory.

Climbing high and sliding fast
With grass straws ripping into backs.
King of the Hill, and other games,
Of Hide and Seek and Sneak Attacks.

And then, of course, there were treasures to be found on the ground when the hay was finally taken to the barn…or when it was consumed by the sheep.

And tunnels under…with whoop and holler
A fortress. Treasures on the ground.
Upon the earth and hid in stubble
A pen knife, long lost…now is found.

The torn end of a handkerchief
A button from a bygone shirt.
Foil that wrapped a stick of gum,
A watch chain pried up from the dirt.

It was true that summer fun must be enjoyed fast because there was always the looming specter of the eight months of school.

Months of heads down at the slate and chalk and late-night work by lamplight.

However, fun must happen fast.
A haystack does not last forever.
It's not for dark and stormy nights,
Or cold and rainy winter weather.

Nodding at the mental picture it gave her, Miss Francine's pencil traveled on amid the jiggle of the buggy pulled by the shaggy, brown pony. She sighed for that summer fun, stored in the memory, so now it would provide a pleasure that could not go away.

Not just a joyful summer day
Of climbing, sliding fun begun.
They're making memories when they play,
And memories last when youth is done.

Memories…decades later…bring a smile
Sharp ends of hay won't itch and prick.
The speed in sliding down is greater,
The burs and dried out pods won't stick.

The wonderful thing about memory is that it conveniently sorts out the best pleasures to retain and often tosses out others that were disagreeable. A whole new picture can be painted.

The fields are now just sunny warm,
The swarm of hungry flies at bay.
Small moments on their golden slide
Become long summer days of play.

Through the magic of the years
Unpleasant memories? There are none!

Moments in the stacks of hay
Become—
Bright pictures in a youthful book.

Become—
A summer packed with fun.
Become—
The dreams of old, gray men.
As they now sit—
And doze and dream in summer sun.

This rhyme had been a difficult assignment in Miss Rosalie's class. Every inflection and hesitation must be just right. Especially that last part. Miss Rosalie would have it no other way. For what did these children know about "old, gray men" and what they would dream of? And why would this rhyme mean anything to them?

That year of 1907 was a magical one, and it became the last one before this particular group began to dissolve.

Daniel, the oldest, was the first to go, and he was to go far away. He was sent to a seminary up north where he would learn a lot of things, and many of them would be from his Bible. His very special Book.

There had been a story about that particular Bible. Ordinarily a boy of his age would not personally own such an expensive book, but his third great grandfather, who he had never heard of, had left this one to him. The Book had been many years finding its way to this particular child.

The old great grandfather, his long-ago relative, was named Daniel Ledbetter. He had been conscripted into the War of 1812, the war in which the fledgling United States would cut the last vestiges of force and the many ties that had bound it to other countries. The "cord" so to speak, had been severed from the motherland, and the new country now breathed on its own. All because of the War of 1812.

The first Daniel had donned the uniform and sword... picked up his firearm and beloved Bible...and had gone to war when called upon. It was the right thing to do.

The old sword now had a few rust spots near the hilt, the firearm had been cleaned and oiled, though the residue of the whale oil had disintegrated long ago. The leaves of the Book had a few rips and some smudges of dirt that indicated strong usage. It had evidently gone with him into battle.

It would have been so wonderful if there had been more information about him. Evidently he was just one of so many. When a person is living in the midst of the fear and the danger, there is often no thought of leaving words to the future for who might wonder about it.

However, when the old man left his earthly life behind, he had instructed that the Book and the weapons be handed down to his first grandson.

The firm of solicitors at that time had tried for years to do this, but it seemed that only girls were being born into that family and after a marriage name change, they were impossible to locate. Or at least very time consuming.

Also, it was a time of national transition and whole families were on the move toward the west. Following the call of the sun, they said.

Young Daniel's own great grandparents had been victims of a sudden disaster, but the grandsons of the first legal solicitors persevered and had eventually found his grandmother, Carlotta Owens, "somewhere out on the prairie." Clearly the next nearest relative.

Challenged by the difficulty, and with the persistence of many solicitors, they had managed to find her and congratulated themselves on their success.

This had happened shortly after Carlotta's son, also named Daniel, had been born. It was then that the inheritance had finally reached its rightful heir. The old Kiowa doctor, Miz Gray Owl, attending young Daniel's birth, had said there would be a surprise about their young Daniel. As it turned out, there had been a number of them.

The boy attended school at the Prairie Academy under the above-mentioned taskmasters named Miss Carmelita and Miss Rosalie. At age twelve he had completed all requirements offered for Certification to Teach.

There was a summer of fun during which he turned thirteen. Shortly after, the boy was sent north to the boarding seminary for higher education. With that move, the "group personality" of the neighborhood children changed.

It was the next year that Miss Josie's twins, Aaron and Adam, were placed with Uncle Jefferson to help with his special Conamara horses. Pioneer life demanded that all men become acquainted with the current most reliable method of travel, and the two boys spent the summer there, learning to break young animals to the rigors of a saddle and the restriction of being harnessed.

That same year, Mutt Cullen, Miss Josie's only daughter, and Priscilla Carpenter, Daniel's sister, had been reined in by their mothers and sent to learn the art of sock darning, patching and adjusting the size of dresses to match growth.

Girls aged eight and nine were deemed to be the perfect age for these lessons, as set forth by Miz O'Grady, who had been "trained by the best." Those lessons consumed a lot of each summer afternoon.

By the end of the summer, the girls were introduced to the mystery of paper patterns and how to create them. Also how to use them to cut new dress fabric.

Sunny and Rainy Day teamed up with Barney Cullen and several of the younger set. The haystacks were still their prime center of interest.

The next summer, Adam and Aaron were moved on to their father's blacksmith shop and introduced to the hammer and anvil, and the art of keeping the coals blazing hot.

Their vacated places in the corral of Uncle Jefferson were filled by James and John, Miss Josie's second set of twins.

By then, Mutt and Prissy were making simple items of clothing for themselves. Skirts, aprons and underwear…and were taught the fancy work of making hankies and scarves. With a sigh, Miz O'Grady agreed to take on the Day twins.

The wonderful summer of 1907 became a fond memory to be tucked away and there, within their memory, the stolen moments of fun became a whole, uninterrupted summer of joy. The mind can do wonderful things with a few pleasant afternoons.

Daniel Carpenter, now boarding at the seminary and accustomed to taking schoolwork seriously, bent his mind toward every subject he could manage. His marks were so high that the professors smiled together and agreed that he could very well be the new nation's next great preacher, and couldn't the country use one?

- END OF EXCERPT -

Additional Book Series by Joann Klusmeyer

The Great I Am Bible Story Series for Kids
6 books

The Young Pioneers Adventure Series for Kids
5 books

The Wentworth Triplets Mystery Series for Young Teens
3 books

The Footsteps in the Canyon Adventure Series for Young Teens
4 books

The Burnt Tree Junction Historical Fiction Series
6 books

The Ozark Mountains Historical Fiction Series
7 books

The Taming the Wilderness Historical Fiction Series
4 books

The Sheltering Stones Historical Fiction Series
5 books

The Trilogy of Wishbone Hollow Historicial Fiction Series
3 books

www.ingramcontent.com/pod-product-compliance
Lightning Source LLC
LaVergne TN
LVHW020534100826
845148LV00010B/1451
9781613147191